GHOSTS
AND
GRISLY THINGS

RAMSEY CAMPBELL

D0061500

TOR®

A TOM DOHERTY ASSOCIATES BOOK
NEW YORK

GHOSTS AND GRISLY THINGS

First published in Great Britain by Pumpkin Books,
an imprint of MeG Enterprises Limited, 1998

Collection and introduction copyright © 1998 by Ramsey Campbell

A Tor Book
Published by Tom Doherty Associates, LLC
175 Fifth Avenue
New York, NY 10010

www.tor.com

Tor® is a registered trademark of Tom Doherty Associates, LLC.

ISBN 0-312-86758-1 (hc)
ISBN 0-312-86757-3 (pbk)

First Tor Hardcover Edition: October 2000
First Tor Trade Paperback Edition: October 2001

Printed in the United States of America

0 9 8 7 6 5 4 3 2 1

Praise for Ramsey Campbell

"Campbell's literate short stories and novels work their way into your consciousness and lurk there, waiting to zap you at odd moments with a jolt of unrefined terror. He writes of our deepest fears in a precise, clear prose that somehow manages to be beautiful and terrifying at the same time."

—The Washington Post Book World

"The most inventive and risk-taking contemporary writer of horror fiction."

—The Sacramento Bee

"Menace has always been his keynote: His stories take place in a world full of threat and insinuation, where even the most contemporary objects shine with a sinister light. The world Ramsey Campbell takes for granted is the world of our darkest nightmares. Horrors in his fiction are never merely invented, they are felt and experienced, and affect the readers for days afterward."

—Peter Straub

"Ramsey Campbell is highly regarded for his sensitive use of the language and his ability to create psychologically complex characters."

—Dean Koontz

"Ramsey Campbell is one of the finest writers of modern horror fiction."

—The San Diego Union-Tribune

"He provides the reader with insights and chills only a master of dark fantasy could achieve."

—Clive Barker

"One of the most distinguished writers in our realm. [His] tales are compact, subtle, allusive, laced with sexual tension, and potently horrific in a manner difficult to define but easy to feel."

—Worlds of Fantasy and Horror

BY RAMSEY CAMPBELL
FROM TOM DOHERTY ASSOCIATES

Ancient Images
Cold Print
The Count of Eleven
Dark Companions
The Doll Who Ate His Mother
The Face That Must Die
Fine Frights (editor)
Ghosts and Grisly Things
The Hungry Moon
Incarnate
Influence
The Last Voice They Hear
The Long Lost
Midnight Sun
The Nameless
Nazareth Hill
Obsession
The One Safe Place
*Pact of Fathers**
The Parasite
Silent Children
Waking Nightmares

*forthcoming

CONTENTS

for Angela and Tony -
some fragments from a flaking brain

INTRODUCTION

AM I OLD YET? Am I jaded? Have I reached the point H. Russell Wakefield reached, and Nigel Kneale, and any number of commentators on my field, when they declared with all the confidence of ignorance that no good work was being done in it any more? Not while writers who've come after me are adding so much of worth to it — let me exhort anyone who needs convincing to start with Thomas Ligotti, Terry Lamsley, Kim Newman and Poppy Z. Brite, four of my particular favourites. I hope I may add some good stuff yet myself. Meanwhile, here's all this, which I'll reminisce about as the mood takes me, in chronological order of writing.

"Through the Walls" (1974) was a part — an odd one, you may think — of the process of working myself up to try a major psychedelic. When I dropped acid for the first time soon afterwards, the experience had thankfully little in common with the tale, though the flashback I suffered in late 1976 had far too much. I originally intended the story for *Superhorror*, the first anthology I edited, but several informed friends — Hugh Lamb, Kathy Murray and T. E. D. Klein, all of them presently less active in the field than they deserve to be — pointed out flaws in the version I showed them. Later I rewrote it, and here is its final form.

"Looking Out" (1974) derives, I suspect, from my mother's increasing reluctance to venture far from her house once Jenny and I were living together. It was a trait that chafed her sister and brother-in-law, whom she regularly arranged to visit only to cancel at the last moment. Many were the arguments we had when I tried to persuade her that my aunt and uncle might be inconvenienced, and great was her pique if they proved to have invited a friend the next time she announced a visit. All that had its comic side, but Nairn's plight became hers too, anticipated by the tale. At least, that's my sense of it, though the notes for its development should be in the library vaults of Liverpool University if anybody wants to challenge my account.

As well as addressing its obvious themes of the difficulties of ageing and of the costs of change, "The Sneering" (1975) is a somewhat bitter celebration of an area of Liverpool where I once attended school — Ryebank Private School, to be precise, from 1953 to 1957. I remember being ragged on my arrival by some seniors and declaring with what must have been insufferable precociousness that I wouldn't stand for it. "Sit down for it, then," one of my tormentors duly responded. My memory and my eleven-plus results suggest it was a pretty good school, though one Irish teacher, a Mrs Toomey or Twomey, berated me in front of the class for having told someone at a bus stop — I've no idea how the information got back to the school — that I wrote stories (true even then) and wanted them to be published in America. Wasn't England good enough for me? she demanded, and it's only now I retort that Ireland seems not to have been for her. She was fond of telling unruly pupils how she had once spanked a rebellious girl on stage in front of the entire school. My readers must decide why this should have lodged in my memory.

"Missed Connection" was written in early 1976, and "The Change" immediately after. The year was nothing if not productive, as can be seen from Joshi's and Dziemianowicz's splendid bibliography, *The Core of Ramsey Campbell*. The first of these two stories prefigures the darkness and oppressiveness of the second, I think. These qualities aren't so appropriate in the first instance, which should have been another of my succinct tales written in tribute to the EC comics of the fifties, but I find "The Change" authentically grim — indeed, for me it's my darkest tale, and surely needs no exegesis by the author.

"This Time" (1978) and "Root Cause" (1979) don't call for much explanation either. The more fiction one writes, I find, the more the slightest incident or passing thought can set about instantly plotting itself. "This Time" began with the idea of counting backwards during the onset of an anaesthetic, and was a tale I worked out pretty fully in advance so that I would have something to write once our first child was born. ("Down There" followed it, and was so intractable that I nearly abandoned it after three days, until a paragraph of the first draft came alive.) The genesis of "Root Cause" must be somewhere in my notebooks, and I leave it to be discovered with a grunt or gasp or cry of triumph by some future researcher. Will that be my spectral finger marking the page for them, or just a length of restless cobweb?

"Welcomeland" (1987) owes its conception to Alan Moore, one of the contemporary British giants — Bryan Talbot and Neil Gaiman and John Coulthart are others — of the comic book. At a party after a signing we did in Peterborough, Alan told me of an abandoned Northern industrial town that a businessman had sought to turn into a theme park until his money ran out. Substances ingested at the party may have helped me to develop the notion as weirdly as it deserved.

We come to 1990, and four tales herein. "The Alternative" is one of the stories I thought of writing on the theme of a life whose positive qualities depend on dreadful nightmares. Maybe in time I'll write another, though this one also discovers a moral theme. I wrote at length about my actual dreams and nightmares in my regular column in the magazine *Necrofile*. "A Street was Chosen" has at its root the kind of trick writers should play on themselves every so often — requiring themselves to use a style they don't ordinarily employ. My task here was to write in the passive voice without undue repetition, and in the form of a scientific report. I found this virtually impossible until I switched from writing longhand, always my way with first drafts, to composing directly onto the computer screen. That's how I write non-fiction, the present ramblings included, and perhaps that's why the method worked for "A Street was Chosen".

"See How They Run" was written for an anthology about psychopaths edited by my old, and now lamented, friend Robert Bloch. Bob was happy with the tale but not the title, which he'd used for a story of his own, and so I retitled mine "For You to Judge". I still preferred my original title, however, and after Bob's death I used it for a reprinting by another much-missed friend, Karl Wagner. Not many days before Bob died I was able to speak to him on the phone for half an hour and tell him he was loved. He told me that he was able to see a pattern in his life. I hope I shall in mine.

"The Same in Any Language" was a response to a request too. A resurrected *Weird Tales*, the legendary pulp magazine, was to publish an issue as a tribute to me, much to my delight. My first glimpse of a copy of *Weird Tales* in a shop window when I was six or seven years old started a yearning which only collecting the magazine could begin to satisfy. Darrell Schweitzer, editor of its latest incarnation, asked me to vary the tone and settings of my stories for the tribute issue as much as I could. Given that "The Change" was included, I imagine he wanted me to be less bleak. I'd wanted to use Spinalonga as a setting in any case, having forgotten that John Ware had already done so in the thirteenth volume of Herbert van Thal's increasingly pornographic Pan books of horror stories, a series later rescued from itself by Steve Jones and his partner in excellence David Sutton. Ware's tale is an old-fashioned ghost story. How about mine?

1991 was the year I finished *The Count of Eleven* — a novel of a serial killer who might have been played by Stan Laurel, as one reviewer delighted me by saying — and the comedy I'd discovered there found its way into that year's short stories. Mind you, there may be some who would take "The Dead Must Die" straight, an unnerving thought. It was written for *Narrow Houses*, Pete Crowther's anthology about superstition, a human failing I take to mean basing one's life on irrationality. Of course my stuff frequently deals with the irrational, but I trust my readers to recognise that I'm writing fiction. Some writers in the field seem happy to increase their sales by pretending otherwise. Mind you, "A Side of the Sea" strikes me now as less fantastic than I took it to be at the time, and in "McGonagall in the Head" I found it difficult to invent worse verse than some of the couplets real people send after the departed. I don't know if any reader needs me to explain that William McGonagall was to poetry what Edward D. Wood of *Plan 9 From Outer Space* was to the cinema. Fans of either will also be rewarded by the poetry and prose of Amanda McKittrick Ros.

In 1992 I had time to complete only one short story, "Between the Floors". That Easter the annual British science fiction convention was held in a Blackpool hotel, where some of the conventioneers were banished to an annexe served by a lift complete with a lugubrious attendant not at all unlike (except in some ways, one hopes) the figure who haunts my tale. What is it about comedians that makes them recur in my stuff? Even the monstrous Hector Woollie in the novel I'm presently writing has ambitions to amuse children. Perhaps I've never felt the same about comedians since reading the nightmarish chapter fourteen of David Storey's *Radcliffe*.

I saw myself into 1993 by finishing "Where They Lived". The idea for it, or more precisely the characters, came to me on a coach ride in Turkey. I overheard nobody like the Lunts on it — indeed, the organiser of the tour had the good taste to play a tape of the *Appassionata* — but I suspect my subconscious had been scheming for a while to create representatives of the kind of English tourist who goes abroad in search of Blackpool. (American readers should understand that Blackpool can be described as a less tasteful Coney Island.) Any number of lines of Luntish dialogue suggested themselves to me all at once. Having scribbled them down, I was casting about for a suitably macabre situation to build around the Lunts when it occurred to me that they were macabre enough in themselves. See if you agree once you've met them — I hope only on the page.

"Going Under" (1994) was done for Nancy Collins' book *Dark Love*. I know it doesn't fit her title very well. I'd somehow convinced myself she was editing an anthology about obsessions, and the tale can claim that preoccupation, I think. Around the time I planned to write it one of the Mersey Tunnels was closed to traffic for a day so that the public could celebrate its anniversary by walking through. I intended to research the experience, but the story grew impatient to be written, and so I saved myself the walk.

"Out of the Woods" dates from the same year. The editor of a Belgian journal approached me to write a story about wood or paper or a Finnish legend for a magazine he was to edit in English to be sold to Finns worldwide. I assure you that I don't invent these anecdotes. He tempted me to fit the project into my schedule by offering a handsome sum, but when he received the story his offer turned out to be less than forthcoming, and I haven't heard from him since. Still, the story went down well at readings, and I later recorded it (along with "The Guide", "Calling Card" and "The Companion") on an audiocassette, *Twilight Tales from Merseyside*, available from BBC Radio Merseyside and in America from Necronomicon Press.

And so to the chunk of unpublished stuff, "Ra*e". It was another tale written to an order that proved less firm than it had promised to be. Jeff Gelb and Lonn Friend, editors of the *Hot Blood* series of anthologies, asked various people to write a long story about one of the seven deadly sins. You will have guessed which attracted me. Alas, for whatever reason, the project failed to find a publisher, and so although I completed the first draft of the tale in early 1996, I saw little point in revising such a lengthy piece to be touted elsewhere. For a while a second volume of *Dark Love* seemed imminent, and apparently both Nancy Collins and her publishers wanted me in it, but it too faded and vanished. Now here is a place for "Ra*e", in final draft at last. My thanks to all those who bought it and the book it rounds off, and who have indulged my determination not to repeat myself, which isn't to say that I've by any means always succeeded. All the same, here's to keeping on trying. The journey isn't over, and I hope to have some odd things to show you on the way.

Ramsey Campbell
Wallasey, Merseyside
16 September 1997

THE SAME IN ANY LANGUAGE

T HE DAY MY FATHER IS TO TAKE ME where the lepers used to live is hotter than ever. Even the old women with black scarves wrapped around their heads sit inside the bus station instead of on the chairs outside the tavernas. Kate fans herself with her straw hat like a basket someone's sat on and gives my father one of those smiles they've made up between them. She's leaning forwards to see if that's our bus when he says "Why do you think they call them lepers, Hugh?"

I can hear what he's going to say, but I have to humour him. "I don't know."

"Because they never stop leaping up and down."

It takes him much longer to say the first four words than the rest of it. I groan because he expects me to, and Kate lets off one of her giggles I keep hearing whenever they stay in my father's and my room at the hotel and send me down for a swim. "If you can't give a grin, give a groan," my father says for about the millionth time, and Kate pokes him with her freckly elbow as if he's too funny for words. She annoys me so much that I say "Lepers don't rhyme with creepers, dad."

"I never thought they did, son. I was just having a laugh. If we can't laugh we might as well be dead, ain't that straight, Kate?" He winks at her thigh and slaps his own instead, and says to me "Since you're so clever, why don't you find out when our bus is coming."

"That's it now."

"And I'm Hercules." He lifts up his fists to make his muscles bulge for Kate and says "You're telling us that tripe spells A Flounder?"

"Elounda, dad. It does. The letter like a Y upside down is how they write an L."

"About time they learned how to write properly, then," he says, staring around to show he doesn't care who hears. "Well, there it is if you really want to trudge round another old ruin instead of having a swim."

1

"I expect he'll be able to do both once we get to the village," Kate says, but I can tell she's hoping I'll just swim. "Will you two gentlemen see me across the road?"

My mother used to link arms with me and my father when he was living with us. "I'd better make sure it's the right bus," I say and run out so fast I can pretend I didn't hear my father calling me back.

A man with skin like a boot is walking backwards in the dust behind the bus, shouting "Elounda" and waving his arms as if he's pulling the bus into the space in line. I sit on a seat opposite two Germans who block the aisle until they've taken off their rucksacks, but my father finds three seats together at the rear. "Aren't you with us, Hugh?" he shouts, and everyone on the bus looks at him.

When I see him getting ready to shout again I walk down the aisle. I'm hoping nobody notices me, but Kate says loudly "It's a pity you ran off like that, Hugh. I was going to ask if you'd like an ice cream."

"No thank you," I say, trying to sound like my mother when she was only just speaking to my father, and step over Kate's legs. As the bus rumbles uphill I turn as much of my back on her as I can, and watch the streets.

Aghios Nikolaos looks as if they haven't finished building it. Some of the tavernas are on the bottom floors of blocks with no roofs, and sometimes there are more tables on the pavements outside than in. The bus goes downhill again as if it's hiccuping, and when it reaches the bottomless pool where young people with no children stay in the hotels with discos, it follows the edge of the bay. I watch the white boats on the blue water, but really I'm seeing the conductor coming down the aisle and feeling as if a lump is growing in my stomach from me wondering what my father will say to him.

The bus is climbing beside the sea when he reaches us. "Three for leper land," my father says.

The conductor stares at him and shrugs. "As far as you go," Kate says, and rubs herself against my father. "All the way."

When the conductor pushes his lips forwards out of his moustache and beard my father begins to get angry, unless he's pretending. "Where you kept your lepers. Spiny Lobster or whatever you call the damned place."

"It's Spinalonga, dad, and it's off the coast from where we're going."

"I know that, and he should." My father is really angry now. "Did you get that?" he says to the conductor. "My ten-year-old can speak your lingo, so don't tell me you can't speak ours."

The conductor looks at me, and I'm afraid he wants me to talk Greek. My mother gave me a little computer that translates words into Greek when you type them, but I've left it at the hotel because my father said it sounded like a bird which only knew one note. "We're going to Elounda, please," I stammer.

"Elounda, boss," the conductor says to me. He takes the money from my father without looking at him and gives me the tickets and change. "Fish is good by the harbour in the evening," he says, and goes to sit next to the driver while the bus swings round the zigzags of the hill road.

My father laughs for the whole bus to hear. "They think you're so important, Hugh, you won't be wanting to go home to your mother."

Kate strokes his head as if he's her pet, then she turns to me. "What do you like most about Greece?"

She's trying to make friends with me like when she kept saying I could call her Kate, only now I see it's for my father's sake. All she's done is make me think how the magic places seemed to have lost their magic because my mother wasn't there with me, even Knossos where Theseus killed the Minotaur. There were just a few corridors left that might have been the maze he was supposed to find his way out of, and my father let me stay in them for a while, but then he lost his temper because all the guided tours were in foreign languages and nobody could tell him how to get back to the coach. We nearly got stuck overnight in Heraklion, when he'd promised to take Kate for dinner that night by the bottomless pool. "I don't know," I mumble, and gaze out the window.

"I like the sun, don't you? And the people when they're being nice, and the lovely clear sea."

It sounds to me as if she's getting ready to send me off swimming again. They met while I was, our second morning at the hotel. When I came out of the sea my father had moved his towel

3

next to hers and she was giggling. I watch Spinalonga Island float over the horizon like a ship made of rock and grey towers, and hope she'll think I'm agreeing with her if that means she'll leave me alone. But she says "I suppose most boys are morbid at your age. Let's hope you'll grow up to be like your father."

She's making it sound as if the leper colony is the only place I've wanted to visit, but it's just another old place I can tell my mother I've been. Kate doesn't want to go there because she doesn't like old places — she said if Knossos was a palace she was glad she's not a queen. I don't speak to her again until the bus has stopped by the harbour.

There aren't many tourists, even in the shops and tavernas lined up along the winding pavement. Greek people who look as if they were born in the sun sit drinking at tables under awnings like stalls in a market. Some priests who I think at first are wearing black hatboxes on their heads march by, and fishermen come up from their boats with octopuses on sticks like big kebabs. The bus turns round in a cloud of dust and petrol fumes while Kate hangs onto my father with one hand and flaps the front of her flowery dress with the other. A boatman stares at the tops of her boobs which make me think of spotted fish and shouts "Spinalonga" with both hands round his mouth.

"We've hours yet," Kate says. "Let's have a drink. Hugh may even get that ice cream if he's good."

If she's going to talk about me as though I'm not there I'll do my best not to be. She and my father sit under an awning and I kick dust on the pavement outside until she says "Come under, Hugh. We don't want you with sunstroke."

I don't want her pretending she's my mother, but if I say so I'll only spoil the day more than she already has. I shuffle to the table next to the one she's sharing with my father and throw myself on a chair. "Well, Hugh," she says, "do you want one?"

"No thank you," I say, even though the thought of an ice cream or a drink starts my mouth trying to drool.

"You can have some of my lager if it ever arrives," my father says at the top of his voice, and stares hard at some Greeks sitting at a table. "Anyone here a waiter?" he says, lifting his hand to his mouth as if he's holding a glass.

When all the people at the table smile and raise their glasses and shout cheerily at him, Kate says "I'll find someone and then I'm going to the little girls' room while you men have a talk."

My father watches her crossing the road and gazes at the doorway of the taverna once she's gone in. He's quiet for a while, then he says "Are you going to be able to say you had a good time?"

I know he wants me to enjoy myself when I'm with him, but I also think what my mother stopped herself from saying to me is true — that he booked the holiday in Greece as a way of scoring off her by taking me somewhere she'd always wanted to go. He stares at the taverna as if he can't move until I let him, and I say "I expect so, if we go to the island."

"That's my boy. Never give in too easily." He smiles at me with one side of his face. "You don't mind if I have some fun as well, do you?"

He's making it sound as though he wouldn't have had much fun if it had just been the two of us, and I think that was how he'd started to feel before he met Kate. "It's your holiday," I say.

He's opening his mouth after another long silence when Kate comes out of the taverna with a man carrying two lagers and a lemonade on a tray. "See that you thank her," my father tells me.

I didn't ask for lemonade. He said I could have some lager. I say "Thank you very much," and feel my throat tightening as I gulp the lemonade, because her eyes are saying that she's won.

"That must have been welcome," she says when I put down the empty glass. "Another? Then I should find yourself something to do. Your father and I may be here for a while."

"Have a swim," my father suggests.

"I haven't brought my cossy."

"Neither have those boys," Kate says, pointing at the harbour. "Don't worry, I've seen boys wearing less."

My father smirks behind his hand, and I can't bear it. I run to the jetty the boys are diving off, and drop my T-shirt and shorts on it and my sandals on top of them, and dive in.

The water's cold, but not for long. It's full of little fish that nibble you if you only float, and it's clearer than tap water, so you can see down to the pebbles and the fish pretending to be them. I chase fish and swim underwater and almost catch an octopus before it squirms out to sea. Then three Greek boys about my age swim over, and we're pointing at ourselves and saying our names when I see Kate and my father kissing.

I know their tongues are in each other's mouths — getting some tongue, the kids at my school call it. I feel like swimming away as far as I can go and never coming back. But Stavros and Stathis and Costas are using their hands to tell me we should see who can swim fastest, so I do that instead. Soon I've forgotten my father and Kate, even when we sit on the jetty for a rest before we have more races. It must be hours later when I realise Kate is calling "Come here a minute."

The sun isn't so hot now. It's reaching under the awning, but she and my father haven't moved back into the shadow. A boatman shouts "Spinalonga" and points at how low the sun is. I don't mind swimming with my new friends instead of going to the island, and I'm about to tell my father so when Kate says "I've been telling your dad he should be proud of you. Come and see what I've got for you."

They've both had a lot to drink. She almost falls across the table as I go to her. Just as I get there I see what she's going to give me, but it's too late. She grabs my head with both hands and sticks a kiss on my mouth.

She tastes of old lager. Her mouth is wet and bigger than mine, and when it squirms it makes me think of an octopus. "Mmm-*mwa*," it says, and then I manage to duck out of her hands, leaving her blinking at me as if her eyes won't quite work. "Nothing wrong with a bit of loving," she says. "You'll find that out when you grow up."

My father knows I don't like to be kissed, but he's frowning at me as if I should have let her. Suddenly I want to get my own back on them in the only way I can think of. "We need to go to the island now."

"Better go to the loo first," my father says. "They wouldn't have one on the island when all their willies had dropped off."

Kate hoots at that while I'm getting dressed, and I feel as if she's laughing at the way my ribs show through my skin however much I eat. I stop myself from shivering in case she or my father makes out that's a reason for us to go back to the hotel. I'm heading for the toilet when my father says "Watch out you don't catch anything in there or we'll have to leave you on the island."

I know there are all sorts of reasons why my parents split up, but just now this is the only one I can think of — my mother not being able to stand his jokes and how the more she told him to finish the more he would do it, as if he couldn't stop himself. I run into the toilet, trying not to look at the pedal bin where you have to drop the used paper, and close my eyes once I've taken aim.

Is today going to be what I remember about Greece? My mother brought me up to believe that even the sunlight here had magic in it, and I expected to feel the ghosts of legends in all the old places. If there isn't any magic in the sunlight, I want there to be some in the dark. The thought seems to make the insides of my eyelids darker, and I can smell the drains. I pull the chain and zip myself up, and then I wonder if my father sent me in here so we'll miss the boat. I nearly break the hook on the door, I'm so desperate to be outside.

The boat is still tied to the harbour, but I can't see the boatman. Kate and my father are holding hands across the table, and my father's looking around as though he means to order another drink. I squeeze my eyes shut so hard that when I open them everything's gone black. The blackness fades along with whatever I wished, and I see the boatman kneeling on the jetty, talking to Stavros. "Spinalonga," I shout.

He looks at me, and I'm afraid he'll say it's too late. I feel tears building up behind my eyes. Then he stands up and holds out a hand towards my father and Kate. "One hour," he says.

Kate's gazing after a bus that has just begun to climb the hill. "We may as well go over as wait for the next bus," my father says, "and then it'll be back to the hotel for dinner."

Kate looks sideways at me. "And after all that he'll be ready for bed," she says like a question she isn't quite admitting to.

"Out like a light, I reckon."

"Fair enough," she says, and uses his arm to get herself up.

The boatman's name is Iannis, and he doesn't speak much English. My father seems to think he's charging too much for the trip until he realises it's that much for all three of us, and then he grins as if he thinks Iannis has cheated himself. "Heave ho then, Janice," he says with a wink at me and Kate.

The boat is about the size of a big rowing-boat. It has a cabin at the front and benches along the sides and a long box in the middle that shakes and smells of petrol. I watch the point of the boat sliding through the water like a knife and feel as if we're on our way to the Greece I've been dreaming of. The white buildings of Elounda shrink until they look like teeth in the mouth of the hills, and then Spinalonga floats up ahead.

It makes me think of an abandoned ship bigger than a liner, a ship so dead that it's standing still in the water without having to be anchored. The evening light seems to shine out of the steep rusty sides and the bony towers and walls high above the sea. I know it was a fort to begin with, but I think it might as well have been built for the lepers. I can imagine them trying to swim to Elounda and drowning because there wasn't enough left of them to swim with, if they didn't just throw themselves off the walls because they couldn't bear what they'd turned into. If I say these things to Kate I bet more than her mouth will squirm — but my father gets in first. "Look, there's the welcoming committee."

Kate gives a shiver that reminds me I'm trying not to feel cold. "Don't say things like that. They're just people like us, probably wishing they hadn't come."

I don't think she can see them any more clearly than I can. Their heads are poking over the wall at the top of the cliff above the little pebbly beach which is the only place a boat can land. There are five or six of them, only I'm not sure they're heads; they might be stones someone has balanced on the wall — they're almost the same colour. I'm wishing I had some binoculars when Kate grabs my father so hard the boat rocks and Iannis waves a finger at her, which doesn't please my father. "You keep your eye on your steering, Janice," he says.

Iannis is already taking the boat towards the beach. He didn't seem to notice the heads on the wall, and when I look again they aren't there. Maybe they belonged to some of the people who are coming down to a boat bigger than Iannis's. That boat chugs away as Iannis's bumps into the jetty. "One hour," he says. "Back here."

He helps Kate onto the jetty while my father glowers at him, then he lifts me out of the boat. As soon as my father steps onto the jetty Iannis pushes the boat out again. "Aren't you staying?" Kate pleads.

He shakes his head and points hard at the beach. "Back here, one hour."

She looks as if she wants to run into the water and climb aboard the boat, but my father shoves his arm round her waist. "Don't worry, you've got two fellers to keep you safe, and neither of them with a girl's name."

The only way up to the fort is through a tunnel that bends in the middle so you can't see the end until you're nearly halfway in. I wonder how long it will take for the rest of the island to be as dark as the middle of the tunnel. When Kate sees the end she runs until she's in the open and stares at the sunlight, which is perched on top of the towers now. "Fancying a climb?" my father says.

She makes a face at him as I walk past her. We're in a kind of street of stone sheds that have mostly caved in. They must be where the lepers lived, but there are only shadows in them now, not even birds. "Don't go too far, Hugh," Kate says.

"I want to go all the way round, otherwise it wasn't worth coming."

"I don't, and I'm sure your father expects you to consider me."

"Now, now, children," my father says. "Hugh can do as he likes as long as he's careful and the same goes for us, eh, Kate?"

I can tell he's surprised when she doesn't laugh. He looks unsure of himself and angry about it, the way he did when he and my mother were getting ready to tell me they were splitting up. I run along the line of huts and think of hiding in one so I can jump out at Kate. Maybe they aren't empty after all; something rattles in one as if bones are crawling about in the dark. It could be a snake under part of the roof that's fallen. I keep running until I come to steps leading up from the street to the top of the island, where most of the light is, and I've started jogging up them when Kate shouts "Stay where we can see you. We don't want you hurting yourself."

"It's all right, Kate, leave him be," my father says. "He's sensible."

"If I'm not allowed to speak to him I don't know why you invited me at all."

I can't help grinning as I sprint to the top of the steps and duck out of sight behind a grassy mound that makes me think of a grave. From up here I can see the whole island, and we aren't alone on it. The path I've run up from leads all round the island, past more huts and towers and a few bigger buildings, and then it goes down to the tunnel. Just before it does it passes the wall above the beach, and between the path and the wall there's a stone yard full of slabs. Some of the slabs have been moved away from holes like long boxes full of soil or darkness. They're by the wall where I thought I saw heads looking over at us. They aren't there now, but I can see heads bobbing down towards the tunnel. Before long they'll be behind Kate and my father.

Iannis is well on his way back to Elounda. His boat is passing one that's heading for the island. Soon the sun will touch the sea. If I went down to the huts I'd see it sink with me and drown. Instead I lie on the mound and look over the island, and see more of the boxy holes hiding behind some of the huts. If I went closer I could see how deep they are, but I quite like not knowing — if I was Greek I expect I'd think they lead to the underworld where all the dead live. Besides, I like being able to look down on my father and Kate and see them trying to see me.

I stay there until Iannis's boat is back at Elounda and the other one has almost reached Spinalonga, and the sun looks as if it's gone down to the sea for a drink. Kate and my father are having an argument. I expect it's about me, though I can't hear what they're saying; the darker it gets between the huts the more Kate waves her arms. I'm getting ready to let my father see me when she screams.

She's jumped back from a hut which has a hole behind it. "Come out, Hugh. I know it's you," she cries.

I can tell what my father's going to say, and I cringe. "Is that you, Hugh? Yoo-hoo," he shouts.

I won't show myself for a joke like that. He leans into the hut through the spiky stone window, then he turns to Kate. "It wasn't Hugh. There's nobody."

I can only just hear him, but I don't have to strain to hear Kate. "Don't tell me that," she cries. "You're both too fond of jokes."

She screams again, because someone's come running up the tunnel. "Everything all right?" this man shouts. "There's a boat about to leave if you've had enough."

"I don't know what you two are doing," Kate says like a duchess to my father, "but I'm going with this gentleman."

My father calls me twice. If I go to him I'll be letting Kate win. "I don't think our man will wait," the new one says.

"It doesn't matter," my father says, so fiercely that I know it does. "We've our own boat coming."

"If there's a bus before you get back I won't be hanging around," Kate warns him.

"Please yourself," my father says, so loud that his voice goes into the tunnel. He stares after her as she marches away; he must be hoping she'll change her mind. But I see her step off the jetty into the boat, and it moves out to sea as if the ripples are pushing it to Elounda.

My father puts a hand to his ear as the sound of the engine fades. "So every bugger's left me now, have they?" he says in a kind of shout at himself. "Well, good riddance."

He's waving his fists as if he wants to punch something, and he sounds as if he's suddenly got drunk. He must have been holding it back while Kate was there. I've never seen him like this. It frightens me, so I stay where I am.

It isn't only my father that frightens me. There's only a little bump of the sun left above the water now, and I'm afraid how dark the island may be once that goes. Bits of sunlight shiver on the water all the way to the island, and I think I see some heads above the wall of the yard full of slabs, against the light. Which side of the wall are they on? The light's too dazzling, it seems to pinch the sides of the heads so they look thinner than any heads I've ever seen. Then I notice a boat setting out from Elounda, and I squint at it until I'm sure it's Iannis's boat.

He's coming early to fetch us. Even that frightens me, because I wonder why he is. Doesn't he want us to be on the island now he realises how dark it's getting? I look at the wall, and the heads have gone. Then the sea puts the sun out, and it feels as if the island is buried in darkness.

I can still see my way down the steps are paler than the dark — and I don't like being alone now I've started shivering. I back off from the mound, because I don't like to touch it, and almost back into a shape with bits of its head poking out and arms that look as if they've dropped off at the elbows. It's a cactus. I'm just standing up when my father says "There you are, Hugh."

He can't see me yet. He must have heard me gasp. I go to the top of the steps, but I can't see him for the dark. Then his voice moves away. "Don't start hiding again. Looks like we've seen the last of Kate, but we've got each other, haven't we?"

He's still drunk. He sounds as if he's talking to somebody nearer to him than I am. "All right, we'll wait on the beach," he says, and his voice echoes. He's gone into the tunnel, and he thinks he's following me. "I'm here, dad," I shout so loud that I squeak.

"I heard you, Hugh. Wait there. I'm coming." He's walking deeper into the tunnel. While he's in there my voice must seem to be coming from beyond the far end. I'm sucking in a breath that tastes dusty, so I can tell him where I am, when he says "Who's that?" with a laugh that almost shakes his words to pieces.

He's met whoever he thought was me when he was heading for the tunnel. I'm holding my breath — I can't breathe or swallow, and I don't know if I feel hot or frozen. "Let me past," he says as if he's trying to make his voice as big as the tunnel. "My son's waiting for me on the beach."

There are so many echoes in the tunnel I'm not sure what I'm hearing besides him. I think there's a lot of shuffling, and the other noise must be voices, because my father says "What kind of language do you call that? You sound drunker than I am. I said my son's waiting."

He's talking even louder as if that'll make him understood. I'm embarrassed, but I'm more afraid for him. "Dad," I nearly scream, and run down the steps as fast as I can without falling.

"See, I told you. That's my son," he says as if he's talking to a crowd of idiots. The shuffling starts moving like a slow march, and he says "All right, we'll all go to the beach together. What's the matter with your friends, too drunk to walk?"

I reach the bottom of the steps, hurting my ankles, and run along the ruined street because I can't stop myself. The shuffling sounds as though it's growing thinner, as if the people with my father are leaving bits of themselves behind, and the voices are changing too — they're looser. Maybe the mouths are getting bigger somehow. But my father's laughing, so loud that he might be trying to think of a joke. "That's what I call a hug. No harder, love, or I won't have any puff left," he says to someone. "Come on then, give us a kiss. They're the same in any language."

All the voices stop, but the shuffling doesn't. I hear it go out of the tunnel and onto the pebbles, and then my father tries to scream as if he's swallowed something that won't let him. I scream for him and dash into the tunnel, slipping on things that weren't on the floor when we first came through, and fall out onto the beach.

My father's in the sea. He's already so far out that the water is up to his neck. About six people who look stuck together and to him are walking him away as if they don't need to breathe when their heads start to sink. Bits of them float away on the waves my father makes as he throws his arms about and gurgles. I try to run after him, but I've got nowhere when his head goes underwater. The sea pushes me back on the beach, and I run crying up and down it until Iannis comes.

It doesn't take him long to find my father once he understands what I'm saying. Iannis wraps me in a blanket and hugs me all the way to Elounda and the police take me back to the hotel. Kate gets my mother's number and calls her, saying she's someone at the hotel who's looking after me because my father's drowned, and I don't care what she says, I just feel numb. I don't start screaming until I'm on the plane back to England, because then I dream that my father has come back to tell a joke. "That's what I call getting some tongue," he says, leaning his face close to mine and showing me what's in his mouth.

GOING UNDER

BLYTHE HAD SHUFFLED ALMOST TO THE TICKET BOOTH when he knew he should have sent the money. Beyond the line of booths another phalanx of walkers, some of them wearing slogans and some not a great deal else, advanced towards the tunnel under the river. While he'd failed to pocket the envelope, he never left his phone at home, and given the pace at which walkers were being admitted to the tunnel, which was closed to traffic for its anniversary, he should have plenty of time to complete a call before he reached the wide semicircular concrete mouth, rendered whiter by the July sun. As he unfolded the phone and tapped his home number on the keyboard the men on either side of him began jogging on the spot, an action which the left-hand man accompanied with a series of low hollow panting hoots. The phone rang five times and addressed Blythe in his own voice.

"Valerie Mason and Steve Blythe. Whatever we're doing, it's keeping us away from the phone, so please leave your name and number and the date and time and we'll tell you what we were up to when we call you back…" Though the message was less than six months old, it and Valerie's giggle at the end of it sounded worn by too much playback. Once the beep had stuttered four times on the way to uttering its longer tone, he spoke.

"Val? Valerie? It's me. I'm just about to start the tunnel walk. Sorry we had a bit of a tiff, but I'm glad you didn't come after all. You were right, I should send her the maintenance and then object. Let them have to explain to the court instead of me. Are you in the darkroom? Come and find out who this is, will you? Don't just listen if you're hearing me. Be fair."

Quite a pack jogged between the booths at that moment, the man to his immediate left taking time to emit a triumphal hoot before announcing to the ticket seller "Aids for AIDS." Blythe turned his head and the phone to motion the woman behind him to pass, because if he stopped talking for more than a couple of seconds the machine would take him to have rung off, but the official in the booth ahead of him poked out his head, which looked squashed flat by his peaked cap. "Quick as you can. Thousands more behind you."

The woman began jogging to encourage Blythe, shaking both filled bags of her ample red singlet. "Get a move on, lover. Give your stocks and shares a rest."

Her companion, who seemed to have donned a dwarf's T-shirt by mistake, entered the jogging competition, her rampant stomach bobbing up and down more than the rest of her. "Put that back in your trousers or you'll be having a heart attack."

At least their voices were keeping the tape activated. "Hold on if you're there, Val. I hope you'll say you are," Blythe said, using two fingers to extract a fiver from the other pocket of his slacks. "I'm just going through the booth."

The official frowned his disagreement, and Blythe breathed hard into the phone while he selected a charity to favour with his entrance fee. "Are you sure you're fit?" the official said.

Blythe imagined being banned on the grounds of ill health from the walk when it was by far his quickest route home. "Fitter than you sitting in a booth all day," he said, not as lightly as he'd meant to, and smoothed the fiver on the counter. "Families in Need will do me."

The official wrote the amount and the recipient on a clipboard with a slowness which suggested he was still considering whether to let Blythe pass, and Blythe breathed harder. When the official tore most of a ticket off a roll and slapped it on the counter Blythe felt released, but the man stayed him with a parting shot. "You won't get far with that, chum."

The phone had worked wherever Blythe had taken it, just as the salesman had promised. In any case, he was still two hundred yards short of the tunnel entrance, into which officials with megaphones were directing the crowd. "Just had to get my ticket, Val. Listen, you've plenty of time to post the cheque, you've almost an hour. Only call me back as soon as you hear this so I know you have, will you? Heard it, I mean. That's if you don't pick it up before I ring off, which I hope you will, answer, that's to say, that's why I'm droning on. I should tell you the envelope's inside my blue visiting suit, not the office suit, the one that says here's your accountant making a special effort so why haven't you got your accounts together. Can you really not hear it's me? You haven't gone out, have you?"

By now his awareness was concentrated in his head, so that he didn't notice that his pace had been influenced by the urgency of his speech until the upper lip of the tunnel swayed to a halt above him. Hot bare arms brushed his in passing as the megaphones began to harangue him. "Keep it moving, please," one crackled, prompting its mate to declare "No stopping now till the far side." An elderly couple faltered and conferred before returning to the booths, but Blythe didn't have that option. "That's you with the phone," a third megaphone blared.

"I know it's me. I don't see anybody else with one." This was meant to amuse Blythe's new neighbours, none of whom betrayed any such response. Not by any means for the first time, though less often since he'd met Valerie, he wished he'd kept some words to himself. "I'm starting the walk now. Please, I'm serious, ring me back the moment you hear this, all right? I'm ringing off now. If I haven't heard from you in fifteen minutes I'll call back," he said, and was in the tunnel.

Its shadow was a solid chill at which his body was uncertain whether to shiver, considering the heat which was building up in the tunnel. At least he felt cool enough to itemise his surroundings, something he liked to do whenever he was confronted by anywhere unfamiliar, though he'd driven through the tunnel several times a week for most of twenty years. Its two lanes accommodated five people abreast now, more or less comfortably if you discounted their body heat. Six feet above them on either side was a railed-off walkway for the use of workmen, with no steps up to either that Blythe had ever been able to locate. Twenty feet overhead was the peak of the arched roof, inset with yard-long slabs of light randomly punctuated with slabs off sick. No doubt he could count them if he wanted to calculate how far he'd gone or had still to go, but just now the sight of several hundred heads bobbing very slowly towards the first curve summed up the prospect vividly enough. Apart from the not quite synchronised drumming of a multitude of soles on concrete and their echoes, the tunnel was almost silent except for the squawks of the megaphones beyond the entrance and the occasional audible breath.

The two women who'd addressed Blythe at the booths were ahead of him, bouncing variously. Maybe they'd once been as slim as his wife Lydia used to be, he thought, not that there was much left of the man she'd married either, or if there was it was buried under all the layers of the person he'd become. The presence of the women, their abundant sunlamped flesh and determined perfume and their wagging buttocks wrapped in satin, reminded him of too much it would do him no good to remember, and he might have let more walkers overtake him if it hadn't been for the pressure looming at his back. That drove him to step up his pace, and he'd established a regular rhythm when his trousers began to chirp.

More people than he was prepared for stared at him, and he felt bound to say "Just my phone" twice. So much for the ticket seller's notion that it wouldn't work in the tunnel. Blythe drew it from his pocket without breaking his stride and ducked one ear to it as he unfolded it. "Hello, love. Thanks for saving my — "

"Less of the slop, Stephen. It's a long time since that worked."

"Ah." He faltered, and had to think which foot he was next putting forward. "Lydia. Apologies. My mistake. I thought — "

"I had enough of your mistakes when we were together, and your apologies, and what you think."

"That pretty well covers it, doesn't it? Were you calling to share anything else with me, or was that it?"

"I wouldn't take that tone with me, particularly now."

"Don't, then," Blythe said, a form of response he remembered as having once amused her. "If you've something to say, spit it out. I'm waiting for a call."

"Up to your old tricks, are you? Can't she stand you never going anywhere without that thing either? Where are you, in the pub as usual trying to calm yourself down?"

"I'm perfectly calm. I couldn't be calmer," Blythe said as though that might counteract the effect she was having on him. "And I may tell you I'm on the charity walk."

Was that a chorus of ironic cheers behind him? Surely they weren't aimed at him, even if they sounded as unimpressed as Lydia, who said "Never did begin at home for you, did it? Has your fancy woman found that out yet?"

He could have pounced on Lydia's syntax again, except that there were more important issues. "I take it you've just spoken to her."

"I haven't and I've no wish to. She's welcome to you and all the joy you bring, but she won't hear me sympathising. I didn't need to speak to her to know where you'd be."

"Then you were wrong, weren't you? And as long as we're discussing Valerie, maybe you and your solicitor friend ought to be aware she makes a lot less than he does now he's a partner in his firm."

"Watch it, big boy."

That was the broader-buttocked of the women. He'd almost trodden on her heels, his aggressiveness having communicated itself to his stride. "Sorry," he said, and without enough thought "Not you, Lyd."

"Don't you dare start calling me that again. Who've you been talking to about his firm? So that's why I haven't had my cheque this month, is it? Let me tell you this from him. Unless that cheque is postmarked today you'll find yourself in prison for non-payment, and that's a promise from both of us."

"Well, that's the first — " Her rising fury had already borne her off, leaving him with a drone in his ear and hot plastic stuck to his cheek. He cleared the line as he tramped around more of the prolonged curve, which showed him thousands of heads and shoulders bobbing down a slope to the point almost a mile away from which, packed closer and closer together, they streamed sluggishly upwards. On some days that mid-point was hazy with exhaust fumes, but the squashed crowd there looked distinct except for a slight wavering which must be an effect of the heat; he wasn't really smelling a faint trace of petrol through the wake of perfume. He bent a fingernail against the keys on the receiver, and back-handed his forehead as drops of sweat full of a fluorescent glare swelled the numbers on the keypad. His home phone had just rung when a man's voice said loudly "They're all the same, these buggers with their gadgets. Can't be doing with them, me."

There was surely no reason for Blythe to feel referred to. "Pick it up, Val," he muttered. "I said I'd ring you back. It's been nearly fifteen minutes. You can't still be doing whatever you were doing. Come out, there's a love." But his voice greeted him again and unspooled its message, followed by Valerie's giggle, which under the circumstances he couldn't help feeling he'd heard once too often. "Are you really not there? I've just had Lydia on, ranting about her maintenance. Says if it isn't posted today her boyfriend the solicitor who gives new meaning to the word solicit will have me locked up. I suppose technically he might be able to, so if you can make absolutely certain you, I know I should have, I know you said, but if you can do that for me, for both of us, nip round the corner and get that bloody envelope in the shit."

The last word came out loudest, and three ranks in front of him glanced back. Of them, only the woman whose T-shirt ended halfway up her midriff retained any concern once she saw him. "Are you all right, old feller?"

"Yes, I'm... No, I'm... Yes, yes." He shook his free hand so extravagantly he saw sweat flying off it, his intention being to wave away his confusion more than her solicitude, but she advanced her lips in a fierce grimace before presenting her substantial rear view to him. He hadn't time to care if she was offended, though she was using the set of her buttocks to convey that she was, exactly as Lydia used to. The ticket seller had been right after all. The tunnel had cut Blythe off, emptying the receiver except for a faint distant moan.

It could be a temporary interruption. He pressed the recall button so hard it felt embedded in his thumb and was attempting to waft people past him when a not unfamiliar voice protested "Don't go standing. There's folk back here who aren't as spry as some."

"When you're my dad's age maybe you won't be so fond of stopping and starting."

Either might be the disliker of gadgets, though both appeared to have devoted a good deal of time and presumably machinery to the production of muscles, not only beneath shoulder level. Blythe tilted his head vigorously, almost losing the bell which was repeating its enfeebled note at his ear. "Don't mind me, just go round me. Just go, will you?"

"Put that bloody thing away and get on with what we're here for," the senior bruiser advised him. "We don't want to be having to carry you. We had his mother conk out on us once through not keeping the pace up."

"Don't mind me. Don't bother about me."

"We're bothered about all the folk you're holding up and putting the strain on."

"We'll be your trainers till we all finish," the expanded youth said.

"Then I ought to stick my feet in you," Blythe mumbled as those very feet gave in to the compulsion to walk. The phone was still ringing, and now it produced his voice. "Valerie Mason and Steve Blythe," it said, and at once had had enough of him.

All the heat of the tunnel rushed into him. He felt his head waver before steadying in a dangerously fragile version of itself, raw with a smell which surely wasn't of exhaust fumes, despite the haze into which the distant walkers were descending. He had to go back beyond the point at which his previous call had lost its hold. He peeled the soggy receiver away from his face and swung round, to be confronted by a mass of flesh as wide and as long as the protracted curve of the tunnel. He could hear more of it being tamped into the unseen mouth by the jabbing of the megaphones. Of the countless heads it was wagging at him, every one that he managed to focus looked prepared to see him trampled underfoot if he didn't keep moving. He could no more force his way back through it than through the concrete wall, but there was no need. He would use a walkway as soon as he found some steps up.

Another wave of heat which felt like the threat of being overwhelmed by the tide of flesh found him, sending him after the rhythmically quivering women. As far ahead as he could see there were no steps onto the walkways, but his never having noticed them while driving needn't mean steps didn't exist; surely a trick of perspective was hiding them from him. He narrowed his eyes until he felt the lids twitch against the eyeballs and his head ache more than his feet were aching. He poked the recall button and lifted the receiver above his head in case that might allow him to hook a call, but the phone at home hadn't even doubled its first ring when his

20

handful of technology went dead as though suffocated by the heat or drowned in the sweat of his fist. As he let it sink past his face, a phone shrilled further down the tunnel.

"They're bloody breeding," the old man growled behind him, but Blythe didn't care what he said. About three hundred yards ahead he saw an aerial extend itself above a woman's scalp as blonde as Lydia's. Whatever had been interfering with his calls, it apparently wasn't present in that stretch of the tunnel. He saw the aerial wag a little with her conversation as she walked at least a hundred yards. As he tramped towards the point where she'd started talking he counted the slabs of light overhead, some of which appeared to be growing unstable with the heat. He had only half as far to go now, however much the saturated heat might weigh him down. It must be his eyes which were flickering, not as many of the lights as seemed to be. He needn't wait until he arrived at the exact point in the tunnel. He only wanted reassurance that Valerie had picked up his message. He thumbed the button and flattened his ear with the receiver. The tone had barely invited him to dial when it was cut off.

He mustn't panic. He hadn't reached where phones worked, that was all. On, trying to ignore the sluggishly retreating haze of body heat which smelled increasingly like exhaust fumes, reminding himself to match the pace of the crowd, though the pair of walkers on each side of him made him feel plagued by double vision. Now he was where the woman's phone had rung, beneath two dead fluorescents separated by one which looked as though it had stolen its glare from both. All three were bumped backwards by their fellows as he jabbed the button, bruised his ear with the earpiece, snatched the receiver away and cleared it, supported it with his other hand before it could slide out of his sweaty grip, split a fingernail against the button, bruised his ear again... Nothing he did raised the dialling tone for longer than it took to mock him.

It couldn't be the phone itself. The woman's had worked, and his was the latest model. He could only think the obstruction was moving, which meant it had to be the crowd that was preventing him from acting. If Lydia's replacement for him took him to court he would lose business because of it, probably the confidence of many of his clients too because they wouldn't understand he took more care with their affairs than he did with his own, and if he went to prison... He'd closed both fists around the phone, because the plastic and his hands were aggravating one another's slipperiness, and tried not to imagine battering his way through the crowd. There were still the walkways, and by the time he found the entrance to one it might make sense to head for the far end of the tunnel. He was trudging forward, each step a dull ache which bypassed his hot swollen body wrapped in far too much sodden material and searched for a sympathetic ache in his hollowed-out head, when the phone rang.

It was so muffled by his grip that he thought for a moment it wasn't his. Ignoring the groans of the muscled duo, he nailed the button and jammed the wet plastic against his cheek. "Steve Blythe. Can you make it quick? I don't know how long this will work."

"It's all right, Steve. I only called to see how you were surviving. Sounds as if you're deep in it. So long as you're giving your brain a few hours off for once. You can tell me all about it when you come home."

"Val. Val, wait. Val, are you there?" Blythe felt a mass of heat which was nearly flesh lurch at him from behind as he missed a step. "Speak to me, Val."

"Calm down, Steve. I'll still be here when you get back. Save your energy. You sound as though you need it."

"I'll be fine. Just tell me you got the message."

"Which message?"

The heat came for him again — he couldn't tell from which direction, nor how fast he was stumbling. "Mine. The one I left while you were doing whatever you were doing."

"I had to go out for some black and white. The machine can't be working properly. There weren't any messages on the tape when I came in just now."

That halted Blythe as if the phone had reached the end of an invisible cord. The vista of walkers wavered into a single flat mass, then steadied and regained some of its perspective. "Never mind. Plenty of time," he said rapidly. "All I wanted — "

A shoulder much more solid than a human body had any right to be rammed his protruding elbow. The impact jerked his arm up, and the shooting pain opened his fist. He saw the phone describe a graceful arc before it clanged against the railing of the right-hand walkway and flew into the crowd some thirty yards ahead. Arms flailed at it as though it was an insect, then it disappeared. "What was that for?" he screamed into the old man's face as it bobbed alongside his. "What are you trying to do to me?"

The son's face crowded Blythe's from the other side, so forcefully it sprayed Blythe's cheek with sweat. "Don't you yell at him, he's got a bad ear. Lucky you weren't knocked down, stopping like that. Better believe you will be if you mix it with my dad."

"Can someone pick up my phone, please?" Blythe called at the top of his voice.

The women directly in front of him added winces to their quivering and covered their ears, but nobody else acknowledged him. "My phone," he pleaded. "Don't step on it. Who can see it? Look for it, can you all? Please pass it back."

"I said about my dad's ear," the man to his left rumbled, lifting a hammer of a fist which for the present he used only to mop his forehead. Blythe fell silent, having seen a hand raised some yards ahead of him to point a finger downwards where the phone must be. At least it was in the middle of the road, in Blythe's immediate path. A few raw steps brought him a glimpse of the aerial, miraculously intact, between the thighs of the singleted woman. He stooped without breaking his stride, and his scalp brushed her left buttock. His finger and thumb closed on the aerial and drew it towards him — only the aerial. He was staggering forward in his crouch when he saw most of the keypad being kicked away to his left, and several other plastic fragments skittering ahead.

As he straightened up, a grasp as hot and soft as flesh yet rough as concrete seemed to close around his skull. The singleted woman had turned on him. "Whose bum do you think you're biting?"

Any number of hysterical replies occurred to him, but he managed to restrain himself. "I'm not after any of that, I'm after this." The words sounded less than ideally chosen once they were out, especially since the aerial in his hand was rising between her legs as though magnetised by her crotch. He whipped it back, the grip on his skull threatening to blind him, and heard himself shouting. "Look at it. Who did this? Who smashed my phone? Where are your brains?"

"Don't look at us," said the woman with the increasingly bare and moist midriff, while the son leaned his dripping face into Blythe's: "Keep the row up if you're after an ear like my dad's." All at once they were irrelevant, and he let the aerial slip from his hand. There was at least one working phone in the tunnel.

As soon as he attempted to edge forward the crowd swung its nearest heads towards him, its eyes blinking away sweat, its mouths panting hotly at him, and started to mutter and grumble. "What's the panic? Wait your turn. We all want to get there. Keep your distance. There's people here, you know," it warned him in several voices, and raised one behind him. "Now where's he scuttling off to? Must be afraid I'll report him for going for my bum."

The obstruction to his calls was about to turn physical if he couldn't find a way to fend it off. "Emergency," he murmured urgently in the nearest unmatched pair of ears, which after hesitating for a second parted their bodies to let him through. "Excuse me. Emergency. Excuse," he repeated, stepping up the intensity, and was able overtake enough people that he must be close to the phone. Which of the clump of blonde heads belonged to it? Only one looked real. "Excuse me," he said, and realising that sounded as if he wanted to get by, took hold of its unexpectedly thin and angular shoulder. "You had the phone just now, didn't you? I mean, you have — "

"Let go."

"Yes. What I'm saying is, you've got — "

"Let go."

"There. I have. Excuse me. My hand's in my pocket, look. What I'm trying to say — "

The woman turned away as much of her sharp face as she'd bothered to incline towards him. "Not me."

"I'm sure it was. Not my phone, not the one that was trodden on, but weren't you talking on the phone before? If it wasn't yours — "

She was surrounded by female heads, he saw, all of them preserving a defiant blankness. Without warning she snapped her head round, her hair lashing his right eye. "Who let you out? Which madhouse have they closed down now?"

"Excuse me. I didn't mean to..." That covered more than he had time to put into words, not least the inadvertent winks which his right eye must appear to be sharing with her. "It's an emergency, you see. If it wasn't you you must have seen who it was with the phone. She was somewhere round here."

All the heads in her clump jeered practically in unison, then used her head to speak. "It's an emergency all right, an emergency that you need locking up. Just you wait till we get out of here and talk to someone."

That made Blythe peer at his watch. Sweat or a tear from his stinging eye bloated the digits, and he had to shake his wrist twice before he was able to distinguish that he would never reach the tunnel exit in time to find a phone outside. The crowd had beaten him — or perhaps not yet, unless he'd failed to notice it sending a message ahead that he was to be stopped. "Emergency. Emergency," he said in a voice whose edge the heat seemed determined to blunt, and when he thought he'd sidled far enough away from the woman who wanted to persuade him he was going mad, let his desperation grow louder. "Emergency. Need to phone. Has anyone a phone? Emergency." A shake or a wave of the heat passed through bunch after bunch of heads, and each time it did so his right eye blinked and smarted. He was trying to sound more official and peremptory when his voice trailed off. At the limit of his vision the packed flesh beneath the unsteady lights had come to a complete stop.

He could only watch the stasis creeping towards him, wavering into place in layer after layer of flesh. It was his worst possible future racing to meet him, and the crowd had been on its side all along. As he heard a murmur advancing down the tunnel from the direction of the unseen exit, he strained his ears to hear what it was saying about him. He was feeling almost calm — for how long, he couldn't predict — when words in an assortment of voices grew distinct. The message was past him before he succeeded in piecing it together. "Someone's collapsed in the middle of the tunnel. They're clearing the way for an ambulance."

"Bastard," Blythe snarled, not knowing if he meant the casualty or the crowd or the ambulance — and instantly knew he should mean none of them, because he was saved from the future he'd almost wished on himself. He began to shoulder his way forward. "Emergency. Make way, please. Make way," he was able to say more officiously, and when that failed to clear his route fast enough "Let me through. I'm a doctor."

He mustn't let himself feel guilty. The ambulance was coming — he could see the far end of the tunnel beginning to turn blue and shiver — and so he was hardly putting the patient at risk. The ambulance was his only hope. Once he was close enough he would be injured, he would be however disabled he needed to seem in order to persuade the crew to take him out of the crowd. "I'm a doctor," he said louder, wishing he was and unmarried too, except that his life was controllable again, everything was under control. "I'm the doctor," he said, better yet, strong enough to part the flesh before him and to blot out the voices that were discussing him. Were they trying to confuse him by dodging ahead of him? They had to be echoes, because he identified the voice of the woman who'd pretended she had no phone. "What's he babbling about now?"

"He's telling everyone he's a doctor."

"I knew it. That's what they do when they're mad."

He needn't let her bother him; nobody around him seemed to hear her — maybe she was fishing for him with her voice. "I'm the doctor," he shouted, seeing the ambulance crawling towards him at the end of the visible stretch of tunnel. For a moment he thought it was crushing bruised people, exhaust fumes turning their pulse blue, against the walls, but of course they were edging out alongside it, making way. His shout had dislodged several voices from beneath the bleary sweat-stained lights. "What did she say he's saying, he's a doctor?"

"Maybe he wanted to examine your bum."

"I know the kind of consultation I'd like to have with him. It was a quack made my dad's ear worse."

Could the crowd around Blythe really not hear them, or was it pretending ignorance until it had him where it wanted him? Wasn't it parting for him more slowly than it should, and weren't its heads only just concealing its contempt for his imposture? The mocking

26

voices settled towards him, thickening the heat which was putting on flesh all around him. He had to use one of the walkways. Now that he had to reach the ambulance as speedily as possible, he was entitled to use them. "I'm the doctor," he repeated fiercely, daring anyone to challenge him, and felt his left shoulder cleaving the saturated air. He'd almost reached the left-hand walkway when a leotarded woman whose muscles struck him as no more likely than her deep voice moved into his path. "Where are you trying to get to, dear?"

"Up behind you. Give me a hand, would you?" Even if she was a psychiatric nurse or warder, he had seniority. "I'm needed. I'm the doctor."

Only her mouth moved, and not much of that. "Nobody's allowed up there unless they work for the tunnel."

He had to climb up before the heat turned into sweaty voices again and trapped him. "I do. I am. There's been a collapse, the tunnel's made them collapse, and they need me."

He'd seen ventriloquists open their mouths wider. Her eyes weren't moving at all, though a drop of sweat was growing on her right eyelashes. "I don't know what you're talking about."

"That's all right, nurse. You aren't required to. Just give me a hand. Give me a leg up," Blythe said, and saw the drop swelling on her untroubled eyelid, swelling until he could see nothing else. If she was real she would blink, she wouldn't stare at him like that. The mass of flesh had made her out of itself to block his plan, but it had miscalculated. He flung himself at her, dug his fingers into her bristly scalp and heaved himself up with all the force his arms could muster.

His heels almost caught her shoulders. They scraped down to her breasts, which gave them enough leverage for him to vault over her. His hands grabbed at the railing, caught it, held on. His feet found the edge of the walkway, and he hauled one leg over the railing, then the other. Below him the nurse was clutching her breasts and emitting a sound which, if it was intended as a cry of pain, failed to impress him. Perhaps it was a signal, because he'd taken only a few steps along the way to freedom when hands commenced trying to seize him.

At first he thought they meant to injure him so that the ambulance would take him, and then he saw how wrong he was. He had an unobstructed view of the ambulance as it rammed its way through the crowd, its blue light pounding like his head, the white arch flaring blue above it as he felt the inside of his skull flaring. There was no sign of anyone collapsed ahead. The ambulance had been sent for Blythe, of course; the message had been passed along that they'd succeeded in driving him crazy. But they couldn't conceal their opinion of him, hot oppressive breathless waves of which rose towards him and would have felt like shame if he hadn't realised how they'd given themselves away: they couldn't hold him in such contempt unless they knew more about him than they feigned to know. He kicked at the grasping fingers and glared about in search of a last hope. It was behind him. The woman with Lydia's hair had abandoned her pretence of having no phone, and he had only to grab the aerial.

He dashed back along the walkway, hanging onto the rail and kicking out at anyone within reach, though his feet so seldom made contact that he couldn't tell how many of the hands and heads were real. The woman who was still trying to convince him he'd injured her breasts flinched, which gratified him. She and the rest of the mob could move when they wanted to, they just hadn't done so for him. The beckoning aerial led his gaze to the face dangling from it. She was staring at him and talking so hard her mouth shaped every syllable. "Here he comes now," she mouthed.

She must be talking to the ambulance. Of course, she'd used the phone before to summon it, because she was another of the nurses. She'd better hand over the phone if she didn't want worse than he was supposed to have done to her colleague. "Here I come all right," he yelled, and heard what sounded like the entire crowd, though perhaps only the tunnel that was his head, echoing him. As he ran the tunnel widened, carrying her further from the walkway, too far for him to grab the aerial over the crowd. They thought they'd beaten him, but they were going to help him again. He vaulted the railing and ran across the mass of flesh.

It wasn't quite as solid as he had assumed, but it would do. The heat of its contempt streamed up at him, rebounding from the dank concrete of his skull. Was it contemptuous of what he was doing or of his failure to act when he could have? He had a sudden notion, so terrible it almost caused him to lose his footing, that when he raised the phone to his ear he would discover the woman had been talking to Valerie. It wasn't true, and only the heat was making him think it. Stepping-stones turned up to him and gave way underfoot — there went some teeth and there, to judge by its yielding, an eye — but he could still trample his way to the phone, however many hands snatched at him.

Then the aerial whipped up out of his reach like a rod that had caught a fish. The hands were pulling him down into their contempt, but they weren't entitled to condemn him: he hadn't done anything they weren't about to do. "I'm you," he screamed, and felt the shoulders on which he'd perched move apart further than his legs could stretch. He whirled his arms, but this wasn't a dream in which he could fly away from everything he was. Too late he saw why the woman had called the ambulance for him. He might have screamed his thanks to her, but he could make no words out of the sounds which countless hands were dragging from his mouth.

THE ALTERNATIVE

HIGHTON WAS DRIVING PAST THE DISUSED HOSPITAL when the car gave up. On the last fifty miles of motorway he had taken it slow, earning himself glances of pity mingled with hostility from the drivers of the Jaguars and Porsches. As he came abreast of the fallen gates the engine began to grate as though a rusty chunk of it were working itself loose, and the smell of fumes grew urgently acrid. The engine died as soon as he touched the brake.

A wind which felt like shards of the icy sun chafed the grass in the overgrown grounds of the hospital as he climbed out of the Vauxhall, rubbing his limbs. He was tempted to leave the car where it was, but the children who smashed windows were likely to set fire to it if he abandoned it overnight. Grasping the wheel with one hand and the crumbling edge of the door with the other, he walked the car home through the housing estate.

All the windows closest to the hospital were boarded up. Soon he encountered signs of life, random windows displaying curtains or, where the glass was broken, cardboard. A pack of bedraggled dogs roamed the estate, fighting over scraps of rotten meat, fleeing yelping out of the communal entrances of the two-storey concrete blocks.

His skin felt grubby with exertion when at last he reached his block. A drunk with an eyeshade pulled down to his brows was lolling at the foot of the concrete stairs. As Highton approached, he staggered away into the communal yard strewn with used condoms and syringes. Someone had recently urinated at the bend of the staircase, and the first flat on the balcony had been broken into; a figure was skulking in the dark at the far side of the littered front room. Highton was opening his mouth to shout when he saw that the man at the wall wasn't alone: bare legs emerging from a skirt as purple as a flower were clasped around his waist above his fallen trousers. The couple must have frozen in the act, hoping Highton wouldn't notice them. "Have fun," he muttered, and hurried past six doors to his.

The 9 on the door, where the red paint had been sun-bleached almost pink, had lost one of its screws and hung head downwards from the other, like a noose. When he pushed it upright, it leaned drunkenly against the 6 as he let himself into the flat. The dim narrow corridor which led past three doors to the kitchen and the bathroom smelled of stale carpet and overcooked vegetables. He closed the front door quietly and eased open the first inner door.

Valerie was lying on the bed which they had moved into the living-room once the children needed separate bedrooms. Apart from the bed and the unmatched chairs the room contained little but shadowy patches lingering on the carpet to show where furniture had stood. At first he thought his wife was asleep, and then, as he tiptoed through the pinkish light to part the curtains, he saw that she was gazing at the corner which had housed the television until the set was repossessed. She gave a start which raised the ghost of a ring from the disconnected telephone, and tossing back her lank hair, smiled shakily at him. "Just remembering," she said.

"We've plenty to remember." When her smile drooped he added hastily "And we'll have more."

"You got the job?"

"Almost."

She sighed as if letting go of the strength which had helped her to wait for him. As her shoulders sagged, she appeared to dwindle. "We'll have to manage."

He lowered himself into a chair, which emitted a weary creak. He ought to go to her, but he knew that if he held her while they were both depressed she would feel like a burden, not like a person at all. "Sometimes I think the bosses choose whoever travelled furthest because that shows how much they want the job," he said. "I was thinking on the way back, I should have another try at getting jobs round here."

Valerie was flicking a lock of hair away from her cheek. "If I can rewire a few properties," he went on, "so people know they shouldn't associate me with those cowboys just because I was fool enough to work for them, the work's bound to build up and we'll move somewhere better. Then we can tell Mr O'Mara that he's welcome to his ratholes."

She was still brushing at her greying hair. "Where are Daniel and Lucy?" he said.

"They said they wouldn't be long," she responded as if his query were an accusation, and he saw her withdraw into herself. He was trying to phrase a question which he wouldn't be afraid to ask when he heard the door creep open behind him. He turned and saw Lucy watching him.

He might have assumed Valerie was mistaken — that their fourteen-year-old had been in her room and was on her way out, since the front door was open — if it weren't for her stance and her expression. She was ready to take to her heels, and her look betrayed that she was wondering how much he knew — whether he recognised her cheap new dress as purple as a flower. She saw that he did, and her face crumpled. The next moment she was out of the flat, slamming the door.

As he shoved himself off the chair, his heart pulsating like a wound, Valerie made a grab at him. How could she think he would harm their daughter? "I only want to bring her back so we can talk," he protested.

She shrank against the headboard of the bed and tried to slap away the lock of hair, her nails scratching her cheek. "Don't leave us again," she said in a low dull voice.

"I'll be as quick as I can," he promised, and had a fleeting impression, which felt like a stab of panic, that she meant something else entirely. The clatter of Lucy's high heels had already reached the staircase. He clawed the front door open and sprinted after her.

He reached ground level just in time to see her disappearing into the identical block on the far side of the littered yard. The drunk with the eyeshade flung an empty bottle at him, and Highton was afraid that the distraction had lost him his daughter. Then he glimpsed a flash of purple beyond a closing door on the balcony, and he ran across the yard and up the stairs, on tiptoe now. As he reached the balcony he heard Lucy's voice and a youth's, muffled by the boards nailed over the window. He was at the door in two strides, and flung it open. But his words choked unspoken in his throat. The youth on the floor was his son Daniel.

The fifteen-year-old blinked at him and appeared to recognise him, for a vague grin brought some animation to his face as he went back to unwinding the cord from his bruised bare scrawny arm. Highton stared appalled at the hypodermic lying beside him on the grimy floorboards, at the money which Lucy was clutching. He felt unable to move and yet in danger of doing so before he could control himself. He heard Valerie pleading "Don't leave us again," and the memory seemed to release him. "No," he tried to shout, and woke.

He was alone in bed, and surrounded by some indeterminate distance by a mass of noises: a hissing and bubbling which made his skin prickle, a sound like an endless expelled breath, a mechanical chirping. When he opened his eyes, the room looked insufficiently solid. "Valerie," he managed to shout.

"Coming." The hissing and bubbling grew shriller and became a pouring sound. As he sat himself up she brought him a mug of coffee. "Don't dawdle in the bathroom or your father will be late for work," she called, and told him "You seemed to want to sleep."

"I'm just drying my hair," Lucy responded above the exhalation.

"Finish on the computer now, Daniel. You know not to start playing before school."

"It's not a game," Daniel called indignantly, but after a few seconds the chirping ceased.

Valerie winked at Highton. "At least all that should have woken you up."

"Thank God for it."

She stooped and holding back her long black hair with one hand, kissed each of his eyes. "Have your shower while I do breakfast."

He sipped the coffee quickly, feeling more present as the roof of his mouth began to peel. The dream had been worse this time, and longer; previously it had been confined to the flat. It must have developed as it had because he would be seeing O'Mara this morning.

As usual when Lucy had used it, the bath was full of foam. Highton cleared the mirror and tidied away Daniel's premature electric razor before sluicing the foam down the plughole with the shower. By the time he went downstairs, Valerie was waving the children off to school. When the microwave oven beeped he grabbed his breakfast and wolfed it, though Valerie wagged a finger at him. "You'll be giving yourself indigestion and nightmares," she said, and he thought of telling her about his recurrent dream. Doing so seemed like inviting bad luck, and he gave her a long kiss to compensate for his secrecy as he left the house.

All along the wide suburban street the flowering cherry was in bloom. Highton inhaled the scent before he drove the Jaguar out of the double garage. He had an uninterrupted run along the dual carriageway into town until the traffic lights halted him at the junction with the road which led to the disused hospital past the flats which O'Mara had bought from the council. When the lights released him Highton felt as if he were emerging from a trance.

The only spaces in the car park were on the ninth floor. Beyond the architectural secrets which the top storeys of the business district shared with the air he saw the old council estate. He put the sight out of his mind as he headed for his office, mentally assembling issues for discussion with O'Mara.

O'Mara was late as usual, and bustled into Highton's office as if he had been kept waiting. He plumped himself on the chair in front of the desk, slung one leg over the other, rubbed his hands together loudly and folded them over his waistcoated stomach, flashing a fat gold ring. Throughout this performance he stared at Highton's chair as if both men were on the wrong sides of the desk. "Tell me all the good news," he demanded, beginning to tap the carpet with the toecaps of his brogues.

"We've identified a few points you overlooked in your accounts."

A hint of wariness disturbed the heavy blandness of O'Mara's round face. "So long as you'll be making me more than I'm paying you."

"It depends whether you decide to follow our advice." Highton picked up the sheet on which he'd made notes for discussion, and blurted out a thought which seemed just to have occurred to him. "You might consider a programme of repairs and improvements to your properties as a tax expense."

O'Mara's face reddened and appeared to puff up. "I can't afford to splash money around now I'm no longer on the council."

"But surely —" Highton said, and heard his voice grow accusing. How could he forget himself like that? It wasn't his job to moralise, only to stay within the law. The dream must have disturbed him more than he knew for him to risk betraying to O'Mara his dislike of the man. "Let me guide you through your accounts," he said.

Half an hour later the landlord was better off by several thousand pounds, but Highton couldn't take much pleasure in it; he kept seeing how exorbitant the rents were. He showed O'Mara to the lift and made himself shake hands, and wiped off the man's sweat with his handkerchief as soon as the lift door closed. The sympathetic grins his partners and the secretaries gave him raised his spirits somewhat, and so did the rest of the day: he set up a company for a client, argued the case of another with the Inland Revenue, helped a third choose a pension plan. He had almost forgotten O'Mara until he returned to his car.

He leaned on the Jaguar and gazed towards O'Mara's streets. Could they really be as bad as he'd dreamed? He felt as if he wasn't entitled to go home until he had seen for himself. When he reached the junction at the edge of the estate he steered the car off the dual carriageway.

Concrete surrounded him, identical streets branching from both sides of the road like a growth which had consumed miles of terraced streets. The late afternoon sky was the same dull white. From the air the place must resemble a huge ugly crystal of some chemical. Perhaps half the windows he passed were boarded up, but he didn't know if he was more disturbed by the spectacle of so many disused homes or the thought of tenants having to live among the abandoned flats. The few people he passed — children who looked starved or unhealthily overweight, teenagers with skin the colour of concrete, older folk hugging bags tightly for fear of being mugged — either glared at him or dodged out of sight. They must take him for someone on O'Mara's payroll, since the landlord never visited his properties in person, and he was uncomfortably aware that his wallet contained a hundred pounds which he'd drawn from the bank at lunchtime. He'd seen enough to show him the district was all that he'd imagined it to be; but when he turned off the main road it was to drive deeper into the maze.

Why should he assume that he was following the street along which he'd turned in his dream? Apart from the numbers on the doors and over the communal entrances, there was little to distinguish one street from another. He was driving past the low nine hundreds; the block on the far side of a junction scattered with broken glass should contain the flat whose number he had dreamed of. He avoided the glass and cruised past the block, and then the car shuddered to a standstill beside a rusty Vauxhall as his foot faltered on the accelerator.

It was by no means the only faded red door he'd seen since leaving the dual carriageway, nor the only door on which a number was askew; but the sight of the 9 dangling upside-down as if the final 3 had been subtracted from it seemed disconcertingly familiar. He switched off the ignition and got clumsily out of the car. Glancing around to reassure himself that nobody was near, he ran across the road and up the stairs.

Of course the concrete staircase looked familiar, since he had already driven past a host of them. He peered around the corner at the top and hurried along the balcony as fast as he could creep. There were seven doors between the stairway and the door with the inverted 9. One glance through the gap between the curtains next to the door would quieten his imagination, he promised himself. He ducked his head towards the gap, trying to fabricate an explanation in case anyone saw him. Then he froze, his fingers digging into the rotten wood of the windowsill. On the carpet a few feet from the window was a telephone, and he'd recognised the number on the dial.

Even stronger than the shock which caused him to gasp aloud was the guilt which overwhelmed him at the sight of the room, the ragged pinkish curtains, the double bed against the wall beyond the unmatched chairs. He felt responsible for all this, and unable to retreat until he'd done his best to change it. He groped for his wallet and counted out fifty pounds, which he stuffed through the slot in the front door. Having kept half the cash made him feel unforgivably mean. He snatched the rest of the notes from his wallet and shoved them into the flat, where they flopped on the hall floor.

The sound, and the prospect of confronting anyone from the flat, sent Highton fleeing like a thief. How could he explain to Valerie what he'd just done when he could hardly believe that he'd done it? He swung the car screeching towards the dual carriageway and drove back to the business district, where he withdrew another hundred pounds from the dispenser in the wall outside the bank.

As he let himself into the house Valerie was coming downstairs laden with the manuals she employed to teach her students word processing. "Hello, stranger," she said.

Highton's stomach flinched. "How do you mean?"

"Just that you're late. Though now you mention it, you do look a bit strange."

"I'm home now," Highton said, feeling even more accused. "I had something to tidy up."

"You can't fool me, you've been visiting your mistress," Valerie said smiling. "I've had to eat so I can run. Everything for you three is by the microwave."

He was relieved not to have to face her while his thoughts were in turmoil, but his relief felt like disloyalty. He listened as the dreamy hum of her car receded, fading sooner than he was expecting. When the oven peeped he called the children downstairs. Lucy came at once, her extravagant earrings jangling; Daniel had to be shouted for three times, and would have worn his personal stereo at the dinner-table if Highton hadn't frowned at him. "Let's hear about your day instead," Highton appealed to both of them.

Daniel had scored a goal in a football match against a rival school and been praised for his science project, Lucy's work on local history had been singled out to be shown to the headmistress. "Now you have to tell us about your day," Lucy said.

"Just the usual, trying to balance the books." Feeling trapped, Highton went on quickly: "So are you both happy?"

Daniel looked puzzled, almost resentful. "Expect so," he said and shrugged.

"Of course we are. You and mummy see that we are."

Highton smiled at her and wondered if she was being sensitive to his emotional needs rather than wholly honest; perhaps it had been an unreasonably direct question to ask people of their ages. Once the dinner things were in the dishwasher Daniel lay on his bed with his headphones on while Lucy finished the homework her class had been set in advance to give them more time at the school disco, and Highton poured himself a large Scotch and put a compact disc of Mozart piano sonatas on the player.

The stream of music and the buzzing in his skull only unsettled him. Had he really donated a hundred pounds to someone he didn't know, with as little thought as he might have dropped a coin beside any of the beggars who were becoming an everyday sight in the downtown streets? In retrospect the gesture seemed so flamboyant as to be offensive. At least the money had been in old notes, and couldn't be traced to him; the idea that whoever lived in the flat might come to the house in search of an explanation terrified him. Worse still was the thought of their asking Valerie or the children. His growing confusion exhausted him, and he would have gone to bed if that hadn't seemed like trying to avoid Valerie when she came home. He refilled his glass and switched on the television, which was more likely than the music to keep him awake, but he found all the programmes discomforting: newscasts and documentaries about poverty and famine and a millionaire who had never paid tax, a film in which a policeman had to hunt down a jewel thief who had been his best friend when they were children in the slums. He turned off the set and waited for the financial report on the radio, in case the broadcast contained information he should know. The programme wasn't over when he fell asleep in the chair.

The next he knew, Valerie was shaking him. "Wake up, I want to talk to you. Why won't you wake up?"

He found himself clinging to the arms of the chair as if by staying immobile he could hold on to his slumber. One of his fingers poked through a tear in the fabric, into the spongy stuffing of the chair. The sensation was so disagreeable that it jerked his eyes open. Valerie was stooping to him, looking in danger of losing her balance and falling back on the bed. "Don't keep going away from me," she begged.

Highton grabbed her wrists to steady her. "What's wrong now? Is it the children?"

"Lucy's in her room. I've spoken to her. Leave her alone, Alan, or she'll be running off again. She only wanted to give Daniel what she could because she can't bear to see him suffer."

Highton blinked at Valerie as she tried to toss back her greying hair. The light from the overhead bulb glared from the walls of the room, except where the shadow of the lampshade lay on them like grime, yet he felt as if they or he weren't fully present. "Where is he?"

"Gone."

"Where?"

"Oh, where do you think?" Her resignation gave way momentarily to anger, and Highton felt deeply ashamed of having left her to fend for herself. "There was some money in the hall," she said as though she was trying to clarify her thoughts. "A hundred pounds that must have been put through our door by mistake. Whoever did that can't be up to any good, and they'll turn nasty if they don't get it back, but Daniel wouldn't listen. He was away with it before we could stop him."

Highton felt that he ought to know where the money had come from, as if he had foreseen it in a dream. The impression was too vague to grasp, and in any case he hadn't time to do so. "How long ago?"

"Ten minutes, maybe quarter of an hour. We didn't see which way he went," Valerie said like an accusation.

"You wouldn't be safe out there this late." Highton squeezed her shoulders through the faded grey checked dress and stood up. "You look after Lucy. I'll find him."

He wouldn't return until he had, he vowed to himself. He closed the front door and picked his way along the unlit balcony to the head of the stairs. Through the windy aperture in the rear wall he could see across the yard. Some of the windows that were lit shouldn't be; he glimpsed the glow of an upturned flashlight beyond one set of makeshift shutters, the flicker of candlelight through another. Daniel and youngsters like him would be in one or more of the abandoned rooms while their suppliers hid at home behind reinforced doors and windows. The knowledge enraged Highton, who launched himself at the stairs, too hastily. His foot missed the step it was reaching for, and he fell headlong.

He was bracing himself to hit concrete, but his impact with the carpet was a greater shock. His fists and his knees wobbled, and the crouch he had instinctively adopted almost collapsed. He stared bewildered at the chair from which he'd toppled forwards, the radio whose voice had grown blurred and distant, the glass of Scotch which seemed exactly half empty, half full. The room and its contents made him feel dislocated, unable to think. He stumbled to the telephone and dialled the number which had lingered in his head.

The number was disconnected. Its monotonous wail reached deep into him. He was pressing the receiver against his ear, and feeling as if he couldn't let go until he had conceived a response to the wail for help, when Valerie came into the room. "Who are you calling so late?"

He hadn't realised she was home. He clutched at the earpiece to muffle the wail and fumbled the receiver onto its rest. "Nobody. Nobody's there," he gabbled. "I mean, just the speaking clock."

"Don't look so disconcerted or you'll have me thinking you're being unfaithful." She gazed at him for several protracted seconds, then she winked. "Only teasing. I know you've just woken up," she said, and went upstairs.

Her affectionateness made him feel guiltier. He switched off the mumbling radio and sat trying to think, until he realised how long he had been sitting and followed Valerie. He was hoping they could make love — at least then he might feel closer to her without having to talk — but she was asleep.

He lay beside her and stared up at the dark. His desire for sleep felt like a compulsion to dream. He didn't know which disturbed him more, his fear of finding out what happened next or his need to do so. Why couldn't he accept that he had simply acted on impulse this afternoon — that he'd donated his cash to some of O'Mara's tenants to compensate for his involvement with the man? Given how cramped the flats were, the presence of a bed as well as a few worn-out chairs in the front room didn't require much imagining, and was he really certain that he had dreamed anything more specific about the place before he had looked in the window today? Had he genuinely recognised the phone number? The memory of seeing it through the window was vivid as a photograph — so vivid that it blotted out any memory of his having seen it before. Trying to recall the dream felt like slipping back into it, and he kept recoiling from the promise of sleep.

When at last he dozed off, the alarm seemed to waken him so immediately that he could hardly believe he was awake. As long as sleep had caught up with him, why couldn't the dream have reached a conclusion? He dozed again, and when he was roused by Daniel and Lucy calling their goodbyes he thought he was dreaming. He sprawled on the floor in his haste to be out of bed and under a reviving shower.

Whatever temperature he set it to, the downpour felt more distant than he would have liked. The breakfast Valerie put in front of him was almost too hot to taste, but he mustn't linger or he would be late for work. He kissed her cheek and ran to the car, feeling obscurely treacherous. Because of his unsettled night he drove as slowly as the traffic would allow. At the junction from which the concrete flats were visible he felt in danger of forgetting which way to go, and had to restrain himself from driving townwards while the lights were against him.

Julie brought him a mug of coffee and the news that a client had cancelled that morning's appointment because one of her boutiques had been looted overnight. Highton set about examining a hairdresser's accounts, but he didn't feel safe with them: in his present state he might overlook something. He dictated letters instead, trusting the secretaries to spot mistakes. Since he had no appointments, should he take the afternoon off and catch up on his sleep? Once Rebecca had collected the tape of his dictation he cleared a space among the files on the desk and propped his hand against his mouth.

The phone jolted him awake. He wondered how they had been able to afford to have it reconnected until he saw that he was in the office. "It's Mrs Highton," Julie's voice told him.

"Yes, I want to talk to her."

A moment later Valerie's breathing seemed to nestle against his cheek. "Next time it will be," he said.

"What's that, Alan?"

"I was talking to someone here." Despite his confusion he could lie about that, and say "What can I do for you?"

"Do I have to make an appointment? I was going to ask if you wanted to meet for lunch."

He couldn't say yes when he hadn't had time to think. "I'm already booked," he lied. "I'm awfully sorry."

"So you should be," Valerie retorted, and laughed. "I just thought when you went out you looked as if you could do with easing up on yourself."

"I will when I can."

"Do, for all our sakes. See you this evening. Don't be late."

"Why should I be?" Highton demanded, hoping that didn't sound guilty. He dropped the receiver onto its cradle and pinched his forehead viciously to quicken his thoughts. He knew why he'd greeted Valerie as he had: because on wakening he'd found himself remembering the last words she had addressed to him. "Why did it have to be money? Why couldn't it have been something that might have meant something to him?"

She meant the cash Daniel had taken from the flat. Highton must have dreamed her words at the moment of wakening, but he couldn't recall doing so, which made them seem unassailably real. He wouldn't be able to function until he had proved to himself that they weren't. He told the secretaries that he wouldn't be more than an hour, and hurried to his car.

By the time he reached the junction he had a plan. He needed only to be shown that the tenants of the flat weren't the victims of his dream. If sounding his horn didn't bring someone to the window he would go up and knock. He could always say he had mistaken the address, and surely nobody would take him for a thief.

The pavements were scattered with chunks of rubble. Icy winds ambushed him at intersections and through gaps in the architecture, carrying tin cans and discarded polystyrene into the path of the Jaguar, dislodging an empty liquor bottle from a balcony. As he came in sight of the block where he'd posted the notes, a wind raised washing on the line outside the flat as if the clothes were welcoming him. Closest to the edge of the balcony was a dress as purple as a flower.

He clung to the wheel and sent the car racing onwards. Not only the purple dress was familiar; beside it was a grey checked dress, more faded by another wash. He trod on the brake at last, having realised that he was speeding through the duplicated streets with no idea of where he was. Before he found a route to the dual carriageway his head was brimming with panic. He succeeded in returning to the car park without mishap, though he couldn't recall driving there. He strode almost blindly into his office, shouting "Leave me alone for a while." But when Julie tapped on the glass to inform him that the rest of the office was going home he was no closer to understanding what had happened or where it might lead.

He depressed the accelerator hard when the lights at the junction with the dual carriageway turned amber, and was dismayed to find that he wasn't so much anxious to be home as even more nervous of being sidetracked. He steered the car into the driveway and was unlocking the garage when Valerie opened the French windows and stepped onto the back patio. "You may as well leave your car out, Alan."

"Why, are we going somewhere?"

"You haven't forgotten. You're teasing." Her amused expression disguised a plea. "You're getting worse, Alan. I've been saying for months that you need to take it easier."

When he didn't respond she marched into the house, and he could only follow her. The sight of Lucy still in her school uniform released his thoughts. "I *was* joking, you know," he called after Valerie. "It's time to meet Lucy's teachers again."

"Don't bother if it's that much trouble," Lucy said.

"Of course it isn't," Highton replied automatically, hearing Valerie tell Daniel "Make sure you're home by nine."

As the family sat down to dinner Highton said to Lucy "You know I like seeing your schoolwork." He saw that she guessed this was a preamble, and he hurried on: "But your mother's right, I've been having to push myself lately. Better too much work than none, eh? Would you mind if I stayed home tonight and had a rest? I can catch up on your achievements next time."

She suppressed her disappointment so swiftly he might almost have believed he hadn't glimpsed it. "I don't mind," she said, and

Valerie refrained from saying whatever she had been about to say to him, rationing herself to a frown.

She and Lucy drove away before Daniel made for the youth club. Now that Highton had created a chance for himself — the only time he could foresee when he was certain to be alone in the house — he felt both anxious to begin and nervous of betraying his eagerness to Daniel. Hadn't he time to conduct an investigation which should already have occurred to him? He leafed through the phone directory to the listing for Highton, but none of the numbers alongside the column of names was the one he'd seen in the flat. Nor could Directory Enquiries help him; a woman with a persistent dry cough explained patiently that she couldn't trace the number, and seemed to suspect he'd made it up.

Whatever he'd been hoping the search would prove, it left him even more confused. As soon as Daniel had left the house, Highton ran Valerie's Toyota out of the garage and unlocked the boot, then he carried Daniel's computer out to the car. The boy wouldn't be without it for long, he told himself, and the insurance money might pay for an upgraded model. He felt unexpectedly mean for removing only the computer, and so he rushed through the house, collecting items which he felt ashamed to be able to afford: the telephone extension in his and Valerie's bedroom, the portable television in the guest room. Dumping them in the boot, he ran back to the house, trying to decide which window to smash.

A burglar would enter through the French windows, but the prospect of so much breakage dismayed him. The thief or his accomplice could have been small enough to climb through the kitchen window. He was picking up a tenderiser mallet to break the glass, and a towel to help muffle the sound, before he realised that he couldn't use anything in the house. He dashed out, locking the front door behind him, and ran on tiptoe around the house.

He mustn't take long. He had to leave the items on the balcony outside the flat and drive to the school in time to appear to have decided to see Lucy's work after all. Once they were home he would discover that he'd been in such a hurry to get to the school that he had forgotten to switch on the burglar alarm. There were tools in the garden shed which an unprepared burglar might use, but how would the burglar open the padlock on the door? Highton had been straining for minutes to snap the hasp, using a branch which he'd managed to twist off the apple tree, when he wondered if he could say that he had left the shed unlocked, though wouldn't he be claiming to have been too careless for even pressure of work to explain? He ran to the garage for a heavy spanner, with which he began to lever at the hasp and then to hammer at it, afraid to make much noise in case it attracted attention. He was still attacking the padlock when the Jaguar swung into the drive and spotlighted him.

Lucy was first out of the car. "They couldn't turn off the fire alarm, so everyone had to go home," she called; then her cheerfulness wavered. "What are you doing?"

He felt paralysed by the headlights. He couldn't hide the spanner. "I lost the key," he said, and remembered that Valerie knew it was on the ring with his keys to her car. "I mean, I snapped it. Bent it. Had to throw it away," he babbled. "I was going to come to the school after all when I — " He had no idea how he would have continued if he hadn't been interrupted, but the interruption was anything but welcome. A police car had drawn up behind the Jaguar.

Valerie climbed out of his car as the two policemen approached. "I wasn't speeding, was I?"

"We weren't following you, madam," the broader of the pair assured her, staring at Highton. "We received a report of someone behaving suspiciously around this house."

"There must be some mistake. That's my husband." But as she laughed, Valerie's gaze strayed to the open boot of her car. "It's all right, Lucy," she said — too late, for the girl was already blurting "What are you doing with Daniel's computer?"

"I'm sure there's a perfectly reasonable explanation," Valerie said in a tone so clear that she might have been addressing not only Lucy and the policemen but also the neighbours who had appeared at several windows. "In any case, it's a domestic matter."

The police stood their ground. "Perhaps the gentleman would like to explain," the thickset policeman said.

"I was just pottering. Can't I potter around my own property?" Highton felt as if the lights were exposing his attempt at humour for the defensiveness it was, and the police obviously thought so;

they stepped forwards, the man who was built like a bouncer declaring "We'll have a look around if you don't mind, to make sure everything's in order."

They stared hard at the spanner and the padlock, they examined all the downstairs locks and bolts. They lingered over the contents of the boot of the Toyota. "These are yours, are they, madam?" the wiry policeman enquired, and looked ready to ask Valerie to produce receipts. Eventually the police left, having expressed dissatisfaction by their ponderousness. "There won't be any reason for us to come back, I hope," the broad policeman commented, and Highton knew that they'd concluded they had cut short an insurance fraud.

Once they had driven away, Valerie glared at the neighbouring houses until the pairs of curtains fell into place. "Don't say anything, Lucy. Help me carry these things into the house." To Highton she said "You look terrible. For God's sake try and get some sleep. Tomorrow we'll talk about what has to be done. We can't go on like this."

He felt too exhausted to argue, too exhausted even to be afraid of sleep. He fumbled through washing his face and brushing his teeth, and crawled into bed. Sleep held itself aloof from him. In a while he heard Daniel and Lucy murmuring in the back garden, obviously about him. The unfamiliar smell of smoke made him flounder to the window, from which he saw them sharing a cigarette. "Don't start smoking or you won't be able to give it up," he cried, and they fled around the house.

Later, as he lay feeling that sleep was gathering just out of reach, Valerie came to bed. When he tried to put an arm round her she moved away, and he heard muffled sobs. He had the notion that somehow her grief wouldn't go to waste, but before he succeeded in grasping the idea, sleep blotted out his thoughts.

Then she was leaning over him and whispering in his ear. "Come and see," she repeated.

Her voice was too low for him to distinguish its tone, but when he opened his eyes he saw she had been crying. He swung his legs off the bed, on which he had been lying fully dressed. "What is it?"

"Nothing bad," she assured him, and he realised that her tears had been of relief. "Come and see."

He followed her into the hall of the flat and saw a portable television near the front door. "Where did that come from?"

"That's part of it. Have you really been asleep in there all this time?" She was too full of her news to wait for an answer. "He didn't spend that money on drugs. That's why you couldn't find him. He bought the television for us and something for himself to keep him straight."

She put a finger to her lips and beckoned him to the door of Daniel's room. Daniel and Lucy were sitting together on the chair in front of the rickety dressing-table, which bore a computer with a small monochrome screen. Both of them were engrossed in the calculations which it was displaying. "I'm teaching them how to use it," Valerie said in his ear. "Once they're old enough to get a job doing it, maybe I can go back to mine."

Though Highton recognised that he shouldn't enquire too closely into how or where Daniel had been able to buy both a computer and a television for a hundred pounds, it looked like a miracle. "Thank God," he said under his breath.

She squeezed his arm and led him back to the front room. "It won't be easy," she said with a strength which he'd feared had deserted her. "The next few days are going to be awful for him. He swears he'll straighten himself out so long as we don't leave him alone for a moment. He means you particularly, Alan. He needs you to be here."

She wasn't referring only to the present, Highton knew. "I will be, I promise," he said, trying to grasp why he felt less sure of himself than he sounded. "Do you mind if I go out for a stroll and a think, seeing as I won't be going anywhere for a while? I won't be long."

"Don't be," she said, and hugged him fiercely.

He would go back to her, he vowed as he descended the dark concrete stairs, just as soon as he understood why he was harbouring any doubt that he would. Not far now, not much farther, he kept telling himself as he tramped through the dark between the broken streetlamps, trying to relax enough to think. When at last he turned and saw only darkness and looming blocks of flats he was seized by panic. Before he could run back to the flat, he awoke.

Valerie had wakened him by sitting up. When he reached for her, desperate to feel that she was there, she slid out of bed without looking at him. "I'm sorry," he mumbled, rubbing his eyes.

She gave him a wavering glance and sat on the far end of the bed. "I don't even want to know what you thought you were doing, but I need to know what's wrong."

"It's as you've been saying, pressure of work."

"You're going to have to tell me more than that, Alan."

He couldn't tell her the truth, but what else might convince her? "I'm not happy about some of the clients I have to work for. One in particular, a landlord called O'Mara."

"You used to talk to me about anything like that," Valerie said as if he had confirmed his disloyalty. She nodded at the open door, past which Lucy was padding on her way to the bathroom. "Wait until we're alone."

Once the bathroom was free Highton made for the shower. If he closed his eyes he could imagine that the water was lukewarm rain, surging at him on a wind between the blocks of flats. He hurried downstairs as soon as he was dressed, not wanting the children to leave the house until he'd bidden them goodbye.

They were still at the table. They stared at their food and then smiled at him, so brightly yet so tentatively that he felt like an invalid whose condition was obvious to everyone except himself. As Valerie put his plate in front of him with a kind of resentful awkwardness, Lucy said "Don't worry about Mr O'Mara."

The side of Highton's hand brushed against the hot plate. The flare of pain was too distant to bother him. "What do you know about O'Mara?"

"Only that he says you're the best accountant in town," she said, flinching from his roughness. "I didn't mean to listen to what you and mummy were saying."

"Never mind that. Where have you come across him?"

"I haven't yet. His son Lionel told me what he said. Lionel goes to our school." She lifted a forkful of scrambled egg to her lips before adding defiantly "He's taking me to the disco."

Highton could see that she was expecting an argument, but he didn't want to upset her now, particularly since there was no need. He finished his breakfast and waited near the front door to give her and Daniel a hug. "Don't let life get you down," he told them, and watched as they walked away beneath the sunlit cherry trees and turned the corner.

Valerie was switching on the dishwasher. "So tell me about this O'Mara," she said with more than a hint of accusation.

"You look after Lucy. I'll deal with him."

"Not in your present state of mind you won't. You need to see someone, Alan. Maybe they'll prescribe some time off work, which we can afford."

That was true, especially since she was a director of the firm. "At the very least I have to tidy things up," he said.

She seemed resigned, even relieved. "Shall I drive you to the office?"

A surge of love almost overwhelmed him, and he would have pulled her to him if he hadn't been afraid that the violence of his emotion would rouse her suspicions. "I don't know how long I'll be," he said. "I'll come back as soon as I can."

Having to be so careful of his words to her distressed him. He yearned to linger until he had somehow communicated his love for her, except that if he stayed any longer he might be unable to leave. He grabbed his overcoat and made for the front door. "We want you back," she said, and for a moment he was certain that she had an inkling of his plan; then he realised that she was referring to the way he had become unfamiliar. He gave her a wordless smile which he just managed to hold steady, and hurried out to the car.

The lights at the junction on the road into town remained green as he approached them, and he drove straight through. For years he had driven through without considering where the side road led, but now there was barely room for anything else in his mind. It wasn't the money he'd left at the flat which had changed the situation, he thought; it was the balance of fortune. Life at the flat had started to grow hopeful because life at the house had taken a turn for the worse. He parked the car and marched himself to the office, thinking how to restore the balance.

"I'm going to have to take some time off. I wish I could be more definite." His partners reassured him that they could handle the extra workload; they didn't seem surprised by his decision. He discussed with them the cases about which they needed information, and when they left him he grabbed the phone. "No, I can't leave a message. I want to speak to Mr O'Mara in person."

Eventually the landlord picked up the car phone. "I hope I'm going to like what you have to tell me, Alan."

"You won't," Highton said, savouring the moment. "I want you to tell your son to stop sniffing around my daughter. I won't have her feeling that she needs to prostitute herself for the family's sake."

For some time O'Mara only spluttered, so extravagantly that Highton imagined being sprayed in the face with saliva. "He won't be going near her again," O'Mara shouted, "but I'll be wanting a few words with her father in private."

"Just so long as you don't send your thugs to do your talking. I'm not one of your tenants," Highton said, and felt reality lurch. "And if you come anywhere near my house the police will want to know why."

When O'Mara began spluttering obscenities Highton cut him off and held onto the receiver as if he couldn't bear to let go until he'd placed one last call. He dialled and closed his eyes, waiting for Valerie's voice. "Look after one another," he said, and set the receiver on its cradle before she could respond. Snatching a fistful of old financial journals from the table in the reception area, he headed for his car.

The lights at the junction seemed almost meaningless. He had to remind himself not to turn left while they were against him. As soon as they changed he drove through the rubbly streets until he found a courtyard entirely surrounded by boarded-up flats. With the tyre-iron he wrenched the number-plates off the Jaguar, then he thrust the rolled-up magazines into the petrol tank. Once they were all soaked he piled them under the car and set fire to them with the dashboard lighter. As he ran out of the courtyard he shoved the plates between the planks over a window, and the numbers fell into the dark.

He was nearly at the flat when he heard the car explode. Surely that would be enough misfortune for his family to suffer. The sound of the explosion spurred him onwards, up the smelly concrete steps, along the balcony. The door of the flat swung inwards as he poked a key from his ring at the lock. "I'm home," he called.

Silence met him. The cramped kitchen and bathroom were deserted, and so were the untidy bedrooms and the front room. The small television in the latter, and the computer in the boy's room next to it, were switched off. He prayed that he wasn't too late — that Daniel had gone wherever Lucy and his mother were so that they could watch over him. Thank heaven the phone wasn't working, or he might have been tempted to make a call which could only confuse and distract him. He lay down on the bed and closed his eyes, wondering if he might dream of his life in the house while he waited for his family to come to him.

OUT OF THE WOODS

T HE GLASS OF SCOTCH GNASHED ITS ICE CUBES as Thirsk set it down on his desk. "I don't care where it comes from, I just want the best price. Are you certain you won't have a drink?"

The visitor shook his head once while the rest of him stayed unmoved. "Not unless you have natural water."

"Been treated, I'm afraid. One of the many prices of civilisation. You won't object if I have another, will you? I don't work or see people this late as a rule."

When the other shook his head again, agitating his hair, which climbed the back of his neck and was entangled like a bristling brownish nest above his skull, Thirsk crossed to the mahogany cabinet, to pour himself what he hoped might prove to be some peace of mind. While he served himself he peered at his visitor, little of whom was to be seen outside the heavy brown ankle-length overcoat except a wrinkled knotted face and gnarled hands, which ornamented the ends of the arms of the chair. Thirsk could think of no reason why any of this should bother him, but — together with the smell of the office, which was no longer quite or only that of new books — it did, so that he fed himself a harsh gulp of Scotch before marching around his desk to plant himself in his extravagant leather chair. It wasn't too late for him to declare that he didn't see salesmen without an appointment, but instead he heard himself demanding "So tell me why we should do business."

"For you to say, Mr Thirsk."

"No reason unless you're offering me a better deal than the bunch who printed all these books."

That was intended to make the other at least glance at the shelves which occupied most of the wall space, but his gaze didn't waver; he seemed not to have blinked since Thirsk had opened the door to his knock. "Do you know where they get their paper?" he said, more softly than ever.

"I already told you that's immaterial. All I know is it's better and cheaper than that recycled stuff."

"Perhaps your readers would care if they knew."

"I doubt it. They're children." The insinuating softness of the other's speech, together with the dark wistful depths of his eyes, seemed to represent an insubstantial adversary with which Thirsk had to struggle, and he raised his voice. "They won't care unless they're put up to it. If you ask me there's a movement not to let children be children any more, but plenty of them still want fairy tales or they wouldn't buy the books I publish."

The ice scraped the glass as he drained his Scotch and stood up, steadying himself with one hand on the desk. "Anyway, I'm not arguing with you. If you want to send me samples of your work and a breakdown of the costs then maybe we can talk."

His tone was meant to make it clear that would never happen, but the other remained seated, pointing at his own torso with one stiff hand. "This is for you to consider."

He wasn't pointing at himself but rather at a book which was propped like a rectangular stone in his lap. He must have been carrying it all the time, its binding camouflaged against his overcoat. He reared up from the chair as if the coat had stiffened and was raising him, and Thirsk couldn't help recoiling from the small gargoyle face immobile as a growth on a tree, the blackened slit of a mouth like a fissure in old bark. When the hands lowered the volume towards him he accepted it, but as soon as he felt the weight he said "You're joking."

"We seldom do that, Mr Thirsk."

"I couldn't afford this kind of production even if I wanted to. I publish fairy tales, I don't live in them. The public don't care if books fall to bits so long as they're cheap, and that goes double for children."

"Perhaps you should help them to care."

"Here, take your book back."

The other held up his hands, displaying knobbly palms. "It is our gift to you," he said in a voice which, soft as it was, seemed to penetrate every corner of the room.

"Then don't look so glum about it." As Thirsk planted the book on his desk he glimpsed a word embossed on the heavy wooden binding. "*Tapioca*, is that some kind of pudding cookbook?"

Whatever filled his visitor's eyes grew deeper. They struck Thirsk as being altogether too large and dark, and for a moment he had the impression of gazing into the gloomy depths of something quite unlike a face. He strode to the door, more quickly than steadily, and threw it open.

The avenue of pines interspersed with rhododendrons stretched a hundred yards to the deserted road into town. For once the sight didn't appeal to him as peaceful. Surely it would when he'd rid himself of his visitor, who he was beginning to suspect was mad; a leaf and maybe other vegetation was tangled in his hair, and wasn't there a mossy tinge to his cracked cheeks? Thirsk stood aside as the other stalked out of the door, overcoat creaking. Too much to drink or not enough, he thought, because as the figure passed along the avenue, beneath clouds which were helping the twilight gather, it appeared to grow taller. A sound behind him — paper rustling — made him glance around the room. The next second he turned back to the avenue, which was as deserted as the road.

Had his visitor dodged into the bushes? They and the trees were as still as fossils. "Get off my property," Thirsk warned, and cleared his throat so as to shout, "or I'll call the police."

By now it was apparent to him that the man hadn't been a printer. He was tempted to hurl the book after him, except that might bring him back. As he stared at the avenue until the trees seemed to inch in unison towards him, he found he was unwilling to search the grounds when it was growing so rapidly dark. "Go back where you came from," he yelled, and slammed the door so hard the floorboards shook.

A chill had accompanied his visitor into the office, and now it felt even colder. Had one of Thirsk's assistants left a window open in the warehouse? Thirsk hurried to the stout door in the back wall of the room. The door opened with an unexpected creak which lingered in his ears as he reached a hand into the dark. The fluorescent tubes stuttered into life, except for one which left the far end of the central aisle unlit. Though all the windows crammed into the space above the shelves were closed tight, the fifty-yard-long room was certainly colder than usual, and there was more of a smell of old paper than he remembered. In the morning he would have to fix the lights: not now, when at least two of the tubes were growing fitful, so that the flickering contents of the shelves kept resembling supine logs multicoloured with lichen, the spines of the dust jackets. He thumbed the light-switch, a block of plastic so cold it felt moist, and as the dark lurched forward, shut it in. For the first time ever he was wishing he could go home from work.

He was already home. The third door of the office led to the rest of his bungalow. When he opened the door, the cold was waiting for him. The heating hadn't failed; he had to snatch his hand away as soon as he touched the nearest radiator. He poured himself an even larger Scotch, and once he'd fired up his throat and his stomach, dumped himself in the chair behind the desk. The unwelcome visit had left him so on edge that all he could do was work.

The late afternoon mail had brought him an armful of packages which he hadn't had time to open. The topmost padded envelope proved to contain the typescript of a children's book by Huntley Dunkley, who sounded familiar. In his present mood, just the title — *The Smog Goblin and the Last Forest* — was enough to put him off. "Send your bloody propaganda somewhere it's wanted," he snarled, grabbing a copy of the Hamelin Books rejection letter. "Fit only for recycling," he pronounced, and scrawled that as a postscript.

Usually one of his assistants would see to the outgoing mail, but he couldn't stand the sight of the typescript a moment longer. Having clipped the letter to it, he stuffed it into a padded envelope and slung it on the desk next to his, and glared at the discarded packing as it tried to climb out of the waste-bin. Presumably the silence of the room emphasised its movements, though he could have imagined it wasn't alone in making a slow deliberate papery sound, an impression sufficiently persuasive that he glanced out of the window.

The light from the office lay on the strip of grass outside but fell short of the trees, which were embedded in a darkness that had sneaked up on him. He knuckled the switch for the security light. The fierce illumination caught hold of the trees and bushes, and he felt an irrational desire to see them shrink back from the blaze which he could summon at the touch of a finger. Instead they stepped almost imperceptibly forward as though urged by their shadows, a mass of secret blackness interrupted by the drive. Just now the bright bare gravel looked as though it was inviting someone or something to emerge onto it, and he turned away so furiously that he almost tripped over an object on the floor.

It was the discarded envelope, writhing slowly on the carpet and extending a torn brown strip of itself like the remains of a finger towards him. He closed one fist on it, squeezing its pulpy innards, and punched it into the bin before grinding it down with his heel. "That's enough," he shouted, not knowing what he was addressing until his gaze fell on the book his visitor had brought him. "Let's see what you are," he said through his teeth, and flung the book open, wood striking wood. Then he let out a gasp that would have been a word if he'd known how he was feeling.

The thick untrimmed pages weren't composed of paper; each was a single almost rectangular dead leaf. For a moment he thought words were printed on the uppermost, and then he saw the marks were scattered twigs, formed into patterns which he could imagine someone more susceptible than himself assuming to be words in a forgotten language. "If this is a joke," he yelled, ignoring how small his voice sounded in the empty room, "you can take it back," and hoisting the book off the desk, ran to the door.

As the cover banged shut like a coffin lid, the tilting of the book rearranged the twigs into a different pattern — into words he was able to read. He fumbled the door open and raised the volume in both hands. By the glare of the security light he saw the title wasn't *Tapioca* but *Tapiola*. What difference did one letter make? "Come and get it," he roared, hurling the book from him.

It struck the grass with a thud which seemed to crush his shout. The cover raised itself an inch and fell shut, and then the book was as still as the trees and their shadows. Beyond the unlit road, and around his property, the forest stretched for miles. The words he'd glimpsed were growing clearer, embedding themselves in his mind. YOU TURNED AWAY ONE MESSENGER. The night sky seemed to lean towards the patch of light which contained him and the book, as though the sky was the forehead of the blackness behind the mass of trees, in which he heard a sudden gust of wind. Its chill found him while he waited to see the trees move, and he was

56

continuing to wait when it subsided. It might have been a huge icy breath.

"Not likely," he said in a voice which the darkness shrank almost to nothing. He backed away and closed the door. The breath of the night had smelled of decaying vegetation, and now the room did. He thought he saw a trace of his own breath in the air. Hugging himself and rubbing his upper arms, he went to his desk for a mouthful of Scotch. As the ice cubes clashed against his teeth, he almost bit through the glass. Beyond the window the lawn was bare. The book had gone, and there wasn't so much as a hint of a footmark on the grass.

"I bet you think that's clever. Let me introduce you to someone who's cleverer." He was speaking aloud so that his voice would keep him company, he realised, but he wouldn't have to feel alone for long. Without glancing away from the window he groped for the phone on his desk, detached the receiver from its housing and jabbed the talk button. He was already keying the number for the police as he brought the receiver to his face.

A sound came to find him. Though the earpiece was emitting it, it wasn't the dialling tone. It could have been a gale passing through a forest, but it seemed close to articulate. He clawed at the button to clear the line, and listened to the welcome silence; then he poked the talk button again, and again. The phone was dead.

And there was movement among the trees. High on the trunks, branches sprang up and waved at him, a series of them rapidly approaching the house. A branch of a tree at the edge of the grass drooped before gesturing triumphantly at him, and then a severed length of the telephone cable which they had all been supporting plummeted onto the grass.

"Having fun, are you?" Thirsk demanded, though his throat was so constricted he barely heard himself. "Time I joined in." He dropped the useless receiver on top of a pile of typescripts and dashed kitchenward, switching on lights as he went. His bedroom lit up, the bathroom and toilet next to it, the large room in which he dined and watched television and listened to music, and finally the kitchen, where he lifted the largest and sharpest knife from the rack on the wall. Outside the window he saw an image of himself almost erased by the forest — an image which grew fainter, then was wiped out entirely as his breath appeared in front of him and condensed on the window.

He saw himself being engulfed by fog in the reflection of a room which had been invaded by trees. The glint of the knife looked feeble as a lantern lost in a forest. "I'm still here," he snarled. Driven by a defiance which he felt more than understood, he stormed back into his office.

He was still there, and for a while, since he couldn't call a taxi. He laid the knife within reach on the desk and drafted a letter to his printer. *...looking forward to the Christmas consignment... any way you keep costs down is fine...* His words seemed insufficiently defiant until he scribbled *It's only paper, only pulp.* Of course he would never send such a letter, and he was about to tear off the page and bin it when he realised how like taking back a challenge that would seem. He drove the knife through the pad, pinning the letter to the desk like a declaration nailed to a door.

At first there was no apparent response. The only visible movement in the room was of his breath. It took him some minutes to be certain that the smell of decaying vegetation had intensified — that the source was in the room with him. Did the colours on the jackets of the new books resemble stains more than they should? His chair trundled backwards and collided with the wall as he reached the shelves, where he dug a finger into the top of the spine of the nearest book.

It came off the shelf at once — the spine did. The cheap glue had failed, exposing bunches of pages which looked aged or worse. His hand swung wildly, hooking another spine at random. That fell away, bearing a patch of its rotten jacket, and his finger poked deep into the pages, which were a solid lump of pulp. He dragged his finger out of it, dislodging both adjacent spines. Their undersides were crawling with insects. He staggered backwards just as sounds began in the warehouse: a ponderous creaking followed by a crash that shook the office.

"Leave my property alone," Thirsk screamed. He ripped the knife out of the pad and pounding across the office, hauled open the door to the warehouse. The bookcases that weren't attached to the walls had fallen together, forming an arched passage, in the darkness of which piles of books were strewn like jagged chunks of chopped timber. Not only books were in that darkness, and his hand clutched at the light-switch before he knew he didn't want to see.

As soon as his hand found the switch, the block came away like a rotten fungus from the wall. The surviving fluorescents lit for an instant before failing in unison with a loud sharp glassy ping, and he glimpsed a shape stalking up the passage of the bookcases towards him. It resembled a totem, carved or rather shaped out of a tree, walking stiffly as a puppet, though it was considerably taller than any puppet had a right to be. It grew as it advanced on him, as if whatever feet it had were picking up or absorbing the books on which they trod. Its disproportionately large head was featureless and unstable as a mass of foliage, and its arms, which were reaching for him, were at least half the length of the warehouse. So much he distinguished before he threw the door in its face. Twisting the key, he wrenched it out of the lock and shied it across the room.

There was silence then, a silence like the quiet at the secret heart of a forest. He heard his pulse and his harsh unsteady breaths. Gripping the knife two-handed, he glared about. Half a dozen spines sagged away from books, spilling grubs, as the telephone let out a hollow exhalation and began to speak in the voice of the wind.

Thirsk shouted louder, drowning out its words. "In here too, are you? Not for long. This is my house, and one of us is leaving." But he wasn't sure why he was rushing to the front door — to eject an intruder, or to confront the source of all the intrusions?

The trees were out there, and the darkness behind them. Neither appeared to have moved. "I know it's you," he yelled. "I know you're out there." He saw his shadow jerking towards the trees before he was aware of heading for them. As he reached the nearest, he slashed at the trunk, slicing off bark. "You're my property and I can do what I like with you," he ranted. "If you don't like it try and stop me, you and your big friend."

He felt his feet leave the gravel for the plushy floor of fallen leaves and pine needles. He was well into the woods, hacking at every tree within reach, when all the lights of the house were extinguished. He whirled around, then discovered he was able to see by the faint glow of the sky, which no longer felt like a presence looming over him. "Is that the best you can do?" he cried, reeling deeper into the woods, no longer knowing or caring where he was. "That's for you, and so's that." When the trees around him began to creak he chopped more savagely at them, daring them to move towards him; when the mounded earth seemed to quiver underfoot he trampled on it, ignoring how the forest had begun to smell as if the earth was being dug up. He might have been miles into the lightless forest when the hand whose enormous fingers he'd just slashed raised itself with an explosive creak, soil and undergrowth and decaying vegetation spilling from its palm, and closed around him.

A STREET WAS CHOSEN

A STREET WAS CHOSEN. Within its parameters, homes were randomly selected. Preliminary research yielded details of the occupants as follows:

A (husband, insurance salesman, 30; wife, 28; infant daughter, 18 months)

B (widow, 67)

C (husband, 73; wife, 75; son, library assistant, 38)

D (mother, bank clerk, 32; daughter, 3)

E (husband, social worker, 35; wife, social worker, 34)

F (electrician, male, 51; assistant, male, 25)

G (husband, 42; wife, industrial chemist, 38; son, 4; infant son, 2)

H (mother, 86; son, teacher, 44; son's wife, headmistress, 41; granddaughter, 12; grandson, 11)

I (window-cleaner, male, 53)

J (tax officer, female, 55)

K (milkman, male, 39)

L (waiter, 43)

It was noted that subjects I-L occupied apartments in the same house.

Further preliminary observation established that:

(a)   subject B wrote letters to newspapers;

(b)   the children of couples A and G visited each other's homes to play;

(c)   granddaughter H sat with child D while mother D was elsewhere on an average of 1 evening per week;

(d)   husband G experienced bouts of temporary impotence lasting between 6 and 8 days;

(e)   elder F performed sexual acts with his partner in order to maintain the relationship;

(f)   subject L had recently been released into the community after treatment for schizophrenia.

It was decided that stimuli should be applied gradually and with caution. During an initial 8-night period, the following actions were taken:

(1,i)   each night a flower was uprooted from the garden of subject B, and all evidence of removal was erased;

(1,ii) the lights in house H were caused to switch on at random intervals for periods of up to 5 minutes between the hours of 3 and 6 in the morning;

(1,iii) on alternate nights, subject I was wakened shortly after entering deep sleep by telephone calls purporting to advertise life insurance;

(1,iv) the tinfoil caps of milk-bottles delivered to subject D were removed after delivery, and feeding nipples substituted.

At the end of 8 days, it was noted that subject B was less inclined than previously to engage her neighbours in conversation, and more prone to argue or to take offence. From the 7th day onwards she was seen to spend extended periods at the windows which overlooked her garden.

Subjects F were employed by couple H to trace the source of an apparent electrical malfunction. It was observed that mother H became increasingly hostile to her son's wife both during this process and after electricians F had failed to locate any fault in the wiring. Observations suggested that she blamed either her daughter-in-law or her grandchildren for tampering with the electricity in order to disturb her sleep.

Subject J was observed to approach subject A in order to obtain names and addresses of insurance companies which advertised by telephone. It was noted that when the list provided by A failed to yield the required explanation, A undertook to make further enquiries on J's behalf.

It was observed that subject D initially responded to the substitution of nipples as if it were a joke. After 2 days, however, she was seen to accuse subject K of the substitution. At the end of the 8-day period she cancelled the delivery and ordered milk from a rival company. It was decided to discontinue the substitution for an indefinite period.

After observations were completed, the following stimuli were applied during a period of 15 days:

(2,i) An anonymous letter based on a computer analysis of B's prose style was published in the free newspaper received by all subjects, objecting to the existence of househusbands and claiming that the writer was aware of two people who committed adultery while their children played together;

(2,ii) Every third night as subject L walked home, he was approached by religious pamphleteers whose faces had been altered to resemble the other tenants of his building in the order I, K, J, I, K;

(2,iii) The dustbin of subjects F was overturned, and pages from a magazine depicting naked prepubertal boys were scattered around it;

(2,iv) The figure of subject I was projected on the bedroom window of subjects E and caused to appear to pass through it while husband E was alone in the room;

(2,v) Brochures advertising old folks' homes were sent on alternate days to son C;

(2,vi) Telephone calls using a simulation of the voice of subject J were made between 3 and 5 in the morning on 6 occasions to house A, complaining that J had just received another advertising call.

At the end of the second period of stimuli, the following observations were made:

After the appearance of the letter in the newspaper, husband G was observed to suffer a bout of impotence lasting 11 days. It was also noted that subject D attempted to befriend wives A and G, who appeared to be suspicious of her motives. As a result of this encounter, increasing strain was recorded within couples A and G.

Subject L was seen to examine the mail addressed to subjects I, J, and K, and also to attempt to view the apartments of these subjects through the keyholes. Whenever any two of these subjects began a conversation while L was in the building, attempts by L to overhear were observed. Also noted was the growing tendency of L to scrutinise the faces of diners while he waited on them in the restaurant.

After the elder of subjects F discovered the pages which had apparently been hidden in the dustbin, several disagreements of increasing length and violence between subjects F were recorded, both subjects accusing the other of responsibility for the material. At the end of 11 days, the younger of the subjects was seen to take up residence beyond the parameters of the present experiment. It was further observed that mother G required her sons to promise to inform her or their father if they were approached in any way by subjects F.

It was noted that subject E did not mention the apparition of subject I to his wife.

After the first delivery of brochures to their son, parents C were observed to cease speaking to him, despite his denial of responsibility for the receipt of the material. It was noted that parents C opened and destroyed all brochures subsequently delivered. Hot meals prepared for son C were left on the table for him for up to 1 hour before his consumption of them.

Husband A was seen twice to request subject J not to telephone his house after 11 o'clock at night. When the calls continued, wife A was observed to threaten J with legal action, despite J's denial of all knowledge. During this confrontation, subject L was seen to accuse J of attempting to distress both himself and wife A. It was recorded that wife A advised him to take up the matter with the landlord of the apartments.

A decision was reached to increase the level of stimuli. The following actions were taken during a 6-day period:

(3,i)   In the absence of subject B, all the furniture in her house was dismantled;

(3,ii)   Several brochures concerning euthanasia and the right to die were addressed to son C;

(3,iii) Whenever husband G succeeded in achieving an erection, the car alarm of subjects A was made to sound;

(3,iv) A box of fireworks labelled as a free sample was delivered to children H. Several fireworks were later removed and were exploded inside the house of subject F;

(3,v) The face of subject B was made to appear above the beds of children G. When infant G fled, he was caused to fall downstairs. Snapping of the neck was observed to occur;

(3,vi) Live insects were introduced into meals which subject L was about to serve to diners;

(3,vii) The outer doors of apartments I and K were painted crimson overnight.

During and after this period, the following observations were made:

After parents C were seen to examine the brochures addressed to their son, it was noted that they placed his belongings outside the house and employed a neighbour to change the external locks. It was observed that when on his return son C attempted to protest that he owned the house, he was refused any response. Later he was found to be sleeping in a public park. Information was received that when his workmates attempted to help him he quit his job. It was observed that although mother C wished to take the son's belongings into the house, father C insisted on their remaining outside.

Grandmother H was seen to attack grandchildren H under the impression that they were responsible for the damage to house F, although the police had accepted evidence that the children could not have been involved. When mother H defended her children from their grandmother, it was noted that she was accused of having succeeded professionally at the expense of her husband. A protracted argument between all five subjects H was observed, after which increases in tension between all subjects were recorded, the greatest increase being between son and wife.

It was observed that when granddaughter H offered to sit with child D, mother D refused to employ her. Mother H was later seen to accuse mother D of attempting to befriend families in the hope of developing a sexual relationship with the father.

Husband G was observed to smash the headlights of car A with a hammer. The ensuing altercation was seen to be terminated when wife G reported that infant G had been injured on the stairs. It was noted that infant G died en route to the nearest hospital.

It was recorded that subject L was unable to determine whether or not the insects placed in the meals he was about to serve were objectively real. It was noted that this confusion caused L to lose his job. Subsequently L was observed to attempt to persuade several of the other subjects that a pattern was discernible in the various recent events, without success. It was noted that L overheard subjects I and K suggesting that L had repainted their doors.

Surviving child G was seen to inform its parents that subject B had driven infant G out of the children's room. It was observed that when mother G confronted B with this, B accused G of having caused the apparition by experimenting on the children with drugs produced in the laboratory where G worked. It was further noted that subjects E attempted to intervene in the argument but were met with hostility bordering on accusation, both by B and G and by several bystanders. When subject I was attracted by the confrontation, husband E was observed to retreat at speed.

It was noted that subject L approached his landlord and tried to persuade him that subjects I, J, and K were conspiring against L. It was further observed that when L was given notice to quit the apartment, L set fire to the building in the absence of the other tenants. Temperatures in excess of 450 degrees Celsius were recorded, and it was observed that L was trapped beneath a fallen lintel. Melting of the flesh was recorded before the subject lost consciousness, and death was subsequently observed.

Husband E was seen to propose a separation from wife E while refusing to explain his motives. The separation was observed to take place and to become permanent.

Preparations for suicide by subject B were observed. It was noted that the previously dismantled chair used by B for support gave way as the subject was seen to decide against this course of action. Dislocation of the neck by hanging was recorded, and death from strangulation ensued after a period of 53 minutes. It was further observed that after 8 days subject F entered house B and discovered the corpse of subject B.

Because of the risk of discovery, it was decided to discontinue the experiment at this stage. Since the results were judged to be inconclusive, it is proposed that several further experiments on larger groups of subjects should be conducted simultaneously. Communities have been chosen at random, and within them a further random selection of streets has been made.

MCGONAGALL IN THE HEAD

H E WAS ON HIS WAY TO BEING A REPORTER. That Monday morning he was early as usual for work, hoping the editor might observe his eagerness. The newspaper office was locked, however, and so Don watched the street through the late October fog of his breath. Buses bearing words and faces scrawled inside their clouded-over windows paraded like a train of elephants through the shopping precinct; girls and young women said "Brrr" to one another before taking refuge in the hot shops where they worked. Half a dozen schoolchildren whose faces looked bruised by the icy air dodged across the road in front of a lorry laden with washing machines, and the screech of brakes awakened in Don's guts a sensation which felt like hunger and nausea combined. Eyewitness Reporter Don Drake, Our Man At The Scene Of The Tragedy... The children skidded onto the pavement, leaving the lorry stalled and fuming, and Tina the receptionist jumped out of her boyfriend's Porsche and waved the rump of her culottes at Don while lingering over a last kiss.

She unlocked the office and switched on the fluorescent lights and ran to press her bottom against the nearest radiator. "Want to warm me up, Don?"

She'd kicked off her left shoe and was rubbing her right calf with her foot. The cuff of her culotte whispered up and down her stockinged thigh, never quite keeping the promise of a glimpse of bare flesh. "Just tell me how," Don said.

"You know where the kettle is, and the coffee's in one of my drawers."

"I knew that was what you meant," he said as his discomfort rose from his groin into his stomach.

When a fist rattled the glass of the door he hurried to let in Ted Mull, who dumped his tweed hat on the counter and rubbed his chest vigorously before unbuttoning his overcoat. "Morning, love's young bloom," he boomed, tilting his face up and opening his lips as though to catch something in flight. "Any for me?"

"Coffee, you mean," Don said.

"What makes you think I was talking to you, squirt?"

"Don't pick on him, Ted. He's doing his best."

"He's trying all right. Just put it on my desk, son, and give us the milk," Ted said on the way to comb the remnants of his hair.

The rest of the team arrived before the editor. Stanley Brady responded to greetings by muttering "Egh" and displaying today's shade and texture of his tongue. Trevor Horrocks, who wasn't much older than Don, blinked anxiously at the editor's door while unwrapping his stringy neck. Bernadette Hain, who wrote the women's page, came last, treating her colleagues to a look of regal disapproval diluted by conscious tolerance. "It isn't what *I'd* call a good morning," she said.

As the clock struck nine the editor strode in, his astrakhan dangling by the sleeve he was about to peel off. "Morning, Mr Davenport," the staff said in a ragged chorus.

"Mng."

That was neutral. "Mg" was ominous, "Mrng" expansive. He waved away Don's offer of coffee and turned to the other desks. "Two minutes."

Precisely two minutes later the reporters trooped into the inner office. One day, Don promised himself, he would hear what the editor had to say at the morning conferences. All he could distinguish through the door were murmurs, which were enough to distract him from Tina except when her perfume spiced the air. He uncovered his screen and keyboard, then he unclipped his gold-plated ballpoint, which he was saving until he needed to take notes, and laid it on his desk. Then the phone on his desk rang, and he was somebody. "*News,*" he announced. "Births, marriages and deaths."

"Deaths?"

"Sorry."

"Sorry?"

"Deaths."

"Is there any limit on how long I can be?"

"Over six feet could be a problem," Don might have said if his professional voice weren't speaking for him. "Entirely up to you, sir," he said. "It's ten pee a word."

"Poetry included?"

"Whatever you want to give me. You can dictate it to me now if you have a credit card."

"I'll cough." The caller did so, sounding as if he was pronouncing the word. "I'll give you my details at the end of the remembrance. Have you pen and paper?"

"Keyboard and monitor."

"Dear me. Are you sure those will serve?"

"You have my word."

"Then here are mine," the caller said, and adopted a tone that suggested he was reading someone else's. "Oh dad we had you all too fast?"

Don had typed the entire line before he grasped what he was being asked. "That fast is fine. Oh dad we had you all —"

"— these years,
But every life must end in cough."

"Tears."

"When we both stepped through life's door,
After mum's yours was the first face we saw.
And if we were unhappy at school
You cheered us up, you cough. Cough, cough."

Don waited for the coughing to subside and said "You cheered us up, you —"

"Played the fool," the caller said with a resentment Don thought unreasonable. "And when we had exams to do —"

"You gave us help to see us cough."

"Through," Don said, typing, resisting the temptation to say "Are you?"

"You gave us each money to buy cough. Couuggh, cough. To buy cough."

Don lifted the receiver away from his ear to put a distance between himself and the harsh dry sound. At that remove the coughing sounded even falser. When the caller repeated "To buy" Don held the receiver at arm's length until he heard the voice continue.

"— a flat,
And lent us more when we needed that.

It took us years to get our degrees,
And it was you who paid most of our fees.
Then you and mum saw us both wed,
First Sue and then your little cough."

Don couldn't resist typing "cough" at the end of the sentence, to be deleted when he went through the text to add punctuation and capital letters and to correct any errors in transcription. There couldn't be much more to come, or he might begin to suspect the call was a joke. "Your little —"

"Frough. Cough. Fred," the caller said, and drew a rattling breath. "Mum sat our babies on her knee,
"And cur. Currough. Currough. Currough."

It *was* a joke. "And gave you one when they had to pee," Don heard himself say, and was so nervous of doing so out loud that he typed the line instead. "And —" he prompted when the coughing trailed off, but there was a breathless silence. "And gave —"

"What about a grave?"

"Nothing," Don said, deciding that the call was serious after all. "On her knee, you were saying, and —"

"And called them each her little flea."

Don gave the receiver a long slow double-take before he typed the line. "Carry on," he said, keeping his face straight, and his voice. "We've got us all now that you've gone,
And our thoughts of you will still go cough, cough, cough."

Don typed the last word without speaking it and waited for the coughs to finish. "Who is the message from and to, please?"

After a silence which seemed longer than was necessary for the caller to catch his breath came the response: "To Terence Bernard Moore from daughter Sue, son Fred, grandchildren cough, cough."

"Twins, eh?" Don muttered. "Flea and flea?"

The silence made him nervous that the caller had heard him, until he — Fred, presumably — said "Hope and Charity."

"And called them Hope and Charitee," Don said under his breath, and more loudly "So I just need the details of your card."

"I'll get them now."

Don waited through a spectacular outburst of coughing and what sounded like the contents of a room being exhaustively overturned, at the end of which he thought the phone had been flung on the floor. Instead the caller said in an aggressively aggrieved voice "I can't lay my hands on it just now."

"Then I'm afraid you'll be too late for —"

"I'll send you a cheque. When must you have it?"

"For Thursday's paper, tomorrow morning."

"I'm writing it now. Goodbye."

"Of course you are," Don commented as the phone went dead, and poised his fingers over the keyboard. It would be the work of a few seconds to delete the entire rigmarole, but he should wait for the morning so as to make sure it had indeed been an elaborate joke. The voice had been too old, he reflected, like someone trying to sound older than they were. He was about to call Tina to look at the incredible doggerel when the editor's face loomed beside his own reflection on the screen. "S," Don hissed, and managed to say not "Sorry" but "Sir?"

"Choking us, is it, Mr Drake, the tie? Finding it hard to talk?"

"No?" Don replied, all he could think of to ask.

"Tidy yourself up, then. We're not at college now, we're in the real world," Mr Davenport said, and watched while Don pulled the noose tighter.

Don had failed at the interview for the rival newspaper because his hair had been too long, and now his bare nape seemed to bristle with being spied on by his colleagues. Everyone had to please the editor, he told himself. Ted Mull had emerged from the inner office booming "Of course I will, sir, you can always count on me" as if he didn't care who overheard his slavishness. As the editor headed for the toilet Trevor Horrocks jumped up, gasping "Oh er Mr Dav" to no effect other than to make Mr Davenport hunch his shoulders, and Don felt better at once. He could rely on his professional voice, and anyone who glimpsed him at his desk would take him for a reporter.

By the end of the day he'd lost count of the births and marriages he'd dealt with, and the rhyming deaths. Why was it death that produced so much doggerel? Perhaps it was a way the living regained control of their lives, even if it meant reducing their experience of death virtually to meaninglessness.

Shops were putting up their shutters as he walked home. The large houses were mostly rest homes, except for those like the one he inhabited, which had been divided into almost as many flats as there were rooms. Otherwise the main difference seemed to be that in houses like his nobody called on anyone else. Cartoon voices climbed from television to television as he raced the time-switched lights up the ragged stairs and let himself into his third of the top floor.

He emptied a can of baked beans and sausages into the pan on the electric ring and fed the toaster its trinity of bread. While he ate dinner he gazed through the windows of the envelopes he'd picked up in the front hall, and having washed up, opened them. The bills weren't quite as greedy as he'd feared, though a reporter's salary would have made them less daunting. He lined up the envelopes on the mantelpiece and tried to read a comic novel, but couldn't lose himself in it, not when he encountered the word "dead" four times in as many pages: dead letters, beat, good, drunk. He abandoned it and strolled down the hill to the pub opposite the graveyard.

It was the Polytechnic's local, where he had been drinking ever since he'd joined the journalism course. Making his way over the bare floorboards of the snug, which was dimmed by the smoke of a crowd worthy of a rush-hour train, felt like coming home. He was taking his first gulp of Letterman's Bitter when a hand clapped him on the shoulder. "Dressing for the part?" Paul Prentiss said.

"What part's that?"

"Don't be modest. You've been seen working at your rag. You look quite the hack."

Don had never cared for the heavy rough humour which went with the chubby scrubbed schoolboyish face, and he liked Prentiss even less for saying "What story are you after at the moment?"

"At the moment all I'm after is a drink."

"I can take a hint." Apparently Don's tone wasn't enough of one, however, because Prentiss bought him another pint and winked over Don's shoulder. "You're in luck, girls. Two real journalists for the price of one. Meet Don Duck, I mean Drake."

Don used the lack of space as an excuse merely to wave his free hand without turning. "So don't keep all the news to yourself, Don," Prentiss said. "What's your big story just now?"

As Don drained his first pint, which made him feel as if his head was separating from the rest of him, he deduced why Prentiss was taunting him. "It was you, wasn't it."

"You're letting the job get on top of you, Don. I'm not a story, I'm real."

"It was you pretending to have lost someone. You shouldn't make fun of the dead."

"Why, can't they keep a straight face? You're never telling us you only deal with dead issues at your rag, when our tutors thought you were so —"

Don took a mouthful of bitter and expelled most of it in Prentiss' face. "You're so funny, I couldn't help it," he said as Prentiss spluttered and mopped himself.

He enjoyed the spectacle until the stocky barman grasped his arm. "I think you've had enough for one night, son. How old are you anyway?"

"Old enough to know when someone's trying to make a fool of me."

"You can do that all by yourself," Prentiss shouted as Don struggled to the door, having drained his tankard. He heaved the door open, receiving the night in his face like a dash of ice water, and stalked into his own fog. DISAGREEMENT BETWEEN JOURNALISTS END IN FRACAS, he thought as he was confronted by the smudged stony messages of the graveyard, BECAUSE ONE WAS A JACKASS. He accepted worse rhymes than that every working day. Surely sometime he would be able to draw on his years spent studying in the library, on all those words.

In the morning he waited outside the *News*. By the time Tina straightened up from the Porsche his lips were stiff, his mouth felt clogged with ice. She ran to her usual radiator, and he followed in her perfumed wake.

"Hello, young lovers, whatever you're up to. Make mine black."

"He isn't in yet, is he, Mr Der —"

"Gagh."

"You're easily pleased."

"Mrng."

Don watched while Tina sorted the mail, delivered by a postman who departed whistling like a blue tit which had almost lost its voice. "Any for me?" Don eventually asked her.

"A pile."

None of the letters and cheques related to yesterday's protracted call. He should have emptied the tankard over Prentiss' head. He called up the eighteen lines of verse on the screen and was grinning wickedly at them when his phone rang. He deleted them and immediately wished he'd waited for the noon mail, but it didn't matter: he could remember every word as if they'd leapt off the screen into his skull. "Births, marriages and deaths," he said.

Of course the noon mail contained nothing from Fred Moore, and Don felt he should be able to relax. The afternoon brought him mostly births and marriages, which was a relief. That night after his tinned dinner he crouched over the television beside the sink in order to switch channels. An album of black and white faces fluttered past until he settled on a comedy, but he couldn't watch for long when the dialogue seemed to be chanted rather than spoken. "Crambojingle, crambojingle," he murmured over and over in bed, and fell asleep wondering where the word came from.

"You'll catch your death one of these days," Tina said next morning, "hanging about in the doorway."

"How's love's young dream today? Time to wake up."

"Gurgh."

"Hmmm."

"Mg."

"Sorry I'm 1 — Mr Dav —"

"God bless you love we miss you chuck."

"God bless you love we miss you chuck," Don confirmed, reminding himself to be professional, not to put words into the caller's mouth, not to listen to rhymes in his head, however tempting they were. Tomorrow was publication day, and then he would have no reason to be uneasy, not that he had now.

That night he went down to the pub, but saw Prentiss through the windows shrouded in breaths. He strolled through the graveyard, where he kept smelling a newly dug grave. Though the stones gleamed darkly over the crystallised turf he was unable to distinguish a single inscription. As he lay in bed his head felt laden with words, but in the morning his mind was blank, thank... "Enough of that stuff," he muttered as he got himself ready for work.

"Gangway, brrr."

The rest of the greetings were lost in the bustle as some of the deliverers came to Tina for their batch of newspapers and had to be sent around the back. Don imagined all the words for which he was responsible that week spreading across the town, having begun to fade at the instant they were printed.

It was almost lunchtime when a caller addressed him in a tone he wasn't prepared for. "Are you answerable for the contents of today's paper?"

"If it's a birth, a marriage or a cough I am."

"Then where's my father?"

Don was instantly suspicious. "What name?"

"The name's Fred Moore, and my father was Terence Bernard."

"I thought you might say that. Not Paul Prentiss, eh?"

"What's that? What are you raving about?"

"Let it rest, Paul, unless you want another in your eye. Haven't you enough news at the *Advertiser* without trying to make a story out of me?"

"Who the devil d'you imagine you're addressing?"

"You've almost got the voice right this time, but you don't fool me. You went on too long last time, that was what gave you away. Nobody living could be that bad for eighteen lines without noticing."

"I don't think you realise —"

"Sew it up, Paul, before you have a heart attack. There may be real people trying to get through to me."

Don heard a strangled sound that suggested his warning about the heart attack had come too late, and then there was only the moaning of the dialling tone. He grinned at the receiver before replacing it and waiting for the phone to ring. Just now all the calls were for the switchboard, interrupting Tina's sorting of the lunchtime mail. Eventually she brought him a single envelope addressed to Deaths in a shaky hand. "Someone must love you," she said, and hurried back to the switchboard as the editor opened his door. "Mr Drake?"

"Mr Davenport?"

76

The editor jerked his permanently frowning slab of face towards his shoulder. "My office, please."

Could this be the chance for which Don had been working? He tried to seem nonchalant yet enthusiastic as he walked into the inner office, where all the furniture seemed to smell of the pipe Mr Davenport was relighting. Without inviting him to sit the editor leaned back in his chair, thumping the underside of the desk with his knees. "Enjoying our work, are we, Mr Drake?"

"Certainly are. Am."

"No ambitions elsewhere?" the editor said through his teeth, making the tobacco in the bowl glow red.

"Elsewhere, well..." Don wished he could use his telephone voice; this one wasn't working too well. "Ambitions, you bet, but when you say elsewhere..."

"Take it slow and steady, Mr Drake. Never try to run before you can walk."

"I'll bet you did. Or didn't, rather."

The editor stared at him over the fierce red glow. At last he said "So what's this I hear about your notices?"

"Something good, would —"

Don's voice seemed to stick on the rhyme. "About a Mr Moore," the editor said.

"A Mr Moore? Which Mr Moore?"

Don felt as if he was being forced to recite doggerel. He gripped his lips with his fingertips as the editor's voice grew thin. "A Mr Fred Moore who has just been on to me, wanting to know what became of his father's obituary."

"If he told you he rang up with it —"

"He didn't, no. His father did."

"His fough —" Don cleared his aching throat and tried again. "His father —"

"His father phoned in his own obituary which I'm assured you copied. Don't ask me why he did, it isn't our business to ask. He knew he was dying, his son says, and almost as soon as he'd spoken to you he coughed himself to death."

The informant could have been Paul Prentiss, Don thought wildly — Prentiss trying to feed the *News* fake news. A single point

77

seemed clear amid the babble of gibberish which the world was threatening to become: whoever the caller had been, he hadn't complained to Mr Davenport about Don's response to his call of a few minutes ago. "We couldn't publish the obituary," Don said, inspired just in time. "We haven't received payment."

The editor gazed at him as if his mind was on something else entirely. "You'd better ascertain what happened to it and let the son know."

"I will," Don promised, and was fleeing towards the door when Mr Davenport said "Try taking these."

"I'm fine, I'm not ill," Don said, "I don't need a pill," and saw too late that the editor was proffering Moore's address and phone number. He clutched them and stumbled out to his desk, where the envelope with the second-class stamp was waiting. As he grabbed it he was afraid he might tear it up, not open, but managed to peel back the flap. The envelope did indeed contain a cheque from T. B. Moore.

Don laid it next to the scrap of paper Mr Davenport had given him, then moved them closer together in an attempt to read them simultaneously without shifting his eyes. As soon as Tina was busy with a call he seized his phone and dialled. "Mr Moore?"

"Who is it?"

Thank God, Don had succeeded in disguising his voice. "I'm calling on behalf of Births, Marriages and Deaths. They've had to go out, he has, I mean, but I can tell you your father's cheque has just this moment arrived."

"Indeed."

"It was second class," Don said, thinking that Moore sounded in the mood to take that as some kind of slur on his father. "I can guarantee your father's piece will be in the *News* next week."

"You'll understand if I make sure, I'm sure."

"You rhyme like your dad," Don managed not to say before breaking the connection. He clipped the cheque and the scrap of paper to the top of his pile of mail, and switched on the monitor. He was hearing the rhythm of T. B. Moore's first line: cough cough, cough cough, cough cough cough cough. He peered at the blank screen and moved his lips, and when the monitor seemed about to flicker in that rhythm he closed his eyes and attempted to mouth. That didn't work either. He couldn't recall a single word of Moore's.

It wasn't urgent, he tried to tell himself. So long as he remembered by next week, nobody would find him out. But his inability to remember felt like a hole in his brain, a vacuum aching to be filled. Moore's rhymes: if Don recalled the rhymes the rest would follow. He was straining to remember just one rhyme when his phone shrilled, and he snatched it up, mumbling a greeting which was all that emerged from the fight of two words to be first past his lips.

"Is that Births, Marriages and Deaths?"

"Yes, this is First and Last Brea —" Don coughed so as to interrupt himself. "Yes."

"I didn't quite hear what you said."

"I deal with the living and —" Don coughed harder. "No tiss says," he managed to pronounce.

"Can I have a remembrance next week?"

"All that you need do is speak."

The woman hesitated, which allowed Don to add "You can pay by credit card, or send a cheque if that's, cough, preferable."

The caller dictated her credit card details at once. "Right, that's done," Don said. "Go on."

"Though it's been years since you said goodbye —"

"Since you went up into the sky... We thought that you would never die..."

The choice of rhymes saved Don — their struggle for priority gave him time to choose only to mouth them. He wiped his forehead with the bristling back of one hand and typed her line. "Go on."

"The thought of you still makes us cry."

Don preferred his lines, but he typed hers. "Go on."

"Each week in church we light a candle —"

He would be fine so long as he didn't type what he was mouthing. He only needed to say "Go on" at the end of each line; his professional voice wouldn't let him down. When the caller finished dictating and said "Is that all right now?" Don managed to confine himself to an affirmative grunt before cutting her off.

His colleagues were returning to their desks with stories from the outside world. Whenever Don had to answer his phone he crouched low over the keyboard so that they wouldn't notice his mouthing outrageous responses to "She is not dead but gone before" and "There never was a sweeter Mum" and "We're glad that now you are at rest." The day was almost spent when Ted Mull stooped to him on the way to the toilet, murmuring "First sign of madness."

"At least it's not badness," Don muttered at his retreating back. Leaving the office was less of a relief than he'd hoped. He'd anticipated being able to think freely once he was alone, but he was surrounded by words. Everything had a name — street, car, lamp, house — and they seemed to be massing between him and the world. He let himself into his house with The Feeling Of A Key and ran upstairs towards The Taste Of Food. He fed himself a few spoonfuls of baked beans out of the can, and felt as though he was feeding himself the late October cold. He needed to relax in order to think, that was it — he needed a drink. He wouldn't be a journalist unless he had a drink.

The pub felt like a refuge from the cold words standing in the dark. The snug wasn't crowded yet, and the barman who had ordered Don out was off duty. Don sat in a corner with a pint and then with another, turning his back on the room so as to whisper. "Dead," he repeated. "Moore must have said dead. I've got dead in my head."

He was searching his brain for a rhyme which he was sure was the key when a fingertip tapped sharply on his shoulder. At some point the snug had filled with drinkers and smoke, and Don felt as though the crowd had forced Paul Prentiss on him. "I want a word," Prentiss said.

"Because you're a —" Don started to retort, and slapped himself across the mouth. He'd told Fred Moore both Prentiss' name and where he worked, and if he didn't keep his promise to Moore the man might well contact the rival paper. "Can't you forget I got you wet?" he babbled. "I'll pay for the damage if you can't cough. You've an empty glass. Let me fill it, you —"

Prentiss was gazing at him with mute amusement. He knew, Don thought: Moore had already been in touch with him. The roar of the crowd — far too many words — engulfed Don. "You can't make me news," he shouted at Prentiss, staggering to his feet. "I'm just here for the booze."

"I should lay off it for a while if I were you."

"I've as much right as you have, you —" Don yelled, backing away from the argument which he was afraid he mightn't be able to stop. He mustn't waste time, he had to remember Moore's words before Prentiss could discover he'd mislaid them. He squirmed through the crowd and lunged into the night.

Dark, stark. Gate, fate. Trees, freeze. Willows, pillows. Walk, stalk. Wreath, teeth. Dates, crates. Earth, berth. Stones, bones. Lines, dines... None of this revived the verses. When he couldn't think for shivering he went home. If the pit in his brain was sucking in reality and reducing it to words, perhaps lying absolutely still in the dark would clear enough space in his overloaded mind for his memory to work.

At some point he fell asleep. He must have continued to rhyme, however, because when icy sunlight wakened him his brain was laden with pairs of words, while his surroundings seemed more aloof than ever. He was going to be late for work. He dashed cold water on himself, shivered into his freezing clothes and ran stiff-faced out of the house.

Though he was almost on time after all, only Tina was in the outer office. Some big local story must have broken overnight, because Don could hear the buzz of discussion beyond Mr Davenport's door. Ted Mull and Bernadette Hain sounded outraged, and for a panicky few moments Don felt sure they were appalled by something he himself had done. "Didn't you get much sleep?" Tina said.

"Why, do I look like a creep?"

"That's not what I said."

"It's what's in your head."

"Be that way," Tina said, turning her back on him.

"It's all I can say," Don protested, almost missing the hook on the wall with his coat in his haste to take refuge at his desk. Once his monitor was switched on he wouldn't need to speak to anyone around him. Just as the screen lit up, Mr Davenport's door opened. "Ah, Mr Drake. Arrived now, have we?"

"Both of us, you mean, or just me?"

"I didn't quite catch what you said."

"I'm trying to talk for the dead," Don muttered even lower as the phone rang on his desk.

He thought it had saved him. He pressed the receiver against his cheekbone, and his jaw dropped as though a bandage had been snatched away. What might he feel compelled to say? "Is that the births column?" a woman said.

"No need to be solemn," Don managed only to mouth as he grunted encouragingly.

"Can I put in a happy event?"

"One that you couldn't —" Don coughed so hard it hurt his throat. "Mm hm," he said.

"To Dee and Desmond Gray, a son..."

Don would be able to cope so long as he mouthed before he typed, he told himself — and then he gaped at the screen. Instead of her line he had typed "A side effect of a bit of fun." He could take the call and attempt afterwards to deduce from the screen what the caller had actually said, except that wouldn't work: he wouldn't be able to stop rhyming until he remembered Moore's words. "Sorry, I'm having a technical hitch. Could you call back a bit later, you —" he gabbled and drowned his last word in the row he made replacing the receiver. As he perched it slightly askew on the rest so that no further calls would be able to reach him, Ted Mull leaned over the monitor at him.

Don thought Mull had noticed his ruse with the phone until the reporter said "I heard what you said to the boss."

"That so? Well, I don't give a toss."

Mull snapped his mouth shut as though he'd caught something in it. "You'll get nowhere with that attitude, my lad."

"Then call me a bounder and a rotter and a cad."

Mull's shiny face was turning several shades of pink and white, putting Don in mind of an iced cake. Bernadette Hain was telling Tina about last night's local outrage — vandalism and, by the sound of it, worse in a graveyard — but Don didn't want to hear; they were more words he would be compelled to rhyme. He closed his eyes and thrust his fingers in his ears, and when he looked again he was alone with Tina.

It was the best he could hope for. He mustn't speak to her. He had to make the most of his chance before she or the editor wondered why Don's phone had ceased to ring. Once Don had reproduced Moore's verses, surely he would no longer need to rhyme — surely he would be able to persuade Mr Davenport to give him a different job. Was it Moore who was filling his head with rhymes in an attempt to recapture his own? The notion felt like inspiration, except that now Don's brain was swarming with the rhymes Moore summoned up: viewer, renewer, lure, cure, immure, boor, endure, spoor... Perhaps if Don thought of every single rhyme for Moore that might release him; perhaps if he wrote them all down... He was staring with shaky eyes at the screen, convinced that there was something else he had to type so as to clear his head, when a voice said "Moore."

Don thought he had spoken aloud until he noticed the newcomer, a man in black with a long mottled face that looked pressed between his bushy sideboards. "The editor's on the phone, but I'll tell him as soon as he's free," Tina was saying to him. "What shall I say it's about?"

"About my father. About his obituary you neglected to publish. I've been trying to speak to someone about it all morning, but it seems that number's out of order. I want to see the obituary before it goes in."

"You want Mr Drake there. Don, this gentleman wants a word."

Don felt his lips twitching. They were going to open, he was going to speak, and that would be the end of him. So this was what his nemesis looked like, Moore's grown-up son, no longer little Fred. "First Sue and then your little Fred," he thought and mouthed, and gasped. "Then you and mum saw us both wed..."

All at once the obituary was as present in his mind as it had been while he copied it down, and he was afraid he mightn't be able to type fast enough to record it before it departed from him. He gave Fred Moore a sickly grin and gestured him to wait until Don finished at the screen, and turned away from the counter as his fingers commenced scuttling over the keyboard. Two lines, four, eight, sixteen... Though they weren't in order, all eighteen lines were there, thank God. Moore's son was clearing his throat harshly, but

Don put the couplets in chronological order before turning back to him.

He didn't trust himself to speak. He went to the counter and lifted the flap and invited Moore in with an ushering gesture, repeating it until Moore stalked frowning through the gap. He gave Moore his chair and stood beside it while the man peered at the screen. "Oh dad we had you all these years," Moore read aloud.

Don heard the late Moore reading the words. Each line seemed to remove a layer of dead words from his mind. As the son pronounced "And our thoughts of you will still go on," Mr Davenport came to his office door, demanding "Is there some problem?"

"Are you the editor?"

"I have that honour. Can I help?"

Moore poked a finger at the monitor, his nail clinking against the screen. "You can see that this is never published."

It didn't matter, Don told himself. Since the verses were out of him, the compulsion must be. He sensed that a change was about to take place in his head. The editor marched over and scowled at the screen. "What exactly is the trouble?"

"We spoke. Fred Moore. You didn't print my father's obituary, and now you're trying to fob me off with this."

"In what way fob?"

Moore swung one hand at Don. "Your clerk's made this up. My father was never responsible for this rubbish. As if we haven't been through enough..."

Don felt all the rhymes rush back into his head. If nobody believed Moore had composed the obituary he might never be rid of them. His lips shifted, but he mustn't speak. He grabbed his pen from his desk as Fred Moore said unevenly "Last night someone dug my father up, and — and now this."

Don clicked the point of the pen out of the barrel and swivelled in search of scrap paper. He mustn't rhyme with Fred Moore's words. This was what your father said, he's still stuck inside my head, he's been here inside since the moment he died... Before he had time to scribble any of that, Mr Davenport confronted him. "You're fired."

No, hired. Give me a chance, don't lead me a dance, don't make me prance... Don shoved his hands against the sides of his skull as if he could squeeze out what had lodged in there, and felt the point of the pen scrape his temple. "Take yourself off to the doctor if you're ill," Mr Davenport said.

Kill. Don felt his temple begin to twinge as ink mixed with his blood. The rhyme was louder than any of the sounds of the office, the humming of the monitor, the gasps of the men, Tina's scream. It was only doggerel, he didn't have to act it out because he could no longer speak it. Perhaps he had, or else go mad.

THROUGH THE WALLS

H UGH PEARS WAS GATHERING MINT in the back yard
when he heard the crash. It sounded like someone hurled
onto a sheet of tin. God, not the children! As he ran through the
kitchen, Chris glanced at him, puzzled; she hadn't recognised the
sound. "You aren't going out now," she protested. "The children
will be home any minute." But he hadn't reached the front door
when they ran in.

"There's a man hurt outside," Linda shouted.

"They nearly ran us over," Andrew shouted louder.

Pears let go of his fear with a gasp of relief. He hurried out. A
red Mini had slewed into the wall of the house next door. The driver
was lifting a figure from the passenger seat. Its head was a raw red
bulb; blood had rusted its hair.

When Pears opened his eyes he'd regained control. The driver
was supporting his passenger, whose forehead was bleeding copiously.
Pears wondered why he should have seen anything else. He wasn't
fond of the sight of blood, but nor was he given to building
nightmares out of it. "Bring him in here," he called. "My wife's a
nurse."

As Pears helped them up the path, he saw the young man in
the ground-floor flat next door gazing expressionlessly at them.
Only his gaze moved, as if he were peering from behind a pale
gaunt mask. If you can't help, Pears raged, then have the decency
to take yourself elsewhere. The gaze followed them blankly,
indifferent as the fog that massed at the edge of the streetlight,
like dim spectators.

Chris sat the man in one of the white wood dining-chairs.
"What happened?" she asked, tilting his head back.

"We skidded on a patch of oil," the driver said. "It looked big
enough for a lorry. I wouldn't have thought they were supposed to
come down a residential street, not a narrow one like this."

"Too many people don't care about that," Chris said.

The passenger was holding his trouser-leg away from his shin down which blood was running incontinently into his shoe. "This'll teach me to wear my seat-belt," he said, shaking.

She cleaned the wound and gave him a compress to hold against it. "I don't think it's serious, but we'd better be sure," she said, turning down the cooker. "I'll drive you to the hospital."

Andrew was sponging blood from the back of the chair. That jarred Pears out of the reverie through which he'd watched Chris caring for the man. The thoughts had streamed through his mind like smoke; he felt vaguely that he would prefer not to remember them. He shook his head. All this nonsense came of boredom, inertia, probably of feeling incapable of helping Chris. Get on with something. He strode into the back yard.

He'd finished gathering the mint when he heard Linda's cry of disgust. A spider, he thought, or a crane-fly or a slug. As he hurried through the kitchen and the dining area he saw, beyond the open front door down the hall, the young man from the flat standing on the pavement, gazing in. If he's what you're saying yuk to, Pears told Linda, I can't say I blame you. But she was staring at the hall wall.

Just inside the front door, the wallpaper had acquired a splotch of blood. Trickles were making their way toward the skirting-board. "Damn," Pears said. "He must have done it as they went out. Get me a cloth, Linda, quick."

He closed the front door. As Pears hid the blood from him, the young man gaped in appalled disbelief. You're absolutely right, Pears told him, we're going to scrape it off and use it for soup.

He dabbed at the blood. Mrs Tarrant can get the worst of it off, she'll be here tomorrow. That's what she's paid for. He scrubbed as hard as he dared. The stain remained, but fainter. Eventually he sat and waited for his dinner, minutely lining up the cutlery, listening to Linda and Andrew playing pole-vaulting in the yard. His mind felt full of rapid formless smoke.

Over dinner Chris asked "What exactly happened?"

"He shouldn't have driven down our road so fast," Andrew said.

"If someone hadn't been so stupid they ran out in front of him, there wouldn't have been an accident," Linda said.

"I didn't see him. He came straight round the corner." He glared at her, the threat of angry tears in his eyes. "I bet you'd have been glad if I'd been run over."

"That's right. No, I wouldn't," Linda amended, trying to head off his mood. She put an arm round him, but he threw her off.

"You're quite right, Andrew," Chris said. "He shouldn't have been driving so fast. But for your own sake you must be more careful how you go."

Pears listened blankly. He heard the words, but it was as though he heard them through a wall; they seemed separate from him. He stared at the table, at the white wood and its reflected hints of the violet and lilac walls. The words affected him in the same way: they were there, that was all.

He gazed at his food as he ate. Wherever he looked, there seemed to be movement at the edge of his eye. Dark spots moved on the walls, as though the kitchen were a sweating cave, or as if the walls were the throat of a chimney, fluttering with soot. When he looked, the movements snapped into corners of the room or behind the furniture. His eyes must be tired. Perhaps he could blame the tree in the next yard, its shadow on the curtain swaying sluggishly, blurred by the gathering November fog. Perhaps he was overworked, though he hadn't thought himself to be more so than anyone else at the bank.

Andrew had been mollified, or nearly. "Sisters," he said witheringly. When he'd eaten his fruit he said "May I leave the table? I'm going to dust Fritz."

Linda had been waiting for a chance at the last word in the argument. She was too much of a young lady now to stick out her tongue. "Aren't you too old for that thing yet?" she demanded. "When are you going to throw away that horrible doll?"

"Linda, you're only two years older," Chris said. "Hardly the voice of maturity."

"Well, *I* didn't want that doll when *I* was eight."

An aunt had brought her Fritz from Germany, but Linda had mislaid the doll behind her bed almost at once, complaining "Alice's father brought her back a lovely German dress." "Give me the doll if you don't want him," Andrew had said. Pears supposed that now it was up to him to intervene. Anything to drag his mind free of the slow heavy dance of the nodding shadow on the curtains, to shake off the darkly teeming walls. "There's nothing horrible about Andrew's doll, Linda," he said.

"There is too. You come and look."

She pulled him into the hall. "Go outside and see," she said. "I used to like to look up at our bedroom when I came home. Now he makes it look nasty. I'll switch on the light so you can see."

She ran upstairs, pleats flirting from her bare thighs. A Majorca tan was fading from her legs. He must talk to Chris about making her wear longer skirts. She was far too enticing. One of these days — What? He snatched his gaze away from Linda as she reached the top of the stairs, and rushed himself out.

As Pears emerged, the young man next door was letting in three others. One displayed a fat hand-rolled multicoloured cigarette for approval. Stupid fools. No wonder the fellow in the flat looked so inert. And him an industrial chemist, if Pears wasn't mis-interpreting his salary cheque: should know better.

When Linda switched on the light, the fog sprang forward, towering blankly on the opposite pavement. It settled clammily on Pears, who shivered and looked up. Fritz the doll was standing on the sill in the centre of the bay window, grinning out. Pears could just see his red knees over the sill, beneath his lederhosen. His raised tankard was halfway to his mouth; his painted wooden face was edged with light. He looked hideous.

Fog crept insinuatingly down Pears' spine, fog was a dwindling blank-faced box around him. The lawn stirred feebly, as if drowned. He tried to shake himself, but shuddered. Good God, he was standing in his own front garden, looking at his own house: what could be so terrible in that? But he could hardly keep his eyes on the doll.

It looked like an overgrown bloated schoolboy mottled with red paint as if its skin were bursting. Beneath the blue glass eyes, the grin had become secretive, knowingly obscene. Its free hand hovered near its flies. It was all the effect of the fog; fog had tinted its face shinily grey, slimy, diseased. It looked swollen with waste that might gush forth at any moment.

Linda read his expression. "See?" she called.

"I must say," Pears said warily, "he looks rather a nasty little man today."

He didn't realise that Andrew was in the bedroom until the boy appeared behind Linda, weeping. He pushed her out of the way and threw up the sash, then he hurled the doll into the road. Pears heard it break.

"Did you see that?" someone said in the flat. "Far out!"

Cretins, Pears snarled. Tears were streaming between Andrew's fingers, Linda was trying to comfort him and fighting to pull his hands away from his face, Chris was hurrying upstairs, irritably shouting "What's going on?" Pears opened the front gate; wet flakes of rust chafed beneath his fingers. He stooped to pick up the doll. Then he recoiled.

The fog had dimmed the streetlights. The shadow of the doll was blurred, the wet road was uneven. He wasn't really seeing a thick dark lumpy fluid, seeping slowly from the doll's cracked head.

The fog was muttering; the sound grew into an open-mouthed snarl. A car swung into the road. Pears reached for the doll, then he pulled back his hand and ran toward the house. Behind him he heard the car grind the doll into splinters.

Andrew had heard it too; Chris was trying to calm him down. "Will you *stay out of this*!" she shouted. Pears gladly took the order for himself. He went into the living-room. Beyond the garden the privet leaves looked thick, coated with fog; he knew how they felt. He drew the curtains and sat in the bay window.

When Chris came down, she stared at him. He frowned enquiringly. If she didn't say what she was thinking, they couldn't talk about it. His mind seemed clearer now; he relaxed, smiling. She sat opposite him, shaking her head. The subdued children trudged into the next room, the playroom; Linda whispered. "It's not my job to run this family single-handed," Chris said.

"I never said it was."

"But you act it. If you don't intend to help at least don't make things more difficult."

She sounded weary. "Have you a migraine?" Pears said.

"It's taken you long enough to notice."

"I'm not feeling too well myself. I expect that hasn't helped my behaviour."

"Your behaviour isn't that unusual."

This was hardly the time to discuss it: if she felt as odd as he did, they would only end up screaming. He moved his chair out of the bay and switched on the television.

He found he couldn't watch for long. The image whirred silently, as his eye refused to aid the illusion of continuous movement. Black-faced minstrels danced and sang, hurtling forward to fill the bulging screen, grimacing with painted lips. Pears reached for the switch. "I'm listening to that," Chris said. He sank back and gazed at the fire. On the edge of his vision colours boiled beneath glass, as if an aquarium had gone mad.

The fire swayed gently, flickering high and vanishing. When he emerged from his reverie, the programme had been ousted by another. A sandy brown desert, a bright amber sky: the colours didn't clamour for attention. Calm now, he looked. Men in khaki shorts were gently spading out a pit. Archaeologists? Two of them were coaxing something from the soil. He leaned closer.

It came up with its arms held stiff at its sides, its skin pulled back from a yellowing fixed smile. The pit was surrounded by fleshless bodies, rigidly contorted or lying supine with their lips wrenched back as if by hooks, grinning.

"So far the mass graves have yielded at least five hundred dead," an announcer was pronouncing. The camera tilted up to show that it had been keeping back a vista of ranked corpses as far as the horizon. In the next room the children were putting toys away. "I don't think we should risk the children seeing this," he said, turning to Chris. As he spoke something moved to the edge of the screen and emerged into the room.

A shadow, of course. When Pears glared at the corner where it had halted, there was nothing. How could television cast a shadow? It must have come from the street. The screen piled up with swarms of brown emaciated manikins. Their dried-out sockets were turned to the sun, their jaws protruded through their skins. He surged out of his chair and switched off the television.

All he achieved was to send the announcer into hiding. "There are almost certainly further graves to be discovered," the man continued, muffled now, as if he'd put his hand over his mouth. Not until Pears heard someone shout "Jesus, that's sick. Turn it off!" did he realise that the voice was persisting in the flat through the wall.

He slumped back, and began to cough. Had the fog managed to insinuate itself into the room? There was a faint unpleasant smell. In the corner a faint shadow remained — an after-image, of course. The smell reminded him of old meat, but wasn't quite like that. Had a mouse died beneath the floor? He'd look tomorrow — he didn't feel at all like searching now. "I think we'd all benefit from an early night," he said. "It's past their bedtimes, anyway."

"Do what you want," Chris said.

Andrew was morosely obedient, and Linda made only a token protest; yet Pears found himself becoming irritable. Suppose Chris noted the smell, what might she find? Nothing, for God's sake. Get to bed.

Reading his mood, the children allowed themselves to be herded quickly to the bathroom. Pears stood outside as they splashed; Linda was trying to wheedle Andrew into her game. We aren't such a bad family, Pears thought. I can hold Chris, we don't need to talk.

Abruptly Linda was out of the bathroom. She ran naked to him, towelled pink, her bald pubes and tentatively swelling breasts framed in her tan, and put her arms around him. "Carry me to bed," she pleaded.

Her hair was warm beneath his chin. She moved against him, soft to his touch, instinctive and guileless as a young animal. As she gazed up at him, sleepy and innocently sensuous, she looked exactly as Chris sometimes did. For a moment of illusion she was Chris, renewed.

"Not tonight, love," he said. "Your mother and I aren't feeling very well."

He smacked her bottom gently. She wriggled with delight, gazing at him.

Suddenly he pushed her away. "Go on, now," he said, close to panic. "We want to get to bed."

He hurried into the bathroom. "Finish your teeth quickly, Andrew, and I'll tuck you in." He leaned against the wall, his nails squeaking on the tiles. As soon as Andrew had closed the door, Pears was seized by a violent and prolonged orgasm.

He lay in bed, making a lair of the darkness. Even there he wasn't safe. When he closed his eyes, grinning faces floated up, plump and sticky. Suppose Chris wanted him to make love to her? That was often the way they expunged their arguments. He could hear her scrubbing the blood from the wall.

Her climbing footsteps seemed to take forever, as if she were sadistically prolonging her approach. She knows, he thought. I've broadcast to her what I've done. He pressed himself as near to his edge of the bed as he could, pretending to sleep.

He held himself still as she slipped into bed. Too still. He moved slightly, muttering. "Hugh?" she said. He glared into the darkness, grinding his teeth silently. "Hugh, listen," she said.

He turned over violently. "What is it?" He hadn't meant to shout.

"Nothing," she said, turning away.

"No, what is it?"

"It doesn't matter."

He could feel her turning restlessly for hours. He held himself rigid, willing her to sleep. She turned against him, rubbery; the bed felt like a tropical tent. When at last she was quiet, he couldn't be sure she wasn't pretending. He didn't dare leave the bed in case he disturbed her. Fog hung in the gap between the curtains, glowing feebly, thick and blank as his mind. His eyes itched hotly. He gazed at nothing.

At breakfast his eyes felt bloated and raw. Around dawn the chattering of birds had suddenly toppled with him into sleep. He stared at his plate. His knife sliced a poached egg; yellow liquid leaked from its pupil. The sounds of Chris and the children nagged at him, annoying as radio voices bumbling against an exhausted battery. He didn't know how he would be able to face work.

"I don't want to go to school today," Andrew said. "I don't feel well."

"Neither do I," Linda said.

"What's the matter with you?" Chris demanded.

They looked at each other, baffled. "Come on, both of you," she said. "No nonsense. Once you come home tonight, you've the whole weekend."

Pears forced himself to look at them directly. They were rummaging for an argument. "Listen, don't fret," he told them. "It won't be so bad, once you're there. I don't always want to go out in the mornings, you know. I don't this morning. But we have to go."

"And what about me?" Chris demanded angrily. "Do you think it's a picnic for me to go shopping, the way they look at you round here? It's an effort of will, I assure you."

He stared at her. "Only last week you said you liked these shops."

She was flushed with anger that she'd let her feelings show. "Well, that's how I feel now," she said defiantly.

"Well," he said, glancing at his watch. "Time's getting on. If I go now, I can walk up with you two. Are you coming?" he asked Chris, rather discouragingly: her revelation had annoyed him, for he didn't know how to handle it.

"I've the washing-up to do. I'll manage, don't worry." When he hesitated she said "I've told you not to worry about me."

Fog was blocking the way just outside the gate, a dull featureless thug. Behind the thickening grey screen, the privet leaves looked fat and plastic. Pears could see nothing he would be able to bear to touch. He gazed back down the hall, past the dining-table to Chris at the sink, and almost retreated. Then he urged the children out. Glancing back at their bright orange curtains, which looked shabby now with fog, he caught sight of the young man in the flat, gazing apathetically through the uncurtained window.

The hinges of the gate shrieked jaggedly; Pears felt as if the sound were being dragged through his ears. The children waited restlessly. "Go on, then," he said, impatient with everything, and strode out, thinking: I should make them want to go, not bully them.

The fog settled on him like wet cobwebs, drawing him deeper into itself. It closed him in with silence. He could hear no sound

from the main road two hundred yards away. His muffled footsteps
clopped; he could hardly hear the children's. Andrew and Linda
were diluted, dissolving smudgily into the fog.

Odd blurs bobbed past: the mirror of a parked car, the
overhanging tips of a tree. They faded, and the street seemed to
fade with them. He was alone with fog. It closed on his face like a
cold soft mask, trickling thickly into his lungs. A single paving-
stone repeated itself underfoot, again and again, in a frame of fog.
He couldn't see the children now. He began coughing uncomfortably.
Nor could he hear them.

He gagged himself with one hand, and strained his ears. All
his senses were muffled; his mouth and nose felt stuffed with wet
smoke. The flat inexorable wall of fog stood close to him, boxing
him in. He opened his mouth to shout, but it filled with a foggy
cough. The children had gone.

As he fought to speak, a dreadful suspicion choked him. He
and the children hadn't been alone in the fog. There had been a
hulking shape that had paced them just behind the blinding wall,
waiting until they became separated. He could feel its stealthy
presence now, somewhere near. Its hands had grabbed the children's
mouths. It had dragged the children into an alley and stuffed gags
into their mouths. Now it was turning to Linda —

He heard the children's muffled screams.

For a moment he was fog, fluid, helpless. Then he smashed
his way blindly forward, toward the cries. The grey slammed against
his eyes, then fell back, acquiring an orange tinge. The children
were waiting beneath the sodium lights of the main road, giggling
nervously. Traffic moved by like a glacier, bleary lights gazing
tearfully ahead. He'd never expected to be so glad to see a traffic
jam.

The children must have been playing hide and seek in the fog,
they must have scared each other. Pears felt angry, and anxious to
be sure that that was what had happened. But to interrogate them,
or to lose his temper, would only cause further unpleasantness: best
to leave it alone. Abruptly, Linda said to Andrew "I'm sorry I was
rude about your doll. I was mean."

"I was growing out of it anyway," Andrew said.

Oddly, they became less reluctant as they neared the school. They ran into the underpass eagerly enough, casting him a last glance as they went, flushed oval portraits in Balaclavas. He strolled to the bank, musing.

They couldn't have felt more reluctant to come out than he had. But now, away from the house, he felt no reluctance at all. At home they were all caught in a tight spiral of neuroses. Now he saw that, he knew how to free them. They must go away at the weekend, into the countryside. The fog stepped back before him, parting.

He enjoyed the day. He joked with those of his colleagues who seemed gloomily befogged, until their polite smiles broke into spontaneity. He'd cleared his desk of the convoluted cases which had been gathering, piling up against his mind. He rang Chris at work. She sounded happier, and said she liked the idea of a day out.

He felt affectionate toward everyone he saw or thought of. Almost everyone. He stole a look at the young industrial chemist's account. No salary cheque had been received this month, and the account was overdrawn. So that's why he sits around all day.

Walking home, Pears felt ashamed of his snooping. It hadn't even gained him anything. He hardly knew the man; he'd spoken to him only once, to ask him to subdue a howling guitar at midnight. These days the chemist's flat was usually silent — inert was more the word. As he reached his road, Pears saw the chemist driven away in a van by one of the friends who'd visited him last night. Pears couldn't help feeling glad to see him go.

At dinner the children cheered the proposal of a day out. "I did feel odd yesterday," Pears said. "And this morning too. It must have been something I ate. Didn't you feel odd, Chris?"

"You know I had a migraine. I don't know about anything else."

"What about you two?" But they didn't know what he meant any more than Chris seemed to; and when he remembered how he'd felt it seemed healthier to forget.

The next day was cold and bright. They drove into North Wales. Slate hills were silver against pastel blue, white watery clouds streaked the horizons. They parked in a village whose name they stumbled over, laughing helplessly. The village seemed full of slim spires, of churches built of plump bricks of creamy dough around rose windows. They sat outside a pub, watching tractors pass, a market in the street opposite, a pony cantering by. "I wish I had a book about ponies," Linda said.

They bought her one, and *Watership Down* for Andrew. As they walked back to the car, Chris said "Do you think there's a hotel?" There was: two cottages knocked together, with a double room and a single free. "I bet you're called Mrs Jones," Linda told the landlady, who was. Andrew ran upstairs to read his book, and later they had to open the bedroom door to let the smell of dinner tempt him down.

After dinner they walked through the village. The streets were full of greetings and good-nights; distant windows came alight on the hills. An elderly couple said good night to them. They put the children to bed. Glancing through Andrew's book, Pears found a poem which he thought was one of the most beautiful things he'd ever read. He read it aloud to them, letting himself go completely into the poem and into the children's eyes; by the end he was almost in tears. The children said good night quietly. Later Chris and he made love tenderly, unhurried, tranquil. They lay and felt the wide night calm around them.

"Now I think about it, you were right," Chris said. "I did feel strange on Thursday."

"In what way?"

She was asleep as soon as she'd said "I don't know why, I was jealous of you and Linda."

On Sunday Mrs Jones invited them to visit a friend's farm. The farmer's children were playing on a collapsed haystack. Andrew and Linda plunged into it shouting, pleading with their parents to join them. Urged on by Mrs Jones and her friends, Pears and Chris climbed the stack, pretending reluctance. At the top Linda began tickling Pears to make him roll down. Feeling her small fingers move over him, he froze for a moment. Then he retaliated, and while Andrew played with the other children — bringing him out of himself, Pears thought, good — he and Linda set about Chris. They rolled to the bottom entangled, laughing.

The farmer's wife insisted they stay for dinner. They drove home leisurely, through thin drifts of mist. The children slept in the back, nestling against Chris. Whenever he caught her eye in the mirror she smiled gently. Even Liverpool seemed refreshed by their outing; the long carriageway of Tuebrook was polished clean by frost and sodium light. The yellow paintwork of their house surged forward from the terrace to greet them. The flat next door was dark. Pears couldn't remember ever having been so pleased to return home.

On Monday evening he hurried home. Chris wouldn't be back for an hour, the children were staying late at school for recorder practice. He'd had enough of the rusty gate. The tin of paint nudged his thigh. Paint now, oil tomorrow. Fog unrolled the street like a carpet for him, yards ahead. A light appeared in the flat next door. He didn't bother looking.

He'd climbed to the loft in search of a paint-brush when the sound began. It was a low rumbling, almost inaudible; for a while he wasn't sure he heard it. Dust stirred wakefully in the dim charred light beneath the roof. The sound seemed to be deep in the walls; momentarily the uncoloured shapes around him in the loft appeared to be vibrating. Surely it couldn't be thunder. Of course, it was a plane approaching overhead.

He had just climbed down to the landing when he felt the sound inside him.

It was growing there. It was a huge rusty lump of metal, sharp-cornered and jagged, exploding slowly from the centre of his cranium, forcing its dull saw-toothed way out through his ears. He could taste it. His mouth tasted full of coins.

Don't let it be starting again! Please, no!

He rushed for the stairs. Downstairs he wouldn't be so close to the sound. But he had to halt at the top, clutching at the banister, for he was plummeting toward the hall like a plane out of control. As he'd moved, his head had gone hurtling uncontrollably forward and down, as if on a cable. Within him metal rasped heavily.

By the time he reached the hall, gripping the banister and holding himself immobile on each step while his momentum subsided, the plane was fading. He sank gingerly into a chair in the living-room. The sound drained lazily away, a murmur, a whisper, cold and rough in his head; he couldn't tell when it began to persist only in his imagination. He sat still. If he didn't move nothing else would happen. It would all fade, he would feel it go and know when it was safe to move. The walls held themselves still, almost trembling with the effort.

Soon he felt there was nothing wrong except the fog, which now had night on its side. The privet hedge was sliced thin by a block of grey. He stood up to draw the curtains, but fell back into his chair. There was something out there he must watch for, to be prepared when it came. Each time he looked the fog had inched more of his surroundings into itself.

Because the window was closed he didn't hear them coming. The fog within the gateway stirred. Two small forms were rising to the surface. They came slowly, like bodies floating up from grey mud. He heard the faint clang of the gate, then they were rushing toward the house. They came to the window and peered in at him, mouthing. Then a key was scrabbling at the front door.

He knew their names, Andrew and Linda. But that didn't help. He struggled to grasp memories before they came in. Andrew was both younger and older than his age, prone to trip over his own feet, over-sensitive. No use. Pears was coldly analysing a stranger, and every phrase was a cliché. And Linda —

Memory deluged him, one image smashing against him again and again. Oh my God. Oh my God. How could he have had such feelings about a ten-year-old child, his own daughter? Even worse, how could he have tried to ignore them, forget them, pretend he'd meant Chris all the time? What was he becoming? Or had this secret self been waiting within him all the time?

Linda ran in, flushed, excited. "Bet you can't guess what we did today," she said.

She was all freed hair and pink flesh, palpitating. He clenched his fists down the sides of his chair, gouging his palms, trying to lock in a threatened explosion of nausea. "Tell me, tell me later," he managed to say. "Go and play."

"But I wanted to tell you," she said, hurt.

"Not now." Each time he spoke another voice, muffled, joined him in chorus. It was his own. He tried to ignore it long enough to speak. "Go, go on," he stammered.

Their sounds in the playroom annoyed him like the bumbling of flies, but at least he'd avoided further speech. He stared emptily at the encroaching fog. He wasn't going mad, he wasn't. But he couldn't bear to think that what he'd been experiencing was real. Yet if he were going mad the horror was himself, dragging him deeper, saving its worst until all his defences were down — not yet even hinting at its worst. His thoughts slithered, eluding him. He wasn't mad. But there were states of mind similar to madness. Suddenly he knew he'd been drugged.

How? In food. The chemist next door — Nonsense. He had neither opportunity nor motive. Detectives always looked for those. But Pears had detected a drug in himself, however it had got there. Chris, experimenting on behalf of the hospital — Rubbish. It was temporary. Bearable. Drugs didn't drive sane people mad, drugs couldn't overcome a strong mind, a mind that wouldn't weaken, that was in control, they couldn't. Perhaps Chris could determine what drug it was, and the antidote. The wall of fog shifted forward, hanging dull and slack, leaving only a cramped strip of dark bedraggled lawn.

The children muttered in the playroom, blurred. Pears lay back gingerly; his head felt thin-shelled, rocking with liquid. He closed his eyes and let sounds pass him by: Andrew's toy train rattling on its cramped line, Linda's padding bare-socked footsteps, Linda's voice. His eyes sprang wide, glaring.

"I want the bunny." That was all she'd said. A frayed stuffed rabbit sat in the corner of the playroom, the children rarely bothered with it now. But Linda had just asked for it.

She hadn't really said "He wants to fuck me."

Or perhaps she had. After all, she needn't have meant her father. Of course she hadn't meant him, Pears thought, his face burning. Then whom had she meant? God, surely nobody! She had just been trying out the word, as children do.

She could have meant Pears. Young girls were supposed to go through a period of sexual love for the father. But wasn't she too young? Perhaps not: perhaps hidden in her mind were pictures of her father pulling off her clothes, his huge hairy body pressing down on her, forcing her wider —

He leapt up snarling. But his rage relieved him of nothing. He had to know. All he could hear now was what he thought she'd said. He strode into the hall, and balked. What could he say? He couldn't accuse her directly, in case his mind had tricked him. But why should his mind play that particular trick? He stood, trying to force himself forward; his hands felt bloated, and spiky with sweat. Andrew's voice squeaked. The playroom door hung immobile, smugly threatening. Linda answered.

She'd said "We want to stick these blocks up here." She hadn't said —

Pears slammed the door wide. The children stared at him: startled? innocent? pretending? Some building blocks were scattered amid the clutter on the floor, but he demanded "What were you saying?"

When Linda gazed at him, perhaps without guile, and opened her mouth, he interrupted savagely "You know what I mean. Just now. What were you saying?"

She looked uneasy now. "I don't know. What was I saying?"

"Leave Andrew out of it, don't try and make him answer for you. Don't drag him into it, you little —"

Her eyes were wider, rimmed with moisture. In a minute she would run to him in tears. He couldn't bear to have her near him. If she touched him — "All right. All right. It doesn't matter," he stammered, to escape. "Just keep quiet," he said, and slammed the door.

He couldn't shake off the suspicion that Linda had got the better of him. She had seduced him again: into silence. She was knowing, evil; her body was. It was taking over, possessing the little girl he'd loved. He mustn't think of her.

The fog had fitted to the windows like the backing of a mirror. A dull discoloured lump of flesh sat in his reflected armchair, staring at him. They were still gazing at each other when he heard Chris's key in the lock.

Fear burned through him. The children might tell her how he'd behaved. She'd know he was going wrong again. His eyes might betray him if she looked closely; drugs were supposed to show in the eyes. If her terror were added to his the onslaught would disintegrate him completely.

101

Wasn't he looking at it the wrong way? The inspiration lifted him to his feet. Being near her should help. It was exactly what he needed. He hurried after her, into the kitchen.

"Hello," he said. "I was going to paint the gate but the fog came down. I'll do it tomorrow without fail. I'll make myself if I have to. Not that I'll have lost interest." He was saying too much, too fast, trying to outrun his muffled other voice. "Do you like that colour paint? Never mind, don't answer, you must be tired. Was your day all right?"

"It was all right." She sounded a little weary. "You can get your own drink, Andrew. Don't start nibbling, Linda, dinner won't be long."

He avoided looking at the children. "Can I help you at all? Have you a migraine?"

"No, not yet." But all of a sudden Pears had. Perhaps she was in fact suffering secretly; but he was experiencing it directly. Perhaps he was imagining what migraine felt like. All he knew was that open metallic sores were burning coldly through his scalp; his cranium felt like a raw wound. Yet somehow he wasn't yet feeling the pain. If he weren't with Chris it might fade. "You don't want me to do anything, do you?" he gabbled, hurrying away, his scalp corroding.

He'd managed to attune himself to the fog, to its untroubled colourless calm, when Chris called him to dinner. He walked down the hall, bearing his calm carefully. That telephone is red. That wall is yellow. No need to touch them with his mind.

In the dining-area he found he felt invulnerable. He smiled surreptitiously. The effect was wearing off. He raised a forkful of dinner to his mouth.

He couldn't taste it. He almost reached into his mouth with the fork to examine the food. Lamb chop, mint sauce, potatoes, sprouts; no taste of any of them, just solids moving in his mouth. It was all right. No need to strain. This was only reaction against what he'd been suffering, what did they call it, sensory overload.

He chewed. Linda was gazing toward him as she ate.

He'd been chewing for hours. Linda gazed at him.

He chewed faster. Faster, faster. No use: he couldn't make Linda move. His time was slowing to a halt. Each moment was only a fraction of the one before. They would never add up to the next; he was trapped in this moment forever. And Linda's pictures of him were creeping toward his mind. "What are you doing?" he shouted. "What do you think you're staring at?"

Linda gasped. "I was just thinking."

Oh no, she couldn't trick him again so easily. Her gaze had been slowing him down, as though time were amber. "Ah," he snarled triumphantly. "And just what were you thinking, eh? Would it have been about me?"

"I was just thinking about my recorder. I played a whole page today." She was nearly crying.

Chris was staring at him. If he went on, she might suspect what had happened to him on Thursday night — when Linda had got the better of him. She mustn't know that, nobody must know, he must wipe it out of his mind. "All right," he told Linda abruptly. "It doesn't matter. Get on with your dinner."

Faces gazed at him. "I'm sorry," he said, to turn them away. "All right!" he shouted. "I'm sorry! I am sorry," he said quietly. Maybe Linda had been telling the truth. At least he'd escaped the trap of the dwindling moment, though his time still felt more intolerably stretched than it had since his childhood. Perhaps that was how Linda's time felt too.

Having eaten all he could, he retreated to the living-room. He lay back in its stillness, letting its shapes and colours lie on his eyes. If he didn't move they would stay still. But they grew harsh, alert. Someone was coming down the hall.

He'd forgotten: he had to get through an entire evening with Chris and the children. Surely the effect would fade before then. He had only to keep still, calm.

Chris read while the children watched television. They were pretending. They knew something was wrong with him, they were watching covertly, until he betrayed himself. But he wasn't going to. Let them watch how calm he was. He closed his eyes.

Which sprang open. Rushing up from their depths there had been a doll whose head was cracked wetly like an egg of blood, a doll with Andrew's face. As Pears glared at Andrew, he glimpsed the cracks fading into the boy's hair.

Worse was waiting for his eyes to close. He stared at the television. Too hectic. He stared at the palely coffee-coloured wall. If he kept his eyes open the images would die away. His eyes twinged, smarting, and he blinked.

Linda sailed up, naked, posturing, ready to engulf him. He gasped, then tried to smile convincingly: he could just have woken from a doze, they couldn't prove anything. He blinked. Chris flashed out at him and was etched on his mind. All her nerves were laid bare; small sharp hooks like dentist's instruments plucked at them. Her head was a mass of buried razor-blades.

He sprang from his chair and stumbled upstairs. If he couldn't see the three of them they wouldn't be able to provoke these nightmares. He lay on the bed. Ahead hung the window, a faint grey smudged rectangle. It was receding from him.

Instead of yielding more light to his eyes it grew fainter, dwindling. The bedroom was enormous and very dark. The floor was crowded with figures, creeping lopsidedly toward him on all fours. The heads of the foremost, grey blurred ovals, were peering at him over the edge of the bed.

Little of his scream escaped between his fingers. His other hand groped for the light-switch, found something, switched it on. The room was defiantly bare. He examined that fact for a long time, until he felt it might be true. The depths of his mind waited for him. It was only a temporary lull. The tide would flood back soon. Each time it returned it was more overpowering.

He was descending the stairs, which felt still in the way a booby-trap might, when a terrible certainty gripped him. The effects must wear off eventually, no drug could last for the rest of one's life; but his nightmares must be imprinted on the house. Exactly as if some dreadful tragedy had happened there, the house was haunted now.

His gaze was drawn to the hall wallpaper. It was faintly speckled with a brownish stain. Blood. That was the beginning of the nightmare, when he'd seen the accident victim. If he could wipe off the last of the blood perhaps it would erase the imprint of his terror. Sickly he felt that the walls were soft within, as if subtly corrupted from their core, by the haunting; but he bent closer.

Peering, he wasn't sure whether the spots were blood or shadow. He sniffed the wall. Still unsure, he touched the stain

104

with his tongue. A faint metallic taste: blood. Before he knew what he intended he was supporting himself, palms flat against the wall, while he licked avidly, searching for the taste.

He threw himself back, but couldn't escape himself. Maybe, he thought in a desperate bid for distraction, that's what the dopey chemist thought I meant to do when he saw me in the hall. Now his fantasy's true.

Chris and the children looked up when he opened the door. His face froze. He didn't know what expression he wore, but dared not alter it in case his face betrayed his terror. A tight mask he'd never seen before was clamped on him. As he paced to his seat the mask tugged painfully at his face, determined to reshape itself. He sat down and had to pass his hand over his face, as if brushing away sweat, in order to change the mask.

"You don't feel well, do you," Chris said. He managed to shake his grinning head. "You ought to lie down," she said.

He realised fully how helpless and alone he was. "No!" he shouted.

"You two had better go and play."

"I want them here." He wanted to keep an eye on Linda. "Stay here," he told them.

He seemed to have earned himself a lull. Someone was knocking and ringing the bell next door, but he could bear that. Now they were banging on the window of the ground-floor flat, several of them talking in low voices. "Come on," one said. "I can't stand this." Pears was glad to hear someone else feeling that, for a change. They were going; the gate clanked. He looked up, smiling emptily, and saw Linda gazing beyond him in horror.

He twisted about. A dark blotch was scuttering over the wall, hectic tendrils quivering. It was — it was a crane-fly; its legs fluttered hysterically, as if in a dying paroxysm. Still the lull. It scuttled into a corner. "I'll get it," he told Chris. She usually dealt with intruding insects; this time he'd do it, to show that he could.

He had trapped the whirring fly, it was trembling violently yet feebly in his fist like an essence of terror, when he glimpsed Chris's expression.

At once she was thrusting the poker deeper into the fire. He opened the window and released the fly, then he gazed at the fog, trying to understand. She wasn't frightened of insects. Then he knew: he'd projected his own fading terror onto her face. His nightmare had lent her a mask. He sat down, smiling at her.

When he looked away her weak smile collapsed into naked terror.

This time her smile wasn't swift enough. He forced himself to look behind him at the corner toward which she'd been glaring. He wouldn't panic, he'd fought through, the effect was fading, vanquished. But as he turned, a faint smell of something like meat touched his nostrils.

The corner was bare. He felt weak with relief, yet uneasily baffled. Briefly he'd dreamed that he was infecting Chris. He must have been right before: he was simply imposing the last of his terror on his perception of her. Mightn't that show that the terror was leaving him? He glanced at her.

She smiled at him. She smiled. She was almost convincing. But he knew what was happening, and reality parted beneath him. The smell filled his nostrils. She hadn't been looking at the corner, but at him. He had already smelled what she smelled: himself. Behind her smile her eyes were transfixed by slivers of growing horror. As if her eyes were mirrors he could see what she saw.

In his chair she saw an eyeless face of mottled bone, grinning at her through its gaping cheeks.

At last he managed to look down at his hand. He felt his neck-bone creak. His hand was still flesh. But he could feel his corpse. It was inside him, slowly corroding its way to the surface, a core of numbness spreading outward, reaching lazily for him. It was unhurried. It had as much time as he.

He suppressed his scream, even though it would say he was still alive. There was worse to come, he realised almost dispassionately. He looked at Andrew and Linda, watching television, sitting still. Still as corpses.

Suddenly he knew, gazing at their immobile faces on which colours flickered lightly, that they were feeling rigor mortis stake its claim on them. Death was squeezing their windpipes experimentally, like a witch in a dream. But it was no dream, for he could smell them. It must be terror that was fluttering trapped in their eyes.

All he could do was close his own. It no longer mattered what was waiting in there. Anything would be more bearable than the sight of his dead children. He closed them out.

Blank.

White.

Nothing.

When he opened his eyes, feeling purged and somehow released, he was in a room with three strangers.

There was a woman, and a small imitation of her: a girl, less haggard, pinker, more plump. There was a small boy who reminded him vaguely of someone. All three of them were pretending his presence in the room was natural — pretending that they knew who this man was. But they didn't, any more than he did.

They were watching him surreptitiously. He had to get out before they moved on him, the stranger. But they would never let him reach the door unless he defended himself.

He caught sight of the poker. Half of it was buried in the fire and red-hot, but the handle was insulated. He stood up gingerly and began to move stealthily toward the fire. He felt the three of them pretending not to watch him. If he used the weapon he would have to close his eyes, though he wouldn't be able to close his ears.

He had to escape. He inched toward the poker, trying to seem casual, aimless. For a moment he was surrounded by the three; his held breath burned in him. But they didn't leap.

The presence of the young girl disturbed him most of all. She was his greatest danger. There was something in her he must destroy; her freshness was deceitful, her soft plumpness was a snare. She was like the walls of the house, whose corrupted cores oozed now, thick with evil. Her innocence was disgusting, intolerable, false. He'd make sure her body could never again lure anyone. He stooped to the fire. As the poker stirred, its nest of cinders fell open, brightening.

Something came howling toward the house.

He jerked and almost fell. He stumbled to the window, knocking the television askew. They'd trapped him in his room

107

until the howling came for him. He shouldered the clinging curtains aside and wrenched up the sash. The howling growled into silence.

A blue glow pulsed through the fog. The fog's dead heart was beating. It took him minutes to discern a blue will-o'-the-wisp, flashing sluggishly. Uniformed men strode toward him out of the fog. No, they were heading for the next house.

He turned to watch, and came face to face with a pinched white almost fleshless mask, peering through the neighbouring window.

It was his own reflection. No: it was his enemy, the man who'd been trying to drive him mad. At last Pears had found him. Now he would make him suffer.

Pears was trying to remember where he'd put the poker when the uniformed men closed around his enemy. Pears snarled in frustration. The white mask was still as they lifted the body to its feet, but the body was breathing. They could have him, so long as they used the poker on him. Pears would give them his. He turned, but the ambulance had gone.

He was staring emptily at the fog when the chemist's friends returned. They were the three he'd seen on Thursday night. He could remember. He let memories drift back as they might, hoping he wouldn't remember anything he couldn't bear.

One of the young men hurried into the flat and rummaged in a rickety chest of drawers. He snatched out a piece of paper, and something else. He moved offstage, and Pears heard a toilet flushing.

As he emerged, one of his friends demanded "Have you got the formula?"

Pears tried to control himself, but already was screaming with laughter. The three glanced sharply at him. "I'm sorry," he gasped, weeping, and was hoarse with laughter again. He ran out, ashamed and spasmodically hilarious, to explain if he could.

One frowned at him from beneath a red mock-leather cap and edged away. "Don't get paranoid," said the one who'd entered the flat. "We aren't going to make this stuff. Neither is anyone else," and he tore up the piece of paper minutely. The fragments swarmed away on the hint of a wind.

"He'd freaked out completely, that guy in there," the third said, winding his long scarf tautly into his fists. "We had to call the ambulance."

"He'd synthesised a new trip," the man in the red cap chattered, released apparently from guilt into speech. "It was too much. It got worse every time you tripped. But he said it was worth learning how to control it."

"The last one was so bad we took him away for the weekend. We thought we'd persuaded him off it. But tonight he was even deeper into it."

"I never took any," said the man with the stretched scarf. "But I was picking up his trip while we were waiting. It was that powerful, being near him could turn you on even if you hadn't taken any. It was bad. We had to call the ambulance."

"I think you had," Pears reassured him, feeling his surroundings start the long slow fall back into familiarity. He remembered the face he'd seen carried away. The eyes had been sunken, passive, immobile, at the mercy of whatever passed before or within them. They had looked exactly like red-cracked glass.

Weeks later he told Chris some of what had happened, and why. Perhaps she believed him. "Did you feel any of it?" he asked. "Anything at all?"

"I don't know."

"Anything you can describe?"

"No."

Perhaps she was telling the truth; he couldn't be sure. Had she forgotten her jealousy of Linda? If so, what should that convey to him? How should he react? Since his experience he seemed to be approaching decisions more and more gently and circuitously, and making fewer.

He carried the paint and brush down the hall. Today would be the rusty gate's last day. The children shouted in the playroom. Had they felt any of it? How could he find out? It would be better to let them forget. Besides, he seemed to have forgotten all he'd ever learned about how to talk to them.

"The shuttlecock's under the stairs," Linda said, muffled.

So it was, behind a tangle of nesting chairs. Andrew ran into the hall, bursting into brighter colour as he entered the path of sunlight. He stooped beneath the stairs, but shrank back at once. "I can't find it," he called, his voice unnaturally high.

What had the boy flinched from? "There it is, Andrew," Pears said, and handed him the shuttlecock.

When Andrew had gone Pears forced himself to stoop beneath the stairs again. Under his hand the wall felt thin, a crust over softness. He made himself look at what he'd glimpsed from the corner of his eye.

It was snarling silently from the dark corner where the underside of the stairs met the floor. It was pale and smooth, and had no eyes that he could see. A mat of grey hair like a lump of dust hung over most of the face. Its mouth was huge and red with an unbroken ring of teeth, gibbous with rage.

He managed to save the tin of paint before it fell, and saw at once what the face must be. Someone had wiped a splotch of red paint with a wad of paper. The matted hair was a tangle of dust.

But the corner was bare. There was no paper beneath the stairs, and the corner was clean of dust.

THIS TIME

A S CROSBY EMERGED FROM THE DENTIST'S he almost tripped over a dog, which vanished behind the bushes. He took more care while crossing the road to the park, for he felt unreal, dreamy. He tongued the hole in his stony jaw and tried to recall what he'd dreamed.

People were walking dogs in Birkenhead Park or being run by them. A man was training an Alsatian called Winston. On the fish-pond the white ducks looked moulded out of the reflections of clouds. He had been counting backwards from thirty; he'd reached fourteen before the anaesthetic worked, and then he'd seemed to begin counting an altogether different set of numbers backward — on and on into the dark. He felt he had arrived eventually, but where?

He walked through the short cut from the pond to his street. On the playing-field beside him, rugby posts were panting in the August heat: H H H. As he opened his front door, pushing back a couple of letters, spacious echoes greeted him.

His face no longer felt stony. The gap in his jaw was plugged with an ache. He was glad he'd drawn today's stint before he had gone to the dentist's — but nevertheless he was anxious not to lose the impressions he'd gathered in the waiting-room: a mother holding her child like a ventriloquist's dummy from which she was determined to coax a brave smile, a teenager who had tried to pretend that the bulge in his cheek was nothing worth noticing, just a sweet. Perhaps Crosby could sketch something for his exhibition.

He gazed across his drawing-board, out of the window. Beyond the long garden, the pond blazed among the trees. The head of the little girl next door kept popping over the seven-foot hedge like a Jack-in-the-box; the seat of her swing was concealed by the hedge. She made him feel all the more unreal, and incapable of sketching the impressions he wanted to fix. When at last he began to sketch he was hardly aware of doing so.

Ten minutes later he had finished. The man's face stared up at him. It was hairless, and looked smooth as a baby's face, as though it had never been spoiled. Was it a face or a mask? It looked too good to be true, especially the eyes.

Was it even worth preserving? It meant nothing at all to him — yet that was why he filed it away, in the hope that he would remember where the impression had come from. His thoughts were dodging aimlessly about his mind, like the echoes in the house.

Never mind: he was visiting Giulia. He would have waited for her in the art gallery, except that he might disturb her at work. Instead he wandered about the park before catching the train, then strolled through Port Sunlight for a while. Along the vistas of the Causeway and the Diamond, the trees were dark and velvety, unrolling their long shadows on the plots of grass. Everything was steeped in evening light: the columns and domes of the Lady Lever Gallery, the half-timbered cottages that looked outlined and latticed in charcoal, their gardens trim as carpet tiles. Even the factories beyond the estate looked to be pouring forth gold smoke, like a lyrical advertisement for cigarettes.

Giulia was wearing her grandmother's apron. "How do you feel?" she said.

"Cut off from everything."

She gave him a wry smile. "That's hardly new, is it?"

He followed her into the kitchen of the cottage; he'd found that he wanted to talk. "I hope you'll be able to eat," she said anxiously.

"Certainly." She was making several of his favourite dishes. They were too old, and had known each other for too long, to express their affection in words.

She emerged from the pantry bearing spices. "So may I take it that your air of gloom is an after-effect of the surgery?"

"No, not really. My book has been out for a month, without a single review. What makes it worse is the trash that gets reviewed — three notices this week for a collection of pornographic comics."

"That's exactly why you shouldn't mind that they don't appreciate you. Few things of any worth are appreciated in their own time, I've told you that before." She frowned exaggeratedly at

112

him. "Now, Thom, you just enjoy being depressed. Some of your work satisfies you, doesn't it? That's all that any genuine artist can hope for."

"I suppose so." He sighed, to make her chide him further. "I wish I had more time to do something special for the exhibition. Instead I'll be wasting a day on this damn television show."

"You'll be reaching a new audience direct rather than via the reviewers. How can that be wasted time?" She said almost wistfully "If I had a television I'd watch you."

They ate in the kitchen, then carried the rest of the wine into the parlour and played chess. One of Crosby's sketches hung above the mantelpiece: an enormous man whose round head resembled a pudding balanced on a larger, and who was devouring a pudding which looked like him. Secretly he felt that Giulia's appreciation was worth all the gushing of reviewers.

When each of them had won a game, they stood close together in the small porch, not quite touching, and lingered over their goodbyes. The rocking of the dim train lulled him, made him feel he might be able to meet all his commitments, after all. As he reached home, close to midnight, someone was walking an off-white dog in the park.

He woke convinced that he had been counting backwards. The series of numbers had seemed very long. He felt frustrated by his inability to concentrate or to trust himself to his intuition; he had no time now to add to the exhibition, when the private view was only two days hence.

But perhaps — He retrieved the sketch of the smooth-faced man from the file and pored over it. Had he dreamed that face too? The enigma annoyed him, but there was another feeling which, if defined, might help him complete the picture. Usually he regarded his subjects with detached yet affectionate humour, like a father or a historian — but he was sure that whatever he felt for the smooth face, it wasn't affection.

The sound of applause, which he thought at first was a flock of birds starting from the trees, roused him. Down by the fish-pond, fishermen appeared to be presenting one another with awards. They were blurred, for Crosby's window was wet, though it didn't seem to have been raining overnight: the park was dry, not a twinkle of rain.

The decks of the Liverpool ferry were crowded with shoppers. White stuffing bulged from splits in the blue sky. A pigeon on the mast of a yacht was modelling the metal bird on the tower of the Liver Building. A naked baby was crawling about behind the legs of the crowd. Of course it must have been a dog.

When he'd overseen the mounting of his exhibition in the Bluecoat Gallery, he sat on a bench in Church Street and watched people. A man with a bowler hat and umbrella danced by as though in search of the rest of his troupe. A scrawny man in a pinstripe suit sat opposite Crosby, his limbs like sticks of mint rock. A whitish dog that looked hairless vanished into the crowd.

By the time he reached home he knew what he was going to draw. An hour later it was done: a chorus line of businessmen, all shapes and sizes, trotting to the office. He liked it enough to copy it for the exhibition before sending it for syndication.

And yet he felt he'd overlooked a more important task. He wandered through the house, feeling like a stranger who had strayed into a gallery full of framed drawings while it was closed to the public. "This is the Michaelangelo room," he muttered wryly. "This is the Cruikshank room. And here is the Crosby room — the smallest room, of course." Even if he was being unfair to himself, the echoes agreed with him.

A stroll in the park might help clear his mind. Perhaps his problem related to the smooth-faced sketch, but he felt there was more to remember. When he went out the twilight was deepening: the intricate lattices of grass-blades merged into a smouldering impressionistic glow; the pond looked solid and dark as soil. He began to follow the path around the water as the last fragments of light in the sky went out.

Before long he felt uneasy. The path was caged by railings, and hemmed in by trees and bushes on grassy banks. It turned constantly back and forth in a series of blind curves. Suppose he rounded a curve and bumped into someone in the dark?

Why should that bother him? It was nothing that an apology couldn't make right. Of course it would be unpleasant to touch an unseen face without warning — but how could he do that when his hands were down by his sides? There was no point in brooding, especially since he knew that if he left the path now, even assuming he could, he would be lost.

He hurried onward, stumbling. Tree-roots forced open the cracked lips of the concrete path. A white blotch on the pond grew suddenly larger, flapping. The grey mass the size of his head which came at Crosby's face was a cloud of midges.

Though the park road was no lighter, he let out a guarded sigh of relief when he emerged from the path. He made his way along the road toward the short cut beside the rugby ground, and had almost reached the dark gap when he faltered, his jaw lolling. A flat white face had peered over next door's hedge at him.

He glared up at the seven-foot hedge. He'd had the impression of a face like a bulldog's, but it had only been a glimpse from the corner of his eye; perhaps it hadn't been a face at all, just a piece of paper fluttering in the grasp of the hedge. But weren't the chains of the swing squeaking faintly to a halt? Surely his neighbours wouldn't let their child play out so late; perhaps a strange child had squeezed through the hedge. Their garden was impenetrably dark. Crosby dodged through the short cut, and was blinded by the streetlamps until he reached them.

Next morning he had been dreaming of fire. He'd turned away in dismay, only to find himself surrounded by gloating eyes. More than that he couldn't recall, and had no time to try. He was already later than he'd meant to leave for the Manchester train.

When he arrived panting at the television studios, he had to wait while an old soldier misheard his name and announced him dolefully over the intercom. For a moment Crosby hoped the show had begun without him, but it wasn't that kind of a show. Eventually the producer appeared; his smile was more like a twitch. A makeup girl dabbed at Crosby's face as though cleaning a dusty waxwork before they rushed him into the studio.

The audience applauded, inspired by a placard, as the host strode onstage, a gleaming young man with a disc-jockey's brittle cheerfulness. Crosby was studying his opponents. The woman who drew feminist cartoons seemed all right, if rather lacking in detachment; but what of her partner on the team, "the wicked wit of Welwyn Garden City"? His hair resembled a shaving-brush, his smile was as thin as his voice; his quips made Crosby think of a cruel child probing wounds.

Crosby's partner was a plump man who made jokes in the tone of a patient describing symptoms. What of Crosby himself? "He draws like an artist surveying today's world from a Victorian time machine," the host said, quoting. "Kindly but critical, amused but never spiteful." It must have been the only quote they could find, but it was true enough: Crosby did feel apart from the time in which he was living, a visiting observer — and never more so than today.

It wasn't only the game that alienated him, though that, now that he saw it, was repulsive enough: whichever team produced the first cartoon on a theme culled from the audience won a point, as did the team which provoked the loudest applause. The whole thing was as vulgar as its name, *Top Draw* — a debased circus with cartoonists instead of clowns.

But he was more disturbed by the blank gaze of the cameras — because they almost reminded him of something else. When had he suffered the judgement of expressionless gazes that pricked his skin with dread? Some childhood ordeal he'd forgotten, perhaps? He was still trying to remember when the show ended. The other team had won.

At least examples of his work had been displayed to the cameras, and the host had mentioned his exhibition, though Crosby doubted that the show's audience would be interested. When he arrived home that night it was raining on a rugby match; bunches of floodlights glared on bony stalks, lines of rain looked like scratches on glass. Even the roar of the crowd seemed indefinably reminiscent — but why did he feel it wasn't savage enough? Shaking his head, to sort out his thoughts or dislodge them entirely, he let himself into his house.

He was drawing his bedroom curtains, and ready to enjoy the ineffectual assault of the rain on the house, when he saw the mark on the window. Momentarily the floodlights and his angle of vision made it resemble the impression which a flat drooping noseless face might have left on the glass. It must be a trick of the rain, which was pelting now; in a few minutes he couldn't even make out where the outline had seemed to be. Then why did he feel that he'd seen such a mark before?

A glimpse of movement in the park distracted him. The trees beyond the hedge were streaming with dim light. When he'd gazed at them so long that they swelled and shifted apart, he caught sight of the man who stood among them, gazing out of the park. It took him longer to distinguish the man's pale companion, for it was on all fours. How could anyone go out walking the dog in such a downpour? Crosby lay in bed and listened uneasily to the rain. Sometimes it sounded like a scratching at the windows; sometimes echoes made it sound to be inside the house.

He slept jerkily, and dreamed he was in bed with his wife, though in reality he had never even thought of marrying. Then he was betraying someone to the expressionless judges in order to save himself, and there was fire again. He spent the next day irritably pondering all this, which seemed just beyond his comprehension, and trying to draw a last piece for the Bluecoat Gallery. He had achieved nothing when it was time to leave for the private view.

It was hardly encouraging. The invited audience sipped sherry, smiled politely at his work or seemed afraid to laugh, talked of other things. He wouldn't have thought that dogs were allowed in here — but whenever he looked around he couldn't be sure that anybody had brought one. When people met his eye, their faces turned hurriedly blank. Again he thought of expressionless judges.

At least Giulia was there, which was a pleasant surprise; of course she would have been sent a ticket at the Lady Lever Gallery. "Don't take any notice of how they looked while you were watching," she said afterward. "They liked it, from what I overheard. They were inhibited, that was all." Perhaps sensing that he was unconvinced, she said "Come to me tomorrow and we'll read the reviews over dinner, if you like."

If only he could discuss his problems with her! How could he, when he had no idea what they were? That night in bed he tried to catch them in the dark. Though he wasn't aware of dreaming, he kept starting awake and wondering not only where he was, but who. Several times he restrained himself from getting up to look out of the window.

In the morning he was exhausted, but the notices revived him. They were more favourable than he would have permitted himself to hope: "...an impressively consistent exhibition..." "...real wit and style..." "...civilized humour of a kind one had ceased to hope for..." Perhaps his elation would help him discern the rest of his problems.

He spread out the sketch before him on the desk. There was a background that would make sense of the smooth face, if only he could draw it. He still had time to include it in his exhibition — but was that why it seemed so urgent to complete the picture?

The sketched eyes outstared him, challenged him to be sure they contained any secret at all. He had not the least idea what he was struggling to draw. Outside in the wind and the rain, trees tossed like the foot of a waterfall. Was it the wind or his awareness that kept fading? His pencil and his head were nodding, starting up. Perhaps he gazed at the smooth face for hours.

When eventually he fell asleep the pencil seemed about to mark the paper, yet he was too exhausted to intervene. Again he dreamed that he was in bed with his wife. He had woken beside her in the dark. She must be having a nightmare, for she was panting, though everything was all right now: he'd betrayed the smooth-faced man to save himself, betrayed the man who had corrupted him. All this was a dream, since he had never been married, and so he could wake up; please let him wake before he lit the candle! But the flint sparked, the wick flared, and he had to turn and look.

His wife lay face up beside him, her mouth gaping. She might have been panting in her sleep, except that her chest was utterly still. No, the sound was coming from the face that quivered above hers, the jowly face with its tongue grey as slime and its tiny pink eyes like pimples sunk in the white flesh. He thought of a bulldog's face, but it was more like a noseless old man's, and its paws on her chest looked like a child's hands.

Crosby woke, for the pencil had snapped in his fingers. The trees in the park were still now, and hardly distinguishable from the night. When he switched on his desk-lamp the reflection of his hand went crawling among the trees. He barely noticed, for he'd caught sight of the sketch. Before falling asleep, or while he had been dreaming, he had filled in the background at last.

Background wasn't precisely the word. The smooth-faced man had a body now, though not to his benefit; it was chained to a stake, and was burning. As Crosby stared at this, not at all sure that he wanted to understand, he remembered his spell under anaesthetic. As he'd drifted away he had begun to count backward, not random numbers but years — centuries of them.

All at once fear choked him, yet he wasn't sure what he feared. Once he was with Giulia he would be able to think. He switched off the desk-lamp and hurried out, contorting himself into his coat. Why did it seem that a dim reflection of his hand stayed in the park?

He strode to the railway station, and kept close to the streetlamps. The downpour had moved on, but rain continued beneath trees. Dockers were yelling inside and outside pubs. The platforms of the station were deserted, but hardly quiet enough; he wished the noises would come out and make themselves clear. The countryside, a glistening blur, dashed past the train. Fireflies of houses and streetlamps swarmed by.

He had just stepped onto the Port Sunlight platform, and was glad to leave behind the foggy light and brownish repetitive seats of the empty carriage, when something darted out of the train and vanished up the passage to the street.

At once his fear was no longer for himself. He ran along the passage, which was deserted, not even a porter. So were the half-timbered streets and avenues; the black and white buildings looked dead as bone. Shadows or rain bruised the pavements beneath trees. Far down a vista, the beam of a headlight stretched between two rows of trees, then broke up and was gone.

Giulia's cottage was rocking like an anchored boat, for he was stumbling toward it at a run. Something pale was waiting for him in the porch: a crumpled pamphlet wet with rain. Not even a pamphlet — just a ball of paper. But perhaps it wasn't rain that had made it wet, for it was also chewed. It was his sketch that had hung on the wall of Giulia's parlour. It must have strayed out through the front door, which was open.

Mightn't she have left it open for him? Yet when he made himself enter, he couldn't bring himself to call out to her. A tap ticked like a beetle in the bathroom to the right of the narrow hall; at the end of the hall, light angled from the kitchen and lay in wedges on the stairs. Amid the smells of cooking was a stench reminiscent both of a zoo and of decay.

He had almost reached the first door — the parlour's — when something dodged out and past him, down the dark hall. He thought of a slavering child on all fours. He kicked out, but it eluded him. He knew instinctively that there was no longer any reason to hurry into the parlour, and it was a long time before he could.

Giulia lay on her back on the floor, in an overturned chair. Her legs dangled from the seat. Her mouth and her eyes were gaping, her lips were wet. Stooping, he felt for her heartbeat. He was touching her at last, but only to confirm that she was dead. After a while he trudged to the kitchen and switched off the cooker.

Eventually he went back to the station. There was nobody to tell, nothing to do. In the empty carriage a lolling face peered out from beneath the seat opposite, drew back whenever he kicked at it. It was venturing closer, and so at last were his memories, but he was beyond caring.

His street was deserted. Light like glaring metal discs lay beneath the streetlamps. Something like a hairless dog vanished into the short cut to the park. No doubt when Crosby looked out of his window, he would see it and its master waiting among the trees.

He was unlocking his empty house when he thought of Giulia. Both the shock and his sense of meaninglessness had faded, and he began to sob dryly. Suddenly he dragged the front door shut, sending echoes fleeing into the house, and strode toward the park.

His memories were flooding back. Perhaps they would help him. He was almost running now, toward the dark beneath the trees, where the smooth-faced man and his familiar were waiting. Once they were face to face, Crosby would remember both the man's name and his own. He'd got the better of the smooth-faced man once before, and this time, by God — even if it killed him — he would finish the job.

THE SNEERING

WHEN THEY'D COME HOME the house had looked unreal, dwarfed by the stalks of the streetlamps, which were more than twice as tall as any of the houses that were left. Even the pavement outside had shrunk, chopped in half by the widened roadway. Beneath the blazing orange light the house looked like cardboard, a doll's house; the dark green curtains were black now, as if charred. It didn't look at all like his pride. "Isn't it nice and bright," Emily had said.

Bright! Seen from a quarter of a mile away the lights were ruthlessly dazzling: stark fluorescent stars pinned to the earth, floating in a swath of cold orange light watery as mist. Outside the house the light was at least as bright as day; it was impossible to look at the searing lamps.

Jack lay in bed. The light had kept him awake again, seeping through the curtains, accumulating thickly in the room. The curtains were open now; he could see the lower stretch of a towering metal stalk, gleaming in the July sunlight. Progress. He let out a short breath, a mirthless comment. Progress was what mattered now, not people.

Not that the lights were the worst. There was the incessant jagged chattering and slow howling of machinery: would they never finish the roadworks? They'd finish a damn sight faster if they spent less time idling, telling vulgar jokes and drinking tea. And when the men had sneaked off home there was still the traffic, roaring by past midnight, past one o'clock, carrying the racket of passengers, shouting drunkenly and singing — the drivers too, no doubt: they didn't care, these people. Once or twice he'd leapt out of bed to try to spot the numbers of the cars, but Emily would say "Oh, leave them. They're only young people." Sometimes he thought she must walk about with her eyes shut.

The machinery was silent. It was Sunday. The day of rest, or so he'd been brought up to believe. But all it meant now was an early start for the cars, gathering speed on the half-mile approach to the motorway: cars packed with ignorant parents and their ill-spoken children, hordes of them from the nearby council estate. At least they would be dropping their litter in the country, instead of outside his house.

He could hear them now, the cars, the constant whirring, racing past only to make way for more. They sounded as if they were in the house. Why couldn't he hear Emily? She'd got up while he was asleep, tired out of wakefulness. Was she making him a pot of tea? It seemed odd that he couldn't hear her.

Still, it was a wonder he could hear anything over the unmannerly din of traffic. The noise had never been so loud before; it filled the house. Suddenly, ominously, he realized why. The front door was open.

Struggling into his dressing-gown, he hurried to the window. Emily was standing outside the shop across the road, peering through the speckled window. She had forgotten it was Sunday.

Well, that was nothing to worry about. Anyone could forget what day it was, with all this noise. It didn't sound like Sunday. He'd best go and meet Emily. It was dim in the pedestrian subway, her walk wasn't always steady now; she might fall. Besides, one never knew what hooligans might be lurking down there.

He dressed hastily, dragging clothes over his limbs. Emily stood hopefully outside the shop. He went downstairs rapidly but warily: his balance wasn't perfect these days. Beneath the hall table with its small vase of flowers, an intruding ball of greasy paper had lodged. He poked it out with one foot and kicked it before him. The road could have it back.

As he emerged he heard a man say "Look at that stupid old cow."

Two men were standing outside his gate. From the man's coarse speech he could tell they were from the estate. They were staring across the road at Emily, almost blocking his view of her. She stood at the edge of the pavement, at a break in the temporary metal fence, waiting for a chance to cross. Her mind was wandering again.

He shoved the men aside. "Who are you frigging pushing?" demanded the one who'd spoken — but Jack was standing on tiptoe at the edge of the traffic, shouting "Emily! Stay there! I'm coming! Emily!"

She couldn't hear him. The traffic whipped his words away, repeatedly shuttered him off from her. She stood peering through a mist that stank of petrol, she made timid advances at gaps in the traffic. She was wearing her blue leaf-patterned dress; gusts from passing cars plucked at it. In her fluttering dress she looked frail as a grey-haired child.

"Stay there, Emily!" He ran to the subway. Outside his gate the two men gaped after him. He clattered down the steps and plunged into the tunnel. The darkness blinded him for a moment, gleaming darkly with graffiti; the chill of the tiled passage touched him. He hurried up the steps on the far side, grabbing the metal rail to quicken his climb. But it was too late. Emily had crossed to the middle of the roadway.

Calling her now would confuse her. There was a lull in the traffic, but she stood on the long concrete island, regaining her breath. Cross now! he willed her desperately. The two men were making to step onto the road. They were going to help the stupid old cow, were they? He ran to the gap in the metal fence. She didn't need them.

She had left the island, and he was running to it, when he saw the car. It came rushing around the curve toward Emily, its wide nose glittering silver. "Emily, watch out!" he shouted.

She turned and stood bewildered in the roadway. The men had seen the car; they retreated to the pavement, gesturing at Emily. "Get back!" they shouted, overlapping, confusing.

He couldn't reach her in time. The car rushed toward her. He saw the driver in his expensive silver-painted frame: young, cocksure, aggressive, well-groomed yet coarse as a workman's hands — everything Jack hated, that threatened him. He should have known it would be such a man that would take Emily from him.

The driver saw Emily, dithering in his path. His sidewhiskered face filled with the most vicious hatred Jack had ever seen. He wrenched at the wheel. The car swooped round Emily, coiling her with a thick swelling tentacle of dust. As she stood trembling, one back wheel thudded against the kerb outside the house. The car

123

slewed across the roadway toward the lamp-standard. Jack glimpsed the hate-filled face in the moment before it became an explosion of blood and glass.

Emily was running aimlessly, frantically, as if her ankles were cuffed together. She staggered dizzily and fell. She lay on the road, sobbing or giggling. The two men went to her, but Jack pushed them away. "We don't want your help, thank you. Nor yours either," he told the drivers emerging from their halted cars. But he accepted Dr Tumilty's help, when the doctor hurried over from glancing at the driver, for Emily was beginning to tremble, and didn't seem to recognize the house. More drivers were gathering to stare at the crash. Soon Jack heard the approaching raucous howl of the police. The only thought he could find in his head was that they had to be deafening in order to shout everyone else's row down.

"What are you doing?"

"Just looking."

She turned from the front-room window to smile at him. Looking at what, for heaven's sake? his frown demanded. "I like watching people go by," she said.

He could see no people: only the relentless cars, dashing harsh sunlight at his house, flinging dust. Still, perhaps he should be grateful she could look. It seemed the doctor had been right: she didn't remember the accident.

That had been a week ago. Luckily the doctor had seen it happen; the police had questioned him. A policeman had interrogated Jack, but had left Emily alone, calmed by a sedative. Jack was glad she hadn't encountered the policeman, his sarcastic deference full of innuendo: "Does your wife take any drugs, sir? I suppose she doesn't drink at all? She wouldn't be under treatment?" He'd stared about the house in envious contempt, as if he had more right to be there than Jack — just as the people from the estate would, if they saw something different from their concrete council houses.

The council — They provided such people with the homes they deserved, but not Jack and Emily, oh no. They'd offered compensation for the inconvenience of road-widening. Charity, that was all that was, and he'd told them so. A new house was what he wanted, in an area as quiet as this had used to be when he'd bought the house — and not near any estates full of rowdies, either. That, or nothing.

Emily was standing up. He started from his reverie. "Where are you going?"

"Over to the shop to buy things."

"It's all right, I'll go. What do you want?"

"Oh, I don't know. I'll see when I get there."

"No, you stay here." He was becoming desperate; he couldn't tell her why he was insisting. "Make me a list. There's no need for you to go."

"But I want to." The rims of her eyes were trembling with tears.

"All right, all right. I'll help you carry things."

She smiled brightly. "I'll get my other basket," she said, and ran upstairs a few steps before she had to slow.

He felt a terrible dry grief. This nervously vulnerable child had been the woman he'd married. "I'll look after you," he'd used to say, "I'll protect you," for he'd loved to see her turn her innocent trusting smile up to him. For a while, when they'd discovered they could have no children, she had become a woman, almost a stranger — neurotically irritable, jealous of her introversion, unpredictably morose. But when he'd retired, the child had possessed her again. He had been delighted, until her memory had begun to fail. It was almost as though his love for the child in her were wiping out the adult. His responsibility for her was heavier, more demanding now.

That was why they had gone to the seaside while the road was widened: because the upheaval upset Emily, the glistening mud like ropes of dung where the pavement had been. "Our house will still be here," she'd said. "They won't have knocked that down" — not like the post office up the road. Their months by the sea had cost the last of their savings, and when they'd returned it was too late to accept the council's offer of compensation, even if he had intended to. But he mustn't blame Emily.

"Here's your basket. Won't you feel silly carrying that? Come on, then, before it gets too hot."

As they reached the gate he took her arm. Sunlight piled on them; he felt as though the clothes he wore were being ironed. Up the road, near where the post office had been, a concrete lamp-standard lay on the new roundabout, protruding rusty twisted roots. A drill yattered, a creaking mechanical shovel hefted and dumped earth. Men stood about, stripped to the waist, dark as foreigners. He pursed his lips in disapproval and ushered Emily to the subway.

The tunnel was scattered with bottles and wrappings, like leavings in a lair. The tiles of the walls were overgrown with a tangle of graffiti: short white words drooled, red words were raw wounds, ragged-edged. Another of the ceiling lights had been smashed; almost the whole of the tunnel was dim, dimmed further by the blazing daylight beyond. Something came rushing out of the dimness.

He pulled Emily back from the mouth of the tunnel. It must be a cyclist — he'd seen them riding through, with no thought for anyone. From the estate, no doubt, where they knew no better. But nobody emerged from the dimness: nothing at all.

A wind, then, or something rolling down the steps on the far side. He hurried Emily through the chill darkness; she almost stumbled. He didn't like the subway. It felt cold as a flooded cave, and the glimmering graffiti seemed to waver like submarine plants: he mustn't overexert himself. The sunlight leapt at him. There was nothing on the steps.

"Oh hello, Mrs Thorpe," the shopwoman said to Emily. "Are you better?" Stupid woman. Jack chattered to her, so that she couldn't disturb his wife. "Have you got everything?" he kept asking Emily. He was anxious to get back to the house, where she would be safe.

They descended the subway steps more slowly, laden now. The passage was thickly dark against the dazzle beyond. "Let's get through quickly," he said. The darkness closed around him, snug and chill; he held Emily's arm more firmly. Cars rumbled overhead. Dark entangled colours shifted. The clatter of their hurry filled the tunnel with sharp fluttering: that must be what he heard, but it sounded like someone rushing toward them. Someone had almost reached them, brutally overbearing in the dark. For a moment, amid the writhing colours and the red filter of his panting hurry, Jack glimpsed a face. It was brief as lightning: eyes gleaming with hatred, with threat.

Jack rested in the sunlight, gripping the metal rail. No wonder he had glimpsed the face of the driver from the accident: he had almost panicked then too. And no wonder he'd panicked just now: suppose roughs had waylaid Emily and himself down there? "I think we'll use the shops on this side in future," he said.

Back in the house he felt ill at ease, somehow threatened. People stared through the windows as if into cages. Were they what Emily liked watching? The sounds of cars seemed too close, aggressively loud.

When the evening began to settle down Jack suggested a walk. They wouldn't use the subway, for the pavements across the road glittered with grit and glass. As he closed the gate carefully behind him a car honked a warning at Emily: impertinence. He took her arm and led her away from the road, into the suburb.

The sounds of the road fell behind. Trees stood in strips of grass laid along the pavements; still leaves floated at the tips of twigs against a calm green sky. He felt at home now. Cars sat placidly in driveways, cars were gathering outside a few of the semi-detached houses; people sat or stood talking in rooms. Did the people on the estate ever talk to each other, or just watch television all day? he wondered, strolling.

They'd strolled for several streets when he saw the boys. There were four of them, young teenagers — not that one could be sure these days, with them all trying to act older than they should be. They were dressed like pop singers: sloppily, not a suit among them. As they slouched they tugged at garden hedges, stripping leaves from privet twigs. "Do you live there?" Jack demanded. "Then just you stop that at once."

"It's not your house," said one, a boy with a burst purple lip; he twisted another twig loose.

"Go on. You just move along or you'll get something you won't forget."

"Oooh, what?" the purple-lipped boy cried, pretending effeminacy. They all began to jeer at Jack, dancing around him, dodging out of reach. Emily stood by the hedge, bewildered. Jack held himself still, waiting for one of them to come close; he could feel blood blazing in his face. "Go on, you young ruffians. If I get hold of you —"

"What'll you do? You're not our father."

"He's too old," one giggled.

Before even Jack knew what was happening Emily leapt at the boy. She'd pulled a pin from her hat; if the boy hadn't flinched back the point would have entered his cheek or his eye. "Mad old bitch," he shouted, retreating. "My father'll do you," he called as the four ran off. "We know where you live."

Jack felt stretched red, pumped full of blood. "We'd better get home now," he said harshly, not looking at her. The dull giant pins of the lamp-standards stood above the roofs, looming closer. The rough chorus of cars grew louder.

A car snarled raggedly past the gate. As Jack started and glanced back, he glimpsed movement in the subway. A pale rounded shape glimmered in the dark mouth, like the tenant of a burrow: someone peering out, framed by the muddle of graffiti. Up to no good, Jack though distractedly. Unlocking the front door, he glanced again at the subway: a brief pale movement vanished. He turned back to the door, which had slammed open as something — a stray wind — shouldered past him.

He sat in the front room. Now, until the streetlamps glared, the drawn curtains were their own dark green. He could still feel his urgent startled heartbeats. "You shouldn't have flown at those boys," he said. "That wasn't necessary."

"I was defending you," she said plaintively.

"I had control of the situation. You shouldn't let these people make you lose your dignity."

"Well, you needn't have spoken to them like that. They were only young, they weren't doing much harm. If you make them resentful they only get into worse trouble."

"Are you really so blind? These people don't have any love for us, you know. I wish you could see what they'll do to this house after we're gone. They'll be grown up by then. It'll be their kind who'll spoil what we've made. And they'll enjoy it, you mark my words." He was saying too much, but it was her fault, with her blind indulgence of the young — thank God they'd never had children. "You just watch these people," he said. "You'll have them taking over the house before we're gone."

"They're only young, it's not their fault." As though this were incontestable proof she said "Like that poor young man who was killed."

He gazed at her speechlessly. Yes, she meant the driver in the crash. She sounded almost as if she were accusing Jack. All he could do was nod: he couldn't risk a retort when he didn't know how much she remembered.

The curtains blackened, soaked with orange light. Emily smiled at him with the generosity of triumph. She parted the curtains and sat gazing out. "I like it now it's bright," she said.

Eventually she went up to bed. He clashed the curtains together and sat pondering sombrely. All this harping on youth — almost as if she wanted to remind him he had been unable to give her children. She should have married one of the men from the estate. To judge from the evidence, they spent half their time stuffing children into their wives.

No, that was unfair. She'd loved and wanted him, she still did. It was Jack she wanted to hold her in bed. He felt ashamed. He'd go to her now. He switched out the light and the orange oozed in.

As he climbed the stairs he heard Emily moaning, in the grip of a dream. The bedroom was full of dim orange twilight, pulsing with passing lights. The bedclothes were so tangled by her writhing it was impossible to decipher her body. "Emily. Emily," he called. Her face rolled on the pillow, turning up to him. A light flashed by. The dim upturned face grinned viciously. It was a man's face.

"You, you —" He grabbed blindly for the light-switch. Emily's face was upturned on the pillow, eyes squeezed into wrinkles against the light, lips quivering. That must be what the flash of light had shown him. "It's nothing, nothing. Go back to sleep," he said sharply. But it was a long time before he was able to join her, and sleep.

He had bought the house when he was sure they could have no children. It had cost their old home and almost the whole of their savings. It was meant to be a present for Emily, a consolation, but she hadn't been delighted: she had thought they should leave their savings to mature with them. But property was an investment — not that he intended ever to sell the house. They had argued coldly for weeks. He couldn't bear this new logical disillusioned Emily: he wanted to see delight fill her eyes. At last he'd bought the house without telling her.

Unlocking the door, he had held his breath. She'd gazed about, and in her eyes there had been only a sad helpless premonition that he'd done the wrong thing. That had been worse than the day the doctor had told him he was sterile. Yet over the years she'd come to love the house, to care for it almost as if it were a child — until now. Now she did nothing but gaze from the window.

She seemed content. She seldom left the house, except for the occasional evening stroll. He shopped alone. The scribbled subway was empty of menace now. Once, returning from the shop, he saw Emily's face intent behind the shivering pane as a juggernaut thundered by. She looked almost like a prisoner.

The imitation daylight fascinated her most — the orange faces glancing at her, the orange flashes of the cars. Sometimes she fell asleep at the window. He thought she was happy, but wasn't sure; he couldn't get past the orange glint in her eyes.

She was turning her back on their home. Curls of dust gathered in corners, the top of the stove looked charred; she never drew the curtains. Her attitude depressed him. In an indefinable way, it felt as though someone were sneering at the house.

When he tried to take over the house-work he felt sneered at: a grown man on his hands and knees with a dustpan — imagine what the men from the estate would say! But he mustn't upset Emily; he didn't know how delicately her mind was balanced now. He swept the floor. His depression stood over him, sneering.

It was as if an intruder were strolling through the house, staring at the flaws, the shabbiness. The intruder stared at Emily, inert before the window; at Jack, who gazed sadly at her as he pretended to read. So much for their companionship. Didn't she enjoy Jack's company any more? He couldn't help not being as lively as he was once. Did she wish he was as lively as the mob outside the window?

He couldn't stand this. He was simply depressing himself with these reveries. He could just make out Emily's face, a faint orange mask in the pane. "Come upstairs now," he said gently.

His words hung before him, displaying their absurdity. The sneering surrounded him as he took her arm. It was coarse, stupid, insensitive; it jeered at them for going to bed only to sleep; but he couldn't find words to fend it off. He lay beside Emily, one arm about her frail waist; her dry slim hand rested on his. It distressed him to feel how light her hand was. The orange dimness sank over him, thick as depression, dragging him down toward a dream of sleeping miserably alone.

It was all right. She was beside him. But something dark hung over her. He squinted, trying to strain back the curdled dimness. It was a face; curly black hair framed its vicious sneer. Jack leapt at it, punching. He felt no impact, but the face burst like a balloon full of blood. The blood faded swiftly as a fireworks star. He knew at once that he hadn't got rid of the face. It was still in the room.

His fist was thrust deep into the blankets. He awoke panting. He tried to slow his heart with his breathing. The orange light hammered at his eyes. He turned over, to hold Emily, to be sure he hadn't disturbed her. She was not there.

At once he knew she'd wandered out on the road. The sneering surrounded him, still and watchful. He fumbled into his dressing-gown, his feet groped for his slippers. He heard the rapid swish of cars. His head was full of the thud of a body against metal, although he had heard no such sound. He ran downstairs. He felt his mouth gaping like a letter-slot, making a harsh sound of despair.

He stumbled down into the dark. He was rushing uncontrollably; he almost fell. Parallelograms of orange light lay stagnant inside the front door. He scrabbled at the lock and bolts, and threw the door open.

The road was bare beneath the saucers of relentless light. Only a blur of dust hung thinly above the surface. Perhaps she was in the subway. His thoughts had fallen behind his headlong search. He had slammed the gate out of his way before he realized she couldn't have bolted the door behind her.

He was awake now, in time. But he was still running, toward the snarl of a car swinging around the curve. He tottered on the edge of the pavement, then regained his balance. When he turned back to the house he saw Emily gazing between the front-room curtains. The car sped round the curve. Its light blinked in the window beside Emily: a pale bright flash, an oval glimpse of light, a face, a sneering face.

He ran into the room. "Will you get away from there and come to bed!" he shouted. His shock, his treacherous imagination, were rushing his words out of control. "Why don't you bring everyone into the garden if you want to look at them? Bring them into the house?"

She turned and stared at him. For an awful moment he was sure she'd forgotten who he was. "I'm Jack! I'm your husband!" but he couldn't bear to say it, to know. After a while she began to walk slowly, painfully toward the stairs.

But perhaps she'd heard what he'd said. The next day several children were playing football on the pavement, using the top of the subway steps as a goal. "Don't play there," she shouted through the open window, "you'll get hurt." They came to the hedge and pointed at her, laughing, making faces. When she didn't chase them they ventured into the garden. Before Jack could intervene she was chasing them wildly, as if she thought the pavement was as wide as it had used to be.

They were returning for another chase when he strode out. "If I see you again I'll get the police to you." He glanced at Emily, and his stomach flooded with raw dismay. Perhaps he was mistaken, but he was sure that as the children had run out of the far end of the subway he'd glimpsed in her eyes a look of longing.

Chasing the children had exhausted them both. She sat at the window; he read. The day was thickly hot and stagnant, nothing moved except the cars. He felt as though he were trapped in someone's gaze.

"These children these days," she said. "It isn't their fault, it's the way they're brought up. Do you know, some parents don't want their children at all?"

What was she trying to say? What was she sidling towards? He nodded, gazing at the book.

"Did you see that little girl before, that we were chasing? She had such a pretty face. It's such a pity."

Surely she wasn't heading where he suspected, surely she knew better. The heat held him limp and still.

"Don't you think it's up to people like us to help these children?" The longing was clear now in her eyes. "The unwanted ones, I mean. We could give them love. Some of them have never had any."

"Love won't feed them," he told the book.

"But we could go without. We always buy the best meat, you know. I've still a little money that I've saved from housekeeping."

He hadn't known that. Why didn't she invest it? But he felt too exhausted even to change the subject with that argument — exhausted, and depressed: she wasn't musing any longer, she was serious. "And we don't really need such a large house," she said.

Before he could recover from this betrayal she said "Don't you think it would be nice to bring up a little girl?"

She had never mentioned adoption before. Nor had he; the idea of a strange child in his house had always seemed disturbing, threatening. Now there was a stronger reason why they couldn't adopt a child: they were too old. "We wouldn't be able to," he said.

"Why not?"

Because we're too old! But when he met her bright trusting childlike gaze, he couldn't tell her. "Too much work. Too exhausting," he said.

"Oh, I wouldn't mind that. I could do it." Every objection he made she demolished. She had more experience of life than most parents, she'd been brought up decently herself, she would love the child more than its own parents could, it would have a good home, they'd keep the child away from bad company. All day she persisted, through dinner, into the evening. Her eyes were moist and bright.

The orange light sank into the room, stifling. Emily's words closed him in. He was trapped, shaking his head at each point she made; he knew he looked absurd. He mustn't remind her they were old, near death. Why must she persist? Couldn't she see there was something he was trying not to say? As he stared at the book the orange light throbbed on his eyes like blood. "We could sell the house, that would leave us some money," she said. "Wouldn't you like a little girl?"

"No," he blurted at the book. "No."

"Oh, why not?"

His answer was too quick for him. "Because the authorities wouldn't let us have one," he shouted, "you stupid old woman!"

Her face didn't change. She turned away and sat forward, toward the window. Her shoulders flinched as though a lash had cut them. "I didn't mean that. I'm sorry," he said, but she only sat closer to the pane.

He must go to her, hold her — except that when he made to stand up he felt intolerably fatuous. Every nuance of his apology echoed in his head; it sounded like a bad actor's worst line, he felt as if he were at the mercy of an audience's contempt. The sense of his own absurdity, more relentless than the heat or the orange light, pushed him back into his chair.

Emily leaned closer to the window. Suddenly he knew she was trying to see her face in the glass. She went to the hall mirror. He saw her see herself, her age, perhaps for the first time. Her face seemed to slump inward. She walked past him without a glance and sat before the window.

"Look here, I'm sorry." He was whining, each word made him feel more contemptible. Perhaps it was her contempt for him that he was feeling. It gathered darkly on him, atrociously depressing.

He couldn't comfort her while he felt like this. In fact, if it were his own depression, it might be affecting her too. He must go upstairs, hoping she would heal by herself. Even to stand up was a struggle. She sat still as he left the room, glancing back miserably at her.

Upstairs he felt a little better. At least he could close his eyes and clear his mind. He lay limply in the heat; orange painted the dark within his eyelids. Emily would get over it. She would have had to realise eventually. He couldn't think for her all the time, he shouted defensively. He couldn't protect her all her life. The orange glow didn't contradict him. It was soothing, empty, calm.

No, not entirely empty. Something was rushing toward him from deep in the emptiness. As it came it breathed depression at him, thick as fumes. It was rushing faster, it was on him. A face was pressed into his, bright with hatred. Before he had time to flinch back, there was nothing — but something was rushing toward him again. It thrust into his face for a moment, grinning. Again. The face. The face. The face.

He woke. His hands were clenched on the sheets. The face was gone, but for a moment, though depression muffled his thoughts, he knew why it had been there. The man had been killed without warning; he meant Jack to feel the sudden ruthless terror of death. And Jack did. He lay inert and appalled.

All of a sudden, for no reason, his depression lifted — as if someone standing over him had moved away. His mind brightened. He scoffed at his dream. What nonsense, he had killed nobody. It took him a while to wonder what Emily was doing.

He needn't run. She would only be sitting at the window. But he fought away the soothing of the orange calm and hurried to the stairs. Emily was in the hall, at the front door. Her hand was on the lock.

"Where are you going?" She glanced up at the sound of his voice. As she saw him her eyes filled with a mixture of disgust and fear. She pulled the door open; orange light spilled over her.

"Emily, wait!" She was on the path. He ran downstairs, almost falling. He was halfway down when the depression engulfed him like sluggish muddy water. At once he knew that it was surrounding Emily, blinding her to him. It had reached its intended victim.

She was running, a small helpless figure beneath the orange glare. The light spoiled her blue dress, staining it patchily black. She was moving headlong, as fast as the threat in his dream. She snatched the gate out of her way. Amid the nocturnal chorus of the city, a car was approaching.

"Stay there, Emily!" Perhaps she heard him; something made her run faster. The light throbbed, his eyes blurred. For a moment he saw something perched on her shoulder, a dark thing as big as her head, trembling and vague as heat. When he blinked his eyes clear it had gone, but he was sure it was still beside her. He was sure he knew its face.

She was on the roadway now, still running — not toward the far pavement, but toward the speeding car. Jack was running too, although he knew he couldn't save her. She was determined to be killed. Even if he caught her, their struggle would take them under the car.

But she mustn't die alone, with the whisper of hatred and depression at her ear. That death would be like his dream, but prolonged endlessly. She must see that he was with her. He ran; the road and the lamp-standards swayed; the orange light pounded, and his breath clawed at his lungs. He had no chance of overtaking her. She wouldn't see him.

Suddenly she slipped and fell. Jack ran faster, panting harshly; he felt the pavement change to roadway underfoot. Perhaps he could drag her out of the way — no, he could hear how fast the car was approaching. He ran to her and cradled her in his arms. She seemed stunned by the pain of her fall, but when her eyes opened he thought she saw him and smiled weakly. He managed to smile too, although he could feel a darkness rushing toward them. Suddenly he wondered: since her tormentor had stayed here, would they be tied here too? Was this only the beginning of their struggle?

He pressed her face into his chest to hide from her what was upon them: the car, and the grinning face inflated with blood.

BETWEEN THE FLOORS

THOUGH THE VIEW FROM HIS WINDOW looked like the end of the world, that wasn't why Jack Latimer was anxious to go downstairs. A straight line divided the sea and the sky, slabs of two shades of the grey of a solitary pigeon gliding back and forth against them like a kite left behind on the beach by the departed summer. As he straightened his tie and smoothed the wings of his shirt collar he spied from the window on a tram eight storeys below him, feeling its way after its whine along the wire into Blackpool. The pane was as good as a mirror, and showed him his eyes waiting to be amused, his black moustache as sleek as his hair, his features rather too small for the face that even workouts at the gym near his flat couldn't reduce. He picked up the key by its six-inch plastic tag from the dressing-table strewn with glossy brochures and let himself out of the functional room.

To his left, through the window of the exit to the fire escape, was what might as well have been exactly the same view of the sea. To his right, eight doors identical with his and interrupted only by framed prints as subdued as the lighting led to the first of a series of fire doors, beyond which the corridor must eventually find its way to the main bank of lifts. There was a lift opposite Jack's room, however, and he barely hesitated before prodding the askew lozenge-shaped button further into its niche in the wall.

Once again he felt as though the summons hadn't reached its destination. A wind mumbled under the door onto the fire escape; otherwise there was silence, not even the sound of a radio or television in any of the rooms. For a minute or two he contented himself with performing an impromptu tap-dance that rattled the key on its tag, but when he found himself compelled to sing he felt he'd waited long enough. "I'm singing in the rain," he crooned, "just sin —" and was stabbing at the button when he heard beyond the door that was grey as the seascape a voice not much louder than the wind. "Gubless us, we're coming as quick as we can. What do they want me to do, get out and push?"

Jack was tempted to retreat into his room so as not to be seen to have rung twice. But he wasn't a child, he was nudging fifty, and he was damned if he would let any petty official intimidate him. As the doors inched open, the scratched outer door withdrawing behind the wall before its twin began to sidle in the opposite direction, he tugged the jacket of his suit down and folded his hands, dangling the plastic tag. The door was still creeping into its hiding-place when the attendant greeted him. "It's the feller they stuck at the top," he said in his low Northern groan. "Don't tell me, it's Mr... Mr Latitude."

"Latimer."

"Aye, well, are we going to stand here arguing about it till some other bugger starts playing with my ding-dong? Step in, there's a dear, and I'll take you to the rest of the royalty."

Jack had been preparing to apologise for his impatience with the lift, but now he was provoked just to laugh, except he couldn't quite manage that either. He stepped over the threshold into the stuffy box that smelled of the square of dusty carpet no wider than a double bed, and felt outnumbered at once.

Since there must be as many of himself as of the attendant in the mirrors facing each other from halfway up the side walls, he could only assume that his uneasiness was to be blamed on the indirect lighting, which was the colour of fog. It and the mirrors displayed the attendant to him, the pouchy globe of a face which Jack had to remind himself wouldn't be as pale in any other light, the uniform which looked as dusty as whatever book was sprawled face down on the folding stool under the handle that controlled the lift, the curly mop of faded red hair that reminded Jack more than ever of the kind of wig which came attached to a seaside hat. "Gubless us," the attendant groaned at the handle, grasping it with both pudgy hands and leaning his weight on it until the doors shut and the lift began to creak downwards, and then he turned to Jack. "That's what I should call you, isn't it? Know why?"

Like his voice, his clump of features — eyes so protruding they made Jack wince, small beaky nose, inverted whitish V of a mouth above a nub of chin — seemed constantly on the point of adopting another expression. Perhaps it was his being half a head shorter than Jack and having to peer up at him from beneath his hairless eyebrows that made him appear sly, but Jack felt like a stooge singled out from an audience. "Why?" he couldn't help asking.

"Isn't that a good word for you folk in the picture palace game?"

It took some seconds for Jack's bewilderment to give way to relief. "Royalty, you mean. That's droll. You ought to be at the end of the pier."

"Gets a bit lonely out there in the cold and the wind, specially after dark."

Though it wasn't as though Jack had wished that on him, he found himself feeling defensive. "The cinemas these days aren't what you'd call palaces," he said, "and we're just managers."

The sixth floor went by with a creaking shudder of the lift, and a bulb guttered behind the number in the line set into the wall above the stool. All of the attendant's heads shook themselves slowly, putting Jack in mind of some fairground sideshow being switched on for the night. Either the attendant resented managers or was unhappy with Jack's self-deprecation, because his mouth drooped even further before he said "On our own, are we?"

"Depends what you mean."

"Aye, it all depends, that's what they say." The attendant had lowered his gaze to Jack's crotch or rather, Jack hoped, to the plastic tag hanging in front of it. "Remember that old song?"

Jack shoved the key into his breast pocket, where the tag felt as though it was probing for his heart. "Yes, it's from —"

"Hit...owl...deep-ends...hawn...hayouuu." The attendant had abandoned his Lancashire accent and was singing in a hideous parody of Cockney without raising his gaze; then he stared Jack in the face. "Was it you I heard doing a song and dance?"

If Jack blushed, surely that couldn't be visible in the grey light. "Did you hear someone?"

"Aye, and I've brought no other body to your floor. Happen it's you should be at end of pier."

"I'll stick to the job I've been doing for getting on for thirty years, thanks all the same."

"Happy in our job, are we?"

The number 3 flickered and went out, and Jack felt close enough to quitting the lift to be able to retort "I don't know about you."

"If truth be told, lad, I'm not so sure about thee either."

This time Jack certainly felt himself redden, though there was no sign of it in the mirror. "What the devil do you mean by that?"

"No need to bring him into it. Just trying to keep us lively while we go down."

The man's face had begun to remind Jack of stage make-up seen closer than it was meant to be seen, so that he wondered if the attendant could have been a seaside comedian before ending up in this job. "When do they let you out?" Jack said.

"Who's that?"

The question was so sharp that Jack almost looked for someone in the mirror. "The manager, I suppose, or whoever comes after you, rather. How long before you get out of here?"

"Depends."

The attendant's gaze had lowered itself again. Jack stared over the mop of red hair, noticing how dusty the light made it look, until the lift stumbled to a halt. When there was no further movement, he said "Aren't we here?"

"Aye, and soon one of us won't be."

Jack was about to ask how soon when the attendant did something with the handle to release the doors. Beyond them was a nondescript stretch of corridor, and Jack lunged for it, glimpsing the ranks of himself disappear as though they were returning inside him. Before he was over the threshold the attendant seized him by one upper arm, in a grip which felt unexpectedly strong and yet somehow diffuse. "Up you go," he muttered in Jack's ear.

Only when Jack almost tripped did he realise that the floor of the lift had come to rest an inch lower than the corridor. "Thanks," he said, and stepping up, glanced back. The attendant had already let go of him, and was out of reach of the light from the corridor. As Jack moved away, digging a finger in his ear to get rid of the sensation of its being clogged with a dusty whisper, he heard the attendant start mumbling to his crowd of grey selves before the doors creaked shut.

Though the corridor changed direction several times on its way to the lobby, it didn't present as much of a challenge as it had when he was carrying his suitcase. The receptionist who had directed Jack to the lift was at the desk, using one of her silver-tipped fingers to trace a route on a street map for two cinema managers Jack didn't recognise. He gave his tie a last adjustment as he crossed the lobby to the bar, where he saw Lucinda Dodd at once.

She was on the far side of the horseshoe overhung by inverted glasses, her plump bare arms resting on the bar-top. Again he thought she had the biggest smile he'd ever seen — almost as wide as her generous face — but now she was directing it at Rex Smythe beside her. "Here's my rival. We were just talking about someone like you, Jack," Rex said in his infuriatingly penetrating voice.

Jack was almost sure he saw Lucinda wincing on his behalf. He took time to greet colleagues at tables as he made his way around the bar, but when he arrived he still hadn't devised a retort witty enough to utter, not least because Rex's unobtrusively styled hair and elegant grey suit made him feel overdressed. "You look like a man after a drink. What'll it be?" Rex said.

"A Scotch will do me, thanks."

"Not even any water? Well, you know yourself best." Rex snapped his fingers once at the young barmaid. "Whenever you're ready, love. The same for the lady, and another of these on the rocks, and a plain Scotch. Better make that a double."

Jack thought Lucinda found Rex's tone as unappealing as the barmaid did. He thanked the young woman for his drink and topped it up with water from a jug on the bar, then nearly spilled it as Rex's glass collided with his. "Here's to the industry," Rex declared. "May it continue to prosper."

"And us," Lucinda said.

"And as many of us as it can support, Lucy, of course. When you've finished that cocktail I'm buying you both dinner in the restaurant."

"I thought we were thinking of going out, Lucy."

"What, and see miles of entertainments closed down for the winter? You want something better than that, don't you, Lucy? Maybe that's more your style, Jack."

141

Lucinda laid her free hand over Jack's. "It does look a bit bitter for walking."

"There's cabs outside."

"I wouldn't dig too deep into your pocket until you see how things are developing," Rex advised him. "Besides, I always think three in a cab is one too many."

"We can come in here for a drink after dinner, Jack."

There was that, and the way Lucinda had only now removed her hand from his, but Jack wasn't sure if these were meant as more than consolations. He lingered over his Scotch, in case he had reason later not to want to be too drunk, until Rex said "Better get in there before there's no room."

The chandeliered oak-panelled dining-room was indeed already almost full. Rex told the head waiter "Smythe party" and cleared his blank look by slipping him a fiver, not quite surreptitiously enough for Rex's guests to be intended not to notice. At the table by a fountain in the middle of an indoor flower-bed Jack ordered the most expensive dishes on the menu, and felt as though Rex was retaliating by insisting on the best wine. Two glasses of that made Jack take advantage of the first lull in the conversation about last year's films. "Who am I like?"

"Are we playing games now?" Rex asked, aligning his fish-knife and fork alongside the bones of his first course. "I wouldn't like to guess. Who are you?"

"You were saying in the bar you'd been talking about someone I was like."

"Ask Lucy. She brought him up."

"He wasn't much like you, Jack," Lucinda said, dabbing at her lips with a capacious linen napkin as if she wished she could use it to hide her face. "It was only... He wasn't really much like you at all."

"Except Lucy and our friend were like you and me, Jack, her with ten screens and him on the other side of town from her with just a triple."

"So what happened to him?"

"He hadn't been in the business anything like as long as you have." Lucinda obviously hoped that answer would do, but Rex fell on the question. "Exactly what you'd expect from last year's takings

142

is what happened. No room for two sites in one town. The company closed the triple and left Lucy with her multiplex."

"If he'd had more experience they said they'd have sent him to me." Lucinda found her wineglass and proposed a hasty toast. "Here's to how it used to be when I came into the business, when what we did for films meant something to the company. To showmanship."

Rex barely touched her glass with his. "To how things have to be," he said, and rang Jack's almost empty glass.

"Nostalgia isn't what it was," Jack said.

While Lucinda looked sympathetic Rex emitted a grunt with which Jack could imagine he greeted any fault in his cinemas or in his staff. The arrival of the main course relieved an awkward silence, and Jack attacked his lobster until Lucinda coaxed him into joining her in reminiscing about favourite films. They'd agreed on *Casablanca* when Rex said "I prefer to concentrate on current product" in the tone of a future director of the company, and Lucinda interested herself in his opinions as though she'd been reminded that he was buying the meal. Jack thought it advisable just to listen or at least to give the appearance of listening while he ate and, particularly, drank, but eventually found himself saying a good deal about the way the company treated its staff and the cinemas it had bought a few years ago, his included, and how all the films he'd had to show since then seemed to consist of excesses of one sort or another. Diners were glancing at him, and he could see that some of those who were managers felt he was speaking for them. Perhaps he might persuade them to own up to that in the bar. He drained his coffee-cup and brandished it for a refill, and considered pointing out that he'd been given a child's cup by mistake. Then Rex was standing up and saying "Are you sure you'll be all right while I have a word with the big boss?"

"You bet your ding-dong," Jack told him, "and thanks." But Rex wasn't talking to him; nor, presumably, when he said "Join us if you like."

Jack succeeded in staying beside Lucinda as far as the lobby, but when Rex strode into the bar she restrained Jack from following. "I should think about having an early night. If you'll excuse me, I'm going to."

"I'll see you up, shall I?"

"That's the idea."

By the sound of it she was only praising him for seeing sense. Once the doors of the lift off the lobby had closed she said "Do you mind if I say something?"

"My pleasure."

"If I were you I'd try and keep on the right side of Rex."

"You aren't me, and it wouldn't be much of a world if you were." He was doing his best to recall if he'd insulted Rex, but couldn't remember anything he'd said. "Never mind Rex. I've had a bellyful of him."

Lucinda glanced down Jack's body, then up at his face. "Well, here I am."

The lift doors opened, and he stumbled towards her, though he realised she had only been announcing her floor. She put one hand on his chest and poked the eighth-floor button, and gave him a kiss so quick he didn't even see it coming. "You get up to bed and sleep it off," she said as the doors intervened between them.

He couldn't believe he'd wasted his chance on thinking about Rex. When the lift opened he stalked along the eighth-floor corridor, muttering. He'd struggled through the last pair of fire doors when he heard sounds besides his own — a soft thud on metal, and then an outburst of thumping and mumbling. Perhaps the attendant had just wakened and was groping to his feet, and Jack had the disconcerting impression that he was fumbling about in total darkness. Why shouldn't he have turned off the light in his box while he snatched a nap? All Jack cared about just now was not coming face to face with him.

Jack had slammed his door behind him, and was feeling about on the furry wall for the light-switch, when he heard the lift creak open. The attendant must have thought he'd just emerged from his room. Jack's thumb scraped against the plastic switch, and the room lit up, empty as ever. At least there had to be other guests on this floor, since the lift must have brought someone up in order to be where it was, or could the attendant have been waiting to hear when Jack returned to his room? One inadvertent step rushed Jack towards a confrontation with him, but he wasn't quite that drunk. His compensatory lurch took him into the bedroom to grimace at himself while he brushed his teeth, then he hung up his clothes and managed to aim at the toilet again before sprawling into bed.

His morning call wakened him. Darkness had gathered and grown stale behind his eyes and in his mouth. He held onto the wall, though its pelt made his fingertips twitch, all the way to the bathroom, where the shower attacked him with various extremes of temperature as he flinched against and away from the tiled wall. He took fifteen minutes to dress himself, hoping that would let him feel more able to face breakfast, and then he guided himself into the corridor, easing the door shut and muffling the key on its tag with one hand. He'd scarcely turned along the corridor when the lift doors wavered open. "Just us, is it?" the attendant said with a kind of morose triumph. "Hobble in then, Mr Lamplighter."

"Latimer," Jack said, and had already had enough. The attendant would hardly have spent the entire night in there, though he looked as though he hadn't seen daylight for considerably too long. When Jack faltered into the lift, the man sagged against the handle to send the lift down, then turned his head with an audible creak to peer at Jack. "What's that on your finger?"

Jack had been trying to withdraw inside himself in order to ignore the mustiness, presumably composed of the smells of old carpet and of the book which appeared not to have moved from the stool, and the way the muffled light seemed to have caused the attendant's face to add to its pudginess, but the question made him unsure of himself. "Which?"

"Looks like it should be a ring."

Again Jack had the sensation of being singled out, this time to be accused of pretending not to be married. He held up the shaky finger that retained a band of paler skin. "I got engaged once, but that was as far as it went."

"Far enough if you ask me. Let it drop now, there's a dear. We don't want to look at that all the way down."

Jack found the other possibilities even less attractive, particularly the sight of the crowd of his own discoloured faces, which looked as poisoned as he was trying not to feel. Nor was he anxious to see the attendant's face wobbling as he enquired "Will we be a busy boy today?"

"I should think they've plenty in store for us. How about you? Busy, I mean?"

"Don't you know who that's up to?"

"Who?" Jack demanded, though the attendant was gazing up at him so hard that his lower lids seemed in danger of peeling away from the eyeballs. Jack closed his eyes and leaned against the back wall, feeling the lift quiver each time it passed a floor, smelling a staleness which seemed increasingly to be of flesh. "If you ask me," the attendant said, "you want something."

Jack kept his mouth shut, but opening his eyes was apparently sufficient encouragement. "Get a good fat breakfast down you," the attendant told him. "That was always my cure when I'd had one of those nights."

Jack managed not to rush for the doors until the lift reached the ground floor, and then he weaved his way along the corridor to the lobby and reeled out through the revolving doors. Far down the tram-lines beneath the ice-coloured sky he could see a roller coaster and a Ferris wheel, so shrunken and immobile that they and the rest of the fairground resembled cheap toys. He thought the slaps of cold wind in his face were doing him some good, but when he returned to the lobby he found the hotel now felt unbearably hot. As he fled to the lifts, the nearest of them emitted several of his colleagues, Lucinda among them. She left the others and came to Jack. "Feeling better?"

"For seeing you, yes."

"What a gentleman. Are you on your way to breakfast?"

Her perfume — sweet but not cloying — tempted him. "If I can join you."

"That was the idea."

Jack dared to take her arm as they entered the dining-room, where he received a faceful of heat laden with the smells of bacon and sausage and fried bread. "Actually, I won't," he babbled, hoping that she didn't think he had recoiled from touching her. "I'd better just — I'll see you at the screening."

He was already sprinting for the lift she'd emerged from. It took him minutes to reach his floor and his room and the toilet. Some time later he lowered himself gingerly onto the bed, and made himself stand up again not much later than he was supposed to, and picked his way into the corridor. He heard the lift gape behind him, but kept on through the fire doors and down the emergency stairs to the ballroom where the conference was taking place.

He hadn't realised that the door off the staircase would open with such a loud clank, nor that it would admit him beside the podium from which the chairman of the company was holding forth. "As I was saying," Mr Begin said while Jack made apologetic faces at him and raised his hands as if someone had stuck a gun in his back, "the future of our industry depends on teamwork. We all need to set examples to our staff..." Even when Jack located an empty seat and made himself small on it, the chairman took some time to finish looking at him, and much longer to repeat most of last year's address.

At last Mr Begin gave way to previews of forthcoming films, and the darkness let Jack close his eyes whenever the spectacle proved too much for him. Explosions that felt like colossal migraines blew up people and buildings and spaceships and planets, men encased in latex demonstrated unlikely ways to walk and unpleasant things to do to people, young couples swamped in golden light and blanketed with music explored each other, actors found objects to fall over or into or through and roared jokes at one another as though to ensure that the audience made as much noise or couldn't hear itself think... After more than an hour the lights went up, and it was time for lunch. Jack was on his way to standing, having found that sitting still had done him some unexpected good, when he saw Mr Begin heading straight for him. "Jack Latimer, isn't it," the chairman said, towering over him even now Jack was on his feet. "Used to be the Grand."

"That's my place."

"Well, Jack, you missed me saying it's been a good year for us overall," Mr Begin said, and at once Jack was hearing him beyond a hollow sound that filled his ears. The chairman had never called him by his first name before, and Jack knew why he was doing so now. He stared at Mr Begin's several ruddy chins that looked gift-wrapped with a bow tie, and scarcely heard the chairman's words for hearing what lay behind them. He heard himself say he got on well with Rex Smythe and call himself a liar, this last after he closed his mouth. "That's the spirit. Teamwork, Jack, keep telling yourself teamwork," Mr Begin said, clapping him on the arm.

Jack rubbed it as he stumbled out of the hotel, into the vicious wind. He caught a tram whose wheels kept up a screech like a circular saw as they followed the lines along the promenade, past miles of stalls boarded up for the winter. Even if the company retained him, what would happen to his assistants? If he could have afforded to take early retirement he would have made way for at least one of them. The fifth fish-and-chip shop he passed convinced him he was hungry, and eating felt like the first real thing that had happened to him all day. He walked back to the hotel, shivering from having left his coat there, feeling steadily less present. In the ballroom he gripped his temples and stared at the floor throughout the afternoon's pep talk on management, and hadn't moved from that position when the room emptied and Lucinda came over to him. "Still nursing your head?"

"Just thinking."

"Nothing too bad, I hope."

"Looks like the Grand won't be seeing me for much longer."

"Oh, Jack." She squatted in the aisle beside him, the skirt of her dark suit inching above her smooth knees. "Is that what Mr Big told you?"

"Not in so many words."

Lucinda rested a hand on his shoulder before she stood up. "We haven't had that drink yet."

"You've seen me when I've had a few."

"Let's make it just a couple."

"And dinner as well?"

"All right, dinner. I'm going up for a shower and then I'll see you in the bar, say at seven."

The notion of her in the shower revived Jack as much as anything could at the moment. The promise which it and her tone seemed to extend to him brought him to his feet, and he escorted her as far as the main lifts, only to see Rex Smythe and Mr Begin waiting. "I'll use my own lift," he said in her ear.

As soon as he thumbed the button on the wall of the deserted corridor the lift doors jerked open, and the attendant stepped back further into the grey light, his unhealthily white faces burgeoning on both sides of him. "I thought it'd have to be you, Mr Hatimer."

Jack was too exhausted to argue. "Almost," he said.

"Nearly got you now, have we? Scuttle in then, before I have to do a disappearing trick."

"I'm glad to hear I'm not your only customer," Jack said, stepping into the grey light and seeing it coat face after face until he turned away from himself.

The attendant fell against the lever, then poked his face over his shoulder at Jack as the lift swayed upwards. "Why's that, old thing?"

"I wouldn't like to think you were going up and down just for me. By the way, you're never telling me they still haven't sent anyone to take over."

"Aren't I? Well, I won't, then."

"Would you like me to see if I can get someone for you?"

"Too late for that."

The attendant was resting his chin on his shoulder as though his neck had locked, a position which appeared not to bother him but which Jack found so painful to observe that he had to struggle not to close his eyes. "So how's your day in the big wide world been?" the attendant said.

He was beginning to put Jack in mind of a ventriloquist's dummy which had twisted itself into a dismaying posture while continuing to talk. "Could have been worse," Jack mumbled so as not to be drawn.

"Not over yet, or is it? Did I feel the sun go down?"

"It's dark, yes."

"Time to play then, eh?"

The attendant winked, turning that side of his face into a mass of wrinkles that looked about to crack like the make-up it increasingly resembled, and shoved the lever up. "Here we are again, happy as can be. We'll neither of us get any higher."

His rearing up to move the lever had made Jack think of a body being yanked by a rope around its broken neck. "Are you sure you're all right?" he stammered.

"As sure as you are."

Once Jack had blundered out of the lift he didn't glance across the corridor until he was in his room. The attendant was turning slowly back and forth and yet keeping his face towards Jack. "I'll be waiting," he said, and levered the doors shut.

Jack slammed his and leaned his forehead against it and groped for the chain, which he fumbled into the socket. He stood there for a while, unable to think what he was trying to do, and then he remembered his date with Lucinda. He laid his grey suit out on the bed, where it appeared to be making him a promise of company in his room, before taking a bath. As long as he lay in the water he found it possible not to think about the day or how he might sneak past the lift attendant. A few minutes before seven he dried himself and got dressed, and was combing his hair a third time when the phone rang.

Whoever it was, they wouldn't make him late for Lucinda. As he snatched the receiver he had to remind himself not to say he was the Grand. "Yes, who's this?"

"Jack?"

"Lucy! I'm just on my way down."

"Actually, Jack, forgive me, but I'm going to have to cancel dinner."

"Who's the problem?"

"Who else could it be? I told the boss I was meeting you, but he didn't offer to treat you as well."

"Shall we have our drink afterwards instead?"

"Mr Begin seems to want my whole evening. Lots to discuss, he says. Never mind, Jack, there's always next year."

"Always has been," Jack muttered, and let the phone drop. He grabbed it again on the only impulse that seemed left to him and dialled Reception. "I've a complaint. Let me speak to the manager."

"You're Mr..." After a pause the receptionist said "Mr Latimer, is it?"

"Last time I looked it was."

"I'm sorry, Mr Latimer. We've been trying to contact you. There's been a slight mistake on the computer, and there was a new girl on the desk when you checked in. You weren't supposed to have that room."

"Where do you want me to be?"

"That wing wasn't meant to be in use this weekend, you see. Someone should have noticed you were there, but the chambermaid didn't mention it till she came off duty. So if we can just move you over to where the rest of your party is staying..."

"I like it where I am. That isn't what I rang about, it's a member of your staff."

"If we could just deal with your room first, and then I'll get you the manager."

"This has waited long enough. I called about the fellow in the lift outside my room."

"I'm afraid I don't understand, sir. If you'd like me to send someone up to help you move —"

"The lift attendant, whatever his name is. He's been in there ever since I got here yesterday, and if you're saying he's been just for me, that's even more ridiculous."

"You must be mistaken, sir. None of our lifts have been manned for years."

"You're as sure of that as you were of which room you put me in, is that right? Tell you what, you speak to the manager and tell him I've been buggered about enough for one weekend or the rest of my life, come to that, and while you're at it tell him nobody knows you've a man in your lift and it's past time someone did something about him, and then one of you call me back."

He had barely replaced the receiver when the phone shrilled at him. If it was the receptionist again, renewing her attempt to persuade him to change rooms — "Yes?"

"Jack?"

"No need to sound as if you don't know."

"Rex Smythe. I thought it might be an idea for us to have a chinwag."

"Whose idea?"

"Mine and the company's. Shall we meet in the bar for a dram? I gather you're free."

For a few seconds Jack was speechless with rage, and then he saw the chance he'd almost missed. "No, come up to my room. There's something I want you to see."

"Is it important?"

"Very." At the moment Jack could think of nothing more important than ensuring Rex saw the attendant too. "Don't use the main lifts. Walk all the way to my end of the hotel, and there's one that brings you right to me."

"I hope this is going to be worth it," Smythe grumbled, which made Jack certain that it was. He hung up the receiver and opening the door, shot the bolt so as it keep it from closing while he crossed the corridor. He thumped on the metal door and shouted "I've reminded the hotel you're in there. They don't seem to know either of us are here."

The doors staggered open, and the attendant peered up at him. He was clinging to the handle as though for support, and his face, whose colour and texture put Jack in mind of mould on an apple, was turned more or less towards the corridor, yet Jack had the decidedly unwelcome impression that he'd twisted his head even further around than before. Nevertheless he spoke, keeping his chin fixed while the rest of his head wobbled up and down. "Mr Hatton."

Jack didn't feel disposed to argue with anyone who looked like that. "Better put it on, then," he said as lightly as he could.

"That's rich. That's good enough for end of pier." The attendant appeared to be laughing silently, his face quaking like a mask about to work itself loose. "Seeing as how you wanted to do me a favour, can I ask you one?"

"What have you in mind?"

"Can I use your...?"

It wasn't the pause which made Jack falter, it was the way the attendant jerked his head to indicate the hotel room, stretching his deeply ridged white neck until Jack had to look away. "God bless us, can't you even use the toilet?" he muttered, and raised his voice. "Go ahead."

He saw the attendant bobbing up at the edge of his vision as though someone had hauled on an invisible rope; then the man rushed across the corridor so fast that Jack hadn't time to look at him. He had the briefest glimpse of a figure on which the grey of the uniform and the white of flesh had somehow become less clearly separated, before the bathroom door slammed and the bolt clicked home like the hammer of a gun. "Keep an eye on the cage, there's a dear," the attendant must have said in transit, because the words were itching in Jack's ears. "Actually —" Jack called, remembering Smythe, and started back into his room just as the lift began to emit a waspish buzz.

He was afraid it was malfunctioning until he grasped that someone was trying to summon it — Rex. "Excuse me, but —" he recommenced, and then several observations silenced him. By the sound of it the attendant was using the shower rather than the toilet, and whatever he was doing in there, Jack could see from the gap beneath the door and the position of the light-switch outside the bathroom that he was doing it in total darkness. When Jack heard the noise the plughole of the bath was making, a prolonged choked gurgle that suggested some not entirely solid mass was being washed into the plumbing, he retreated into the corridor, almost falling over backwards in his haste. The lift was buzzing irritably, and it occurred to him that his nearest ally was Rex. The thought was enough to send him into the lift. He shoved the handle down, and the doors shut off the corridor at once.

He could have done without quite so much movement around him: the strip of indicator lights flickering one by one like candles that wouldn't stay lit, the shifting of his pack of faces leading into nothingness at both edges of his vision, the stool wobbling from his having bumped into it as he'd taken refuge in the lift, and now folding its unsteady legs and throwing the book on the worn-out carpet. As the book fell open Jack saw it was a biography of Tony Hancock, but it was the word written in faded ink on the title page that caught his attention. It must be the owner's name — Hatton.

"Don't you even know your own name?" Jack demanded, and then another possibility occurred to him. As he raised his head he glimpsed all his reflections shifting. He hadn't time to glance at them, because the lift was almost at the fourth floor, where he heard Rex grousing — but as he shoved the lever up to halt the lift, then exerted the extra pressure which opened the doors, he couldn't avoid noticing that his suit looked grey as a uniform in the dim light, which had also rendered the mark of his engagement ring invisible. None of this need matter, because the doors were opening, and Rex's surprise at the sight of him would restore Jack to himself.

Rex took one step towards the lift, staring directly into Jack's face, then he grimaced and recoiled, waving a hand in front of his nose. "Forget it. I'll phone him," he said.

"Rex, wait. It's me."

Smythe gave no more sign of hearing him than he had of recognising him. Jack heard him shoulder the nearest pair of fire doors out of his way, and tried to follow. The light from the corridor felt like fire on his whitening skin. The doors in the deserted corridor bumped shut, and he flinched back into the lift. His reflections met him like two packs of cards collapsing towards him, vanishing as they came. He heaved at the lever, which took more of his energy to move now, and sent the lift reeling upwards. It still belonged to the attendant more than to him — but as the cage began to quiver to a halt he wondered what might come dripping and gurgling to find him if he called whatever was left of it out of his room.

WHERE THEY LIVED

THE HATCHARDS HAD JUST CROSSED Ataturk Bulvari when a shoeshine boy commenced rubbing the straps of Don's sandals with a cloth. "Your shoes very dirty, sir."

"All right, son, they're only sandals. He'll be polishing my feet next, Maggie. Not the kind of feet you'd want in bed with you." As he walked faster towards the sun-bleached concrete seafront the boy pursued him like a terrier, and Don felt the cloth catch the nail of one big toe. "That's all, son, would you mind? They're going in the sea, so you might as well not bother."

"He has to make a living somehow, Don. If he was a beggar you'd only look away from him."

"You know I hadn't any Turkish money until we went to the bank. What did you want me to give that woman, a travellers' cheque?" He dug in the pocket of his shorts for change, muttering "Have this if it'll help you mind your own business," and jangled the coins for Maggie's benefit before he dropped them into the small thin grubby hand. "I hope you heard that," he said as he tramped puffing after her.

She pulled her sun-hat lower, netting her forehead with shadows. "Oh yes, I'm getting expert at hearing what you don't want me to hear."

"I meant the donation, and you know I — We'll look for her on the way back to the hotel if you like." He was reaching out a hand for one of Maggie's, and about to say "Let's start again like we said we would" when a man shouted at his back "Hey, English."

Only a policeman took that tone, Don thought — one of the policemen he'd seen strolling through the town as if all they needed to keep order were the guns they wore. This one must have observed Don appearing to taunt the shoeshine boy, or assumed he was pestering Maggie, and if Don couldn't clarify the situation, where might he end up? "Wait," he called, images of a communal jail-cell with plumbing even worse than the hotel provided crowding into his overheated head. When he turned, however, he saw two tourists bearing down on him.

They might have spent their marriage growing more alike. They looked like body-builders who had settled at some point for plumpness. They had identical pale blue eyes and marble grins, and over their swimwear both wore open buttonless shirts printed with cartoon figures brandishing bubbling cocktails. Their peeling skins were all the colours of new plaster, and oily with lotion. The woman's cropped hair was the same greying red as the strips under the man's nose and above his ears. Cameras bounced on their stomachs as they overtook the Hatchards. "Thank all the saints for someone who speaks English like a native," the woman said in a voice that would have carried across the street. "We were beginning to think we were the only people in town."

Her husband's shout had expressed enthusiasm, Don gathered now, because the man said in the same tone "Gareth and Trixie Lunt. Hotel's just as bad. Run by characters who bring you boiled fruit juice if you ask for tea, that's if you can make yourself heard above the Huns and God knows what else the hotel's full of."

"My friends call me Trick."

"We're Don Hatchard and —"

Maggie swung round from watching a man in an embroidered cap leading a bear on a chain up the dusty slope beyond the promenade. "I'm Maggie," she said, and when Trixie Lunt tittered behind her hand, added with the ostentatious patience she ordinarily reserved for Don "Did I miss something?"

"Just how you can tell you're married, having to fight to get a word past the old man. Don't tell me, china. No, silver."

"I'm afraid I don't —"

"Never only crystal."

"I'm still not —"

"Are you saying ivory? Look at them, Gar, ivory. You wouldn't think it in a million years."

"If you mean anniversaries," Maggie said, "I wouldn't know. It's been nearly twenty."

"Then Don should be ashamed of himself. If Gar missed any he'd know about it till the next one. When was the last time Don bought you something nice?"

"Oh, he has his moments."

"We'll make this one then, won't we, Gar?"

"Actually," Don said, "we were just —"

Trixie retreated a step and seized her husband's arm and rubbed her left cheek as though Don had slapped it. "Don't let us interrupt anything, I'm sure. We were going to ask you to take our photograph."

"Don's better with technology than I am."

"Mine's so simple even a man can't get it wrong. Just look through my hole, Don, and find us in the little lit-up bit, then you squeeze my button till you feel it stick and poke it down."

While the Lunts posed, intensifying their grins and plumping their arms around each other, Don surreptitiously wiped the sweaty back of the camera on his shorts, earning himself a sympathetic grimace from Maggie. He moved so as to frame the Lunts against a rank of bootblacks sitting on low stools behind elaborate brass stands and a stallholder brushing peaches with a small birch broom. The shutter release gave before he thought it would, and he was considering a retake when Trixie strode up to him and bumped him with her leopard-skinned breasts as she retrieved the camera. "Now we'll get you."

Don stood beside Maggie and took her hand, and realised he'd forgotten how it felt — slim and smooth and cooler than the relentlessly hot day. As he stroked it with his thumb she responded with a squeeze which he was almost sure was more affectionate than a request for him to stop. The camera clicked, and Lunt produced a notebook. "We'll need your address."

Maggie relinquished Don's hand at once, from which he assumed she was telling him to give the information. "Well, would you believe it," Trixie said when he had. "You don't live far from us at all. We'll have to deliver your snap personally."

Several seconds later Lunt broke the silence. "First time?"

"I'm the only one who'd put up with him," Maggie said.

"Ha," Lunt commented, and after a pause, "ha. I'm sure Don knows I was asking if you'd been before."

"We've wanted to, but the children never did. This year we decided they were old enough to go off on their own, so we have."

"You ought to have let them know who's in charge," Lunt told him. "So you won't know the best place to eat in town."

"We only flew in yesterday."

"Then we'll show you," Trixie cried. "We'll take you now."

"Actually, we were going —"

"I wouldn't mind some lunch."

"You tell him, Maggie," Trixie said. "Come with us and you'll never eat anywhere else."

Her husband led the way, and whenever anyone looked like approaching them — proprietors of the seafood restaurants by the harbour, stallholders selling imitation Rolexes and Gucci T-shirts in the pedestrian precinct near the mosque, owners of leather shops seeking customers in the crowds constricted by the arches flanking a mediaeval tower — he said "No thank you" with such authority that those addressed fell back. The narrow street beyond the arches was the Old Bazaar, and Don thought Lunt was conducting them along it towards the market area, where kebabs lay on grills outside restaurants which Maggie had proposed visiting. Instead Lunt marched up an alley. "I bet you're thanking us already," Trixie said.

It was full of would-be English restaurants. Nearest was the Englisch Pub, outside which a blackboard advertised Watneys Red Baral and rost beef and Yorkshire pudding. "Can't expect them to spell when half the yobs at home can't either," Lunt thundered, having caught Don's eye. "They do food that isn't only fit for pigs, that's the appeal."

"Actually, I'm not as hungry as I thought I was."

"We like trying the local cuisine," Don said.

"We'll see how long that lasts. Turkey, isn't that what the Yanks call a dead loss?" Lunt said loudly as a young man with large eyes the same deep brown as his skin opened the door of the pub. "You'll want a drink at least. Is it gin for the ladies? Two of them with tonic, and two pints of your best for the lads."

By the time the drinks were brought to the outside table Trixie had ascertained the name of the Hatchards' hotel. "What are you doing tomorrow?" she enquired, ice-cubes clicking against her display of teeth.

"Taking it easy by the pool," Maggie said at once.

"If you're after conversation, we're at the Turkish Paradise, ha ha. Or are you here on your own so you'll stay together?"

"Does it show?"

"When you've seen as many marriages fall apart as Gar and me have it does. We've found it helps for the hens to go off for a natter, and the same for the cocks if they're that way inclined."

"I expect Don and I will discuss it."

The Lunts had a good deal more to say, but nothing which Don thought he needed to be aware of. When he and Maggie had downed their drinks he felt justified in not offering to buy another round. They left the Lunts groaning and yawning and complaining at the non-appearance of the waiter, and when they were alone in the crowd Maggie said "Suddenly I like you better."

"In that case I'm glad we met them."

"Just let's make sure we never do again."

She took his hand as they arrived at the road beyond the funfair with which the market merged. Once they were across the dual carriageway, which was divided by cacti and interrupted by a roundabout where rights of way seemed chancy as roulette, she kept hold of his hand for long enough to convince him that things might be improving. They plodded up the slope of the pulverised pavement to their hotel, above which horses grazed within the frameworks of new buildings, the most nearly completed of which sprouted concrete weeds bristling with cables, the pillars of unbuilt walls. Don expected Maggie to head for the poolside bar, but she collected their key from Reception. "Coming up?"

"Try and stop me." As she let them into the small sparsely furnished room he added "Maybe all we need is time to get used to being just us again."

"Forever hopeful," she said, less encouragingly than he would have liked. Nevertheless she wriggled out of her swimsuit and lay on her bed and gazed at him, so that he undressed and pushed his bed against hers. He knelt between her legs and kissed her mottled breasts, and experienced a surge of affection for their wrinkles. Beyond foreplay, however, the situation was as frustrating as it had been all year: both he and Maggie had put on too much weight for him to be able to reach as deep into her as he used to. Before long he was aware only of their stomachs smacking together and the sweat pouring off him. "Never mind," Maggie said as, having fallen out of her a second time, he began to manipulate himself.

"I won't if you don't."

"It's something else we have to see if we can get used to. Come again?"

Don refrained from saying "I wish I could", but "And if we can't?" or "Such as what else?" seemed equally inadvisable. "So long as we're used to each other," he said.

After they'd taken turns to stand on the tiled bathroom floor to use the curtainless shower, they dozed on their united beds, their bodies touching carelessly, until a huge blurred recorded voice singing the praises of Allah wakened them. They ate in a restaurant where a boy in a fez turned a spit with one hand and clattered a bell to attract customers with the other. During the meal all the power failed for hundreds of yards, and in the moments before waiters lit candles on the tables the only light came from the sun drowning in the Aegean. "I wonder what we can do tomorrow to top this," Don said.

"Anything except what I told them we'd do," Maggie responded, more sharply than he thought was called for.

The muezzin roused them before dawn, and a morning chorus of nausea resounding through the pipes kept them awake. They were alone on the patio for breakfast of boiled eggs and goat's cheese. Don sensed she was holding him responsible for something, but if he asked what was wrong she would blame him for not knowing. Over his second apple tea he risked saying "So..."

"I fancy one of those boat trips out of the harbour."

Skewered chickens drooped on spits outside restaurants; a teenage youth with a hint of muscles was brushing a poster for a Schwartznegger film in Turkish onto the mediaeval tower. Don dropped a coin on the plate in front of a young mother sitting cross-legged in the dust beside the tower, but when he said "No thank you" as a man with silk scarves draped over his arm commenced an approach, Maggie shot a frown at him.

Several medium-sized motorboats were swaying not quite in unison a few yards out from the pebbly beach. The boat Maggie chose because all the people queuing for it were Turkish was the last to leave. They'd waded through the shallows and were being helped under the awning onto the bench that surrounded the deck when a voice shouted "Hold the boat. You with the boat, wait for us."

"Don't look," Don muttered. "They'll see it's not their sort of day out."

He heard a concerted wallowing behind him, then the boat lurched. "Here, here, don't go starting your engine till we've parked ourselves," Lunt yelled. "We've paid your feller, your partner, whatever the two of you are."

"Make room for two big ones," Trixie bellowed.

Don and Maggie sat still, hoping that the other passengers would close the gaps on either side of them, making space elsewhere on the bench. When the family beside Don backed away from him his mouth opened, and he found himself addressing Maggie, more loudly when she gave him an uncomprehending look. "Garababry splento," he persisted. "Parrawarra akkabroddle prothny binoth."

He was praying that the Lunts would take him for a foreigner, but his performance brought him a scowl from a Turk with a rectangular ebony moustache, who appeared to suspect Don of mocking his countrymen. That dismayed Don less than being joined by the Lunts. "Don't bother trying to learn that jabber," Lunt advised him. "They understand our lingo fast enough when they want to fleece us of our shekels."

Though the boat was already a hundred yards into the deeper water Don might have asked to disembark or even swum for the shore with Maggie, except that she had turned her back on him to watch the captain while he manoeuvred the boat out of the bay and spoke extensively in Turkish. "I speak English," he promised at last. "Name is Bekir."

"What's he on about now?" Trixie demanded, gazing straight at him.

"He's telling us his name," Don said.

"He'd be better off keeping quiet about it," Lunt declared. "Sounds a bit too much like bugger for my taste. I've never seen such a lot as these for pawing other men. You could get a few sly fingers up your arse round here if you ask me."

161

"I'll bet you're thanking the saints we came, or by the look of it you'd have had no-one to talk to. Except each other, and we'll see you do that, won't we, Gar?"

So the Lunts did as the boat chugged fuming through the uneven sea, until Don felt that the sunlight, like their questions, was probing for him. He assumed Maggie shared the feeling, but she kept her hand away from him. Two protracted hours later, as an island rose into view, Trixie wanted to know if he and Maggie still made love. "Why on earth should you assume any different?" he blurted.

"We've heard that before, haven't we, Gar? A man who doesn't want to own up there's a problem. Some friendly advice, Mag — sometimes it takes more than one to solve it."

"Really."

Don told himself that she was inching away from the Lunts, not from him. He was almost relieved when Lunt set about haranguing the captain, who had substituted a cassette of Turkish music for the collection of American hits which had just ended. "Can't we do without that heathen racket? Our friends won't like it any more than we do."

"Perhaps you wouldn't mind just speaking for yourself," Maggie said.

"Well, pardon us, I'm sure," Trixie said, and as loudly to the captain "As long as it's a barbecue I hope we're getting good plain food. I don't want to end up using your excuse for a toilet, thank you very much."

"A waiter was saying it's too many cold drinks in the heat that upsets people's stomachs," Maggie said with a pointed glance at the latest bottle of beer in Trixie's fist. "He said you should hold it in your mouth before you swallow it."

"Gar said they were dirty buggers," Trixie squealed, wincing in delight, and nudged Don with a quivering elbow.

Several passengers dived off the boat as it glided into a cove, one of them catching the rope thrown by the captain and tying it to a ring embedded in the rocky beach. "Shall we?" Don suggested, first turning away from the Lunts, and had to swivel his gaze twice towards the water before Maggie deigned to understand.

The shock of his plunge was assuaged in seconds. He swam near the Turks, thinking their presence should keep the Lunts away, then realised that Maggie was staying at a distance from him too. He swam with his face in the gentle waves, hearing the constant undertone of pebbles grinding together on the sea-bed, and was almost in a trance when he felt her hand lay itself on his spine and trail between his legs as he moved. Was it the water that made it seem plumper than usual? As it wriggled like an octopus he turned over and came face to face with Trixie Lunt, whose hand floated up and bumped its knuckles against his flattened crotch. "What do you — Where's Maggie?" he spluttered.

Trixie wiped her grin with the back of her hand. "She's all right, she's with my big feller."

Don's question had been provoked to some extent by guilt, and that was one of the emotions which sent him floundering past the seaward side of the boat. Against the silent chatter of sunlight on the waves he saw Lunt standing waist-deep in the sea and shouting over Maggie as she heaved herself to her knees. "You keep your eyes for your own women," Lunt was shouting at the moustached Turk. "I know you. I've seen you hanging around the hotel."

As the man and his two friends stepped forward, kicking waves aside, the captain called to them in a tone which Don thought sounded altogether too encouraging. His stomach felt inextricably knotted by the time he grasped that the captain was summoning everyone to the barbecue. He stayed in the water with Maggie, wishing she would look at him, until the Lunts and all the Turks had been served, then he paddled ashore with her to collect bread and salad and half a chicken each. As soon as they were seated on a rock the Lunts came over. "Try not to look so nervous. If things turn ugly I'll deal with them," Lunt said. "I've handled a good few men in my time."

"He used to drill them in the army. You never saw such a knees-up."

For a while the Hatchards used their food as an excuse not to talk, then Maggie dropped her greasy paper plate and shoved herself to her feet. "I'm going to lie down."

"See, you should have eaten where we told you," Trixie said.

"Nothing to do with it," Don retorted, and tore at the remains of Maggie's chicken with his teeth to demonstrate.

"You can have mine to chew if you're that starved."

"I've got all I want, thank you," Don said, and devoted himself to gnawing. On his way to the boat he complimented the captain loudly on the food, realising too late that his comment could be interpreted as a rebuke to Maggie as well as to the Lunts. "Let me be," she groaned when he tried to stroke her forehead, and stretched her body away from him along the bench.

She had to sit up when the rest of the passengers boarded. Don could tell she was determined not to be sick while the Lunts were watching, but it was an impossible resolve; she spent much of the last hour of the voyage with her head over the side of the boat. The Lunts took a great deal of persuading not to assist her to the hotel, but Don managed to do so alone, almost losing the way in the littered side streets Maggie insisted on keeping to. In their room she lowered herself onto her bed and looked as if she meant to wave the entire world away with one hand.

That was her for the next day as well. Don ate at the hotel and confined himself to the pool area, where waiters asked after Maggie and sketched sun-hats with their fingers above their heads. She had him bring her bottles of water, but whenever he asked if he could do anything else for her, he received at best a stare.

A cock-crow awoke him next day to find her giving him the same look. "What's wrong?" he said through the night's accumulation in his mouth. "How are you feeling?"

"Can't you tell?"

"You sound better," he risked saying. "Shall we do something today?"

"What are you suggesting?"

"What would you like to do besides avoiding you know who?"

"You think that'll take care of it, do you?"

"Unless you've a better idea."

"My idea would have been not to let them take our photograph."

"We didn't know what they were like then."

"Precisely." After a pause she said even more accusingly "Didn't we?"

"Do you want me to tell them to have it developed here and, I don't know, leave it at Reception for us?"

"Oh yes, I'm sure they'd trust the locals with their film."

"We could say, we could say there was a film place another Yorkshire pudding fan had recommended to us."

"What good would that do? They'll still have our address."

"Not much we can do about that, unless you feel like asking for it back."

"It wasn't me who was so anxious to give it to them."

"I didn't notice you trying to stop me," he said, and was tempted to add that he hadn't noticed her trying to avoid Lunt in the sea. "You can't expect me to ask for it. It isn't done."

"It's been a while since I've expected much of you at all."

The dawn showed him her face slackening under the weight of their marriage, wrinkles multiplying as he watched. He must look the same to her. "If there's nothing we can do there's nothing we can do," she said, and turned towards the wall.

What she meant was clear enough to him. It hung unspoken between them as they explored the market which had sprung up overnight in all the streets around the hotel. At Ephesus, where the marble of the ruins hurled back the sunlight, he thought of phoning the Lunts' hotel to discover how long they were staying. At Didyma the stumps of columns leading to the temple of the oracle towered over him as he considered venturing to the hotel instead of attempting to conquer the local phone system. At Pamukkale, where they swam in fizzing water which had drowned an ancient portico, he felt all Maggie's silences weighing him down, and vowed to present her with a plan at dinner.

He was sitting on the narrow concrete balcony outside their room that evening, and watching an old man lead his camel up the road which became a rubbly path, when he saw the Lunts marching towards the hotel. "Thank God for a civilised face," Gareth bellowed, and Trixie yelled "What have you done with her? Don't tell us she's still heaving."

"My wife's in the shower."

"Well, when she comes out," Trixie shouted despite having strode closer, "tell her you're both joining us for dinner."

"I'm afraid we've already booked a table at a Turkish place."

"So if you don't show up," Lunt roared, "they'll think it was the will of Allah. It's our last night. We thought you'd want to help us celebrate."

"I promised Maggie we'd go to her favourite restaurant," Don said, wondering how many lies that encompassed. "While you're here I don't suppose you've got our photograph."

"I haven't finished my roll yet. We didn't find much else worth taking."

"We told you we'd bring it to you at home."

Looking down on them emboldened Don. "No, don't do that. Just send it if you want us to have it."

Lunt fixed him with a stare Don could imagine him thrusting in the faces of new recruits. "If you think again we'll be drinking until the bus leaves for the airport. You know where we'll be."

Don watched them tramp away, swinging their arms, dwindling, gone for good. He felt able to indulge in some pity for them. Now he had plenty to tell Maggie, and he saved it until they were in the restaurant where the boy with the fez rang the bell — saved it until they'd ordered a second bottle of the special reserve, which cost all of five pounds. "Did you hear me talking when you were in the shower?" he asked as the waiter pulled the cork.

"If I had I'd have answered, wouldn't I?"

"Not to you, to guess who. Guess who's going home tonight so we won't need to spend next week watching for them."

"Did you ask?"

Don had raised his glass for hers to chime against, but when she didn't respond he half emptied it. "Ask?"

"For God's sake, Don. For our address."

"Of course I — would have if I'd needed to. I got him to promise they wouldn't come, just send the picture."

"And you believed him."

"What's your reason not to trust him?"

"How much reason do you need? You can tell just by looking at them."

Don could have probed further, but his anger was growing more diffuse. "So what do you want me to make him do, tear it up in front of us?"

"I'm not making anyone do anything. It wasn't me who handed them our address on a plate in the first place."

The remainder of their conversation consisted of the scraping of utensils on china and the thumps of glasses on the table. They had another week together here, Don told himself as they trudged to the hotel, but he could see that wouldn't be enough. As Maggie pulled off her dress in the room he thought of making love to her, and knew that he would fail, not only because he was too drunk. "I'm going for a walk," he blurted.

"I notice you wait until I can't."

"What's stopping you?" he would have retorted, except that an argument now would solve even less than usual. He stalked out, holding his head erect as if to keep his rage steady, and down the randomly lamplit road to the side turning which led to the Turkish Paradise Hotel.

The coach to the airport wouldn't be making its rounds for hours. The forecourt surrounded on three sides by single-storey concrete blocks was empty even of the luggage of the departing guests. Don could hear the murmur of an open-air restaurant beyond the rooms. He went straight to the Reception window at the near end of the left-hand concrete block, and had to slap a bell to summon a large bald Turk from an inner office. "Are Mr and Mrs Lunt here?"

The man touched the dangling key to room 18 and shook his head. "Back later."

"Can I wait for them in the restaurant?"

"Round there," the man said, indicating the end of the right-hand block, and withdrew into the office.

It occurred to Don that the man was loath to spend any more time with a friend of the Lunts than was absolutely necessary. Don reached across the sill and grasping the key and its brass persuader, lifted them off the hook. The bunch of his shadows fanned out and merged like the props in an obscure magic trick as he crossed to room 18, which was directly opposite Reception. He remembered looking down on Lunt, the wallet in the man's breast pocket leaving

167

no room for a notebook. Before his sense of the impossibility of what he planned to do overtook him, he poked the key in the lock and turned it. Glancing back, he stepped in and closed the door behind him. "Attaboy," he muttered, "or maybe Ataturk." An object crouching at the level of his shins tripped him and sent him sprawling into the dark.

He landed face down on a bed whose crumpled sheets smelled thickly of perfume and felt sodden with sweat. He writhed upright and sat on the edge, rubbing his shins and brandishing the brass club of the key, until he could see around the dim room. It was empty except for two suitcases, one of which had tripped him. By stooping until his face was inches from them he ascertained that neither label identified which Lunt each case belonged to. He heaved his assailant onto the bed, jarring a protest out of the sketches of hangers in the doorless wardrobe, and fumbled for the zipper.

At first he thought the case was locked, the zipper was so stiff. Abruptly it tore along half the length of its track, opening the case as far as the handle. Shirts bulged out of the gap, releasing such a smell of lotion that he thought the Lunts had crept into the room behind him. He flexed his shoulders and dragged the zipper all the way. The canvas lid reared up, exposing Lunt's stale underwear. Don was rubbing his fingers on his shirt preparatory to rummaging when he saw the notebook peeking out of a nest of used socks. He fished it out between finger and thumb and hurried to the window.

The margins of the pages were a staircase of initial letters, and it took him mere seconds to locate H. That page and its reverse were full of names and addresses, but he only had time to observe that they didn't include his and Maggie's. Theirs was all by itself on the next page, which he ripped out at once. Doing so revealed that what he'd almost noticed about the names and addresses on the previous page was equally true of those on the I pages, and of as much of the book as he dared linger to examine. Virtually every address, including those listed only under first names, had been crossed out.

Shame at having torn out the page almost made him replace it, then he stuffed it into his pocket. He returned the book to its sweaty niche and struggled to zip the case shut, and had to reopen it so as to extract an escaping arm from the teeth. Hauling the case off the bed, he dumped it where it had lain in wait for him. The memory, and his growing need to urinate, revived his anger. He kicked open the bathroom door and unzipping himself, aimed into the glimmering pedestal. "This'll teach you to keep whatever you didn't keep off my wife," he snarled.

It didn't work. He inched forward and stood wider-legged, but couldn't produce a drop. He smelled the Lunts in the dark and felt as though they'd seized him by his useless crotch. He packed himself away and waddled aching to the door. Sneaking into the deserted forecourt, he hurried bow-legged to Reception, where he craned over the sill and hooked the key into place with an expertness born of urgency. He limped out of the gate as if the pain in his bladder was a leash and swerved away from the main road. Once he was beyond the glow of the forecourt he bowed over a lump of rubble shaped like an ancient helmet and let himself out, but the pressure in his bladder was its own defeat. He clenched his eyelids and gritted his teeth, and at last was rewarded by a jet so fierce it splashed his ankles. He was luxuriating in the sensation of release when he heard footsteps closing in on him.

If the Lunts had returned, they couldn't touch him. Surely they wouldn't recognise his back view in the gloom. The footsteps continued to approach, and he had to look, still spouting. Behind him were the moustached Turk and his two friends from the boat.

Don felt his buttocks squeezing together, his mouth opening helplessly. He was about to burst into the gibberish he'd spoken on the boat. He'd lost his balance, and as his shoulder bruised itself against the forecourt wall his penis and its jet swung towards them. "Yes, look at it," he heard himself yelling in a parade-ground voice. "Hardly worth having, is it? Might as well be a woman. Tom Thumb, she used to call it when she wanted it, and that was a long time ago."

He felt sick, tingling with nervousness, and hadn't the least idea what he might do next. He could see only the watching faces and eyes, darkened further by the shadow of the wall. He felt his penis trying to shrink as it worked. Then the three brayed wordlessly in contempt and strolled into the forecourt. Don leaned his forehead against the wall and vomited, and remembered Lunt wielding his ballpoint in the notebook like a weapon. He should have torn out the next page too in case it retained an impression of his and Maggie's address.

"Don Hatchard?"

"Who wants him?"

"The name's Lunt. We met this year in Turkey. I've got something for him and his wife."

"You'll need the new address. Are you ready?"

"Fire away." A sound of scribbling fierce enough to be audible over the phone responded to the details. "That's close enough to drive to," Lunt declared.

"I'm glad to hear that. Is it something Mrs Hatchard asked for?"

"Now you mention it, I wouldn't be surprised."

Don broke the connection. "It'll be something for her to remember me by," he said in a voice that sounded very much like Lunt's, and as grim.

ROOT CAUSE

I SAT BEHIND MY SECOND PINT OF BEER and pretended to be unaware. Over by the billiard table a man in motorcycle leathers was selling a Japanese television, next to the fruit machine three sharp-faced youths in impeccable pastel suits seemed to be muttering about the supermarket across the road. Whenever I glanced at my book in case they thought I was watching, Vladimir said "We're waiting for Godot." They must have suspected I could hear them, for suddenly all three were staring at me across the archipelago of tables, the frayed beermats and greying ashtrays. I headed for the door while gulping the last of the beer. In the doorway a girl of about sixteen was loitering. I hurried, anxious not to be late for work, and had reached the wasteland of the intersection when I saw the children beneath the overpass.

They were clambering up the concrete pillars as though the tangled graffiti were vines, toward the roadway overhead. Precisely because I was nervous, I had to intervene. I mustn't flinch away because their lives weren't like mine.

As I reached the concrete island in the middle of the crossroads, the children came scrambling down. They had almost dodged into the traffic before they saw I wasn't following. "He isn't anyone," said a ten-year-old, the daytime mother of the group. "He's only the library man."

"You mustn't play under there. You might hurt yourselves." I felt absurdly pompous, but I could only be true to myself. "If you come to the library I'll find you some books to read."

"Come here till I tell you something," the ten-year-old hissed to the others. When she'd finished whispering, one boy peered beadily at me. "Are you a queer, mister?" he said.

"Certainly not." But I knew how my middle-class accent, stiffened by years of elocution classes, must sound. The concrete gloom pressed down, the muffled hissing of cars overhead made the pillars sound like trees, and I was afraid that if I went toward

171

the children they would run into the traffic without looking. "Don't come to the library if you don't want to," I said, turning away.

Of course I hoped that would lure them in. Certainly the library needed enlivening. Presumably the plate-glass walls had been intended to attract readers to the tens of thousands of new books, but when I arrived the place was almost deserted. The librarian gave me and the clock a sharp glance, and I hurried to deposit my coat in the staffroom, burping loudly enough to wake an old man who was dozing over the racing pages.

When I emerged, the children were swaggering toward the junior section. The uniformed attendant went after them at once, eager as a policeman on his first beat. Within a minute they were eluding him in four directions, punching the books as they ran, until the shelves looked gap-toothed. The librarian helped chase them while I served a pregnant woman who was returning an armful of overdue books. I didn't charge her a fine, for she already had three children, and I'd seen her husband a few minutes ago, drinking away his unemployment benefit in the Viscount of Knowsley. All at once my neck felt exposed and red-hot, for the librarian was frowning at me, but she hadn't seen me waive the rules. "Brian, did you tell those children to come in here?"

"Yes I did, Mrs Smullen. They didn't seem to have anywhere else to go."

"They most certainly have. They ought to be at school. If they choose to play truant, they mustn't think they have a refuge here. And apart from that, you saw how they behaved."

If the attendant had left them alone they might have found themselves books to read, but I refrained from saying so: I was on probation at the library for the first six months. As the afternoon wore on I stuck labels in books, dealt with a few readers, woke up a snoring drunk, read a landlord's letter to an old lady. The girl who had been loitering in the doorway of the Viscount sat waiting for her mother, a plump pink woman with the fixed thoughtless smile of an inflatable doll. At last the mother appeared in the lobby, beside a man who was averting his face, and beckoned her daughter out. I tried to watch where they went, but Mrs Smullen was saying "You weren't to know about those children, I suppose. You'll learn when you're been here a few weeks. I know it comes as a shock that anyone can live the way these people do."

But they had no choice, I thought as I waited for the bus that night outside the library. They were trapped here in the new town, miles out of the city from which they'd been rehoused. Half the firms which had promised jobs had set up factories elsewhere instead. That was why the overpass was empty now, robbed of the heavy traffic which had been supposed to feed the town.

The April twilight settled on the tower blocks — you couldn't tell it was Spring out here, except by the green tips of the saplings beside the intersection — and I grew nervous in case the bus had broken down, leaving me to wait another hour. Nothing moved on the narrow fenced-in pavements, the pale roads. Few people went out at night here, for there was nowhere to go. The overpass stood like a huge grey humped insect, a dozen legs supporting its midriff, and I found its utter stillness oppressive. It was enough to make me nervous all by itself.

Ten minutes later it was smudged by darkness. Now it looked like a petrified clump of trees. If I stared at it long enough I thought that the children were back again, clambering. Once I was sure that they were, and made a fool of myself by hurrying to look. For a moment I thought they had dodged across to the trees and were peering out at me, as if anyone could hide there: the saplings were no thicker than the poles which were teaching them posture.

I didn't give them a second glance, for I had almost missed the bus. The driver grudgingly opened the doors, then sped up the overpass ramp. I could never understand why buses used the overpass, especially now when the roads were deserted. As the bus reached the top he grimaced — perhaps at the sight of the miles of tower blocks with their racks of windows, or the way the bus juddered in a stray wind, or the only other passenger, who was complaining to nobody in particular that his nose was bleeding again. Neither of them worried me. Now that I was on the bus, I felt safe.

I felt safe until the next morning, when I saw the police cars outside the supermarket. The shattered hole beside the main lock made it clear what had happened, but I already knew. A policeman was talking to the manager, who wore a dark suit and five o'clock shadow. "Nine televisions, eight music centres," the manager was saying, like a belated carol of Christmas spending. I hurried into the library as if I were the culprit, averting my face.

I felt as if I were, but what could I have done? I had only suspicions to offer, and yesterday I would have had even less. Certainly I had no proof. Still, I felt on edge to speak to the police as I unlocked the front door to let in the old men. In they trooped, to squabble over first read of the newspapers.

I was stamping books at the counter when the police found the guard dog on the island beneath the overpass. As they carried it back to the supermarket I saw how its glassy-eyed head lolled, how the fur of its throat was darkly matted. I was angry, but I was more afraid, and very glad to be helping someone search for books when the police came to ask the librarian if she'd noticed anything suspicious yesterday. Until they left, I was afraid they would ask me.

And as soon as they left I was furious with myself, of course. The three youths would never have known that l was the one who had told the police. But then, I realised as lunchtime approached, they weren't the type that would need to be sure, and that made me nervous enough to stay away from the Viscount of Owsley in case they had seen the police in the library.

I was too tense to stay with Mrs Smullen when we closed for lunch. Instead I went walking among the tower blocks. Draughty doorless entranceways gaped everywhere; broken glass glittered on stairs, graffiti dwarfed the walls. Here and there I passed terraces with ragged lawns and crippled fences; most of the houses were boarded up. On one of the few larger areas of green I saw children dragging a large plastic letter K and an N through the mud, which explained what had happened to the Viscount. Around the green, injured saplings tried to lean on splintered poles. It occurred to me that the only untouched saplings I'd seen were by the overpass.

I was on edge all day, and glad to leave. A teacher reserved all our junior books on ancient Britain for a school project, the teenage girl and her doll-faced mother strolled along opposite sides of the main road, slowing whenever they heard a car. That night as I waited for the bus I saw how the road stood over the place where the dog had been found, like a spider photographed in the act of seizing its prey. Had the thieves hidden the dog over there, or had it dragged itself? I found that until the bus was beyond the overpass, everything made me nervous — the way the driver grinned to himself, the smell of the raw meat which the woman at the far end of the bus must be carrying, even the distant chanting that drifted up from below, no doubt football songs in the Viscount. Once they'd begun singing football songs when I was in the pub, and I'd felt more out of place than ever.

At least next day was Thursday, my day off in the week. That afternoon I sat for a while on the pavilion and watched the bowlers, old soldiers and retired businessmen whose moustaches were neat as the green. I could almost believe there was nothing more important than the unhurried click of bowls. Later I strolled through the house of the family which owned the estate: elegant roped-off rooms, portraits safe in the past. Usually while I was there I could pretend I had stepped back in time, but now the house reminded me how I was trying to forget about tomorrow.

When I arrived at the library, it was worse. Overnight half the windows had been smashed. Mrs Smullen watched the workmen, her lips pursed, as they nailed boards over the gaps. She looked furious with everyone — no doubt the police had wakened her during the night — and I hardly dared to say good morning. Besides, I was trying to ignore a secret fear that the windows had been smashed as a warning to me.

Now there was no daylight in the library. I was boxed in with relentless fluorescent light, like a laboratory animal. At lunchtime I sat on the far side of the staffroom from Mrs Smullen and tried to hush the pages of the Vonnegut novel I was reading. I was afraid to show my face in the Viscount of Owly.

All at once, halfway through the afternoon, I was enough on edge to say "Shouldn't we do something about that girl?"

She was sitting at a bare table, waiting for her doll-faced mother and whoever she might bring. "What do you suggest we do?" Mrs Smullen said.

I ignored her sarcastic emphasis. "Well, I don't know, but surely there must be something," I pleaded, fighting to keep my voice

175

low. "She can't be more than sixteen years old, and her mother seems to sell her to anyone who comes along."

"As a matter of fact I happen to know she's thirteen." Before I could react to that, she turned on me. "But what exactly are you implying? Are you alleging that I would allow my library to used in that way?"

I might have been too shocked to pretend that I wasn't. In particular her words dismayed me: suggest, imply, allege — the language of a cautious newspaper. I hadn't replied when a woman came in with an armful of books. "See to the counter, please," Mrs Smullen said.

The books were overdue, and I felt frustrated enough to take a sadistic delight in counting up the fines. When I announced the total, the woman stared unblinking at me. "My friend owed more than that the other day, and you didn't charge her," she said.

Mrs Smullen intervened at once. "We aren't authorised to waive fines. If your friend wasn't charged it must have been an oversight, and she should count herself lucky."

When the woman had gone, leaving her ticket with the unpaid fine and muttering that she'd rather watch television anyway, Mrs Smullen demanded "Is that true? Have you been waiving fines?"

"Well, there was one lady, that woman's friend." In fact there had been several. "She was pregnant for the umpteenth time, and her husband's unemployed."

"I pay quite enough tax to keep people like her without encouraging them. Because you're new I'll overlook this, but if it happens again I shall have to mention it in your probationary report," she said, turning away.

I might have retorted that it was also public money that paid her wages, but of course I didn't dare. Instead I tried to lose myself in work, though I was neurotically aware of every one of her movements, wherever she was in the library. The sky darkened, the fluorescent light seemed to intensify, the glossy spines of books glared discordantly. By the time Mrs Smullen went for her afternoon break, it was pouring with rain.

As soon as the staffroom door closed behind her, I glanced about. Apart from the old men snoozing and mumbling at the tables, the library was deserted, and I didn't think that anyone else would come in until the rain eased off. I hurried to the phone at once, and called the police.

Immediately I heard a voice, I told it about the young girl and her mother. I'd hoped that would make me feel I had achieved something at last, but I only felt uncomfortably furtive, as guilty as if I were making a hoax call. Of course I didn't give my name, and wouldn't let the owner of the voice put me through to someone else. I replaced the receiver hastily, and spent five minutes worrying in case Mrs Smullen had heard the ring.

The girl at the table had found a picture book of Spain and was leafing through it rather wistfully, but I couldn't spare much time to watch her, for I was too busy watching for the police. Whenever the library doors opened, my stomach felt wrenched. I might have been the person they were looking for, not her at all.

I was glad when Mrs Smullen reappeared. At least I could take refuge in the staffroom. But I couldn't read; I could only gaze out at the dark afternoon, the streaming road, a few cars ascending the overpass, their headlights swollen with rain. I was so nervous that I saw a figure being slashed with knives beneath the overpass. It must have been the shadow of a sapling, knives of rain and headlights. The rain made the graffiti on the pillars resemble huge blotchy faces.

When I emerged from the staffroom, the girl had gone. For a moment I felt guiltily relieved, then I realised that it didn't mean the police would stay away. Suppose they assumed the call had been a hoax? Suppose they recognised my voice? I was afraid to look up when the door opened, and by the time the library closed I was near panic. It was almost a relief to stand outside in the last of the rain and wait for the bus, even though I couldn't help peering across at the overpass. I saw nothing unusual, even when I hurried to the window of the bus and stared down from the overpass. There were only the saplings, glistening darkly.

I didn't sleep well that night. I dreamed I was in the staffroom, unable to look away from the overpass outside the window, while someone came into the room behind me. I jerked awake when I felt an icy touch on my throat. After that I couldn't sleep at all, and perhaps that was why, next morning on the bus, the noise of the engine seemed to turn into chanting as the bus reached the overpass.

At least there was no sign of the young girl. Perhaps Saturday was her day off. I managed to behave as if everything was normal: I asked people to keep their voices down, told readers I would put out the returned books in a few minutes, said "Staff only behind the counter" when they tried to grab returned books from the trolley. Mrs Smullen could have had no reason to suspect that anything was wrong, until I came out of the staffroom at the end of my morning break and saw her talking to the police.

My reaction gave me away. I hesitated long enough in the doorway for her to see that I wanted to hide. I snatched a handful of reservation cards and tried to look as if I were searching for the books on the shelves, but as soon as the police left she hunted me down. "Was it you who called the police?"

"Well, somebody had to do something..." I kept my voice low, and wished that she would do the same; readers were glancing at her. "You said she was only thirteen..."

"Let me make one thing perfectly clear to you." Her face was growing red, her voice was rising. "I am in charge of this library. From now on you will do exactly as I say, no more and no less. If that girl comes in here again you will tell her to leave at once."

"But that won't achieve anything," I hissed. "She'll only go elsewhere. What are the police going to do about her?"

"Will you go back to the counter and get on with your work." She turned her back on me at once and strode to her desk.

When I had to give a reader his tickets, I almost dropped them. My fingers felt swollen, my face was burning. Not only had all the readers heard Mrs Smullen, some of them had given her approving smiles. When she went into the staffroom for her break I mouthed obscenities at her, but that didn't make me feel any less enraged. I was still standing at the counter, digging my fingers viciously among the book cards and readers' tickets, when the three sharp-faced youths came in.

They hardly glanced at me, but one of them murmured something. All of them sniggered as they sat down at the table furthest from the counter. They began to mutter, heads close together, a low blurred sound like the noise of a fly trapped in a room. Even if they had been three other people I would have found it nerve-racking. As soon as an old man turned to glare at them I strode over. "Will you keep your voices down, please," I said, my lips trembling.

They took their time before they looked at me, smirking. "All right, squire," one said. "You won't even know we're here."

As soon as I turned away they burst out laughing and resumed talking. All at once I felt safe: they were on my territory here, I was in charge of the library while Mrs Smullen was away, whatever she might think. "That's enough," I said with all the violence I felt. "I told you to keep quiet. Get out and make your plans somewhere else."

"And what'll you do? Hit us with a book?" one said. As they rose to their feet, the chair-legs screeched over the linoleum. They were no longer smirking, because I'd revealed that I knew about them. One of them reached in his inside breast pocket, and my face and throat already felt raw.

Before he could withdraw his hand, the library attendant returned from a surreptitious visit to the Viscount of Owl. He saw what was happening, and intervened at once. "Go on, the lot of you," he snarled, exhaling beer over me and the youths alike. "Don't try it. I'll have the law on you." For a moment the youth stood there like Napoleon, then the three of them marched out, kicking all the chairs within reach.

I was relieved that the attendant had intervened — not only because he'd prevented whatever they might have done to me, but also because he had decoyed their hostility away from me. At least, I hoped he had. Certainly Mrs Smullen assumed that I had been helping him throw out some troublemakers. It wasn't until the library closed for the night, and I was waiting for the bus, that I realised fully how blind my hope was. The youths had every reason to cut me up like the dog, and now was their chance.

I hid beneath the overpass and watched for the bus, but I felt by no means safe. Clouds were blackening the twilight; it was very dark among the pillars. I was surrounded by graffiti, incomprehensible as runes. They were confusing the edge of my vision, for there seemed to be too many pillars, disfigured by huge looming faces. I wouldn't look up, even though I kept thinking that children were clambering overhead; I knew it must be an illusion of the graffiti — no children ever had such bright red mouths. I had enough trouble convincing myself that the spidery saplings weren't fat and darkly glistening.

When the bus came in sight I felt safe at last, but not for long. As soon as I sat down I caught sight of the driver's face in his mirror. The bus was racing up the overpass, and he was grinning mirthlessly, grinning like a wooden mask. He looked insane.

As the bus reached the top, it swerved. For a moment I was sure he was going to drive straight through the concrete railing. When I opened my eyes, we were a hundred yards beyond the overpass, and he looked perfectly normal, almost expressionless. Perhaps it was only my lingering nervousness that had made him look anything else.

My nervousness wouldn't go away. It loomed over me all Sunday while I tried to enjoy the Spring among the large scrubbed houses near my home. I thought of calling Mrs Smullen in the morning to say I was ill, but I knew she wouldn't believe me. My probationary report would no doubt be bad enough as it was.

I didn't get much sleep. On Monday I was tense long before I arrived at the library. Everything made me anxious, even a child who had fallen near the overpass and was crying about his bloody knees. But there was a surprise waiting for me. Someone had been sent on relief from another library, to make the staff up to three.

Mrs Smullen must have known in advance, but it didn't matter that she hadn't mentioned it to me; I was too relieved not to be on my own with her. Jack, the new man, was an expansive sort who asked the readers what they thought of the books they were returning, something Mrs Smullen never did. He joked with everyone, even with Mrs Smullen until her face made it clear that joking was against the rules. I felt at ease for the first time in days.

Perhaps Mrs Smullen resented our rapport. Halfway through the morning she showed me an item in the local newspaper. The woman I hadn't charged fines had been arrested for shoplifting; her flat had proved to be full of stolen goods. "I hope that will make you think a little," Mrs Smullen said, but I was depressed less by the report than by how triumphant she seemed. When Jack saw I was depressed he winked at me, and I felt better.

"Coming for a drink, old son?" he said at lunchtime. I didn't mind going to the Cunt of Owl now that there were two of us. Jack challenged me to a game of billiards, which I lost hilariously. He insisted on a third round of beer, and we were gulping it down with barely a minute to go before the library opened when the three youths appeared at the far end of the bar.

I choked on my beer, and stood coughing and spluttering while Jack thumped me between the shoulders. One youth was dawdling ominously toward me along the bar, but it didn't feel at all like a scene in a Western to me. Then one of his companions caught his elbow and muttered something that turned him back, and at once I felt impressive as John Wayne. I wasn't scared of them or of Mrs Smullen. I took my time finishing my drink; I wasn't about to start coughing again.

When we returned to the library it was already open, and the doll-faced woman was flouncing out with her daughter. "You pack while I tell Reg we have to stay with him," the mother was saying. So the police and Mrs Smullen had made them move elsewhere, but what had that achieved? Still, I felt resigned to its inevitability, thanks to the beer.

The beer helped me amble through the next hour or so, chatting with readers and fumbling for their tickets in the narrow metal trays, but by the time I went for my afternoon break I felt sleepy. I sat and blinked at the rain that was striping the staffroom window. Before long I was nodding. I thought there were too many pillars in the gloom beneath the overpass, but then I saw that what I'd taken for a mass of pillars was something else: a glistening tangle of roots or branches or entrails, that were reaching for me. They might have caught me if I hadn't been woken by a crash of glass.

I sat and stared, and couldn't move. Just a couple of feet in front of me, the staffroom window had been smashed. I heard footsteps running away, and the clang of a metal bar thrown on the pavement, but I could only stare at my reflection in the fragment that remained of the window. I could feel glass in my throat, which was wet and growing wetter. Reflected against the streaming overpass, my chest was darkening with a stain.

Mrs Smullen strode in almost at once. I managed to stand up, my feet crunching broken glass, so that she could see what had happened to me, but she hardly spared me a glance. She seemed almost to blame me for the damage. Perhaps she was right — no doubt the broken window was the revenge of the sharp-faced youths — but couldn't she see that my throat had been cut? At last I ventured to the mirror above the sink, and made myself look. There was a tiny splinter of glass under my chin, but no blood. My chest was soaked with rain.

Perhaps I should have been able to laugh at my panic, but the anticlimax only worried me: it seemed the worst was yet to happen. After all, I would have to wait by myself for the bus. The hammering of workmen at the staffroom window resounded through the library. Before long it felt as though they were hammering my ears.

But I didn't have to wait for the bus. Though he didn't live near me, Jack offered me a lift home. I felt limp with relief, even when he headed unnecessarily for the overpass. "Here goes the roller coaster," he cried.

As the car reached the top, it veered alarmingly. I thought there must be a cross-wind, though I couldn't feel one. I glanced at Jack to make some such remark, and at once I was afraid to speak. He was grinning stiffly, showing his teeth. His eyes were fixed as glass.

I watched him, because I couldn't look away, until we were off the overpass. At once his expression began to fade, and a hundred yards further on he looked at me. "What's up?" he said.

He seemed back to normal. "What were you thinking about when you made that face?" I said, trying to relax.

"What face?"

"You made a face just now on the overpass."

"Did I? I'll take your word for it, old son. I can't recall thinking of anything. This bloody place, I expect."

He obviously thought he hadn't told me anything, but I felt he had: it was just that I couldn't define it, especially while his hand kept touching my leg whenever he changed gear. Soon he let his hand rest on the gear lever and my thigh, until I drew away. Once I was alone I tried to pinpoint what I should have noticed, but my mind felt like a lump in my head. That night I kept waking, convinced that the prickling of my throat meant it had been slashed.

Next morning I almost fell asleep on the bus, but I alighted before it reached the overpass. Though I couldn't see the driver's face, I was almost sure that he lost control for a moment at the top. I didn't feel any more confident for having escaped the bus. As I hurried past the intersection the buds of the saplings looked too green, violent as neon.

Jack clapped me on the shoulder when he arrived. "How are you today, old son?" I tried to stay away from him and Mrs Smullen; I didn't feel at ease with either of them. Old ladies jostled in front of the shelves of romances, the attendant threw out several children for giggling at picture books. I searched for adult books on ancient Britain for the class that was coming in later. Through one of the remaining windows I could see the overpass, rearing up as if to pounce.

When I went for my morning break I wasn't conscious of taking a handful of the history books with me. I sat in the boarded-up staffroom and tried to relax. Flats in the tower blocks must feel like this, like cells. More than the glaring light, it bothered me that I couldn't watch the overpass. I closed my eyes and tried to find a reason for all the tension and frustration I was suffering. If I could understand them, perhaps they would go away. If they lingered they would grow worse, and I couldn't imagine what I would do then.

My hands were clenching. They clenched on the books, which I realised at last I was holding — and suddenly I realised what I'd overlooked.

For a while I stared at the unopened books. I had to know, and yet I was afraid to find out. Eventually I turned to the index of the first book. There wasn't much to find: most of England had been Celtic in the fourth century, the Druids had performed human sacrifices in sacred groves. Perhaps I was wrong, perhaps my impressions had no historical basis after all. In any case, how long could an area of land retain its character? Could any influence survive so long?

I opened the second book, and there it was: a Roman description of a sacred grove. Barbaric rites — "barbara ritu sacra deorum" — every tree sprinkled with human gore, altars heaped with entrails. Trees were carved to represent gods — "simulacra maesta deorum" — and I knew how the Romans must have felt to be hemmed in by the huge looming faces, for I had felt it myself. I was sure of myself now. Jack had said more than he knew when he'd called it a bloody place.

I was sure of myself, but not of what to do. Who could I tell? What could I say? I hurried out of the staffroom, trying to think whether there was anything at the intersection that might convince people, and saw the school bus full of children in the distance. It was heading for the library — for the overpass.

At once my sense of danger was so intense that I began to shake. There wasn't time to explain to anyone. I had to act, I mustn't fail again. My whole body was tingling with apprehension, and yet deep down I felt relieved, capable of dealing with the miles of concrete and everything within them at last. All at once everything seemed clear and simple. The bus came speeding down the long straight road as I ran panting toward the intersection. Before I reached it, my lungs felt raw.

By the time I stumbled to the far side of the intersection, the bus was only yards away. I stood in front of the overpass and gestured wildly for the driver to go around. When the grin formed slowly on his face I knew what I'd failed to anticipate, but it was too late. As he drove straight at me my vision blurred, and the saplings seemed to bend toward me like the tendrils of a carnivorous plant. As the bus knocked me down into darkness, I thought I heard the children chanting.

But perhaps I was wrong. Perhaps I was wrong about everything. When he came to visit me in the hospital, the driver said that the steering had locked. He'd managed to brake, though not in time to prevent the impact from fracturing three of my ribs. Perhaps he had been grimacing as he fought the wheel, not grinning at all.

Yes, I think I was wrong. Now that I read over what I've written, I think that the unfamiliarity of everything distorted my view of it — of the intersection most of all. I can hear the birds in the trees outside the window, singing with their bright red beaks, and it seems to me that the saplings by the intersection may be the most important factor in the lives of all those people. When they grow into trees, surely their green must brighten those lives. Once I leave the hospital, I must do what I can to help the saplings grow as they should.

LOOKING OUT

THE FIRST TIME NAIRN SAW THE FIGURES in his house, he thought the landlord had won.

Nairn hammered his stick triumphantly on the pavement as he neared home. Even his legs weren't hobbling him so much; he was almost striding. The girl at the supermarket had tried to cow him: "I can't let you have this sugar. You haven't bought enough goods. You can see the sign, a pound for a pound." I can read well enough, he'd thought, in my day we went to school to learn. When she continued to refuse he'd thumped the sugar down on her counter, and the bag had split. "You can't sell that to anyone else now," he'd pointed out. "It's damaged goods." She still hadn't sold it to him, bitch in the manger that she was, but they both knew she was the loser. He was smiling as he arrived home.

He was reaching in his pocket for the key, smiling more broadly as he remembered that for the first time in months he wouldn't be greeted by the scrabble of rats nagging at the house, when a movement in his bedroom caught his attention. He glanced up in time to see a group of dim-faced figures peering out at him.

At once he was hurrying toward the house, slashing his stick through the net of grass which overgrew the path. He locked the front door behind him and hobbled toward the back, kicking a letter along the hall. When he'd locked the back door he leaned on his stick, smiling grimly. Let them try to get out now without his seeing who they were. Both doors had mortice-locks. The intruders would get the keys over his dead body. No doubt they were capable of that, if they were like most people today. But let them try to explain away his corpse. Eventually, when they'd still made no sound, he crept upstairs in search of them.

The house was empty. It took Nairn some time, his heart labouring despite his resolve, to be convinced of that. They weren't hiding behind his dressing-table, and they couldn't be under the bed: the bedclothes didn't hang so as to conceal anyone, they were

186

folded over in the centre of the double bed for warmth. But nor could anyone hide in the other two bedrooms; the door of one was missing, the other room was crowded with furniture and trunks unbrokenly coated with dust.

Nairn crept back through the house. Even he, knowing where to tread, couldn't avoid making the loose boards spring and creak beneath the mangy carpets. Nobody could have left the house before he locked the back door without his hearing them.

He was stooping to pick up the letter from the hall floor when he realised what he must have seen. Through the fanlight above the front door he could see people bunched in the window of the first-floor flat opposite. He'd glimpsed their reflections in his bedroom, staring out, possessive and darkly faceless. Let them watch, he thought. They won't see much. They'd love to come in and look round, I know. Over my dead body. He took the letter into the living-room, his feet gritting on coal-dust.

It was from the landlord. Nairn could tell by the envelope, by the misspellings and the handwriting, which was that of an ignorant man. The sort who thinks everyone as ignorant as himself, Nairn thought. On his last visit the landlord had scurried through the house, not even waiting for Nairn to catch up; he'd stared at the bedroom door leaning next to the frame from which its hinges had rusted free, he'd peered at the damp peeling away the sitting-room wallpaper, he'd gazed into Nairn's bedroom, sniffing. "I'm sorry to hear you've a cold," Nairn had said satirically. The man had offered to ask friends to do the repairs, but Nairn knew what that meant: sending his friends to sneer at the way the old fool couldn't cope, to snoop and report back. "I'll see to it myself," Nairn had said, "when I have the money and time."

The following day he'd had the mortice locks fitted. Since then he'd had three letters from the landlord, and here was the fourth. He tore it up unopened and built a small pile of coal over it in the grate. Soon the brownish walls and ragged floor were fluttering about him, amid the darkness; a cold fire flickered in the mirror on the wall. He sat gazing at the sputtering coal. If the landlord and his friends thought they'd picked a helpless victim, they'd find out how mistaken they were.

On the day the next letter arrived, he saw the face.

The postman was crossing the road to the flats opposite when Nairn returned from collecting his pension. "Good day," Nairn said, but the man didn't touch his cap, though he couldn't have been more than twenty. Watching him pass, Nairn saw that the first-floor flat was still curtained. You'll have to get up earlier than that to catch me, he thought. He turned toward his house, and saw it staring down at him from his bedroom window.

The face seemed to be perched on top of a shapeless heap of grey material. The body must be hidden within the mass, Nairn thought, even though he found it impossible to distinguish the material: they couldn't trick him into believing anything else, his eyes might be growing weak but not his mind. The face, however, he could make out clearly enough: a thing of bone and discoloured sucked-in skin, patched with colourless hair that was sodden with sweat, grinning out at him. The dark October sky drifted across it and peeled away, leaving the wide mirthless grin untouched.

Nairn limped toward the house, stamping his stick. He locked the doors and searched. When he'd searched twice and found the building empty, he knew the landlord and his friends were responsible. Nobody else would have keys to the house. The man was trying to frighten Nairn out. He'd soon see who he was dealing with. Nairn strode unsteadily back to the hall, drubbing dust from the carpet with his stick.

Though Nairn's name was still misspelled on the envelope, the letter wasn't from the landlord. It was officially franked, from the courts: a summons. Another attempt to frighten him. He halved the unopened envelope slowly and deliberately, until the pile was too thick to tear. He couldn't bear a man who was underhand. If the landlord had anything to say to him, let him come and say it to his face.

It took him most of the day to drag the bed into a position from which, lying down, he could watch his bedroom door. He'd managed to manhandle chairs to block the front and back doors, skinning the walls as he did so. He lay on the bed in the dark, resting sleeplessly. The bedroom door, which he'd closed fast, merged with dimness; closed fast, it hung in the darkness, distant and invisible. He lay waiting for the dark and the silence to burst open. He must hear a chair fall first. He saw the grey shapeless mass advancing toward his room, bearing the yellowed grinning face toward him. "Come on!" he shouted furiously, but only his voice clattered flatly about the house.

Nothing came that night nor the nights following. But each time he made to pull the chair away from the front door, he halted. Maybe they thought he was a fool, who'd go out and give them the chance to get in. He knew they were watching. He was sure they were in the first-floor flat opposite. If the people there felt about him as he felt about them, they would be delighted to see him beaten. Besides, the landlord owned them. No doubt he thought Nairn hadn't noticed him collecting rent from the flats.

When at last he had to go out he gathered dust in a dustpan beforehand and spread it over the sashes of the windows and on the floor in front of the exterior doors. Perhaps their footprints would betray them; the landlord's shoe-soles were imprinted in the mud of the lawn. Let them explain that away.

Nairn collected his pension and shopped on the same journey. Long before he reached home he was exhausted; the November wind tugged viciously at his wheeled basket, like a dog. His legs ached dully, and the pain left him no room to be surprised to see his bedroom crowded with figures.

The face was there, protruding from its grey mass and grinning. The other figures, four or five of them, clustered dimly behind it, staring out. Nairn was sure that they were all sneering down at him. He stared up at the window, clenching his fist on his stick, to see how long they dared taunt him.

At last he hurled himself forward, nearly falling, and wrenched open the front door. They hadn't time to descend the stairs, and nobody was halted in flight on the staircase; but his bedroom was empty. He hardly bothered to search the house and confirm that the dust on the sashes was undisturbed. He already knew that the dust before the door was untouched.

They were very clever. Too clever for their own good. They'd shown they could enter his house whenever he was out without leaving a trace. But they had overlooked one possibility: that he would never go out. Then let them try to take over his house. "Over my dead body," he shouted, sending his voice to stake his claim on every recess of the building.

They didn't believe him, didn't they? He stumped into the kitchen and grabbing the rat poison, thumped his way upstairs and dropped the packet triumphantly by the bed. Let them try to bully him out now, let them lay a finger on him, they'd see what would happen.

He spread his food more thinly on his plate. He sat nearer to a smaller fire. He tore up a letter. He lay in his cocoon and heard the restless sounds of the house tiptoeing toward him through the dark. He saw the sunken patched face grinning at him, perched atop the grey mass. He started awake and saw it at the end of his bed, hulking. But it was only the dawn, creeping into his room like a cloud of dust.

Soon he'd used up all his coal. He sprinkled a last crackle of dust from the coal-scuttle and watched the fire dimming again to somnolent pink. About to brew a cup of tea, he controlled himself. He'd only start nibbling at food if he went into the kitchen. He wasn't a rat. And he didn't need tea just to cheer himself up. He could keep warm in bed.

The first thing he saw when he entered his room was the packet of poison. He stared at it, confused. Had he intended to use that on himself? Oh no, they wouldn't drive him to that. They thought they could win that way, did they? He'd bent stiffly to pick up the poison when, reflected in the muddy sky in the window, he saw the figures behind him.

There were five of them, converging swiftly on him, a fluttering heartbeat away. He twisted about; his stick slipped on a board, and he fell. By the time he'd levered his throbbing body to its feet it was useless to pursue them; he hadn't even glimpsed which way they'd fled.

They were showing him how bold they could be, were they? His fury mounted in time with the pulsing of his bruises. Their spies had told them he had to go out now to get coal, had they? Then he wouldn't move from this room except for the calls of nature.

Nor did he. He lay thinking: if they want to get me out now they'll have to carry me, bed and all. Such big brave fellows, it should be easy for them to carry an old man downstairs. They'll see what sort of old man they're dealing with if they try.

The house creaked like a boat, the light swelled and drained away; Nairn drifted. Once he heard a sound at the front door, a metallic snap. He reached the window in time to see that it had been the postman, but after that he sat in a chair at the bedroom window, wrapped in his blankets. They would have to come through the front garden to reach the house. Even they wouldn't dare to be seen climbing over the back-yard wall.

His mouth, his throat, his stomach felt like parchment. His body seemed light as paper. They won't blow me away, he thought. The postman stared back at Nairn's window, frowning. No, they haven't got rid of me, Nairn told him. Frown all you like.

The walls of the room looked, and moved, like a stormy sky. As the December clouds sailed by Nairn felt them pulling gently at him, coaxing him out of his room. You won't get me out, he thought. Not you or anybody else. He kept his eyes on the garden gate, through which any intruders must pass; he ignored the stealthily pacing creak of the floorboards, ignored his bedroom door as it fumbled in its frame.

Once, downstairs, something fell, its hollow clatter cackling through the house. Nairn turned sharply and saw his wife lying on the bed, a grey stick-figure gasping open-mouthed but voicelessly. Only in his dreams had the doctor let him see her like that. He turned his back on the room, on the walls that rose slowly like smoke, and felt the room turn with him like a staggering roundabout. His unkempt beard crawled moistly on his cheeks. As he gripped the arms of the chair and fought dry nausea, he caught sight of figures in the flat opposite, watching him. Keep watching, he told them. You won't see me blow away.

When he saw the policeman ring the bell of the flat, when someone came to the street door and pointed to Nairn's room, he knew they thought they'd won. He was hardly surprised, as the dark sky began to hang lower like damp paper, to see the landlord drive up and join the watchers.

Nairn tried to hook the poison toward him, but his stick flew from his hand and slid under the bed, and he had to crawl to the poison. Never mind the stick. He didn't need that to beat them. He grasped the chair, fell back on the floor and the second time managed to clamber in, wrapping the blankets about himself.

The watchers were standing outside the flats, no doubt to taunt him. No, because now he could see what they'd been waiting for: an ambulance. They were striding toward the house, two ambulance-men, the policeman, a man from the flat, the landlord. Even now the landlord didn't dare tackle Nairn alone. This time he'd tricked himself, for there would be witnesses to what he'd made Nairn do. Nairn gripped the poison beneath the blanket like a concealed weapon.

They were knocking on the front door, knocking louder, battering. That's right, Nairn thought, break it down. Eventually they did so, by the sound of it. He heard their footsteps beating the boards of the hall, knocking on the house to show how hollow it was. As their tread came thudding upstairs he remembered the day the landlord had given him the key, remembered his wife running up the stairs, agog at the size of the house.

As they strode across the landing he tried to rise and face them, but his legs trembled and threw him back into the chair. To face them would give them the satisfaction of being acknowledged, anyway. Better to ignore them. He turned to the window as his bedroom door slammed back, and saw the five of them hurry into the room, spreading out to converge on him. He cupped his hand to his mouth and swallowed the poison.

There's your house, he told the landlord. You didn't believe it would be over my dead body, did you? Try and make your tenants forget this was my house now, if you can. He grinned at himself in the glass of the window, as the blackening sky reached out for him. He saw the five of them at his back, staring. He saw his own starved hair-patched face grinning through the window, above the grey shapeless swathe of the blankets.

Then the poison clamped the grin to his face.

THE DEAD MUST DIE

S SOON AS I PUSH THE DOORS OPEN I know I am in
the presence of evil. The lobby walls are white as innocence, but
the place stinks of deceit. It is crowded with lost souls who wander
aimlessly or talk to one another in low voices as though they are in
church. Sensitivity to atmospheres is yet another gift which the mass of
mankind has abandoned. I breathe a prayer and cross the threshold,
steeling myself against the unhealthy heat which refutes the pretence of
healing, the disinfectant stench bespeaking the presence of corruption,
the closeness of so much unredeemed flesh.

Except I single myself out I may pass unnoticed. I silently intone
the Twenty-third Psalm, and am halfway through the fifth verse when
I reach the lifts. I step into the nearest, thumbing the number of the
floor to which I have been called. The doors are closing when they
spring back as if possessed, and two men dressed like choirboys push
in a trolley laden with a draped form that is sucking up blood.

The doors shut, embracing the heat which now I understand is
meant to dull the senses, and the lift shudders as though revolted by
the burden it is being made to carry. But the cage rises, humming
smugly to itself, and I close my eyes and attempt not to breathe in the
stink of devil's incense that reminds me I am in a place which might be
a chapel of rest if it were not teeming with unholy corrupt life. "Aren't
you well?" one of the surpliced attendants says.

His clammy breath in my ear is like a shameful kiss. I step
back from him and shake one finger at the thing on the trolley,
mumbling "Can't stand..."

"You get used to it," he says with a laugh which I gather is
intended to express sympathy but which shows me that he sees no
deeper into me than I desire. I pray God that all his kind here will be
as gullible, as indeed their employment in this place suggests.

The lift stops, and I button the doors open, resisting the instinct
to let them close and burst the dangling sac of blood. The temptation
to perform good works in haste, at the expense of the greater good,

is one of the Adversary's subtlest tricks. As the attendants rush the trolley away the other lift releases a stream of visitors in the direction I am pointed by an arrow on the wall. I let them pass so as to move more swiftly to my goal; but when I emerge I see the way is guarded.

A uniformed woman sits like a wicked child cast out of a schoolroom at a desk in the corridor. She is playing the scribe, noting on a clipboard the names of all who pass. Some she appears to have turned back, for they are slumped against the walls, their faces sagging with the heat. I grip my case more firmly and stride forwards, silently repeating the psalm, and the woman raises first her face and then her eyebrows. "Visiting?"

"As you see."

She shakes her head like a beast that has been struck across the face. "Whom?"

"Paul Vincent."

"Relative?"

"A *caring* relative."

She lowers her gaze to her list as though my emphasis has crushed her. "Name?"

"George Saint."

Presumably this is as nothing to her, for she merely grunts and sets it down. When I make to pass, however, she emits a more bestial grunt and bars my way with a hand luxurious with fat and jewellery. "Two visitors maximum even in the private rooms. You'll have to wait."

I see myself driving a nail through her outstretched palm, and I press my free hand against my thigh. "I have come a long way to be here."

"Then I imagine you'll be staying for a while." When I refrain from contradicting her she says "You needn't be afraid you won't see Mr Vincent again. He's our star patient, getting better every day."

That is a taunt even if she is unaware the Adversary is using her voice. "When his wife wrote to me," I say loudly, "she said he was not expected to live."

"These days we can perform miracles."

Perhaps the triumph in her voice means only that she suspects I would have profited by my brother's death. I retreat for fear of venting my wrath upon her, and I am beyond the lolling visitors when the door of Paul's room opens and my niece Mary looks around for me. "Yes, it was him," she calls into the room. "Hello, Uncle —"

I interrupt before she can arouse suspicion by pronouncing my name from my former life. "Mary. I must wait until someone makes way for me."

"I'll stay out here if you want to see dad."

The guardian of the corridor turns to ensure that she doesn't reenter the room, and I wait until Mary comes forward. I have not set eyes on her for fifteen years — not since she would sit on my lap while I told her about Our Lord — and if I had any doubts about my mission they vanish at the sight of her. She is paler and thinner than she ought to be, and I believe I glimpse a knowing look in her eyes before she says "Dad will be pleased you've come to see him."

I detect no guile in this, and pray that knowingness is only a façade which she feels bound to present to the world. "I hope he can find it in his heart to welcome me."

"He says it's up to the individual what they believe."

For a moment I assume she is defending her father out of misplaced loyalty, and then I grasp that she thinks I was apologising for my faith, though she has no idea of its strength. I must surmise that she is not beyond redemption, however insidious are the influences which surround her. When she says "I'll wait here" I stride past the desk of the false scribe, repeating the fourth verse of the psalm under my breath, and enter the room.

My brother is lying in a bed, his eyes upturned to Heaven. His wife Penelope sits beside him, holding his hand. Their stillness almost persuades me that I am not needed here, and I succumb to a craven feeling of relief. Then my brother's head wavers up from the pillow, and his eyes, which are watery and veinous, light up with a blasphemous parody of intelligence and life. "Thomas," he whispers.

I want to proclaim my outrage with all my voice, but instead I advance to the foot of the bed and gaze solemnly at him. That appears to satisfy him, and his head sinks back. "Thank you for coming, Thomas," says his wife.

Her gratitude is as bogus as everything else in this evil chamber. She must have felt bound to contact me when my brother was at death's door. His eyes close, and he expels a long slow breath. "He waited for you," Penelope tells me.

Though that sounds as if she is holding me responsible for the unnatural prolongation of his life, I am filled with a hope that it has come to an end. His wide pasty face has collapsed as though it is no longer anything but a mask, and he has folded his hands on his chest. Then his hands stir, betraying their mockery of piety, as his chest rises and falls. He is dead, yet he breathes. He has joined the Undead.

How can God's daylight allow such a thing to be? When I attempt to recall how long it has been since I last saw the sun, it seems to me that the sky has been overcast for weeks before I was called to my brother. And the sun and the air were darkened by reason of the smoke of the pit, and there is no sunlight to combat the room's Godless light, which celebrates the flush of my brother's cheeks that gives him the appearance of a whore rouged with the blood of her victims. I turn away in revulsion and confront his wife, who says "I didn't know if you would come. I wasn't even sure we had your right address."

Nor have they, God be thanked. "I felt I had to," I confess.

"You're still born again, then. You're still of the same mind."

"We are all of His mind, however we regard ourselves. There is no birth nor death but proceeds from Him."

At least she has the grace to look embarrassed, though only because in these faithless days God is the dirtiest of words. "We've become quite friendly with the Beynons," she says defensively. "The donor's family."

The heat and stink coagulate in my throat, and for some seconds I cannot swallow for the thought of my brother with part of a corpse sewn up inside him. "Have you visited the grave?" I croak.

"Whose?"

"What you call the donor."

"Why, no," she says as though it is I who am in the wrong. "We don't want to intrude."

"Where is he buried?"

"She. Kidneys don't have a sex, you know. She's in the churchyard near where you used to have your flat."

"A short walk from where I am staying. If there is no objection I shall pay my respects."

"I expect you'll do whatever you think is right," she says in a tone which suggests I ought to be ashamed of doing so. "I hope you don't mind staying in a hotel, by the way. I've my hands full getting the house ready for Paul to come home."

She must take me for a fool if she imagines I assume that otherwise I would be welcome in her house when everything about myself is a reproach. I succeed in sounding casual. "When is that to be?"

"The doctors say Sunday."

The word should choke them. "I shall be in church."

"Come over afterwards to say goodbye to Paul if you have time."

She clearly hopes the opposite, and I may let her think her wish is granted. Sometimes a venial sin is justified in the prosecution of His work. "I have troubled you enough for the nonce," I tell her. "Beynon, you said. What Christian name?"

She seems reluctant to answer, but perhaps she senses that I am prepared to demand the information of my brother, for she replies "Bernadette."

It is indeed Christian — the name of the saint to whom His Blessed Mother chose to appear — which makes the mutilation yet more blasphemous. "May God watch over you and Paul," I curse, and retreat into the corridor.

Only Mary and the guard remain. The guard is studying her clipboard as though it holds a sacred text, while Mary leans against the wall. As I approach, her eyes open and her pale undernourished face attempts to counterfeit a smile. "How was dad?"

I needn't lie. "I am more concerned with how you are, Mary."

"I'm all right. I'm fine," she says, failing to conceal her evasiveness.

I raise my case against my chest so that neither she nor the guard can see what I am carrying, and reach in. "Will you wear this to please me?" I say, and hand Mary the twin of the cross which I never remove.

She hesitates, and I feel as if the Adversary has seized me by the throat. If she is unable to take hold of the cross I shall know she is already a victim of the Undead. Then she holds out a hand palm upwards and suffers me to lay the cross on it. "It's a bit heavy," she complains.

The childishness of her protest convinces me that she is still fundamentally innocent, and I offer up a silent prayer of thanks. "Wear it always," I exhort her. "If anyone tries to dissuade you, do not hesitate to contact me."

"I like wearing pretty things."

I am taken unawares by a wave of grief for her. "I'll buy you a pretty cross if you promise to wear this one at night until I do, and say your prayers."

"Do I really have to, Unc —"

I interrupt her, though the guard appears to be trying not to overhear, by taking the cross from her hand and touching it to her lips before lifting the cord over her head. "Wear it until you get home at least, for His sake."

She looks rebellious, as children can be. I walk quickly to the lifts and step into the nearest before she has time to argue. Perhaps if my brother or his wife attempts to influence her not to wear the cross she will turn her rebelliousness against them. I say another prayer for her as I pass through the lobby and out of that place.

As I entered it had seemed an anteroom to Hell, but now I find it little different from its surroundings. In less time than it takes me to repeat the psalm I am in the shadow of chemical factories discharging their poisons into a sky the colour of sin. Behind them, on the bank of a filthy river, chimneys spout flames that dance and struggle, and I think of machines that begin to consume souls at the hour of death. Opposite the tract of factories gaunt terraces like cell-blocks extending as far as the eye can see face one another across pinched streets with narrow pavements unrelieved except by tainted plots of grass. Broken glass surrounds every streetlamp, and I see that the denizens of these streets abhor the light. How many of them may be Undead, freed by the shrouding of the sun to walk by day?

It takes me half an hour's unbroken march to come in sight of the hotel near the factories. I comfort myself by repeating the psalm aloud, and whenever anyone approaches within earshot they pass by on the other side. I raise my voice to let them know they have betrayed themselves. Their dull self-absorbed faces are pale as tissue paper — a tissue of lies.

A few cheap shops huddle opposite the hotel, and I buy vegetables from a greengrocer whose hands are calloused with toil and who wears a small cross at her throat. As I enter the hotel's dim and dismal hall, where the walls are a mass of advertisements for gluttony and other forms of self-indulgence, the landlady accosts me. "I'm afraid cooking isn't allowed in the rooms, Mr Saint," she says, slowly wringing her colourless hands in a pretence of regret.

"Nor do I propose it, Mrs Trollope."

"And I still have to charge for meals even if you don't take them."

"We must all be guided by our consciences, Mrs *Trollope*." Since she has no answer to this I say "If I may have my key I need trouble you no further."

She thrusts at me the cudgel to which the key is attached, and I climb the shabby stairs to my cheerless room, which smells of must and stale smoke and nights of solitary lechery. I hang my overcoat in the nondescript wardrobe and fall to my knees between the sink and the bed. When I feel I have prayed out the evils of the day I eat half a cabbage and two raw potatoes, savouring the taste of God's earth and the gritting of it between my teeth. The vegetables are as wholesome as can be expected in this place, and at least they were sold to me by a believer. Anything that is served in the hotel will have been touched by blood.

Night has fallen. The factories howl and glare with evil light. Hordes who have squandered their day in the factories shuffle into the narrow streets as if their shadows are dragging them home, while their neighbours swarm to take their places in the workshops of pollution. Then the land is quiet until the young begin to prowl, quaffing wine and smashing bottles in the roadways, if indeed the wine has not undergone some sacrilegious transubstantiation. After a time the corpse-lights of the factories show only lost souls fleeing after their shadows through a lurid icy rain, and I have prayed enough that I crave sleep.

I use the communal bathroom, which is full of warm fog and a suggestive smell of perfumed soap, and then I set about defending my room. I rub garlic around the inside of the door and windows, and employ the cloves to plug the taps and the sink. I hang a cross above the bed and another at its foot, and lay a cross on the frayed carpet at each side. Though thus protected, I am reluctant to switch off the lamp while I sense the land is teeming with corruption. Even the miserly light of the room seems preferable to the unholy glow outside the faded curtains. I kneel to recite Psalm 130, pummelling my breasts and temples as I raise my voice, and when I feel Him answer me in my depths I lay me down to sleep.

But the Adversary has sent his minions to beset me. As I cried out my left-hand neighbour buffeted the wall in a vain attempt to interrupt my supplication, and now I hear Mrs Trollope's voice, first beneath my window and then much closer. I think that she has scaled the outer wall, as the Undead are known to do, until I realise that she is at my door. "I hope you won't be keeping that light on much longer, Mr Saint," she says.

I hold my peace, hoping that she will conclude I am not to be awakened by trifles. Then she begins to smite the door with a clumsiness which suggests to me that she is the worse, if such is possible, for drink. "I know you're in there, Mr Saint," she bawls. "Put that light out or I'll put you out."

When I tire of her blustering I grasp the cord above the bed. As I pull it, darkness descends like the outpouring of a cloaca. A muffled discussion ensues in the corridor outside my room; no doubt the Adversary's minions are plotting further ways to disturb me. Let them seek to enter — they will find me armed. But nothing transpires except the closing of several doors, and so I lie on my back and take a cross in each hand.

In the fullness of time I slumber, as best I can while maintaining a vigil over my hands for fear that the Adversary may endeavour to loosen their grasp and trick them into repudiating the cross. When the sky begins to pale with the dawn I rise and pray that the sun may sear away the pall which darkens the land. Hours later only an enfeebled glow has seeped through the shroud, which I see is the colour of the corpse-lights, as though some poisonous exhalation has grown solid overnight to snuff out the day.

I venture to the bathroom in order to do the penance of voiding myself, then I scour my body at the sink in my room. I plan to spend the greater portion of the day in prayer. The Adversary will have none of this, however. I have scarcely fallen to my knees when he sends his trollop to besiege me. "I want a word with you, Mr Saint," she shouts.

"Have it, then."

"I can't hear you. I won't talk through a door."

"I thought that was a favourite pastime of yours," I say, and fling the door open. "Now you see me, madam."

I have revealed only my right-hand side when she falls back and shields her eyes like Eve after eating the apple. "For God's sake, Mr Saint, cover yourself up."

"We are all naked before Him." Smirking at her hypocrisy, I hold a cross in front of myself. "Now I am as clothed as any man need be."

She stays out of sight and raises her voice. "I'm afraid I must ask you to leave at once."

"May I ask who requires it of you?"

She stamps her foot, shaking the floor. "Let me remind you this is my house."

"It's worthy of your name."

"I don't know what this room smells of, but I want it out, and you. I've had complaints about the row you made all night, snoring and carrying on like I don't know what."

"Why, madam, I took you as my model."

She stamps so hard that the crosses on the floor spring up. "I'm giving you ten minutes to pay up and get out and then I'm calling the police."

So the scheme is to have me cast out before I can fulfil my mission. It would be the work of moments to pursue her and cut her down, but how many of her creatures might I have to put an end to, thereby perhaps drawing unwelcome attention to myself? Shall I abase myself and plead to be allowed to stay two further nights? The notion sticks in my gullet, and then I know that He has not forsaken me, for all at once I see where I may take refuge.

201

My cases are packed in five minutes, and in less than ten I am downstairs, jangling the bell of ill repute which stands on the counter. When Mrs Trollope pokes her face through the hole in the wall above it I cast my coins before her. "I think you will find that fits the bill."

"Haven't you any notes?"

"I thought silver more appropriate. Please count it."

She glowers and with a Jew's gesture scoops the coins together so as to pick them up with both thumbs and forefingers and drop them onto two piles. "That seems to be right," she grudgingly admits.

Can she really not have noticed there are thirty coins? "Wholly," I assure her, and depart out of that house, shaking off the dust of my feet.

The railway station where I arrived is five minutes' forced march distant, up a steep hill between extravagant windows choked with finery. The flesh of the crowds around me seems no less discoloured and artificial than that of the cheap sculptures modelling luxury in the stores which steep the pavements in alluring light. In the station the voice of a false oracle echoes through the vault, sending the lost fleeing hither and thither. As I slide my suitcase into a locker I am reminded of the ungodly practice of cremation. The thought fuels my anger as I set out on the first stage of my task.

The churchyard crowns a hill ribbed with mean streets. While the spire still points to Heaven, many of the gravestones have been overturned, perhaps by the revels of the Undead. Stone angels display mutilated wrists, as thieves in heathen countries do, so that I wonder if this may be yet another symptom of the undermining of our Christian ways by the influx of the heathen. Let it never be forgotten that the Undead originated in lands less Christian than ours.

A few mourners, if that is what they are, loiter morosely near wreaths, and a pair of silent workmen are spading out a grave. Rather than draw attention to myself by enquiring of the labourers where I should go I play the aimless visitor, wandering the stone rows, at whose junctions wire baskets are piled with empty bottles and withered flowers. I am halfway across the churchyard when a funeral arrives at the new grave, and I watch the mourners weep more copiously than is Christian. By the time I reach my goal, a family grave near the top of the churchyard, a vicious wind has cleared the place except for myself.

The Beynon plot is marked by a granite obelisk. Gilded names and dates are etched on the shaft, and the lowest name is Bernadette. As I would expect of a family which allowed her helpless body to be violated, no prayer has been inscribed on her behalf. Her yearning to be hallowed is as clear to me as though she is murmuring a plea in my ear. I kick the pharisaical wreath away from the obelisk and grind the flowers underfoot before falling to my knees on her mound. "The Day of Judgment shall find thee whole," I vow, and immediately I sense her gratitude. I grub her mound open with my hands and bury a cross as deep as I can to keep her safe.

I stay at prayer until the hellish lights of the town begin to waken; then I make for the church. I know that tonight the Undead must exert all their powers against me. I pass through the porch and open my flask to collect holy water from the font, and my heart quails within me. The church is starkly furnished with thin pews and an altar. How shall I go unnoticed when the priest locks the church for the night?

As I stopper the flask I hear footsteps on the gravel path outside the porch. I run to the sole refuge the place affords and crouch behind the altar. The inner door opens, and footsteps approach. Should I not declare myself and my mission, and crave sanctuary against the Undead? If the priest doubts my mission he is no priest, and I must strike him down before the altar he has desecrated. Yet I have little stomach for such an act in God's house, and breathe a prayer as the footsteps halt at the altar.

In a very few minutes the priest, having presumably breathed a perfunctory prayer, retreats along the aisle; then I hear him stop at the font and mutter what sounds all too like profanity. How can a man of the cloth let slip such a word, above all in church? I prepare to follow him and cut him down like the fig tree that beareth no fruit but cumbereth the ground. But darkness falls inside the church, the inner door closes, and I hear the false priest lock the outer door.

At once the church is no longer dark. A faint evil glow rises from the town, transforming the saints in the window above me into swarthy heathens and encrusting the pews with a dimness that appears to crawl. I should be safest where I am, guarded by the altar. I grasp two crosses and lie down on stone with my case for a pillow, and try to pray myself to sleep in order to be ready for the morrow's task. Out of the depths have I cr

A crash of glass! I leap up, brandishing the crosses, and stumble against the altar. The sainted window is intact. I have slumbered; was the sound only in my dream? No, for there comes an outburst of bestial yelling beyond the window, and the thump of gravestones on the earth. The Undead are abroad to trouble my sleep.

When I begin to pronounce an exorcism with all my voice the clamour falters momentarily, then redoubles. The Undead dance and jeer while their hands, if hands they are, belabour the wall of the church. More glass shatters, and I replace the cross in my right hand with my blade. If anything enters the building I shall shed its foul gore.

Perhaps the church is secure against evil, however, because the Undead content themselves with lupine baying in a vain bid to blot out my exorcism. When I grow so hoarse that I can barely whisper, their uproar subsides. I hear them shambling away, toppling gravestones as perhaps they seep back into their graves. I am seized by a fit of coughing, and when at last I am able to contain myself I strain my ears, distrusting the silence. Much later I sink to the floor behind the alt

"Who's there? Is someone there?"

The voice is in the church. The door has been unlocked. I have slept longer than I meant to, until a snore wakened me. Too late I understand that the Undead have achieved their purpose after all. I try to remain absolutely still, praying silently that I need not use my blade, as the priest comes up the aisle. He is almost at the altar — he has only to lean over it to see me. Then he turns on his heel and trots away, and I hear him on the gravel that surrounds the church.

I drop the blade into my case as I run on tiptoe to the porch. The priest has yet to reappear around the building; he must be searching among the graves beyond the far end of the church for the sleeper he overheard. I dart over the grass and crouch behind an angel, only to be overwhelmed by the sense that I am in a position for my bowels to betray me. I hear the priest marching over the gravel, muttering and rubbing his hands together, having presumably righted the gravestones. As he arrives at the porch, a loud and lengthy noisome wind escapes me. The pollution of the land must have inured him, for without hesitation he reenters the church.

I compose myself and follow him. I mean to spend my time in prayer and fasting until I must be about my mission. The priest is replenishing the font, and gives me a sharp glance. "God be with you," I bid him as I cross myself.

Perhaps he recognises that I feel it to be more appropriate that I should wish him this than the reverse; he can hardly bring himself to respond "And with you." I make my way to the foremost pew and kneel, scorning the luxury of the kneeler. I shall pray silently until the priest says Mass, and th

Something is thrust between my ribs. The Undead have invaded the church and turned my weapons against me. "Retro me, Satanas!" I scream, and find myself surrounded by churchgoers, one of whom has elbowed me. All of them, and the priest in the pulpit, are staring at me. If his sermon and his celebration of the Mass had been sincere I would not have slumbered. "Pray continue," I say with a wave of my hand.

When he tires of striving to force me to avert my gaze he recommences prating to the congregation on the subjects of forgiveness and tolerance. In this land there is far too much of both, and almost all of it misdirected. I keep myself awake by gripping crosses so that their corners dig into my palms, though the false priest appears to frown on crosses. The Mass ends and the congregation straggles out while I remain on my knees. I have by no means done praying when the priest sidles up to me. "Are you in need of help, my son?"

"Psalm Twenty-eight, verse seven."

"I'm sorry, I'm not too familiar —"

"The Lord is my strength and my shield. My heart trusted in him, and I am helped."

He scowls at the rebuff or at having revealed his ignorance, and stalks off to gather prayer-books; then he loiters about the church until I finish praying, although I continue until it is almost dark. It seems that, like the landlady, he is being used to drive me out and rob me of a day's grace, and there are moments when I have to struggle to contain my wrath. When at last I succeed in relaxing my grip on the crosses and return them to my case I perform a solemn obeisance before the altar; then I glare so fiercely at the priest that he feigns a sudden interest in the contents of a hymnal as I stride out of the church.

The grubby light is draining into the vile landscape. As I make my way downhill through the blackened furtive terraces the tethered flames jerk above the soiled roofs, and I see I am descending into Hell. The sight of a telephone box diverts me along a terrace whose windows are shrouded with net curtains like the dusty webs of a dozen or more enormous spiders. The box is derelict; holes gape where its instrument and light should be. No doubt the denizens of the land are anxious to prevent anyone less irredeemable than themselves from communicating with the outside world, though surely I saw telephones in use when I arrived at the railway station.

As I enter its vault the voice of the oracle proclaims the name of the town where I live. This is so transparently intended as a temptation that I scoff aloud. Few are there to hear me, and most of them are supine on benches after some debauch. I walk to the nearest telephone and dial the number of my brother's house before turning my back to the wall.

The bell ceases its measured tolling. "Vincent," says Paul's wife.

"It is I."

"Oh, yes," she says discouragingly. "Calling to say goodbye?"

"That is what I understand you wanted me to do."

"Did I? Paul's home, but he's in bed resting. I'll tell him you rang."

"Perhaps," I suggest after mouthing a prayer, "I could say goodbye to Mary."

"She isn't here. She's at a friend's, watching videos."

My prayer is answered. I need not wait until tomorrow, when Mary will be at college. Nevertheless Penelope's tone is too defiant for me to allow it to pass unreproved. "On a Sunday?" I rebuke her.

"She's been working hard all day helping me to get the house ready for her father."

"Working on the Sabbath is a poor excuse for self-indulgence," I declare, and am abruptly overwhelmed by the panic I experienced on Mary's behalf at the hospital. "Besides, when I last saw her she hardly looked fit for work."

"I suppose you think that's funny."

"I assure you I am not smiling."

"Do you ever?" Penelope says, and with a sudden weariness which I suspect is counterfeit: "This sort of conversation's why I'm glad Paul's in bed. I don't want you upsetting him, or Mary either."

"I fail to see how one can upset somebody by enquiring after their health."

"You know perfectly well what I mean. Or if you don't I'll tell you, because I'm proud of her. She's become a lot more responsible since she nearly lost her father. When you saw her she'd just given a pint of blood."

I shudder so violently that I almost kick my case away, and my knees scrape together. Even worse than the revelation is my sense that I ought to have known — that only my fears on Mary's behalf had prevented me from realising the Undead were already battening on her. I sway against the wall, and the oracle names my home again. "It sounds as if it's time to go," Penelope says in my ear.

If there is one thing the Father of Lies can be trusted sooner or later to do, it is to contradict himself. The attempt to lure me home has rebounded on my enemies. I hang up the receiver as a response to her and snatching my case, leave the station at a run.

My brother's house is hidden among the terraces opposite the factories. As I stride up the street which leads to it, my shadow lengthens ahead of me. I will not allow myself to feel that it is leading me into darkness; rather am I forcing it onwards between windows black as the pit or flickering with light from screens around which pallid faces cluster. Some of the faces rise as though from feeding and gaze dead-eyed at me. Each step I take brings me closer to a black panic which, it appears, I can fend off only by outrunning it. I force myself to slow down and intone the psalms until their rhythm imparts discipline to my walk.

My brother lives in our parents' old house. It, and the square of which it is a part, seemed like a haven to me until I began to perceive the errors of my life. Now I see it is an unhallowed sepulchre concealed deep in a monstrous graveyard. I unlatch the gate and venture past the willow into the garden, where the cloying scent of flowers cannot disguise the tell-tale smell of turned earth. I have taken out my largest cross, and I hammer with it on the front door.

In a moment my brother's voice, feeble when it should be mute, calls out "Who's that, love?"

"I'll see. You rest," Penelope says beyond the door. At once it is flung open, and her frown multiplies at the sight of me. "I thought you —"

"Is Mary home yet?"

"No, I told you —"

I need hear no more. I raise the cross above my head. If I had any doubts, the fear which immediately fills her eyes would show me what she is. I bring the cross down with all my force, and one arm of it strikes her left temple, which splinters and begins to leak. A second blow shatters her throat as she attempts to cry out. She is already falling to her knees like a slaughtered beast, making obeisance too late, and I slam the door as I step into the hall. I am raising the cross to deliver a final blow when her eyes go out, and she topples over backwards, still kneeling, so that I hear her knees creak and then snap like pistol shots. If she were alive I am sure she would scream.

I stoop to wipe the bloodied cross on her breast, and then I hear the voice of my dead brother. "Penelope? Penelope?"

The sound infects me with terror, but also rekindles my wrath. As I straighten my back I repeat the Twenty-third Psalm aloud. I have just reached the foot of the stairs when my brother's walking corpse gropes out of his room and advances to the banister on legs that should no longer move. Grotesquely, it is wearing pyjamas instead of a shroud. "Thomas, what are you —" it says in a voice like a wind in a churchyard, and its eyes focus, though they must be rotting from within, on what is left of Paul's wife. "My God, what's happened to — Thomas, what have you —"

I am not interrupting. Its brain must be rotting too, and able to recall only fragments of living speech. The thing is no longer my brother, although may I be right to have heard a plea when it took His name in vain? "God help you, Paul, if you can understand me. I'll save you," I cry, and spring up the stairs.

The suffused remains of its eyes turn to me as if they can hardly focus. I hope it will welcome the end, or else I expect it to recoil before the advance of the cross in my hand. The Adversary has clouded my thoughts, so that I am unprepared when the face of the thing that was once my brother darkens as though all the blood it has consumed is rushing to its brain, and it flies at me, snarling like a wild beast, seeking whom it may devour.

My case is open. I drop it beside me on the stair and snatch out the flask of holy water. I barely have time to unscrew the cap when the Undead thing is upon me. I retreat a step and dash holy water into its eyes. It staggers, moaning, and falls on its back on the stairs. Before it can recover I seize my blade from the case and plunge the point deep between the thing's ribs.

The stolen blood gushes high as though grateful for release. I lean all my weight on the blade, and feel it penetrate the stair beneath as the Undead corpse writhes like an impaled insect, fluttering its hands. When at last it ceases moving I withdraw the blade and hammer the stake in its place, hearing ribs splinter.

The foul but necessary work is not yet done. I unbutton the thing's jacket and cutting open the flesh beneath the lower ribs, widen the incision with my hands. By digging with the blade I am able to lay bare the kidneys. One is slightly smaller, and my instincts tell me this belongs to the victim of the Undead. I hack it free and prise it out of its raw nest, and pray over it before wrapping it in the bag which contained the potatoes. I place the bag in my case and trudge downstairs, bearing the cross before me.

I am almost at the front door when I catch sight of the directory beside the telephone. I leave my gory fingerprints on the page that lists Blood. Long before the prints can be identified my task will be done. The key to a mortice lock protrudes from a keyhole inside the front door, and I lock the door behind me as I leave, then I break off the shaft of the key in the lock. Now Mary must seek help with entering the house, and I pray she will not be the first to see how my brother and his wife have been redeemed. I should like to be with her when she sees them, but there is still much to do. In the morning I shall ask the greengrocer where I can buy a pretty cross to have sent to my niece.

My shadow follows me out of the dead terraces and turns ahead of me. It leads me past the station and uphill to the church. It seems to me that the shadow is my own black soul, urging me to redeem it with further good works. For the moment the churchyard is silent; the Undead must be elsewhere. I make my way swiftly to the Beynon grave and withdrawing the cross from the mound, place the stolen organ in the hole before covering it with the cross and with earth.

Now I shall keep watch here until the morning. I could go now and destroy the house of vampirism, but I mean to strike down those who administer this iniquity. Whatsoever soul it shall be that eateth any manner of blood, even that soul shall be cut off. The victims such as Mary I shall spare, and the town of the Undead shall rise up against me, nor shall I escape. Let my exploit and my martyrdom act as a sign to the righteous, that they may destroy the false healers, the vampires whose uniforms mock sanctity, the halls of intensive care which are factories of mutilation. I am not alone. Our time has come.

A SIDE OF THE SEA

I'M AMONG THE FIRST TO USE THE TOILET, one of two wheeled sheds parked at the edge of a segment of concrete, but it takes the two coachloads of passengers so long that I need to join the queue again. Beyond the hedge behind the toilets, fields and a few lonely trees turn greener as the sky fills with black clouds. Lorries rush down the slope into the dip in the road and out again with a sound like waves. The plumbing sounds like waves too when at last the queue leads me back into the shed, and I'm just splashing the urinal when I seem to hear the building engulfed by the sea. People scream, but I feel safe until I venture to the exit and see it's a cloudburst so fierce that spikes of rain are leaping off the concrete. Passengers holding coats over their heads dash to the nearest vehicle, the coach I'm supposed to be on, and I can see that long before they all finish clambering up the steps I'll be drenched. I sprint to the further coach and drag myself up the steps beside the driver's seat while trying to wipe my drowned spectacles on my jacket. "Someone took my seat," I say for the benefit of anyone who ought to be informed.

"You weren't on this coach," says a blur.

"That's what I mean. Someone from this one stole my place."

The downpour roars on the metal roof, and I'm about to protest "You wouldn't make me go out in that" when the blur retreats along the aisle and knocks on the rear window. Presumably it uses signs to tell someone on my coach that they'll exchange passengers at the next stop, because it calls "Find yourself a seat" to me.

I put on my spectacles, though the lenses are still wet. Beneath the racks laden with swimming costumes wrapped in beach towels, passengers are rubbing their hair dry and turning the windows greyer with every breath. Someone near the back is trying to lead a chorus of "We're going to the sea, sea, sea" without much success. The lenses of my spectacles are blurring, transforming the passengers into statues sitting underwater, all of them gazing blankly at me. I can't see where I'm to sit until a hand begins to wave extravagantly halfway down the coach. "Here," the owner of the hand shouts. "Here, my dear."

He's wearing a flowery shirt and shorts which are even more florid. His clothes are pasted to him by the rain, so that they resemble wallpaper. He has a large round face which seems to be about to sink into its plumpness, and hands so fat they have dimples for knuckles, and a stomach which rests on the tops of his thighs. As I sit down he squeezes himself against the window to make room. I rub my spectacles to rid them of fog and spots of dried rain, and as I hook them over my ears my seat-mate cranes his head around to me. "What's the game?" he says.

The coach lurches forward, and the person who went to the rear window — a grey-suited woman with severely restrained black hair — nods curtly at me as she returns to her seat by the driver. If she's in charge of the day trip, surely she oughtn't to ignore what I've just been asked. "What do you mean?" I say loudly, hoping that will bring her.

"Name. Name of the game. Both the same. Your name, your game."

It takes me longer to understand than it takes my neighbour to say all this, and longer still to decide if responding is advisable. Maybe an answer is all he requires, and then he won't bother me. "Ah, you want my name. It's Henry."

"Henry." He swings his head back and forth, and I think he's contradicting me until I realise he's looking for something. He focuses on the befogged window across the aisle with an expression of relief. "Can't see the scen'ry," he crows. "Henry who? Henry what else too?"

I don't see why he should demand my surname, and so I tell him the first I can think of which might shut him up. "Hancock."

"Hancock goes to Bangkok," he cries at once.

I find his triumph so annoying that although I was planning to keep quiet in the hope that he would, I say "No, I want to see the sea."

"See the sea," he repeats, giving me a plump nudge as if I meant to imitate his rhyming. "Like me. You'll be like me."

"Hush for a bit now, Algernon," says my neighbour across the aisle, a woman who is knitting into a large open handbag. "We don't want you filling up Henry's head until he's got no room to think."

"Shush and hush. Don't gush. Crush your rush." My seat-mate's voice dwindles with each word. "Algernon. Algy. Alg," he murmurs almost inaudibly, then he all but shouts at me "Al's your pal."

"Of course you are," the woman soothes him, her knitting clicking quicker. "Give the glass a wipe now and see what you can see."

She gazes at him until he rubs the window with his hairy forearm, then she turns to me. Her gleaming eyes are very pale. "And what do you think of all this rain?"

My answer seems to be important to her. She raises her eyebrows, crinkling her papery forehead below her hair, which looks like curled shavings of tin. "It's a bit wet," I offer.

"That's how God made it. It wouldn't be rain if it was dry." I smile and shrug in agreement, but apparently that isn't enough for her. "You can see that, can't you?" she says, halting her needles.

"I'm sure you're right."

"It isn't a question of what I am." Her eyebrows are starting to tremble from being held high. "It makes the sea, you might want to remember. Without the rain we'd all be living in the desert. We'd be eating dates for breakfast and wearing dish-cloths on our heads and sitting on camels instead of a coach."

"There's that," I say to placate her.

She scrutinises my face before she lets her eyebrows down and recommences knitting. I'm watching the road beyond the wide sweeps of the windscreen wipers, though all I can see are lights like half-eaten strawberry sweets, when she says "Do you think it'll still be raining when we get to the beach?"

"I don't know."

"But is that what you *think*, what you're *thinking*?"

"I suppose I am."

"I know you are," she says in the soothing tone she used on Algernon. "Shall we see what we can do about it?"

"About my thinking?"

She drops the shapeless knitting into her handbag and wags a finger at me. "Henry," she rebukes me. "About the rain."

"Not much, I should think."

"Never let yourself despair, Henry. Just put your hands together."

I assume that's a generalised recommendation until she clasps her hands together and gazes unblinking at mine. "Henry, Henry, Henry," she says.

I'm afraid that if she keeps that up she'll provoke my seat-mate into rhyming, and so I fold my hands. Raising her gaze towards the drumming on the roof, she says "Heavenly Father..."

I glare piously at my knuckles, but that doesn't satisfy her. "Heavenly Father," she repeats slowly and firmly, raising her eyebrows at me.

"Heavenly Father," I mouth.

"Heavenly Father, we thank Thee for the sun that Thou sendest after the rain."

I'm steeling myself in case Algernon settles on a word of hers, but it's her neighbour, a bony man with a wedge-shaped face that looks as though it was lengthened by someone tugging its knob of a chin, who responds. "Heheavenly Fahatheher," he says, "wehe thahank Thehee fohor teehee suhun thahat Thououow sehehehendest ahafteherherher teehee raihaihain."

He has folded his hands on his chest and rolled his eyes up so that only the whites are visible, shivering in their sockets, and the woman seems to be as unsure as I am whether he is doing his best to pray. "If it be Thy will," she says more loudly, "let it be sunny at the beach."

"Ihif ihit behe Thyhy wihihill, lehet ihihit be, hehe, hehe, *suhuhuhunny* ahat thehe be, hehe, heheach."

His lips are twitching. He could be struggling either to pray or not to grin. At least he has drawn the woman's attention away from me, and I no longer bother to mouth. "We ask Thee on behalf of Thy child Henry," she bellows, "that the weather forecasters may have read Thy signs aright."

Her words might let me feel protected if it weren't for the prospect of hearing her neighbour turn my name into something else. As he says "Wehe ahahask" I flex my fingers, preparing to stick them in my ears, whatever the woman will think of me for doing so. Just then, as if I've inadvertently betrayed my thoughts, someone behind me touches my shoulder.

Pain flares in my skull as I twist around. The man standing in the aisle is resting his other hand on the head-rest of my seat. His fingers must have snagged my hair, though he appears not to have noticed. His ruddy big-boned mug has protruding ears for handles. "I'd like to pray if you want to change places," he says.

I shove myself to my feet as the coach speeds downhill. The seat he has vacated is four rows further back. While I stumble towards it, clutching at head-rests, everyone in the intervening seats watches me. Hedges stream by like smoke beyond the obscured windows, and the greyness by which the passengers are framed puts me in mind of a photograph. For some reason that idea disturbs me, but once I reach the seat I feel safer.

My new neighbour is a small neat woman with cropped red hair who is hugging a large canvas tote bag. I return her glancing smile as I sink onto the seat. Through the uproar of the downpour I hear prayers like a battle of words which the knitting woman and her new ally are winning. The sound of rain begins to fade, and the praying soars triumphantly before subsiding. In the relative quiet I'm able to hear the voice of the passenger next to the window across the aisle, a moon-faced man with the left half of his scalp combed flat, the right half bristling. "Smudge Cottages," he's muttering. "Blob Hill."

His seat-mate, a squat man who is either examining his own bitten fingers or counting on them, grunts and tries to squash himself smaller. "Blotch Woods," the moon-faced man declares, "Fog Field, Splosh Road," and leans forward to look at me for agreement. Just in time I realise that he's naming everything he sees through the clouded windows, and I nod and grin until he sits back. I turn away with the grin stuck to my face, and my seat-mate assumes it's aimed at her, because she responds with the twin of her earlier smile. "Best to keep your mind occupied on a trip like this," she says.

"I suppose."

"Oh, I think so."

I take it she's referring to the moon-faced man until she claps her hands and says "So what shall we do?"

I struggle to come up with a suggestion before she does, but my mind has grown as foggy as the windows. "I know," she says, "we'll show each other our things."

"Things. Ah, well, I —"

She slaps my knee playfully and gives me the smile. "Things we take with us wherever we go, silly. What did you think I meant? Here, I'll show you what I have in mind."

She lifts her bag and lowers her face, and I'm reminded of a horse feeding. She twirls the bag by its handles and cocks her head, then snatches out a photograph. "Sea," she says.

It isn't the sea at all. It's a bedroom so tidy it might never have been slept in. Either a painting of blue sky or a mirror faces a window across the single bed, and a framed square of perfectly symmetrical embroidery hangs above the headboard. Of course she said "See" — she didn't try to trick me. "Well, there you are," I say, handing back the photograph.

"Now you have to show me one or pay a forfeit."

Though she flashes the smile, a pain seems to tug at my skull. I don't like the sound of the game she has started to play; I only have one photograph. I'm suddenly too nervous to be able to resist dragging my wallet from my inside pocket and taking out the photograph.

"That's nice. Your daughter. What's her name?"

I shake my aching head. "Not my daughter."

"Your wife?"

Shaking makes the ache worse. "My mother."

"That's even nicer." The smile must have a variety of meanings, because the woman adds through it "You should have brought her to the seaside instead of just a photograph."

"She can't get about any more."

"So you look after her like a good boy, I can tell. And someone's taken over while you give yourself a day off."

I keep my head still in the hope that the ache will fade. "Did she use to take you to the sea?" the woman wants to know.

The questions are causing the ache; they feel like a teacher pulling my hair. "No, we never went too far," I say, though talking

216

has begun to hurt as well. "She used to say I didn't need holidays when I had her."

"And was she right?"

When I nod as hard as I dare the woman says "Shall I tell you what else I think?"

"I expect so."

"I think going to the seaside will be even more of an adventure at your age."

I think so too, and her saying "Look, the sun's coming out for you" begins to make me feel safe. Then she says "I'll just show you one more of my things and then I'll let you off."

She spends some time rummaging in her bag. It's this business with photographs that has made me nervous, because I'm growing surer that I've seen a picture somewhere of the people on the coach. When she hands me a photograph I'm afraid this might be the one, but it's another picture of her bedroom. Clothes — underwear and scarves and shoes — cover the bed and the floor. There's a pair of everything, arranged so that the photograph is divided into two identical halves. Down the centre of the bed are six bras, their cups on either side of the dividing line; three pairs are face down, three face up. "What do you say to that?" the woman urges me.

I can't seem to grasp whether the bras with their tips pointing up or those showing their insides represent more of an absence. "Very neat," I manage to respond.

She gives me a smile as quick as the movement with which she snatches the photograph, and I don't like to wonder what the smile means, any more than I care to imagine what other photographs she may have in her bag. In a bid to avoid meeting her eyes I stare through the window across the aisle. The last of the rain is worming its way off the glass, and the people in the window-seats are erasing the communal breath.

We must be almost at the seaside. Through a patch like a grey hand squelched and dripping down the window I see a row of tall white hotels and then two fish-and-chip shops. "Room Street," moon-face says, "Fried Bunch," while his neighbour grabs his own right ear with his left hand and blocks his left ear with his upper arm. Are my fellow passengers a troupe of performers on their way to a seaside engagement? Is that why their faces seem familiar? If they're rehearsing, I wish they would stop. "Flag Holes," says lunar lineaments, "Stubble Humps," and I feel he is snatching reality away from me and making it his before I can perceive it. What will he do to my sea?

The coach swings into a layby alongside the golf course and halts with a gasp. "Car Clump," says selenophysiognomy, but I don't care. When the other coach draws up behind this one I'll be able to return to my own seat. The driver lets the front door puff open and tramps clanking down the steps, and I turn to watch for my vehicle. Then my neck jerks, and the pain in my skull feels like a pin driven so deep into my spine that I can't move my head.

A woman is sitting in the middle of the back row with her feet propped against the seats on either side of the aisle. Her striped pink dress is raised above her waist, and I can see into her. I feel as though the bearded purplish avenue is drawing me in, as though the coach and the passengers and their hubbub have become a tunnel down which I'll go rushing helplessly unless I can look away. Just in time I glimpse the one sight which is able to distract my attention — the other coach. It races around the bend at the edge of the golf course and flashes its lights, and I succeed in swivelling my head. I grab the head-rest in front of me so as to heave myself to my feet as soon as my coach stops. But the coach races past without slowing and disappears over the slope of the road.

I clench my fists and my eyes and my mouth in order not to attract attention to myself. I can't prevent my eyes from twitching open, however, because I have hardly drawn breath when the coach starts to move. Surely there hasn't been time for the driver to climb aboard — and as the coach swerves out of the layby I seem to glimpse a figure running beside the murky windows and waving vainly as it is left behind.

Now I know what kind of company I'm in. They aren't actors, but I know why I would have seen photographs of them in newspapers. Asylums have days out, even asylums where the criminally insane are locked up, though the public aren't supposed to know they do. It must have been a nurse I gave my name to when I got on this coach. Why didn't she prevent whoever's in the driver's seat from starting the engine? She must be afraid to intervene while the vehicle is moving, and I can't do anything, I'm afraid to draw attention to myself. I'll be able to keep quiet so long as we end up by the sea.

The woman next to me smiles, and then she smiles, and then she smiles, and I make myself smile at her, and smile, and smile; what harm can there be in a smile? Moon-dial is naming everything we pass — "Bucket Bunches, Toddler Splash, Bloat Boats, Wheel Baldies" — but I can cope with this, because he won't be able to bother me once I've left the coach as soon as we get to the beach. The man beside the knitting woman is multiplying syllables again, and I can hear Algernon rhyming and someone else singing "God save our gracious" over and over to any number of tunes as if she can't progress to the next word until she finds the melody, but I mustn't let all this oppress me; above all, I mustn't look back.

Through the windscreen, far away down the aisle, I see sunlit hotels giving way to dunes ahead, and then water shines beyond the dunes. As I take a breath which I mean to hold until my silent wish is granted, the woman beside me smiles and says "Do you mind if I ask you one question?"

The road curves, and I see the other coach. It's parked at the edge of the dunes, and the passengers are climbing down the steps. "Not any more," I say.

"Who's looking after your mother while you're out for the day?"

Algernon has opened a window, and I can hear the waves. They sound exactly like my mother's breathing, which I thought I'd never hear again. Once I lay my head in a hollow between two dunes I shall feel safe. I'm resisting the urge to run along the aisle so as to be first off the coach when the man in the driver's seat honks the horn and passes the parked vehicle without even slowing. "We haven't stopped," I cry. "We have to stop."

"Sand Bumps," says satellite-features. "Screech Air." The woman smiles at me and then smiles at me. The rhyming and the prayers and the syllabic babble and "God save our gracious" and all the other tangled sounds are conspiring to steal my breath and weigh me down in my seat. "Stop," I scream and clawing myself out of the seat, lurch towards the front of the coach.

I've drawn attention to myself. There's no turning back now. I grab the knitting woman's needles, cracking her hands and cutting off her prayer of thanks, and poke at anyone who looks as if they might try to catch hold of me. The driver brakes and glances at me as I reach him. Now he looks like the proper driver, but how do I know that isn't a trick?

"Knit, knit," I cry — I used to shout that at my mother whenever I was afraid she was about to stop moving — and jab his face. "Snail," I announce, because that's what he looks like with the needles in his face. As he waves his hands frantically at them I heave him out of the seat and grab the wheel. The coach ploughs through the dunes, and I suffer a pang of regret until I understand that the beach and the sea are so much bigger than I am, too big for me to harm. They're waiting for me. They will take me back where I was safe.

MISSED CONNECTION

OUTSIDE THE TRAIN THE NIGHT ROCKED LIKE A SEA. Distant lights bobbed up and sailed away, waves of earth surged up violently and sank. The hurtling train swayed wildly. In the aisle crowds collided; people grabbed one another, clutching for support; their noise was deafening. But Ted had reached the door, and was wrenching it open.

"Oh no you don't," a voice said.

He woke. Was he home at last, and in bed? But already the jumble of sound had rushed into his ears: the harsh clicking repetitions of the tracks, the ebb and flow of tangled voices. He was still on the train.

He opened his eyes to glance at his watch. God, time seemed to have waited for him while he'd slept. Across the aisle the compulsive talker never faltered. "They're not what they used to be," he was saying. "Nothing is these days." Hadn't he said that before? No, Ted silenced himself: no déjà vu, thank you. He'd had enough philosophy of time this term to last him the rest of his life.

The train hadn't even left the city yet. Perhaps it had halted while Ted was asleep. He shifted so that he could look out of the window, trying to be stealthy: whenever he moved, the fat woman next to him encroached further. Specks of a new rain glittered on the windows. Beneath streetlamps, gleams of orange light drifted across the mirrors of streets, drawn by the movement of the train. At the end of a street, another train passed.

No, it couldn't have been. What, then? Momentarily he'd seen windows passing beyond a street, a glimpse of moving frames like a strip of film pulled through a gate. An unlit bus, probably. It had seemed to pace the train, but the far ends of streets were deserted now. Someone trod on his toe.

Jesus, it was the whining child. He'd stood up to rummage another toy out of the suitcase. "Watch the man's feet," his mother shouted. "Just you sit down and shut up or I'll belt you one." "Aw,

221

I wanna get something else," the child whined. "I wanna play."
God, Ted hoped they weren't going to keep up their double act for
the rest of the journey. How much longer? He bared his watch. It
had stopped.

Well, that was great. Just fantastic. Now he couldn't tell how
long he had still to suffer; he hadn't been home by this route before.
All he needed now was for the train to stall. Anything might happen
on the railway; the train wouldn't have been so crowded if there
hadn't been some foul-up elsewhere; the public address system had
mumbled an explanation. How long would he have to be stifled by
this crowd?

He glanced warily at them. The child toyed with a gadget; his
face grew petulant, preparing to whine. The mother ignored him
ostentatiously and pored over a love story. The fat woman settled
herself again; her lapful of carriers crackled and rustled. The sounds
were close, flattened; all sounds were — a perpetual coughing, the
stream of logorrhoea across the aisle, the loud underlying tangle of
conversations, mixed blurrily with the rush of the train. People spilled
from the corridors into the aisle, swaying expressionlessly as wax.
Stale smoke drifted in, to hang in the trapped June heat. Ted pressed
himself closer to the window, trying to make even the tiniest gap
between himself and the fat woman. He couldn't stand much more
of this.

He must be overtired; he felt on edge, somehow vulnerable.
The university term had been taxing. Still, he needn't be neurotic.
The journey wouldn't last forever. He turned to the window, drawing
into himself, itching with sweat.

The city was petering out. Jagged icicles of streetlamps hung
beneath shades, houses gaped. A distant train crossed a vague street.
Again? It had seemed to pass through a derelict alley. Perhaps a
terrace walling off the end of a street had looked like a carriage. Or
perhaps it had been the train on which he was trapped, reflected
somehow. The night was seeping into the city; it swept away the
last walls, and filled the windows of the train.

It made them into mirrors. The reflected carriage closed him
in. The fat woman sat forward; her lap rustled loudly. Her reflection
appeared, multiplied by the double glazing: her two noses overlapped,

her four lips opened moistly. All the faces became explosions of flesh, far too much of it, surrounding him wherever he looked, hot and oily and luxuriantly featured. His own face had exploded too. He must distract himself. He dragged Robbe-Grillet from his pocket.

The child whined, the man talked, talked; the tracks chattered rapidly. Ted read the same words over and over, but they became increasingly meaningless; Ted read the same words over and over, but they became increasingly meaningless. He found himself hoping to find they had changed. He stared glumly through the window, which was thickly veined with rain. Then he peered closer. This time there certainly was a train out there.

It was perhaps two hundred yards away, and racing neck and neck with his own train. It squirmed a little, distorted by the watery veins. He strained to see more clearly. There was something odd about the train. The dimness of its windows could be an effect of the downpour. But why were the windows flickering, appearing and vanishing, like an incompetently projected film? Of course — the train was passing through a forest.

He gazed fascinated. The image seemed hypnotic; it drew him. He grew unaware of the stifling carriage, the rush of noise. The dim rectangular will-o'-the-wisps swayed jerkily between the glistening pillars of the trees. The forest was thinning. As a child might, he looked forward to the sight of the unobscured train. The trees fell back, giving way to a field. But nothing at all emerged.

He gasped, and craned back to peer at the swiftly dwindling forest, as though the train might be lurking in there like an animal. But there was only the long edge of the forest, fleeing backwards. The bare fields spread around him, soaked and glittering.

He wished he could ask someone whether they had seen it too. But when he'd gasped, the mother and child had gaped only at him. Again he felt nervously vulnerable: as though his skin were drawn too tight, and thinning. Around him they coughed, whined, shouted, chattered incessantly; tracks clattered. Now he felt more than stifled by the crowd, he felt alienated. Hadn't he felt so earlier, before he'd had the dream? He couldn't talk to anyone; he was trapped in his own mind. The crowd was a huge muddled entity, hemming him in with flesh and noise.

He wanted a sandwich. He wanted to use the toilet. In fact he simply wanted to prove somehow that he wasn't helpless: even lean out of a window for a while. "Will you keep my seat?" he asked the fat woman, but she was asleep, jaw dangling. "Will you keep my seat?" he asked the mother, but she only murmured vaguely, shrugging. The child gaped at him. When Ted stood up anyway, the nearest of the standing passengers gazed speculatively at his place. He sat down again, muttering.

The fat woman snorted deep in her throat, as though choking rhythmically; she rolled against him. God! He shoved her away, but she rolled closer. He thrust his shoulder against hers and braced his feet. The mother and child stared at him. He gazed from the window, to ignore them.

The rain was thinning. Beside the train the ground soared abruptly; an embankment glistened with dim grass and flowers, skimming by. It pressed reflections closer to him; the faces overgrown with flesh became more solid. Surely he must be nearly home. Shouldn't the train reach a station soon? The embankment sank, wind cleared rain from the glass. The ground flattened and became fields, and a train matched the speed of his own.

It wasn't the same train, not the one from the trees. Its lights were dim, but why not? Of course, he thought gladly: it was being shunted into a siding. No doubt they shunted many trains at night, that was why the other train had vanished. But this train was closer, hardly a hundred yards away; and it was not empty. Dim faces rode in the dim carriages, bobbing slightly.

Perhaps the train was a reflection, on rain or mist. On bare fields? Sweat crept over him, making his skin uneasy; he felt a vague panic. It couldn't be a reflection, for the seat opposite him on the other train was empty. There was something wrong with the faces. Ahead the ground swooped up, carrying a road over a bridge. He heard his own train plunge into a short tunnel. But there wasn't a bridge for the other train, it was heading straight for — The bridge swept over him, shouting; then fields sailed by. They were deserted. There was no second train.

Oh God, he was hallucinating. He hadn't taken many drugs in his time, surely too few to cause a flashback. Was he having a breakdown? For a moment he was unsure which train he was riding. Sweat stifled him; the noise of the carriage enclosed him, impalpable and roaring.

Oh come on, one needn't be mad to hallucinate. He'd decided earlier that he was overtired. Didn't tiredness sometimes force dreams into one's waking life? In any case, the train need not have been a hallucination. Its track must have curved beside the road, the bridge had prevented him from seeing where it had gone. The explanations soothed him, but still unease was planted deep in him. A thought lurked, something that had happened before, that he'd forgotten. It didn't matter. He must be near the end of the journey.

The crowd shifted restlessly, rocking; voices jumbled. Drifts of smoke sank through the ponderous heat, the cougher persisted harshly. The child banged his feet repetitively beneath his seat, the mother stared emptily away, the talker rattled on. Soon be home now, soon.

Outside the ground was rising. The luxuriant faces stared back from the window with their overlapping eyes. It's all right, nothing's wrong. But as the ground walled off the landscape, Ted felt panic growing. The embankment rushed by. He was waiting for it to sink, so that he could see what lay beyond. There was nothing, nothing lying in wait; why should there be? The embankment began to descend. Wind tugged the last lines of rain from the window. The embankment sped away behind, into the dark. At once its place was taken by a train.

It was much closer: less than fifty yards away. And it looked disturbingly similar to the last train. Though the dim carriages were crowded, their aisles clogged with people, the seat opposite Ted's was empty.

Panic threaded him like wire; his body felt unstable. There was something very odd about that train. Dim and vague though they were, the faces of its passengers looked even more abnormal than his own train's exploded reflections. Some were very pale, others looked vividly stained. The shapes of all of them were wrong.

His panic blazed up. He hardly knew where he was. He swayed, borne helplessly over clattering tracks; he was on one of the trains. He saw faces, flesh exploding beyond glass; they might be reflections, or — The fat woman sagged against him, snatching him back to himself for a moment. He was trapped in the hot suffocating carriage. A train, dim and flickering as though full of candlelight, was keeping pace with him. Within its windows, all the vague deformed faces were staring straight at him.

He struggled to rise. He had to get away. Where? If he found a guard, perhaps — He must get away from the window, from the staring vaguenesses. He fought to thrust back the fat woman; she was pinning him to the seat. Sweat clothed him. He was still struggling to free himself when he saw that the two trains were converging. They were going to collide.

"Ay, well," the talkative man said. "Not long now. We're nearly there."

He'd said that before: just before Ted had fallen asleep. Everything was wrong; there was no reality to hold the nightmare back. "Christ!" Ted screamed. One or two people stared at him, someone laughed; their eyes had gone dead.

He wrenched himself free. The fat woman toppled toward the window, snoring convulsively. He staggered down the aisle, hurled against seats and people by the swaying of the carriage. He glanced fearfully toward the window, and his mind grew numb. Perhaps it already was, for he thought that the ground had fallen away, leaving the other train still racing alongside, and closing.

He shouldered wildly through the crowd. People muttered resentfully. They moved aside sluggishly; some stood in his path, staring at him. The trains were almost touching now. A maze of hot moist flesh hindered him, choking the aisle, swaying repeatedly into his path. He clawed through. Behind him the muttering grew resentful, furious; a hand grabbed him. But he'd reached the end of the carriage.

Outside the door a dim distorted face lolled toward him, staring. He hurled himself toward the far door, against the swaying. He must throw himself clear. Any injury would be preferable to meeting his vague mounting dread. He wrenched at the handle.

"Oh no you don't," a voice said, and the trains collided.

There was no sound, and immediately no light. The trains seemed less to collide than to merge. In the absolute darkness, an image lit up in Ted's mind: a wrecked train lying beside a track, and himself crawling away from an open door. At once the image began to dwindle. He tried to hold onto it, but he was being borne away into the darkness. He wasn't the lone survivor, after all. They had come back to take him with them, they resented his escape. The image fled, was a point of light, went out.

He was lying back in his seat. He felt the carriage swaying, amid total silence. He kept his eyes closed as long as he could. When he opened them at last he tried to scream; but as he saw more, he tried to stay absolutely quiet, still, invisible. Perhaps that would make it all go away.

But the fat woman slumped against him. Without looking, he could make out that she had lost part of her face. The aisles were still crowded; objects swayed there. Outside the windows was nothing but darkness. Opposite him the mother's jaw hung far too wide. But despite their appearance his companions were moving, though slowly as clockwork on the point of running down, in the dim unsteady light. The child's body moved jerkily, and in the object dangling on its neck, a mouth began to whine.

THE CHANGE

A S SOON AS HE REACHED THE FLAT Don started writing. Walking home, he'd shaped the chapter in his mind. What transformations does the werewolf undergo? he wrote. The new streetlamp by the bus-stop snapped alight as the October evening dimmed. Does he literally change into another creature, or is it simply a regression?

"How's it coming?" Margaret asked when she came in.

"Pretty well." It was, though she'd distracted him. He stared out at the bluish lamp and searched for the end of his sentence.

After dinner, during which his mind had been constructing paragraphs, he hurried back to his desk. The bluish light washed out the lines of ink; the rest of the page looked arctically indifferent, far too wide to fill. His prepared paragraphs grew feeble. When he closed the curtains and wrote a little, his sentences seemed dull. Tomorrow was Saturday. He'd begin early.

He had forgotten the queues at the bus-stop. He went unshaven to his desk, but already shoppers were chattering about the crowds they would avoid. They were less than three yards from him, and the glass seemed very thin. He was sure the noise grew worse each week. Still, he could ignore it, use the silences.

Aren't we all still primitive? he wrote. Hasn't civilisation — Children whined, tugging at their mothers. Hasn't civilisation — Now the mothers were shaking the children, cuffing them, shouting. Hasn't bloody civilisation — A bus bore the queue away, but as many people missed the bus and began complaining loudly, repetitively.

"Yes, it's going all right," he told Margaret, and pretended to turn back to check a reference. He wasn't lying. Just a temporary block.

Hasn't civilisation simply trapped and repressed our primitive instincts? he managed to stutter at last. But the more strongly Scarved crowds were massing outside, chanting football slogans. There's tribal

228

behaviour for you. But the more strongly Youths stared in at him, shouting inanities. If only there was room in the bedroom for his desk, if only they had erected the bus-stop just a few houses away — He forced himself to keep his head down. But the more strongly primitive instincts are repressed the more savage their occasional outburst will be, whether in mass murder or actual lycanthropy. God, that was enough. Sunday would be better.

Sunday was full of children, playing itinerant games. He abandoned writing, and researched in library books while Margaret wrote her case reports. He was glad he'd taken time off to read the books. Now he had new insights, which would mean a stronger chapter.

Monday was hectic. The most complicated tax assessments were being calculated, now that all the information had arrived. Taxpayers phoned, demanding why they were waiting; the office rang incessantly. "Inland Revenue," Don and his colleagues kept saying. "Inland Revenue." Still, he managed to calculate three labyrinthine assessments.

He felt more confident on the way home. He was already on the third chapter, and his publisher had said that this book should be more commercial than his first. Perhaps it would pay for a house, then Margaret could give up social work and have her baby; perhaps he could even write full time. He strode home, determined to improve the book. Dissolving bars of gold floated in the deep blue sky, beyond the tower blocks.

He was surprised how well the opening chapters read. He substituted phrases here and there. The words grew pale as bluish light invaded his desk-lamp's. When the text gave out, his mind went on. His nib scratched faintly. At the end of the second paragraph he gazed out, frowning.

The street had the unnatural stillness of a snowscape. Street and houses stretched away in both directions, gleaming faintly blue. The cross-street on his right was lit similarly; the corner house had no shadow. The pavement seemed oppressively close with no garden intervening. Everything looked unreal, glary with lightning.

He was so aware of the silence now that it distracted him. He must get an idea moving before the silence gave way, before someone came to stare. Write, for God's sake write. Repression, regression, lycanthropy. It sounded like a ditty in his mind.

Animal traits of primitive man. Distrust of the unfamiliar produces a savage response. He scribbled, but there seemed to be no continuity; his thoughts were flowing faster than his ink. Someone crossed at the intersection, walking oddly. He glared at the shadowless corner, but it was deserted. At the edge of his vision the figure had looked as odd as the light. He scribbled, crossing out and muttering to deafen himself to the silence. As he wrote the end of a paragraph, a face peered at him, inches from his. Margaret had tiptoed up to smile. He crumpled the book as he slammed it shut, but managed to smile as she came in.

Later he thought an idea was stirring, a paragraph assembling. Margaret began to tell him about her latest case. "Right, yes, all right," he muttered and sat at the window, his back to her. The blank page blotted thought from his mind. The bluish light tainted the page and the desk, like a sour indefinable taste.

The light bothered him. It changed his view of the quiet street which he'd used to enjoy while working. This new staged street was unpleasantly compelling. Passers-by looked discoloured, almost artificial. If he drew the curtains, footsteps conjured up caricatures which strolled across his mind. If he sat at the dining-table he could still hear any footsteps, and was nearer Margaret, the rustling of her case reports, her laughter as she read a book.

His head was beginning to feel like the approach of a storm; he wasn't sure how long it had felt that way. The first sign of violence was almost a relief. It was Thursday night, and he was straining at a constipated paragraph. When someone arrived at the bus-stop, Don forced himself not to look. He gazed at the blot which had gathered at the end of his last word, where he'd rested his pen. The blot had started to look like an obstacle he would never be able to pass. The bluish light appeared to be making it grow, and there was another blot on the edge of his vision — another man at the bus-stop. If he looked he would never be able to write, he knew. At last he glanced up, to get it over with, and then he stared. Something was wrong.

They looked almost like two strangers at a bus-stop, their backs to each other. One shrugged his shoulders loosely, as though he was feeling the cold; the other stretched, baring huge calloused hands. Their faces were neutral as masks. All at once Don saw that was just a pretence. Each man was waiting for the other to make a move. They were wary as animals in a cage.

Now he could see how whenever one shifted the other turned towards him, almost imperceptibly. The light had changed their faces into plastic, bluish plastic masks that might at any moment slip awry. Suddenly Don's mouth tasted sour, for he'd realised that the men were turning their backs on the roadway; before they came face to face they would see him. He was protected by the window, and anyway he could retreat to Margaret. But the sound of her rustling pages seemed very far away. Now the masks were almost facing him, and a roar was growing — the sound of a bus. He managed to gulp back a sigh of relief before Margaret could notice that anything was wrong. How could he explain to her when he didn't understand it himself?

When the men had boarded the bus, making way stiffly for each other, he closed the curtains hastily. His fingers were trembling, and he had to go into the kitchen to splash cold water on his face. Trying to appear nonchalant as he passed Margaret, he felt as false as the masks in the street.

A face came towards the window, grinning. It was discoloured, shiny, plastic; its eyes shone, unnaturally blue. As it reached the window it cracked like an egg from forehead to chin, and its contents leapt at him, smashing the glass and his dream. Beside him Margaret was sound asleep. He lay in his own dark and wondered what was true about the dream.

The next night he pretended to write, and watched. His suspicion was absurd, but fascinating. As he gazed unblinking at the people by the bus-stop they looked increasingly deformed; their heads were out of proportion, or their faces lopsided; their dangling hands looked swollen and clumsy. Christ, nobody was perfect; the clinical light simply emphasised imperfections, or his eyes were tired. Yet the people looked self-conscious, pretending to be normal. That light would make anyone feel awkward. He would be glad of Saturday and daylight.

He'd forgotten the crowds again. Once they would have set him scribbling his impressions in his notebook; now their mannerisms looked studied and ugly, their behaviour uncivilised. The women were mannequins, in hideous taste: hives of artificially senile hair squatted on their heads, their eyes looked enlarged with blue paint. The men were louder and more brutal, hardly bothering to pretend at all.

Margaret returned, laden with shopping. "I saw your book in the supermarket. I improved their display."

"Good, fine," he snarled, and tried to reconstruct the sentence she had ruined. He was gripping his pen so hard it almost cracked.

On Sunday afternoon he managed a page, as late sunlight turned the street amber. In one case, he wrote, a man interested in transmogrification took LSD and "became" a tiger — even to seeing a tiger in the mirror. Doesn't this show how fragile human personality is? Too many rhetorical questions in this book. Very little pressure is needed to break the shell of civilisation — five minutes more of that bloody radio upstairs was about all it would take. There was no silence anywhere, except the strained unnerving quiet of the street at night.

Next week Margaret was on call. After being surrounded by the office phones all day, he was even more on edge for the shrilling of the phone. Yet when she was called out he was surprised to find that he felt relieved. The flat was genuinely silent, for the people overhead were out too. Though he was tired from persuading irate callers that they owed tax, he uncapped his pen and sat at the window.

Why is the full moon important to lycanthropy? Does moonlight relate to a racial memory, a primitive fear? Its connotations might stir up the primitive elements of the personality, most violently where they were most repressed, or possibly where they were closest to the surface. Come to think, it must be rather like the light outside his window.

There was his suspicion again, and yet he had no evidence. He'd seen how the light caricatured people, and perhaps its spotlighting made them uneasy. But how could a streetlight make anyone more savage — for example, the gang of youths he could hear approaching loudly? It was absurd. Nevertheless his palms were growing slick with apprehension, and he could hardly keep hold of his pen.

When they came abreast of the window they halted and began to jeer at him, at his pose behind the desk. Teeth gleamed metallically in the discoloured faces, their eyes glittered like glass. For a moment he was helpless with panic, then he realised that the glass protected him. He held that thought steady, though his head was thumping. Let them try to break through, he'd rip their throats out on the glass, drag their faces over the splinters. He sat grinning at the plastic puppets while they jeered and gestured jerkily. At last they dawdled away, shouting threats.

He sat coated with the light, and felt rather sick. He seemed unable to clear his mind of a jumble of images: glass, flesh, blood, screams. He got up to find a book, any distraction at all, and then he saw his bluish shadow. Its long hands dangled, its distorted head poked forward. As he stooped to peer closer he felt as if it was dragging him down, stretching his hands down to meet its own. All at once he darted to the light-switch. He clawed the curtains shut and left the light burning, then he went into the bedroom and sat for a long time on the bed. He held his face as though it was a mask that was slipping.

On Thursday the bus home was delayed by a car crash. While the other passengers stared at blood and deformed metal, Don was uneasily watching the night seep across the sky. When he reached home the house looked worse than he'd feared: thin, cardboardy, bricks blackened by the light — not much of a refuge at all.

He was overworked, that was why he felt nervous. He must find time to relax. He'd be all right once he was inside with the curtains drawn, away from the dead light that seemed to have soaked into everything, even his fingers as they fumbled with the key. He glanced up to see who was watching him from the upstairs flat, then he looked away hastily. Maybe someone up there was really as deformed as that; he never met the tenants, they had a separate entrance. No, surely the figure must have looked like that because of a flaw in the glass.

In his flat he listened to the footsteps overhead, and couldn't tell if anything was wrong with them. Eventually he cooked the dinner

Margaret had left him when she was called away. He tried to write, but the fragility of the silence made him too nervous. When he held his breath, he could hear the jungle of sound beyond the curtains: snarls of cars, the low thunder of planes, shouts, things falling, shrieks of metal, cries. The bluish flat stood emptily behind him.

The last singers were spilling out of pubs. Surely Margaret would be home soon. Wasn't that Margaret now? No, the hurrying footsteps were too uneven and too numerous: a man and a woman. He could hear the man shouting incoherently, almost wordlessly. Now the woman was running, and the man was stumbling heavily after her. When he caught her outside the window she began to scream.

Don squirmed in his chair. She was screaming abuse, not with fear. He could stand it, surely it wouldn't last long, her screeching voice that seemed to be in the room with him, scraping his nerves. All at once a body thumped the window; the frame shook. They were fighting, snarling. Christ! He struggled to his feet and forced himself to reach towards the curtains.

Then he saw the shadows, and barely managed not to cry out himself. Though the curtains blurred them, they were all too clear to him. As they clawed at each other, he was sure their arms were lengthening. Surely their heads were swelling like balloons and changing shape; perhaps that was why they sounded as though they never could have formed words. The window juddered and he flinched back, terrified they might sense him beyond the glass. For a moment he saw their mouths lunging at each other's faces, tearing.

All at once there was silence. Footsteps stumbled away, he couldn't tell whose. It took him a long time to part the curtains, and much longer to open the front door. But the street was deserted, and he might have doubted everything he'd seen but for a smear of blood on the window. He ran for tissues and wiped it away, shuddering. The lamp stood behind him, bright and ruthless; its dead eye gazed from the pane. He was surrounded. He could only take refuge in bed and try to keep his eyes closed.

The next day he rang the Engineering Department (Mechanical & Lighting) from the office, and told them where he lived. "What exactly have you put in those lights?"

The girl was probably just a clerk. "No, they're not mercury vapour," he said. "You might think they were, but not if you had to live with them, I can tell you. Will you connect me with someone who knows?"

Perhaps she felt insulted, or perhaps his tone disturbed her. "Never mind why I want to know. You don't want me to know, do you? Well, I know there's something else in them, let me tell you, and I'll be in touch with someone who can do something about it."

As he slammed the receiver down, he saw that his colleagues were staring at him. What was wrong with them? Had the politeness which the job demanded possessed them completely? Were they scared of a bit of honest rage?

On the way home he wandered until he found a derelict area, though the start of winter time had made him more nervous. Already the sky was black, an hour earlier than yesterday, and he was dismayed to find he dreaded going home. Outside his flat the lamp stood waiting, in a street that looked alien as the moon. Nobody was in sight. He unlocked the front door, then he lifted the brick he was carrying and hurled it at the lamp. As the bulb shattered, he closed the door quickly. He spent the evening pretending to write, and stared out at the dark.

Saturday brought back the crowds. Their faces were pink putty, all too malleable. He cursed himself for wasting last night's dark. If he went to the library for quiet he would have walked two miles for nothing: there would be crowds there too. If only he could afford to move! But it was only the cheap rent here that was allowing him and Margaret to save.

She emerged from the mass of putty faces and dumped shopping on the table. "Isn't it going well?"

"What do you mean, isn't it going well? It won't go better for questions like that, will it? Yes, of course it's going well!" There was no point in telling her the truth; he had enough to bear without her anxiety. That evening he wrote a few paragraphs, but they were cumbersome and clumsy.

On Sunday he tried to relax, but whenever Margaret spoke he felt there was an idea at the edge of his mind, waiting to be glimpsed and written. "Yes, later, later," he muttered, trying vainly to recapture

235

the idea. That night she turned restlessly in bed for hours. He lay beside her and wondered uneasily what had gone wrong with the dark.

His lack of sleep nagged him on Monday. His skull felt tight and fragile. Whenever he tried to add up a column of figures, a telephone rang, his colleagues laughed inanely, a fragment of conversation came into focus. People wandered from desk to desk. His surroundings were constantly restless, distracting.

One of his taxpayers called and refused to believe he owed four hundred pounds. Don sensed how the man's hands were clenching, seeking a victim, reaching for him. There was no need to panic, not with the length of the telephone cable between them. He couldn't be bothered to conceal his feelings. "You owe the money. There's nothing I can do."

"You bastards," the man was screaming, "you f—" as Don put down the receiver.

Some of his colleagues were staring at him. Maybe they could have done better, except that they probably wouldn't even have realised they were threatened. Did they honestly believe that words and printed forms were answers to the violence? Couldn't they see how false it all was? Only his triumph over the streetlamp helped him through the day.

He walked most of the way home, enjoying the darkness where lamps were smashed. As he neared his street the bluish light closed in. It didn't matter, it couldn't reach his home now. When he began to run, anxious to take refuge, his footsteps sounded flat and false as the light. He turned the corner into his street. Outside his flat the lamp was lit.

It craned its bony concrete neck, a tall thin ghost, its face blazing. It had defeated him. However many times he destroyed it, it would return. He locked himself in and grabbed blindly for the light-switch.

After dinner he sat at his desk and read his chapters, in case Margaret suspected he had failed. The words on the bluish pages seemed meaningless; even his handwriting looked unfamiliar. His hot eyes felt unfamiliar too.

And now it was Margaret's noises. They sounded forced, unnervingly artificial, sound effects. When he frowned at her she muted them, which only made them more infuriating. Her eyes were red, but he couldn't help it if she was distressed while he felt as he did, besieged deep in himself. "I'm going to bed," she said eventually, like a rebuke. When he couldn't bear sitting alone any longer, she was still awake. He lay with his back to her in order to discourage conversation, which would distract him. Something was certainly wrong with the dark.

In the morning, when she'd gone to work, he saw what he must do. Since he had no chance of writing at weekends or in the evenings, he must give up his daytime job, which was false anyway. His book was more important, it would say things that needed saying — they would be clear when the time came to write them. In the shaving mirror his grin looked weaker than he felt.

He grinned more widely as he phoned to report himself sick. That falseness was enjoyable. He sat grinning at his desk, waiting for words. But he couldn't reach back to the self who had written the chapters; however deep in his mind he groped, there was nothing but a dialogue. Isn't it going well? No, it isn't going well. No, it isn't, no, it isn't, no, it isn't going well. Repression, regression, lycanthropy. Putty faces bobbed past the window. Now here was the bluish light, moulding them into caricatures or worse. Repression, regression, lycanthropy.

"You're home early," Margaret said. He stared at her, probing for the implication, until she looked away.

After dinner she watched television in the bedroom, with the sound turned to a whisper. He followed her, to place more distance between himself and the tinged curtains. As soon as he switched off the light, the living-room was a dead bluish box. When he clawed at the switch, the bluish tinge seemed to have invaded the light of the room.

"You've left the light on."

"Leave it on!" He couldn't tell her why. He was trapped in himself, and his shell felt brittle. In a way it was a relief to be cut off from her that way; at least he needn't struggle to explain. She stared at the screen, she swallowed aspirin, she glanced at him and flinched from his indifferent gaze. Shrunken figures jerked about as though they were trying to escape the box of the television, and they felt as real as he did. After a while Margaret slipped into bed and hid her face. He supposed she was crying.

He lay beside her. Voices crowded his mind, shouting. Repression, regression, lycanthropy. Margaret's hand crept around his waist, but he couldn't bear to be touched; he shook her off. Perhaps she was asleep. Around him the room was faintly luminous. He gazed at it suspiciously until his eyelids drooped.

When he woke, he seemed hardly to have slept. Perhaps the revelation had woken him, for he knew at last what was wrong with the dark. It had developed a faint bluish tinge. How could the light penetrate the closed door? Was it reaching beneath the door for him? Or had the colour settled on his eyeballs, seeped into them?

It hadn't trapped him yet. He sneaked into his clothes. Margaret was a vague draped huddle, dimly bluish. He tiptoed to the front door and let himself out, then he began to run.

At the tower blocks he slowed. Concrete, honeycombed with curtained rectangles, massed above him. Orange sodium mushrooms glared along the paths, blackening the grass. The light outside his flat was worse than that; it was worse than moonlight, because it infected everyone, not just the few. That was why he'd felt so strange lately. It had been transforming him.

He must go back for Margaret. They must leave now, this minute. Tomorrow they'd find somewhere else to live, draw on their savings; they could come back in daylight for their possessions. He must go back, he'd left her alone with the light. He ran, closing his eyes against the light as far as he could.

As he reached the street he heard someone padding towards him — padding like an animal. He dodged into an alley almost opposite the flat, but the padding turned aside somewhere. He grinned at the dark; he could outwit the light now that he knew its secret. But as soon as he emerged into the street he sensed that he was being watched.

He saw the face almost at once. It was staring at him between curtains, beside a reflection of the lamp. The face was a luminous dead mask, full of the light. He could see the animal staring out through the eyes. The mask was inside his flat, staring out at him. He made himself go forward, or perhaps the light was forcing him.

Certainly it had won. His head felt cold and hollow, cut off from his trudging. The eyes widened in the mask; the creature was ready to fly at him. The mask writhed, changing.

Suddenly he caught sight of his shadow. The light was urging it towards the window. Its claws were dangling, its head swelled forward eagerly, and this time there was nothing familiar to hold him back, no light he could switch on to change the dead street and the shadow. There was only the enemy in his home. He was the shadow, one hand dangling near the gutter. He snatched up the brick and smashing the window, struggled in through the splintering frame.

The creature backed away, into a corner. For a moment it seemed to be beaten. But when he leapt, hurling the curtains aside, it fought him with its claws. He struggled with it, breaking it, biting, tearing. At last it was still. He staggered blindly into the bedroom, mopping blood from his eyes with the rags of his sleeve.

He switched on the light, but couldn't tell what colour it was. He felt like a hollow shell. When at last he noticed that the bed was empty, it took him a very long time to force himself to look in the living-room. As he looked, he became less and less sure of what he was seeing. As to who was seeing it, he had no idea at all.

WELCOMELAND

S LADE HAD BEEN DRIVING ALL DAY when he came to the road home. The sign isolated by the sullenly green landscape of overgrown canals and weedy fields had changed. Instead of the name of the town there was a yellow pointer, startlingly bright beneath the dull June sky, for the theme park. Presumably vandals had damaged it, for only the final syllables remained: MELAND. He mightn't have another chance to see what he'd helped to build. He'd found nothing on his drive north that his clients might want to buy or invest in. He lifted his foot from the brake and let the car carry him onward.

Suppressed gleams darted through the clogged canals, across the cranium of the landscape. The sun was a ball of mist that kept failing to form in the sky. The railway blocked Slade's view as he approached the town. He caught himself expecting to see the town laid out below him, but of course he'd only ever seen it like that from the train. The railway was as deserted as the road had been for the last hour of his drive.

The road sloped toward the bridge under the railway, between banks so untended that weeds lashed the car. The mouth of the bridge had been made into a gateway: gates painted gold were folded back against the wall of the embankment. The shrill darkness in the middle of the tunnel was so thick that Slade reached to turn on his headlamps. Then the car left its echoes behind and showed him the town, and he couldn't help sighing. It looked as if the building of the park had got no further than the gates.

He'd bought shares in the project when his father had forwarded the prospectus, with Slade's new address scribbled across it so harshly that the envelope had been torn in several places. He'd hoped the park might revive his father and the town now that employment, like Slade, had moved down south. Now his father was dead, and the entrepreneur had gone bankrupt soon after the shares had been issued, and the main street was shabbier than ever: the pavements were turning green, the net curtains of the gardenless terraces were grey as old cobwebs, the displays in the shop windows that interrupted the ranks of cramped houses had been drained of colour. Slade had to assume this was early closing day, for he could see nobody at all.

The town hadn't looked so unwelcoming when he'd left, but he felt as if it had. Nevertheless he owed the place a visit, the one he should have made when his father was dying, if only Slade had known he was, if only they hadn't become estranged when Slade's mother had died... "If only" just about summed up the town, he thought bitterly as he drove to the hotel.

The squat black building was broad as four houses and four storeys high. He'd often sheltered under the iron and glass awning from the rain, but whatever the place had been called in those days, it wasn't the Old Hotel. The revolving doors stumbled round their track with a chorus of stifled moans and let him into the dark brown lobby, where the only illumination came from a large skylight over the stairs. The thin grey-haired young woman at the desk tapped her chin several times in the rhythm of some tune she must be hearing (dum-da-dum-da-dum-da-dum), squared a stack of papers, and then she looked toward him with a smile and a raising of eyebrows. "Hello, may I help you?"

"Sorry, yes, of course." Slade stepped forward to let her see him. "I'd like a room for the night."

"What would you like?"

"Pardon? Something at the top," Slade stammered, beginning to blush as he tried not to stare at her vacant eyes.

"I'm sure we can accommodate you."

He didn't doubt it, since the keyboard behind her was full. "I'll fill in one of your forms then, shall I?"

"Thank you, sir, that's fine."

There was a pad of them in front of her, but no pen. Slade uncapped his fountain pen and completed the top form, then pushed the pad between her hands as they groped over the counter. "Room twenty will be at the top, won't it?" he said, too loudly. "Could I have that one?"

"If there's anything else we can do to make you more at home, just let us know."

241

He assumed that meant yes. "I'll get the key, shall I?"

"Thank you very much," she said, and thumped a bell on the counter. Perhaps she'd misheard him, but the man who opened the door between the stairs and the desk seemed to have heard Slade clearly enough, for he only poked his dim face toward the lobby before closing the door again. Slade leaned across the desk, his cheeks stiff with blushing, and managed to hook the key with one finger, almost swaying against the receptionist as he lunged. Working all day in the indirect light hadn't done her complexion any good, to put it mildly, and now he saw that the papers she was fidgeting with were blank. "That's done it," he babbled, and scrambled toward the stairs.

The upper floors were lit only by windows. Murky sunlight was retreating over ranks of featureless white doors. If the hotel was conserving electricity, that didn't seem to augur well for the health of the town. All the same, when he stepped into the room that smelled of stale carpet and crossed to the window to let in some air, he had his first sight of the park.

A terrace led away from the main road some hundred yards from the hotel, and there the side streets ended. The railway enclosed a mile or more of bulky unfamiliar buildings, of which he could distinguish little more than that they bore names on their roofs. All the names were turned away from him, but this must be the park. It was full of people, grouped among the buildings, and the railway had been made into a ride; cars with grinning mouths were stranded in dips in the track.

Surely there weren't people in the cars. They must be dummies, stored up there out of the way. Their long grey hair flapped, their heads swayed unanimously in the wind. They seemed more lively than the waiting crowd, but just now that didn't concern him. He was willing the house where he'd spent the first half of his life to have survived the rebuilding.

As he turned from the window he saw the card above the bedside phone. DIAL 9 FOR PARK INFORMATION, it said. He dialled and waited as the room settled back into staleness. Eventually he demanded "Park Information?"

"Hello, may I help you?"

The response was so immediate that the speaker must have been waiting silently for him. As he stiffened to fend off the unexpectedness the voice said "May we ask how you heard of our attraction?"

"I bought some shares," Slade said, distracted by wondering where he knew the man's voice from. "I'm from here, actually. Wanted to do what I could for the old place."

"We all have to return to our roots. No profit in delaying."

"I wanted to ask about the park," Slade interrupted, resenting the way the voice had abandoned its official function. "Where does it end? What's still standing?"

"Less has changed than you might think."

"Would you know if Hope Street's still there?"

"Whatever people wanted most has been preserved, wherever they felt truly at home," the voice said, and even more maddeningly, "It's best if you go and look for yourself."

"When will the park be open?" Slade almost shouted.

"When you get there, never fear."

Slade gave up, and flung the receiver into the air, a theatrical gesture which made him blush furiously but which failed to silence the guilt the voice had awakened. He'd moved to London in order to live with the only woman he'd ever shared a bed with, and when they'd parted amicably less than a year later he had been unable to go home: his parents would have insisted that the breakup proved them right about her and the relationship. His father had blamed him for breaking his mother's heart, and the men hadn't spoken since her death. The way Slade's father had stared at him over her grave had withered Slade's feelings for good, but you prospered better without feelings, he'd often told himself. Now that he was home he felt compelled to make his peace with his memories.

He sent himself out of the room before his thoughts could weigh him down. The receptionist was fidgeting with her papers. As Slade stepped into the lobby the bellman's door opened, the shadowy face peered out and withdrew. Slade was at the revolving doors when the receptionist said "Hello, may I help you?" He struggled out through the doors, his face blazing.

The street was still deserted. The deadened sky appeared to hover just above the slate roofs like a ghost of the smoke of the derelict factories. Even his car looked abandoned, grey with the grime of his drive. It was the only car on the road.

Was the park somehow soundproofed so as not to annoy the residents? Even if the rides hadn't begun, surely he ought to be able to hear the crowd beyond the houses. He felt as if the entire town were holding its breath. As he hurried along the buckled mossy pavement, his footsteps sounded metallic, mechanical. He turned the curve that led the road to the town hall. Among the scrawny houses of the terrace opposite him, there was a lit shop.

It was the bakery, where his mother would buy cakes for the family each weekend. The taste of his favourite cake, sponge and cream and jam, filled his mouth at the thought. He could see the baker, looking older but not as old as Slade would have expected, serving a woman in the buttery light that seemed brighter than electricity, brighter than Slade had ever seen the shop before. The sight and the taste made him feel that if he opened the shop door he could step into memory, buy cakes as a homecoming surprise and walk home, back into the warmth of having tea beside the coal fire, the long quiet evenings with his parents when he had been growing up but hadn't yet outgrown them.

He wasn't entitled to imagine that, since he'd ensured it couldn't happen. His mouth went dry, the taste vanished. He passed the shop without crossing the road, averting his face lest the baker should call out to him. As he passed, the light went out. Perhaps it had been a ray of sunlight, though he could see no gap in the clouds.

Someone at the town hall should know if his home was intact. There must be people in the hall, for he could hear a muffled waltz. He went up the worn steps and between the pillars of the token portico. The double doors were too large for the building, which was about the size of the hotel, and seemed at first too heavy or too swollen for him to shift. Then the rusty handles yielded to his weight, and the doors shuddered inward. The lobby was unlit and deserted.

He could still hear the waltz. A track of grey daylight stretched ahead of him and showed him an architect's model on a table in the middle of the lobby. He followed his vague shadow over the wedge of lit carpet. The model had been vandalised, so thoroughly it was impossible to see what view of the town it represented. If it had shown streets as well as rides, there was no way of telling where either ended or began.

He made his way past the unattended information desk toward the music. A minute's stumbling along the dark corridor brought him to the ballroom. The only light beyond the dusty glass doors came from high transoms, but couples were waltzing on the bare floor to music that sounded oddly more distant than ever. In the dimness their faces were grey blotches. It must be some kind of old folks' treat, he reassured himself, for more than half of the dancers were bald. Loath to trouble them, he turned back toward the lobby.

The area outside the wedge of daylight was almost indistinguishably dim. He could just make out the side of the information desk that faced away from the public. Someone appeared to be crouched beside the chair behind the desk. If the figure had fallen there Slade ought to find out what was wrong, but the position of the figure was so dismayingly haphazard that he could only believe it was a dummy. The dancers were still whirling sluggishly, always in the same direction, as if they might never stop. He glanced about, craving reassurance, and caught sight of a sliver of light at the end of the corridor — the gap around a door.

It must lead to the park. He almost tripped on the carpet as he headed for the door. It was open because it had been vandalised: it was half off its hinges, and he had to strain to lift it clear of the rucked carpet. He thought of having to go back through the building, and heaved at the door so savagely that it ripped the sodden carpet. He squeezed through the gap, his face throbbing with embarrassment, and ran.

He was so anxious to be away from the damage he'd caused that at first he hardly observed where he was going. Nobody was about, that was the main thing. He'd run some hundred yards between the derelict houses before he wondered where the crowd he'd seen from the hotel might be. He halted clumsily and stared around him. He was already in the park.

It seemed they had tried to preserve as much of the town as they could. Clumps of three or four terraced houses had been left standing in no apparent pattern, with signs on their roofs. He still couldn't read the signs, even those that were facing him; they might have been vandalised — many of the windows were smashed — or left uncompleted. If it hadn't been for the roundabout he saw between the houses, he might not have realised he was in the park.

It wasn't the desolation that troubled him so much as the impression that the town was yet struggling to change, to live. If his home was involved in this transformation, he wasn't sure that he wanted to see, but he didn't think he could leave without seeing. He made his way over the rubble between two blocks of houses.

The sky was darker than it had been when he'd entered the town hall. The gathering twilight slowed him down, and so did sights in the park. Two supine poles, each with a huge red smiling mouth at one end, might have been intended to support a screen, and perhaps the section of a helter-skelter choked with mud was all that had been delivered, though it seemed to corkscrew straight down into the earth. He wondered if any ride except the roundabout had been completed, and then he realised with a jerk of the heart that he had been passing the sideshows for minutes. They were in the houses, and so was the crowd.

At least, he assumed those were players seated around a Bingo counter inside the section of terrace ahead, though the figures in the dimness were so still that he couldn't be certain. He preferred to sidle past rather than go closer to look. The roundabout was behind him now, and he thought he saw a relatively clear path toward where his old house should be. But the sight of the dungeon inside the next jagged fragment of terrace froze him.

It wasn't just a dungeon, it was a torture chamber. Half-naked dummies were chained to the walls. Signs hung around their necks: one was a RAPIST, another a CHILD MOLESTER. A woman with curlers like worms in her hair was prodding one dummy's armpit with a red-hot poker, a man in a cloth cap was wrenching out his victim's teeth. All the figures, not just the victims, were absolutely motionless. If this was someone's idea of waxworks, Slade didn't see the point. He had been staring so hard and so long that the figures appeared to be staggering, unable to hold their poses, when he heard something come to life behind him.

He felt as if the dimness in which his feet were sunk had become mud. Even if the sounds hadn't been so large he would have preferred not to see what was making them, wheezing feebly and scraping and thudding like a giant heart straining to revive. He forced his head to turn, his neck creaking, but at first he could see only how dark the place had grown while he had been preoccupied with the dungeon. He glimpsed movement as large as a house between the smudged outlines of the buildings, and shrank into himself. But it was only the roundabout, plodding in the dark.

He couldn't quite laugh at his dread. The horses were moving as if they could hardly raise themselves and yearned to fall more quickly and finally than they could. There were figures on their backs, and now he realised he had glimpsed the figures earlier, in which case they must have been sitting immobile: waiting for the dark? They weren't going anywhere, they were no threat to him, he could look away and make for the house — but when he did he recoiled, so violently he almost fell. The torturers in the dungeon were stirring. They were turning their heads toward him.

He couldn't see much of their faces, and that didn't seem to be only the fault of the dark. He began to sink into a crouch as if they mightn't see him, he was close to squeezing his eyes shut as though that would make him invisible, the way he'd believed it would when he was a child. Then he flung himself aside, out of range of any eyes that might be searching for him, and fled.

Though the night was thickening, he could see more than he wanted to see. One block of unlit houses had been turned into a shooting gallery, although at first he didn't realise that the six disembodied heads nodding forward in unison were meant to be targets. They must be, not least because all six had the same face — a face he knew from somewhere. He stumbled past the heads as the six of them leaned toward him out of the dark beyond the figures that were aiming at them. He felt as if the staring heads were pleading with him to intervene. He was so desperate to outdistance his clinging dismay that he almost fell into the canal.

He hadn't noticed it at first because a section had been walled in to make a tunnel. It must be a Tunnel of Love: a gondola was inching its way out of the weedy mouth, bringing a sound of choked slopping and a smell of unhealthy growth. Slade could just distinguish the heads of the couple in the gondola. They looked as if they hadn't seen daylight for years.

He swallowed a shriek and retreated alongside the canal, toward the main road. As he slithered along the overgrown stony margin, flailing his arms to keep his balance, he remembered where he'd seen the face on the targets: in a photograph. It was the entrepreneur's face. The man had died of a heart attack soon after he'd gone bankrupt, and hadn't he gone bankrupt shortly after persuading the townsfolk to invest whatever money they had? Slade began to mutter desperately, apologising for whatever he might have helped to cause if it had harmed the town, if anyone who might be listening resented it. He'd only been trying to do his best for the town, he was sorry if it had gone wrong. He was still apologising breathlessly as he sprawled up a heap of debris and onto the bridge that carried the main road over the canal.

He fled along the unlit road, past the town hall and the sound of the relentless waltz in the dark. The aproned baker was serving at his counter, performing the same movements for almost certainly the same customer, and Slade felt as though that was his fault somehow, as though he ought to have accepted the offer of light. He mustn't confuse himself with that, he must get to his car and drive, anywhere so long as it was out of this place. It occurred to him that anyone who could leave the town had done so — and then, as he came in sight of his car, he thought of the blind woman in the hotel.

He mustn't leave her. She mustn't be aware of what had happened to the town, whatever that was. She hadn't even switched on the lights of the hotel. He shoved desperately at the revolving doors, which felt crusty and brittle under his hands, and staggered into the lobby. He grabbed the edges of the doorway to steady himself while his eyes adjusted to the murk that swarmed like darkness giving birth. The receptionist was at her desk, tapping her chin in the rhythm of the melody inside her head. She shuffled papers and glanced up. "Hello, may I help you?"

"No, I want — " Slade called across the lobby, and faltered as his voice came flatly back to him.

"What would you like?"

He was afraid to go closer. He'd remembered the bellman, who must be waiting to open the door beside the desk and who might even come out now that it was dark. That wasn't why Slade couldn't speak, however. He'd realised that the echo of his voice sounded disconcertingly like the voice on the hotel phone. "I'm sure we can accommodate you," the receptionist said.

She was only trying to welcome a guest, Slade reassured himself. He was still trying to urge himself forward when she said "Thank you, sir, that's fine."

She must be on the phone, otherwise she wouldn't be saying "If there's anything else we can do to make you more at home, just let us know." Now she would put down the phone Slade couldn't see, and he would go to her, now that she'd said "Thank you very much" — and then she thumped the bell on the counter.

Slade fought his way out of the rusty trap of the revolving doors as the bellman poked his glimmering face into the lobby. The receptionist was only as sightless as the rest of the townsfolk, he thought like a scream of hysterical laughter. He'd realised something else: the tune she was tapping. Dum, dum-da-dum, dum-da-dum-da-dum-da-dum. It was Chopin: the Dead March.

He dragged his keys out of his pocket, ripping stitches loose, as he ran to his car. The key wouldn't fit the lock. Of course it would — he was inserting it somehow the wrong way. It crunched into the slot, which sounded rusty, just as he realised why the angle was wrong. Both tyres on that side of the car were flat. The wheels were resting on their metal rims.

He didn't need the car, he could run. Surely the townsfolk couldn't move very fast or, to judge by his observations, very far. He fled to the tunnel that led under the railway. But even if he made himself venture through the shrilly whispering dark in there to the gates, it would be no use. The gates were shut, and several bars thicker than his arm had slid across them into sockets in the wall.

He turned away as if he was falling, as if the pressure of the scream he was suppressing was starving his brain. The road was still deserted. The only other way out of the town was at the far end. He ran, his lungs rusty and aching, past houses where families appeared to be dining in the dark, past the town hall with its smothered waltz, over the bridge toward which a gondola was floundering, bearing a couple whose heads, lolled apart from each other and then knocked their mouths together with a hollow bony sound. The curve of the road cut off his view of the far side of town until he was almost there. The last of the houses came in sight, and he tried to tell himself that it was only darkness that blocked the road. But it was solid, and high as the roofs.

Whether it was a pile of rubble or an imperfectly built wall, it was certainly too dangerous to climb. Slade turned away, feeling steeped in despair thick as pitch, and saw his house.

Was it his panic that made it appear to glow faintly in the midst of the terrace? Otherwise it looked exactly like its neighbours, a bedroom window above a curtained parlour beside a nondescript front door with a narrow fanlight. He didn't care how he was able to see it, he was too grateful that he was. As he fled toward it he had the sudden notion that his father might have changed the lock since Slade had left, that Slade's key would no longer let him in.

The lock yielded easily. The door opened wide and showed him the dark hall, which led past the stairs to the parlour on the left, the kitchen at the back. The house felt more familiar than anything else in the world, and it was the only refuge available to him, yet he was afraid to step forward. He was afraid his parents might be there, compulsively repeating some everyday task, blind to him and the state of themselves — though if what was left of them could be aware of him, that might be even worse.

Then he thought he heard movement in the street, and he stumbled to the parlour door and pushed it open. The parlour was deserted, the couch and chairs were as grey as the hearth they faced, yet the stagnant dimness seemed tense, poised to reveal that the room wasn't empty after all. The kitchen with its wooden chairs that pressed against the bare table between the oven and the sink seemed breathless with imminence too. But he was almost sure that he heard movement, slow and stealthy, somewhere outside the house. He scrambled back to the front door and closed it as silently as he could, then he groped his way upstairs.

The bathroom window was a dull rectangle which gleamed faintly in the mirror like a lid that was opening. The bath looked as if it were brimming with tar. Even that was less dismaying than his parents' bedroom: suppose he found them in the bed, struggling to make love like fleshless puppets? He felt as if he were shrinking, reverting to the age he'd been when his father had shouted at him not to open their door. His hands fluttered at it now and inched it far enough to show him their empty bed, and then he dodged into his room.

His bed was still there, his chest of drawers, his wardrobe hardly wide enough for him to hide in any longer. He shouldered the door of the room closed tight and huddled against it. He felt suddenly as though if he went to the bed he might awaken and discover he had been dreaming of the town, just a nightmare about growing up. He mustn't take refuge in the bed, it would be too like retreating into his childhood — and then he realised he already had.

He'd been left alone in the house just once when he was a child. He'd awakened and blundered through the empty rooms, every one of which seemed to be concealing some terror that was about to show itself. He remembered how that had felt: exactly as the house felt now. He'd retraced the memory without realising. Then a neighbour who'd been meant to keep an eye on him had looked in to reassure him, but he prayed that wouldn't happen now, that nobody would come to keep him company. Surely his house couldn't be where they felt most at home.

"Never fear," the voice on the phone had advised him — but Slade had. The night couldn't last forever, he told himself desperately, pressing himself against the door. The sun would rise, the bars would slide back to let the gates open, and even if they didn't he would be able to see a way out. But he felt as if there was nowhere to go: he couldn't recall the faces of his colleagues, the name of the London firm, even the name of the street where he lived. He didn't need to remember those now, he needed only to stay awake until dawn. Surely the rest of the town was too busy to welcome him home, unless it was his fear that was bringing the movement he could hear in the street. It sounded like a wordless crowd which could barely walk but which was determined to try. They couldn't move fast, he thought like a last prayer, they would have to stop when the sun came up — but clearer than that was the thought of how endless the night could seem when you were a child.

SEE HOW THEY RUN

THROUGH THE READING OF THE CHARGES Foulsham felt as if the man in the dock was watching him. December sunshine like ice transmuted into illumination slanted through the high windows of the courtroom, spotlighting the murderer. With his round slightly pouting face and large dark moist eyes Fishwick resembled a schoolboy caught red-handed, Foulsham thought, except that surely no schoolboy would have confronted the prospect of retribution with such a look of imperfectly concealed amusement mingled with impatience.

The indictment was completed. "How do you plead?"

"Not guilty," Fishwick said in a high clear voice with just a hint of mischievous emphasis on the first word. Foulsham had the impression that he was tempted to take a bow, but instead Fishwick folded his arms and glanced from the prosecuting counsel to the defence, cueing their speeches so deftly that Foulsham felt his own lips twitch.

"... a series of atrocities so cold-blooded that the jury may find it almost impossible to believe that any human being could be capable of them..." "...evidence that a brilliant mind was tragically damaged by a lifetime of abuse ..." Fishwick met both submissions with precisely the same attitude, eyebrows slightly raised, a forefinger drumming on his upper arm as though he were commenting in code on the proceedings. His look of lofty patience didn't change as one of the policemen who had arrested him gave evidence, and Foulsham sensed that Fishwick was eager to get to the meat of the case. But the judge adjourned the trial for the day, and Fishwick contented himself with a faint anticipatory smirk.

The jurors were escorted past the horde of reporters and through the business district to their hotel. Rather to Foulsham's surprise, none of his fellow jurors mentioned Fishwick, neither over dinner nor afterwards, when the jury congregated in the cavernous lounge as if they were reluctant to be alone. Few of the jurors showed much enthusiasm for breakfast, so that Foulsham felt slightly guilty for clearing his plate. He was the last to leave the table and the first to reach the door of the hotel, telling himself that he wanted to be done with the day's ordeal. Even the sight of a newsvendor's placard which proclaimed FISHWICK JURY SEE HORROR PICTURES TODAY failed to deter him.

Several of the jurors emitted sounds of distress as the pictures were passed along the front row. A tobacconist shook his head over them, a gesture which seemed on the point of growing uncontrollable. Some of Foulsham's companions on the back row craned forwards for a preview, but Foulsham restrained himself; they were here to be dispassionate, after all. As the pictures came towards him, their progress marked by growls of outrage and murmurs of dismay, he began to feel unprepared, in danger of performing clumsily in front of the massed audience. When at last the pictures reached him he gazed at them for some time without looking up.

They weren't as bad as he had secretly feared. Indeed, what struck him most was their economy and skill. With just a few strokes of a black felt-tipped pen, and the occasional embellishment of red, Fishwick had captured everything he wanted to convey about his subjects: the grotesqueness which had overtaken their gait as they attempted to escape once he'd severed a muscle; the way the crippled dance of each victim gradually turned into a crawl — into less than that once Fishwick had dealt with both arms. No doubt he'd been as skilful with the blade as he was with the pen. Foulsham was reexamining the pictures when the optician next to him nudged him. "The rest of us have to look too, you know."

Foulsham waited several seconds before looking up. Everyone in the courtroom was watching the optician now — everyone but Fishwick. This time there was no question that the man in the dock was gazing straight at Foulsham, whose face stiffened into a mask he wanted to believe was expressionless. He was struggling to look away when the last juror gave an appalled cry and began to crumple the pictures. The judge hammered an admonition, the usher rushed to reclaim the evidence, and Fishwick stared at Foulsham as if they were sharing a joke. The flurry of activity let Foulsham look away, and he did his best to copy the judge's expression of rebuke tempered with sympathy for the distressed woman.

That night he couldn't get to sleep for hours. Whenever he closed his eyes he saw the sketches Fishwick had made. The trial wouldn't last forever, he reminded himself; soon his life would return to normal. Every so often, as he lay in the dark which smelled of bath soap and disinfectant and carpet shampoo, the taps in the bathroom released a gout of water with a choking sound. Each time that happened, the pictures in his head lurched closer, and he felt as if he was being watched. Would he feel like that over Christmas if, as seemed likely, the trial were to continue into the new year? But it lacked almost a week to Christmas when Fishwick was called to the witness box, and Fishwick chose that moment, much to the discomfiture of his lawyer, to plead guilty after all.

The development brought gasps from the public gallery, an exodus from the press benches, mutters of disbelief and anger from the jury; but Foulsham experienced only relief. When the court rose as though to celebrate the turn of events he thought the case was over until he saw that the judge was withdrawing to speak to the lawyers. "The swine," the tobacconist whispered fiercely, glaring at Fishwick. "He made all those people testify for nothing."

Soon the judge and the lawyers returned. It had apparently been decided that the defence should call several psychiatrists to state their views of Fishwick's mental condition. The first of them had scarcely opened his mouth, however, when Fishwick began to express impatience as severe as Foulsham sensed more than one of the jurors were suffering. The man in the dock protruded his tongue like a caricature of a madman and emitted a creditable imitation of a jolly banjo which all but drowned out the psychiatrist's voice. Eventually the judge had Fishwick removed from the court, though not without a struggle, and the psychiatrists were heard.

Fishwick's mother had died giving birth to him, and his father had never forgiven him. The boy's first schoolteacher had seen the father tearing up pictures Fishwick had painted for him. There was some evidence that the father had been prone to uncontrollable fits of violence against the child, though the boy had always insisted that he had broken his own leg by falling downstairs. All of Fishwick's achievements as a young man seemed to have antagonised the father — his exercising his leg for years until he was able to conceal his limp, his enrolment in an art college, the praise which his teachers heaped on him and which he valued less than a word of encouragement from his father. He'd been in his twenties, and still living with his father, when a gallery had offered to exhibit his work. Nobody knew what his father had said which had caused Fishwick to destroy all his paintings in despair and to overcome his disgust at working in his father's shop in order to learn the art of butchery. Before long he had been able to rent a bed-sitter, and thirteen months after moving into it he'd tracked down one of his former schoolfellows who used to call him Quasimodo on account of his limp and his dispirited slouch. Four victims later, Fishwick had made away with his father and the law had caught up with him.

Very little of this had been leaked to the press. Foulsham found himself imagining Fishwick brooding sleeplessly in a cheerless room, his creative nature and his need to prove himself festering within him until he was unable to resist the compulsion to carry out an act which would make him feel meaningful. The other jurors were less impressed. "I might have felt some sympathy for him if he'd gone straight for his father," the hairdresser declared once they were in the jury room.

Fishwick had taken pains to refine his technique first, Foulsham thought, and might have said so if the tobacconist hadn't responded. "I've no sympathy for that cold fish," the man said between puffs at a briar. "You can see he's still enjoying himself. He only pleaded not guilty so that all those people would have to be reminded what they went through."

"We can't be sure of that," Foulsham protested.

"More worried about him than about his victims, are you?" the tobacconist demanded, and the optician intervened. "I know it seems incredible that anyone could enjoy doing what he did," she said to Foulsham, "but that creature's not like us."

Foulsham would have liked to be convinced of that. After all, if Fishwick weren't insane, mustn't that mean anyone was capable of such behaviour? "I think he pleaded guilty when he realised that everyone was going to hear all those things about him he wanted to keep secret," he said. "I think he thought that if he pleaded guilty the psychiatrists wouldn't be called."

The eleven stared at him. "You think too much," the tobacconist said.

The hairdresser broke the awkward silence by clearing her throat. "I never thought I'd say this, but I wish they'd bring back hanging just for him."

"That's the Christmas present he deserves," said the veterinarian who had crumpled the evidence.

The foreman of the jury, a bank manager, proposed that it was time to discuss what they'd learned at the trial. "Personally, I don't mind where they lock him up so long as they throw away the key."

His suggestion didn't satisfy most of the jurors. The prosecuting counsel had questioned the significance of the psychiatric evidence, and the judge had hinted broadly in his summing-up that it was inconclusive. It took all the jurors apart from Foulsham less than half an hour to dismiss the notion that Fishwick might have been unable to distinguish right from wrong, and then they gazed expectantly at Foulsham, who had a disconcerting sense that Fishwick was awaiting his decision too. "I don't suppose it matters where they lock him up," he began, and got no further; the rest of the jury responded with cheers and applause, which sounded ironic to him. Five minutes later they'd agreed to recommend a life sentence for each of Fishwick's crimes. "That should keep him out of mischief," the bank manager exulted.

As the jury filed into the courtroom Fishwick leaned forwards to scrutinise their faces. His own was blank. The foreman stood up to announce the verdict, and Foulsham was suddenly grateful to have that done on his behalf. He hoped Fishwick would be put away for good. When the judge confirmed six consecutive life sentences, Foulsham released a breath which he hadn't been aware of holding. Fishwick had shaken his head when asked if he had anything to say before sentence was passed, and his face seemed to lose its definition as he listened to the judge's pronouncement. His gaze trailed across the jury as he was led out of the dock.

Once Foulsham was out of the building, in the crowded streets above which glowing Santas had been strung up, he didn't feel as liberated as he'd hoped. Presumably that would happen when sleep had caught up with him. Just now he was uncomfortably aware how all the mannequins in the store windows had been twisted into posing. Whenever shoppers turned from gazing into a window he thought they were emerging from the display. As he dodged through the shopping precinct, trying to avoid shoppers rendered angular by packages, families mined with small children, clumps of onlookers surrounding the open suitcases of street traders, he felt as if the maze of bodies were crippling his progress.

Foulsham's had obviously been thriving in his absence. The shop was full of people buying Christmas cards and rolled-up posters and framed prints. "Are you glad it's over?" Annette asked him. "He won't ever be let out, will he?"

"Was he as horrible as the papers made out?" Jackie was eager to know.

"I can't say. I didn't see them," Foulsham admitted, experiencing a surge of panic as Jackie produced a pile of tabloids from under the counter. "I'd rather forget," he said hastily.

"You don't need to read about it, Mr Foulsham, you lived through it," Annette said. "You look as though Christmas can't come too soon for you."

"If I oversleep tomorrow I'll be in on Monday," Foulsham promised, and trudged out of the shop.

All the taxis were taken, and so he had to wait almost half an hour for a bus. If he hadn't been so exhausted he might have walked home. As the bus laboured uphill he clung to the dangling strap which was looped around his wrist and stared at a grimacing rubber clown whose limbs were struggling to unbend from the bag into which they'd been forced. Bodies swayed against him like meat in a butcher's lorry, until he was afraid of being trapped out of reach of the doors when the bus came to his stop.

As he climbed his street, where frost glittered as if the tarmac was reflecting the sky, he heard children singing carols in the distance or on television. He let himself into the house on the brow of the hill, and the poodles in the ground-floor flat began to yap as though he was a stranger. They continued barking while he sorted through the mail which had accumulated on the hall table: bills, advertisements, Christmas cards from people he hadn't heard from since last year. "Only me, Mrs Hutton," he called as he heard her and her stick plodding through her rooms towards the clamour. Jingling his keys as further proof of his identity, and feeling unexpectedly like a jailor, he hurried upstairs and unlocked his door.

Landscapes greeted him. Two large framed paintings flanked the window of the main room: a cliff baring strata of ancient stone above a deserted beach, fields spiky with hedgerows and tufted with sheep below a horizon where a spire poked at fat clouds as though to pop them; beyond the window, the glow of streetlamps streamed downhill into a pool of light miles wide from which pairs of headlight beams were flocking. The pleasure and the sense of all-embracing calm which he habitually experienced on coming home seemed to be standing back from him. He dumped his suitcase in the bedroom and hung up his coat, then he took the radio into the kitchen.

He didn't feel like eating much. He finished off a slice of toast laden with baked beans, and wondered whether Fishwick had eaten yet, and what his meal might be. As soon as he'd sluiced plate and fork he made for his armchair with the radio. Before long, however, he'd had enough of the jazz age. Usually the dance music of that era roused his nostalgia for innocence, not least because the music was older than he was, but just now it seemed too good to be true. So did the views on the wall and beyond the window, and the programmes on the television — the redemption of a cartoon Scrooge, commercials chortling "Ho ho ho", an appeal on behalf of people who would be on their own at Christmas, a choir reiterating "Let nothing you display", the syntax of which he couldn't grasp. As his mind fumbled with it, his eyelids drooped. He nodded as though agreeing with himself that he had better switch off the television, and then he was asleep.

Fishwick wakened him. Agony flared through his right leg. As he lurched out of the chair, trying to blink away the blur which coated his eyes, he was afraid the leg would fail him. He collapsed back into the chair, thrusting the leg in front of him, digging his fingers into the calf in an attempt to massage away the cramp. When at last he was able to bend the leg without having to grit his teeth, he set about recalling what had invaded his sleep.

The nine o'clock news had been ending. It must have been a newsreader who had spoken Fishwick's name. Foulsham hadn't been fully awake, after all; no wonder he'd imagined that the voice sounded like the murderer's. Perhaps it had been the hint of amusement which his imagination had seized upon, though would a newsreader have sounded amused? He switched off the television and waited for the news on the local radio station, twinges in his leg ensuring that he stayed awake.

He'd forgotten that there was no ten o'clock news. He attempted to phone the radio station, but five minutes of hanging on brought him only a message like an old record on which the needle had stuck, advising him to try later. By eleven he'd hobbled to bed. The newsreader raced through accounts of violence and drunken driving, then rustled her script. "Some news just in," she said. "Police report that convicted murderer Desmond Fishwick has taken his own life while in custody. Full details in our next bulletin."

That would be at midnight. Foulsham tried to stay awake, not least because he didn't understand how, if the local station had only just received the news, the national network could have broadcast it more than ninety minutes earlier. But when midnight came he was asleep. He wakened in the early hours and heard voices gabbling beside him, insomniacs trying to assert themselves on a phone-in programme before the presenter cut them short. Foulsham switched off the radio and imagined the city riddled with cells in which people lay or paced, listening to the babble of their own caged obsessions. At least one of them — Fishwick — had put himself out of his misery. Foulsham massaged his leg until the ache relented sufficiently to let sleep overtake him.

The morning newscast said that Fishwick had killed himself last night, but little else. The tabloids were less reticent, Foulsham discovered once he'd dressed and hurried to the newsagent's. MANIAC'S BLOODY SUICIDE. SAVAGE KILLER SAVAGES HIMSELF. HE BIT OFF MORE THAN HE COULD CHEW. Fishwick had gnawed the veins out of his arms and died from loss of blood.

He must have been insane to do that to himself, Foulsham thought, clutching his heavy collar shut against a vicious wind as he limped downhill. While bathing he'd been tempted to take the day off, but now he didn't want to be alone with the images which the news had planted in him. Everyone around him on the bus seemed to be reading one or other of the tabloids which displayed Fishwick's face on the front page like posters for the suicide, and he felt as though all the paper eyes were watching him. Once he was off the bus he stuffed his newspaper into the nearest bin.

Annette and Jackie met him with smiles which looked encouraging yet guarded, and he knew they'd heard about the death. The shop was already full of customers buying last-minute cards and presents for people they'd almost forgotten, and it was late morning before the staff had time for a talk. Foulsham braced himself for the onslaught of questions and comments, only to find that Jackie and Annette were avoiding the subject of Fishwick, waiting for him to raise it so that they would know how he felt, not suspecting that he didn't know himself. He tried to lose himself in the business of the shop, to prove to them that they needn't be so careful of him; he'd never realised how much their teasing and joking meant to him. But they hardly spoke to him until the last customer had departed, and then he sensed that they'd discussed what to say to him. "Don't you let it matter to you, Mr Foulsham. He didn't," Annette said.

"Don't you dare let it spoil your evening," Jackie told him.

She was referring to the staff's annual dinner. While he hadn't quite forgotten about it, he seemed to have gained an impression that it hadn't much to do with him. He locked the shop and headed for home to get changed. After twenty minutes of waiting in a bus queue whose disgruntled mutters felt like flies bumbling mindlessly around him he walked home, the climb aggravating his limp.

He put on his dress shirt and bow tie and slipped his dark suit out of the bag in which it had been hanging since its January visit to the cleaners. As soon as he was dressed he went out again, away from the sounds of Mrs Hutton's three-legged trudge and of the dogs, which hadn't stopped barking since he had entered the house. Nor did he care for the way Mrs Hutton had opened her door and peered at him with a suspiciousness which hadn't entirely vanished when she saw him.

He was at the restaurant half an hour before the rest of the party. He sat at the bar, sipping a Scotch and then another, thinking of people who must do so every night in preference to sitting alone at home, though might some of them be trying to avoid doing something worse? He was glad when his party arrived, Annette and her husband, Jackie and her new boyfriend, even though Annette's greeting as he stood up disconcerted him. "Are you all right, Mr Foulsham?" she said, and he felt unpleasantly wary until he realised that she must be referring to his limp.

By the time the turkey arrived at the table the party had opened a third bottle of wine and the conversation had floated loose. "What was he like, Mr Foulsham," Jackie's boyfriend said, "the feller you put away?"

Annette coughed delicately. "Mr Foulsham may not want to talk about it."

"It's all right, Annette. Perhaps I should. He was —" Foulsham said, and trailed off, wishing that he'd taken advantage of the refuge she was offering. "Maybe he was just someone whose mind gave way."

"I hope you've no regrets," Annette's husband said. "You should be proud."

"Of what?"

"Of stopping the killing. He won't kill anyone else."

Foulsham couldn't argue with that, and yet he felt uneasy, especially when Jackie's boyfriend continued to interrogate him. If Fishwick didn't matter, as Annette had insisted when Foulsham was closing the shop, why was everyone so interested in hearing about him? He felt as though they were resurrecting the murderer, in Foulsham's mind if nowhere else. He tried to describe Fishwick, and retailed as much of his own experience of the trial as he judged they could stomach. All that he left unsaid seemed to gather in his mind, especially the thought of Fishwick extracting the veins from his arms.

Annette and her husband gave him a lift home. He meant to invite them up for coffee and brandy, but the poodles started yapping the moment he climbed out of the car. "Me again, Mrs Hutton," he slurred as he hauled himself along the banister. He switched on the light in his main room and gazed at the landscapes on the wall, but his mind couldn't grasp them. He brushed his teeth and drank as much water as he could take, then he huddled under the blankets, willing the poodles to shut up.

He didn't sleep for long. He kept wakening with a stale rusty taste in his mouth. He'd drunk too much, that was why he felt so hot and sticky and closed in. When he eased himself out of bed and tiptoed to the bathroom the dogs began to bark. He rinsed out his mouth but was unable to determine if the water which he spat into the sink was discoloured. He crept out of the bathroom with a glass of water in each hand and crawled shivering into bed, trying not to grind his teeth as pictures which he would have given a good deal not to see rushed at him out of the dark.

In the morning he felt as though he hadn't slept at all. He lay in the creeping sunlight, too exhausted either to sleep or to get up, until he heard the year's sole Sunday delivery sprawl on the doormat. He washed and dressed gingerly, cursing the poodles, whose yapping felt like knives emerging from his skull, and stumbled down to the hall.

He lined up the new cards on his mantelpiece, where there was just enough room for them. Last year he'd had to stick cards onto a length of parcel tape and hang them from the cornice. This year cards from businesses outnumbered those from friends, unless tomorrow restored the balance. He was signing cards in response to some of the Sunday delivery when he heard Mrs Hutton and the poodles leave the house.

He limped to the window and looked down on her. The two leashes were bunched in her left hand, her right was clenched on her stick. She was leaning backwards as the dogs ran her downhill, and he had never seen her look so crippled. He turned away, unsure why he found the spectacle disturbing. Perhaps he should catch up on his sleep while the dogs weren't there to trouble it, except that if he slept now he might be guaranteeing himself another restless night. The prospect of being alone in the early hours and unable to sleep made him so nervous that he grabbed the phone before he had thought who he could ask to visit.

Nobody had time for him today. Of the people ranked on the mantelpiece, two weren't at home, two were fluttery with festive preparations, one was about to drive several hundred miles to collect his parents, one was almost incoherent with a hangover. All of them invited Foulsham to visit them over Christmas, most of them sounding sincere, but that wouldn't take care of Sunday. He put on his overcoat and gloves and hurried downhill by a route designed to avoid Mrs Hutton, and bought his Sunday paper on the way to a pub lunch.

The Bloody Mary wasn't quite the remedy he was hoping for. The sight of the liquid discomforted him, and so did the scraping of the ice cubes against his teeth. Nor was he altogether happy with his lunch; the leg of chicken put him in mind of the process of severing it from the body. When he'd eaten as much as he could hold down, he fled.

The papery sky was smudged with darker clouds, images too nearly erased to be distinguishable. Its light seemed to permeate the city, reducing its fabric to little more than cardboard. He felt more present than anything around him, a sensation which he didn't relish. He closed his eyes until he thought of someone to visit, a couple who'd lived in the house next to his and whose Christmas card invited him to drop in whenever he was passing their new address.

A double-decker bus on which he was the only passenger carried him across town and deposited him at the edge of the new suburb. The streets of squat houses which looked squashed by their tall roofs were deserted, presumably cleared by the Christmas television shows he glimpsed through windows, and his isolation made him feel watched. He limped into the suburb, glancing at the street names.

He hadn't realised the suburb was so extensive. At the end of almost an hour of limping and occasionally resting, he still hadn't found the address. The couple weren't on the phone, or he would have tried to contact them. He might have abandoned the quest if he hadn't felt convinced that he was about to come face to face with the name which, he had to admit, had slipped his mind. He hobbled across an intersection and then across its twin, where a glance to the left halted him. Was that the street he was looking for? Certainly the name seemed familiar. He strolled along the pavement, trying to conceal his limp, and stopped outside a house.

Though he recognised the number, it hadn't been on the card. His gaze crawled up the side of the house and came to rest on the window set into the roof. At once he knew that he'd heard the address read aloud in the courtroom. It was where Fishwick had lived.

As Foulsham gazed fascinated at the small high window he imagined Fishwick gloating over the sketches he'd brought home, knowing that the widow from whom he rented the bed-sitter was downstairs and unaware of his secret. He came to himself with a shudder, and stumbled away, almost falling. He was so anxious to put the city between himself and Fishwick's room that he couldn't bear to wait for one of the infrequent Sunday buses. By the time he reached home he was gritting his teeth so as not to scream at the ache in his leg. "Shut up," he snarled at the alarmed poodles, "or I'll —" and stumbled upstairs.

The lamps of the city were springing alight. Usually he enjoyed the spectacle, but now he felt compelled to look for Fishwick's window among the distant roofs. Though he couldn't locate it, he was certain that the windows were mutually visible. How often might Fishwick have gazed across the city towards him? Foulsham searched for tasks to distract himself — cleaned the oven, dusted the furniture and the tops of the picture-frames, polished all his shoes, lined up the tins on the kitchen shelves in alphabetical order. When he could no longer ignore the barking which his every movement provoked, he went downstairs and rapped on Mrs Hutton's door.

She seemed reluctant to face him. Eventually he heard her shooing the poodles into her kitchen before she came to peer out at him. "Been having a good time, have we?" she demanded.

"It's the season," he said without an inkling of why he should need to justify himself. "Am I bothering your pets somehow?"

"Maybe they don't recognise your walk since you did whatever you did to yourself."

"It happened while I was asleep." He'd meant to engage her in conversation so that she would feel bound to invite him in — he was hoping that would give the dogs a chance to grow used to him again — but he couldn't pursue his intentions when she was so openly hostile, apparently because she felt entitled to the only limp in the building. "Happy Christmas to you and yours," he flung at her, and hobbled back to his floor.

He wrote out his Christmas card list in case he had overlooked anyone, only to discover that he couldn't recall some of the names to which he had already addressed cards. When he began doodling, slashing at the page so as to sketch stick-figures whose agonised contortions felt like a revenge he was taking, he turned the sheet over and tried to read a book. The yapping distracted him, as did the sound of Mrs Hutton's limp; he was sure she was exaggerating it to lay claim to the gait or to mock him. He switched on the radio and searched the wavebands, coming to rest at a choir which was wishing the listener a merry Christmas. He turned up the volume to blot out the noise from below, until Mrs Hutton thumped on her ceiling and the yapping of the poodles began to lurch repetitively at him as they leapt, trying to reach the enemy she was identifying with her stick.

Even his bed was no refuge. He felt as though the window on the far side of the city was an eye spying on him out of the dark, reminding him of all that he was trying not to think of before he risked sleep. During the night he found himself surrounded by capering figures which seemed determined to show him how much life was left in them — how vigorously, if unconventionally, they could dance. He managed to struggle awake at last, and lay afraid to move until the rusty taste like a memory of blood had faded from his mouth.

He couldn't go on like this. In the morning he was so tired that he felt as if he was washing someone else's face and hands. He thought he could feel his nerves swarming. He bared his teeth at the yapping of the dogs and tried to recapture a thought he'd glimpsed while lying absolutely still, afraid to move, in the hours before dawn. What had almost occurred to him about Fishwick's death?

The yapping receded as he limped downhill. On the bus a woman eyed him as if she suspected him of feigning the limp in a vain attempt to persuade her to give up her seat. The city streets seemed full of people who were staring at him, though he failed to catch them in the act. When Jackie and Annette converged on the shop as he arrived he prayed they wouldn't mention his limp. They gazed at his face instead, making him feel they were trying to ignore his leg. "We can cope, Mr Foulsham," Annette said, "if you want to start your Christmas early."

"You deserve it," Jackie added.

What were they trying to do to him? They'd reminded him how often he might be on his own during the next few days, a prospect which filled him with dread. How could he ease his mind in the time left to him? "You'll have to put up with another day of me," he told them as he unlocked the door.

Their concern for him made him feel as if his every move was being observed. Even the Christmas Eve crowds failed to occupy his mind, especially once Annette took advantage of a lull in the day's business to approach him. "We thought we'd give you your present now in case you want to change your mind about going home."

"That's thoughtful of you. Thank you both," he said and retreated into the office, wondering if they were doing their best to get rid of him because something about him was playing on their nerves. He used the phone to order them a bouquet each, a present which he gave them every Christmas but which this year he'd almost forgotten, and then he picked at the parcel until he was able to see what it was.

It was a book of detective stories. He couldn't imagine what had led them to conclude that it was an appropriate present, but it did seem to have a message for him. He gazed at the exposed spine and realised what any detective would have established days ago. Hearing Fishwick's name in the night had been the start of his troubles, yet he hadn't ascertained the time of Fishwick's death.

He phoned the radio station and was put through to the newsroom. A reporter gave him all the information which the police had released. Foulsham thanked her dully and called the local newspaper, hoping they might contradict her somehow, but of course they confirmed what she'd told him. Fishwick had died just before nine-thirty on the night when his name had wakened Foulsham, and the media hadn't been informed until almost an hour later.

He sat at his bare desk, his cindery eyes glaring at nothing, then he stumbled out of the cell of an office. The sounds and the heat of the shop seemed to rush at him and recede in waves on which the faces of Annette and Jackie and the customers were floating. He felt isolated, singled out — felt as he had throughout the trial.

Yet if he couldn't be certain that he had been singled out then, why should he let himself feel that way now without trying to prove himself wrong? "I think I will go early after all," he told Jackie and Annette.

Some of the shops were already closing. The streets were almost blocked with people who seemed simultaneously distant from him and too close, their insect eyes and neon faces shining. When at last he reached the alley between two office buildings near the courts, he thought he was too late. But though the shop was locked, he was just in time to catch the hairdresser. As she emerged from a back room, adjusting the strap of a shoulder-bag stuffed with presents, he tapped on the glass of the door.

She shook her head and pointed to the sign which hung against the glass. Didn't she recognise him? His reflection seemed clear enough to him, like a photograph of himself holding the sign at his chest, even if the placard looked more real than he did. "Foulsham," he shouted, his voice echoing from the close walls. "I was behind you on the jury. Can I have a word?"

"What about?"

He grimaced and mimed glancing both ways along the alley, and she stepped forward, halting as far from the door as the door was tall. "Well?"

"I don't want to shout."

She hesitated and then came to the door. He felt unexpectedly powerful, the winner of a game they had been playing. "I remember you now," she said as she unbolted the door. "You're the one who claimed to be sharing the thoughts of that monster."

She stepped back as an icy wind cut through the alley, and he felt as though the weather was on his side, almost an extension of himself. "Well, spit it out," she said as he closed the door behind him.

She was ranging about the shop, checking that the electric helmets which made him think of some outdated mental treatment were switched off, opening and closing cabinets in which blades glinted, peering beneath the chairs which put him in mind of a death cell. "Can you remember exactly when you heard what happened?" he said.

She picked up a tuft of bluish hair and dropped it in a pedal bin. "What did?"

"He killed himself."

"Oh, that? I thought you meant something important." The bin snapped shut like a trap. "I heard about it on the news. I really can't say when."

"Heard about it, though, not read it."

"That's what I said. Why should it matter to you?"

He couldn't miss her emphasis on the last word, and he felt that both her contempt and the question had wakened something in him. He'd thought he wanted to reassure himself that he hadn't been alone in sensing Fishwick's death, but suddenly he felt altogether more purposeful. "Because it's part of us," he said.

"It's no part of me, I assure you. And I don't think I was the only member of the jury who thought you were too concerned with that fiend for your own good."

An unfamiliar expression took hold of Foulsham's face. "Who else did?"

"If I were you, Mr Whatever-your-name-is, I'd seek help, and quick. You'll have to excuse me. I'm not about to let that monster spoil my Christmas." She pursed her lips and said "I'm off to meet some normal people."

Either she thought she'd said too much or his expression and his stillness were unnerving her. "Please leave," she said more shrilly. "Leave now or I'll call the police."

She might have been heading for the door so as to open it for him. He only wanted to stay until he'd grasped why he was there. The sight of her striding to the door reminded him that speed was the one advantage she had over him. Pure instinct came to his aid, and all at once he seemed capable of anything. He saw himself opening the nearest cabinet, he felt his finger and thumb slip through the chilly rings of the handles of the scissors, and lunging at her was the completion of these movements. Even then he thought he meant only to drive her away from the door, but he was reckoning without his limp. As he floundered towards her he lost his balance, and the points of the scissors entered her right leg behind the knee.

She gave an outraged scream and tried to hobble to the door, the scissors wagging in the patch of flesh and blood revealed by the growing hole in the leg of her patterned tights. The next moment she let out a wail so despairing that he almost felt sorry for her, and fell to her knees, well out of reach of the door. As she craned her head over her shoulder to see how badly she was injured, her eyes were the eyes of an animal caught in a trap. She extended one shaky hand to pull out the scissors, but he was too quick for her. "Let me," he said, taking hold of her thin wrist.

He thought he was going to withdraw the scissors, but as soon as his finger and thumb were through the rings he experienced an overwhelming surge of power which reminded him of how he'd felt as the verdict of the jury was announced. He leaned on the scissors and exerted all the strength he could, and after a while the blades closed with a sound which, though muffled, seemed intensely satisfying.

Either the shock or her struggles and shrieks appeared to have exhausted her. He had time to lower the blinds over the door and windows and to put on one of the plastic aprons which she and her staff must wear. When she saw him returning with the scissors, however, she tried to fight him off while shoving herself with her uninjured leg towards the door. Since he didn't like her watching him — it was his turn to watch — he stopped her doing so, and screaming. She continued moving for some time after he would have expected her to be incapable of movement, though she obviously didn't realise that she was retreating from the door. By the time she finally subsided he had to admit that the game had grown messy and even a little dull.

He washed his hands until they were clean as a baby's, then he parcelled up the apron and the scissors in the wrapping which had contained his present. He let himself out of the shop and limped towards the bus-stops, the book under one arm, the tools of his secret under the other. It wasn't until passers-by smiled in response to him that he realised what his expression was, though it didn't feel like his own smile, any more than he felt personally involved in the incident at the hairdresser's. Even the memory of all the jurors' names didn't feel like his. At least, he thought, he wouldn't be alone over Christmas, and in future he would try to be less hasty. After all, he and whoever he visited next would have more to discuss.

RA*E

"YOU'RE JOKING, LAURA. You're just doing your best to madden your mother and me. You're not going out like that either."

"Dad, I've already changed once."

"And not for the better, but it was better than this. Toddle off to your room again and don't come back down until you've finished trying to provoke us."

"I'll be late. I am already. There isn't another bus for an hour unless I go across the golf course."

"You know that's not an option, so don't give your mother more to worry about than she already has. You shouldn't have wasted all that time arguing."

"Wilf —"

"See how your mother is now. Perhaps she can be permitted a chance to speak before you have your next say. What is it, Claire?"

"I think she can probably go like that rather than be waiting in the dark. I know you'd give her a lift if you weren't on patrol. I only wish I could."

"Well, Laura, you've succeeded in getting round your mother and made her feel guilty for not being able to drive into the bargain. I'm sorry, Claire, that's how it seems to me, but then I'm just the man round here. Since my feelings aren't to be allowed for, I'll have to try and keep them to myself."

"Thanks, mum," Laura said swiftly, and presented her with a quick hug and kiss. Claire had a momentary closeup of her small pale face garnished with freckles above the pert snub nose, of large dark eyes with extravagant lashes which always reminded her how Laura used to gaze up at her from the pram. Then the fourteen-year-old darted out of the room, her sleek straight hair as red as Claire's five years ago swaying across the nape of her slim neck as her abbreviated skirt whirled around the inches of bare thigh above her black stockings. "Thanks, dad," she called, and was out of the front door, admitting a snatch of the whir of a lawnmower and a whiff of the scented May evening.

Wilf had turned his back as she'd swung away from her mother. He sat down heavily in the armchair beside the Welsh dresser on which ranks of photographs of Laura as a baby and a toddler and a little girl were drawn up. He tugged at the knees of his jogging pants as he subsided, and dragged a hand across his bristling eyebrows before using it to smooth his greying hair. "Better now?" said Claire in the hope of dislodging his mood.

He raised his lined wide face until his Adam's apple was almost as prominent as the two knuckles of his chin. "I was serious."

"Oh, now, Wilf, I really don't think you can say your feelings are swept under the carpet all that much. But do remember you aren't the only —"

"About how she dresses, and don't bother telling me you used to dress that way."

"I could again if you like."

"I'm still serious. You were older, old enough your parents couldn't stop us marrying. Besides which, girls weren't in the kind of danger they are these days."

"That's why we have folk like you patrolling. Most people are as decent as they used to be, and three of them live in this house."

He lowered his head as if his thoughts had weighed it down, and peered at her beneath his eyebrows. "Never mind hiding in there," she said with the laugh she had increasingly to use on him. "Instead of thinking whatever you're thinking, why don't you start your patrol early if you're so worried and see her onto the bus."

"By God, you two are alike," he said, slapping his thighs so hard she winced, and pushed himself to his feet.

"That's us women for you."

The front door thumped shut, and Claire expelled a long breath through her nose. If only he wouldn't disapprove quite so openly and automatically of all that Laura was becoming — "What's wrong?" she blurted, because he had tramped back in.

"Nothing you've spotted." He played the xylophone of the stripped pine banisters as he climbed the stairs to the parental bedroom. She'd begun to wonder what was taking him so long when he reappeared, drumming his fingernails on his neighbourhood patrol badge, which he'd pinned to his black top over his heart. "Found it in with your baubles," he said. "Now maybe I've some chance of being taken notice of."

In the photograph he seemed determined to look younger, hence threatening. It still made her want to smile, and to prevent herself she asked "Who's out there at the moment, do you know?"

"Your friend Mr Gummer for one."

"No friend of mine. He'd better not come hanging round here if he sees you're away."

"You'd hope putting on one of these badges would make him into a pillar," Wilf said as he let himself out of the house.

Claire followed to close the filigreed gate at the end of their cobbled path after him, and watched him trot along the street of large twinned houses and garages nestling against them. Perhaps she was being unfair, but Duncan Gummer was the kind of person — no, the only person — who made her wish that those who offered to patrol had to be vetted rather than merely to live in the small suburb. Abruptly she wanted him to show himself and loiter outside her house as he often found an excuse to do while he was on patrol: she could tell him she'd sent Wilf away and see how he reacted. She had a vision of his moist lower lip exposing itself, his clasped hands dangling over his stomach, their inverted prayer indicating his crotch. She wriggled her shoulders to shrug off the image and sent herself into the house to finish icing Laura's cake.

She was halfway through piping the pink letters onto the snow-white disc when she faltered, unable to think how to cross the t of "Happy Birthday" without breaking her script. How had she done it twelve months ago and all the times before? She particularly wanted this cake to be special, because she knew she wouldn't be decorating many more. Perhaps it was the shrilling of an alarm somewhere beyond the long back garden with its borders illuminated by flowers that was putting her off, a rapid bleeping like an Engaged tone speeded up. She imagined trying to place a call only to meet such a response — a sound that panic seemed to be rendering frantic. Nervousness was gaining control of her hands now that Wilf had aggravated the anxiety she experienced just about whenever Laura left the house.

She'd spent some time in flexing her fingers and laying down the plastic tool again for fear of spoiling the inscription — long enough for the back garden to fill up with the shadow of the house — before she decided to go out and look for him. Laura would be fine at the school disco, and on the bus home with her friends, so long as she'd caught the bus there. Having set the alarm — she needn't programme the lights to switch themselves on, she would only be out for a few minutes — Claire draped a linen jacket over her shoulders and walked to the end of the road.

The Chung boys were sluicing the family Lancia with buckets of soapy water and a great deal of Cantonese chatter. Several mowers were rehearsing a drowsy chorus against the improvised percussion of at least two pairs of shears. The most intrusive sound, though not the loudest, was the unanswered plea of the alarm. When Claire reached the junction she saw that the convulsive light that accompanied the noise was several hundred yards away along the cross street, close to the pole of the deserted bus stop at the far end, against the baize humps of the golf course. As she saw all this, the alarm gave up. She turned from it and caught sight of Wilf.

He mustn't have seen her, she thought, because he was striding away. Shrunken by distance, and obviously unaware that his trousers were a little lower than they might be — mere like a building worker's than any outfit of the architect he was — he looked unexpectedly vulnerable. She couldn't imagine his tackling anyone with more than words, but then members of the patrol weren't supposed to use force, only to alert the police. She felt a surge of the old affection, however determined he seemed these days to give it no purchase on his stiff exterior, as she cupped her hands about her mouth. "Wilf."

At first she thought he hadn't heard her. Two mowers had travelled the length of their lawns before he swung round and marched towards her, his face drawn into a mask of concern. "What is it? What's wrong?"

"Nothing, I hope. I just wanted to know if you saw her onto the bus."

"She wasn't there."

"Are you sure?" Claire couldn't help asking. "She'd have been in time for it, wouldn't she?"

"If it came."

"Don't say that. How else could she have gone?"

"Maybe she got herself picked up."

"She'd never have gone in anybody's car she didn't know, not Laura."

"You'd hope not. That's what I meant, a lift from a friend who was going, their parents, rather."

The trouble was that none of Laura's friends would have needed to be driven past the bus stop. Perhaps this had occurred to Wilf, who was staring down the street past Claire. A glance showed her that the streetlamp by the bus stop had acknowledged the growing darkness. The isolated metal flag gleamed like a knife against the secretive mounds of the golf course. "She should be there by now," Claire said.

"You'd imagine so."

It was only a turn of phrase, but it made her suspect herself of being less anxious than he felt there was reason to be. "She won't like it, but she'll have to put up with it," she declared.

"I don't know what you mean."

"I'm going to phone to make sure she's arrived."

"That's — yes, I should."

"Are you coming to hear? You aren't due on the street for a few minutes yet."

"I thought I'd send your favourite man Mr Gummer home early. You're right, though, I ought to be with you for the peace of mind."

If he had just the average share, she reflected, she might have more herself. It took her several minutes to reach the phone, as a preamble to doing which she had to walk home not unduly fast and unbutton the alarm, by which time there was surely no point in calling except to assure herself there wasn't. The phone at the disco went unanswered long enough for Wilf to turn away and rub his face twice; then a girl's voice younger than Claire was expecting, and backed by music loud enough to distort it, said "Sin Tans."

"Hello, St Anne's. This is Laura Maynard's mother. Could I have a quick word with her?"

"Who? Oh, Lor." As Claire deduced this wasn't a mild oath but a version of Laura's name, the girl said "I'll just see."

She was gone at once, presumably laying the receiver down with the mouth toward the music, so that it amplified itself like a dramatic soundtrack in a film. Claire had thought of a question to justify the call and no doubt to annoy Laura — they'd established when she must be home, but not with whom or how — when the girl returned. "Mrs Maynard," she shouted over an upsurge of the music, "she's not here yet, her friend Hannah says."

"You obviously wouldn't know if her bus happened to run."

"Yes, Hannah was on it, but it was early at Lor's stop."

"I understand," said Claire, compelled to sound more like a grown-up than she felt. "Could you ask her to ring home the moment she gets there? The moment you see her, I mean."

"I will, Mrs Maynard."

"Thanks. You're very —" The line went dead, and Claire hung up the receiver beside the stairs, next to the oval mirror in which Wilf was raising his hunched head. Two steps like the heaviness of his expression rendered palpable brought him round to face her. "She's not there, then," he said.

"Not yet."

"Not much we can do, is there? Not till she gets home, and then I'll be having a good few words."

"Don't work yourself up till we know what happened. You always assume it's her fault. I may just nip out to see..."

"I can look if you like while you're waiting for her to call. See what?"

"She'll speak to the machine if we aren't here. I know she wouldn't go across the golf course by herself, but maybe someone she knew went with her if they missed the bus too. If anyone's still playing I can ask if they saw her. It's better than sitting at home thinking things there's no need to think."

"I'll come with you, shall I? If there are any golfers they may be miles apart."

He so visibly welcomed being motivated that she couldn't have refused him. "You set the lights and everything while I go on ahead," she told him.

The twilight was quieter, and almost dark. The mowers had gone to bed. Though she could hear no sound of play from the golf course she made for it, having glanced back to see that Wilf was following, far enough behind that she had a moment of hoping a call from Laura had delayed him. By the time he emerged from their street Claire was nearly at the bus stop.

Smaller flags led away from it, starting at the first hole. The clubhouse was nearby, though screened by one of the thick lines of trees that had been grown to complicate the golf. Claire heard the whop of a club across the miles of grass and sandy hollows, and the approach of a bus, reminding her that it was at least an hour since Laura had left the house. "Come on, Wilf," she urged, and stepped off the concrete onto the turf.

Tines of light from the clubhouse protruded through the trees; one thin beam pricked the corner of her eye. A stroke that sounded muffled by a divot echoed out of the gloom. "I'll find them," she called, pointing towards the invisible game, "while you see if anyone at the clubhouse can help. Show them your badge."

Her last words jerked as she began to jog up a slope towards a copse. Having panted as far as the clump, she glanced at Wilf. "Get a move on," she exhorted, but her words only made him turn to her. She waved him onward and lurched down the far side of the slope.

Her cry brought Wilf stumbling towards her, halting when she regained her balance. "What now?" he demanded, his nervousness crowding into his voice. "What have you —"

"Nearly fell in a bunker, that's all," she said, grateful to have an excuse for even a forced laugh. She took a step which placed the bulk of the copse between her and Wilf and cut off the light from the clubhouse, and looked down.

This time she didn't cry out. "Wilf," she said with the suddenly unfamiliar object she used for speech; then she raised her voice until it became part of the agony she was experiencing. "Wilf," she repeated, and slid down into the bunker.

The slope gave way beneath her feet, and she felt as if the world had done so. The darkness that rose to meet her was the end of the lights of the world. It couldn't blind her to the sight below her, though her mind was doing its best to think that the figure in the depths of the sandpit wasn't Laura — was the child of some poor mother who would scream or faint or go mad when she saw. None of this happened, and in a moment Laura was close enough to touch.

She was lying face down in the hollow. Her skirt had been pulled above her waist, and her legs forced so wide that her panties cut into her stockinged legs just above the knees. The patch of sand between her thighs was stained dark red, and the top of her right leg glistened as if a large snail had crawled down it. Her fists were pressed together above her head in a flurry of sand.

Claire fell to her knees, sand grinding against them, and took hold of Laura's shoulders. She had never known them feel so thin and delicate; she seemed unable to be gentle enough. As Laura's face reluctantly ceased nestling in the slope, Claire heard the whisper of a breath. It was only sand rustling out of Laura's hair — more of the sand which filled her nostrils and her gaping mouth and even her open eyes.

Claire was brushing sand out of Laura's eyelashes, to give herself a moment before the glare of her emotions set about shrivelling her brain — she was remembering Laura at four years old on a day at the seaside, her small sunlit face releasing a tear as Claire dabbed a grain of sand out of her eye — when she heard Wilf above the bunker. "Where are —" he said, then "Oh, you're — What —"

She shrank into herself while she awaited his reaction. When it came, his wordless roar expressed outrage and grief enough for her as well. She looked up to see him clutching at his heart, and heard cloth tear. He was twisting the badge, digging the pin into his chest. "Don't," she pleaded. "That won't help."

He wavered at the top of the bunker as if he might fall, then he trudged down the outside of the hollow to slither in and kneel beside her. She felt his arms tremble about her and Laura before gripping them in a hug whose fierceness summed up his helplessness. "Be careful of her," she hardly knew she said.

"I did it."

She almost wrenched herself free of him, his words were so ill-chosen. "What are you saying?"

"If I hadn't made her miss her bus by going on at her..."

"Oh, Wilf." She could think of nothing more to say, because she agreed with him. His arms slackened as though he felt unworthy to hold her and Laura; she couldn't tell if he was even touching her. One of them would have to get up and fetch someone — he would, because she found she couldn't bear the thought of leaving Laura to grow cold as the night was growing. But there was no need for him to go. Someone was observing them from above the bunker.

The emotion this set off started her eyes burning, and she might have scrambled up the slope to launch herself at the intruder if he hadn't spoken. "What are you people up to in there? This is private property. Please take your —" His voice faltered as he peered down. "Dear Christ, what's happened here?" he said, and was irrelevant to her fury — had been as soon as she'd grasped he wasn't the culprit. Nothing but finding them might bring to an end the blaze of rage which had begun to consume every feeling she would otherwise have had.

"Mrs Maynard."

She could pretend she hadn't heard, Claire thought, and carry on plodding. But a supermarket assistant who was loading the shelves with bottles of Scotch and gin nodded his head at her. "There's a lady wants to speak to you."

"Mrs Maynard, it is you, isn't it? It's Daisy Gummer."

Claire knew that. She was considering speeding her trolley out of the aisle when her exit was blocked by a trolley with a little girl hanging onto one side — a six- or seven-year-old in the school uniform Laura had worn at that age. Claire's hands clenched, and she swung her trolley round to point at her summoner.

Mrs Gummer was in her wheelchair, a wire basket on her lap. The jacket and trousers of her orange suit seemed designed to betray as little of her shape as possible. Her silver curls were beginning to unwind and grow dull. Her large pale puffed-up face made to crumple as her eyes met Claire's, then rendered itself into an emblem of strength. "Has to be done, eh?" she declared with a surplus of heartiness. "It's not the men who go out hunting any longer."

The little this meant to Claire included the possibility that the old woman's son wasn't with her, not that his absence was any reason to linger. Before Claire could devise a reply that would double as a farewell, Mrs Gummer said "Still fixing up people's affairs for them, are you? Still tidying up after them?"

"If that's what you want to say accountants do."

"Nothing wrong with using any tricks you know," Mrs Gummer said, performing a wink that involved pinching her right eye with most of that side of her face. "Duncan's done a few with my money at his bank." As though preparing to reveal some of them, she leaned over her lapful of tins. "What I was going to say was you keep working. Keep your mind occupied. I wished I'd had a job when we lost his father."

"That would have helped you forget, would it?"

"I don't know about forget. Come to terms would be about the size of it."

"And what sort of terms would you suggest I come to?" Claire heard herself being unpleasant, perhaps unreasonable, but these were merely hints of the feelings that constantly lay in wait for her. "Please. Do tell me whatever you think I should know."

The old woman's gaze wavered and focused beyond her, and Claire had an excuse to move out of the way of whoever was there. Then she heard him say "Here's the soap you like, mother, that's gentle on your skin. Who's your friend you've been talking to?"

"You know Mrs Maynard. We were just talking about..." Apparently emboldened by the presence of her son, Mrs Gummer brought her gaze to bear on the other woman. "How long has it been now, you poor thing?"

"Three months and a week and two days."

"Have they found the swine yet?"

"They say not."

"I know what I'd do to him if I got hold of him, chair or no chair." Mrs Gummer dealt its arms a blow each with her fists, perhaps reflecting on the difficulties involved in her proposal, before refraining from some of another wink as she said "They'll be testing the men round here soon though, won't they? It isn't just fingerprints and blood these days, is it?"

The possibility that the old woman was taking a secret delight in this sickened Claire, who was gripping her trolley to steer it away when Duncan Gummer said "I shouldn't imagine they think he's from our neighbourhood, mother."

He'd taken his position behind the wheelchair and was regarding Claire, his eyes even moister than his display of lower lip. "They've told you that, have they?" she demanded. "That's the latest bulletin for the patrol."

"Not officially, no, Mrs Maynard. I'm sure Mr Maynard would have told you if they had. I was just thinking myself that this evil maniac would surely have had enough sense, not that I'm suggesting he has sense like ordinary folk unless he does and that's part of how he's evil, he'd have kept his, his activities well away from home, would you not think?" He looked away from her silence as a load of bottles jangled onto a shelf, and let his lip sag further. "What I've been meaning to say to you," he muttered, "I can't blame myself enough for not being out that night when I was meant to be on patrol."

"Don't listen to him. It's not true."

"Mother, you mustn't —"

"It was my fault for being such a worn-out old crock."

"That's what I meant. You weren't to know. You mustn't take it on yourself."

"He thought I was turning my toes up when all I was was passed out from finishing the bottle."

"Can't be helped," Claire said for the Gummers to take how they liked, and turned away, to be confronted by the liquor shelves and her inability to recall how much gin was left at home. She was letting her hand stray along the relevant shelf when Mrs Gummer said "You grab it if that's what you need. I know I did when his father left us."

Claire snatched her hand back and drove her trolley to the checkout as fast as the shoppers she encountered would allow. She couldn't risk growing like Mrs Gummer while Laura went unavenged. Time enough when the law had taken its course for her to collapse into herself. She arranged her face to signify that she was too preoccupied to talk to the checkout girl, and imitated smiling at her before wheeling out the trolley onto the sunlit concrete field of the car park.

Tasks helped advance the process of continuing to be alive, but tasks came to an end. At least riding on the free bus from the supermarket to the stop by the golf course was followed by having to drag her wheeled basket home. She might have waited for Wilf to drive her if waiting in the empty house hadn't proved too much for her. His need to go back to work had forced her to do so herself, and on the whole she was glad of it, as long as she could do the computations and the paperwork while leaving her colleagues to deal face to face with clients. She didn't want people sympathising with her, softening the feelings she was determined to hoard.

As she let herself into the house the alarm cried to be silenced before it could raise its voice. Once that would have meant Laura wasn't home from school, and Claire would have been anxious unless she knew why. She wouldn't have believed the removal of that anxiety would have left such a wound in her, too deep to touch. She quelled the alarm and hugged the lumpy basket to her while she laboured to transport it over the expensive carpet of the suddenly muggy hall to the kitchen, where she set about loading the refrigerator. She left the freezer until last, because as soon as she opened it, all she could see was Laura's birthday cake.

She'd thought of serving it after the funeral, but she would have felt bound to scrape off the inscription. That still ended at the unfinished letter — the cross she had never made. She'd considered burying the cake in the back garden, but that would have been too final too soon; keeping it seemed to promise that in time she would be able to celebrate the fate of Laura's destroyer. She reached into its icy nest and moved it gently to the back of the freezer so as to wall it in with packages. While Wilf rarely opened the freezer, she could do without having to explain to him.

He ought to be home soon. She might have made a start on the work she'd brought home from the office, except that she knew she would become aware of trying to distract herself from the emptiness of the house. She wandered through the front room, past the black chunks of silence that were the hi-fi and videorecorder and television, and the shelves of bound classics she'd hoped might encourage Laura to read more, and stood at the window. The street was deserted, but she felt compelled to watch — to remember. Remember what, for pity's sake? She'd lost patience with herself, and was stepping back to prove she had some control, when she saw what she should have realised in the supermarket, and grew still as a cat which had seen a mouse.

"Wilf?"

"Love?"

"What would you do..."

"Carry on. We've never had secrets from each other, have we? Whatever it is, you can say."

"What would you do if you knew who'd, who it was who did that to Laura?"

"Tell the police."

"Suppose you hadn't any proof they'd think was proof?"

"Still tell them. They'll sort out if there's proof or not. If you tell them they'll have to follow it up, won't they? That's what we pay them for, those that do, that you haven't fixed up not to pay tax."

"I'd be best phoning and not saying who I am, wouldn't I? That way they can't find out how much I really know."

"Whatever you say, love."

He had to agree with her, since he wasn't there: he'd left home an hour ago to be early at a building site. She couldn't really have had such a conversation with him when he would have insisted on learning why she was suspicious, and then at the very least would have thought she was taking umbrage which in fact she was too old and used up to take. She knew better, however. If Duncan Gummer had been as obsessed with her as she'd assumed him to be, how could he have needed his mother to identify her at the supermarket? Now Claire knew he'd used his patrolling as an excuse to loiter near the house because he'd been obsessed with Laura, a thought which turned her hands into claws. She had to force them to relax before she was able to programme the alarm.

The suburb was well awake. All the surviving children were on their way to school; a few were even walking. The neighbourhood's postman for the last four months had stopped for a chat with a group of mothers being tugged at by small children. Less than a week ago Claire would have been instantly suspicious of him — of any man in the suburb and probably beyond it too — but now there was only room in her mind for one. She even managed a smile at the postman as she headed for the golf course.

The old footpath, bare as a strip of skin amid the turf, led past the first bunker, and she made herself glance in. It was unmarked, unstained. "We're going to get him," she whispered to the virgin sand, and strode along the path to the main road.

A phone box stood next to the golf course, presenting its single opaque side to a bus stop. Claire pulled the reluctant door shut after her and took out her handkerchief, which she wadded over the mouthpiece of the receiver. Having typed the digits that would prevent her call from being traced, she rang the police. As soon as a female voice, more efficient than welcoming, announced itself she said "I want to talk about the Laura Maynard case."

"Hold on, madam, I'll put you through to —"

"No, you listen." Now that she was past the most difficult utterance — describing Laura as a case — Claire was in control. "I know who did it. I saw him."

"Madam, if I can ask you just to —"

"Write this down, or if you can't do that, remember it. It's his name and address." Claire gave the information twice and immediately cut off the call, which brought her plan of action to so definite an end that she almost forgot to pocket her handkerchief before hanging the phone up. She stepped out beneath a sky which seemed enlarged and brightened, and had only to walk to the stop to be in time for an approaching bus. As she grasped the metal pole and swung herself onto the platform of the bus she was reminded how it felt to step onto a fairground ride. "All the way," she said, and rode to the office.

"Claire? I'm back."

"I was wondering where on earth you'd got to. Come and sit and have a drink. I've something I've been wanting to —"

"I'm with someone, so —"

"Who?"

"No need to sound like that. Someone you know. Detective Inspector Bairns."

"Come in too, Inspector, if you don't mind me leaving off your first bit. I don't suppose you'll have a drink."

"I won't, thanks, Mrs Maynard, not in the course of the job. Thank you for asking."

She wasn't sure she had — she was too aware of the policeman he'd made of himself. His tread was light for such a stocky fellow; the features huddled between his high forehead and potato chin were slow to betray any expression, never including a smile in her limited experience, but his eyes were constantly searching. "Do have one yourselves," he said.

"I'll get them, Claire. I can see you're ready for a refill."

"You'll have the Inspector thinking I've turned to the bottle."

"Nobody would blame you, Mrs Maynard, or at any rate I wouldn't." Bairns lowered himself into the twin of her massive leather armchair and glanced at Wilf. "Nothing soft either, thanks," he responded before settling his attention on Claire.

She smiled and raised her eyebrows and leaned forward, none of which brought her an answer. "So you'll have some news for me," she risked saying.

"Unfortunately, Mrs Maynard, I have to —"

Wilf came between them to hand Claire her drink on his way to the couch, and in that moment she wished she could see the policeman's eyes. "Sorry," she said for Wilf as he moved on, and had a sudden piercing sense that she might be expected to apologise for herself. "You were saying, please, go on."

"Only that regrettably we still have nothing definite."

"You haven't. Nothing at all."

"I do understand how these things seem, believe me. If we can't make an immediate arrest then as far as the victim's family is concerned the investigation may as well be taking forever."

"When you say not immediate you mean..."

"I appreciate it's been the best part of four months."

"No, what I'm getting at, you mean you've an idea of who it is and you're working on having a reason to show for arresting him."

"I wish I could tell you that."

"Tell me the reason. Us, not just me, obviously, but that's what you mean about telling."

"Sadly not, Mrs Maynard. I meant that so far, and I do stress it's only so far, we've had no useful leads. But you have my word we don't give up on a case like this."

"No leads at all." Claire fed herself a gulp of gin, and shivered as the ice-cubes knocked a chill into her teeth. "I can't believe you've had none."

"We and our colleagues elsewhere questioned everyone with a recorded history of even remotely similar behaviour, I do assure you." The policeman looked at his hands piled on his stomach, then met her eyes again, his face having absorbed any hint of expression. "I may as well mention we received an anonymous tip last week."

"You did." Claire almost raised her glass again, but wasn't sure what the action might seem to imply. "I suppose you need time to get ready to follow something like that up."

"It's been dealt with, Mrs Maynard."

"Oh." There was no question that she needed a drink before saying "Good. And..."

"We're sure it was a vindictive call. The informant was a woman who must bear some kind of grudge against the chap. Felt rebuffed by him in some way, most likely. She didn't offer anything in the way of evidence, just his name and address."

"So that's enough of an excuse not to bother with anything she said."

"I understand your anger, but please don't let it make you feel we would be less than thorough. Of course we interviewed him, and the person who provided his alibi, and we've no reason to doubt either."

Claire had — Mrs Gummer had admitted to having been asleep — but how could she introduce that point or discover the story the old woman was telling now? "So if there's no news," she said to release some of her anger before her words got out of control, "why are you here?"

"I was wondering if either of you might have remembered anything further to tell me. Anything at all, no matter how minor it may seem. Sometimes that's all that's needed to start us filling in the picture."

"I've told you all I can. Don't you think I'd have told you more if I could?"

"Mr Maynard?"

"I'd have to say the same as my wife."

"I'll leave you then if you'll excuse me. Perhaps it might be worth your discussing what I asked when I'm gone. I hope, Mrs Maynard..." Bairns was out of his chair and had one foot in the hall before he said "I hope at least you can accept we're doing everything the law allows."

She did, and her rage focused itself again, letting her accompany him to the gate and send him on his way. The closing of his car door sounded like a single decisive blow of a weapon, and was followed by the reddening of the rear lights. The car was shrinking along the road when she saw Duncan Gummer at the junction — saw him wave to Bairns as if he was giving him a comradely sign. The next moment his patrolling took him out of view, but she could still see him, as close and clear in her mind as her rage.

"Who is this? Hello?"

"It's Claire Maynard."

"It wasn't you that kept ringing off when my mother answered, was it?"

"Why would I have done that, Mr Gummer?"

"No reason at all, of course. My apologies. It's got us both a little, well, not her any longer, she's sound asleep. What can I do for you?"

"I wanted to discuss an idea I had which I think might be profitable."

"I don't normally talk business outside business hours, but with you I'm happy to make an exception. Would you like to meet now?"

"Why don't you come here and keep me company. We can talk over a couple of drinks."

"That sounds ideal. Give me ten minutes."

"No more than that, I hope. And I shouldn't bother troubling your mother if she needs her sleep."

"Don't worry, I'm with you. Softly does it. I'm all in favour of not disturbing anyone who doesn't have to be."

"I'll be waiting," Claire said with a sweetness she imagined she could taste. It made her sick. She heard him terminate the call, and listened to the contented purring of the receiver, the sound of a cat which had trapped its prey. When she became aware of holding the receiver for something to do while she risked growing unhelpfully tense she hooked it and went to pour herself a necessary drink.

She loaded ice into the tumbler, the silver teeth of the tongs grating on the cubes, then filled the remaining two-thirds of the glass almost to the top. More room needed to be made for tonic, and she saw the best way to do that. The tumbler was nearly at her lips when she opened the gin bottle and returned the contents to it. She mustn't lose control now. To prove she had it, she crunched the ice cubes one by one, each of them sending an intensified chill through her jaw into her skull until her brain felt composed of impregnable metal. She had just popped the last cube into her mouth when she saw Gummer's glossy black Rover draw up outside the house. She bit the cube into three chunks which she was just able to swallow, bringing tears to her eyes. They were going to be the last tears Gummer would cause her to shed, and her knuckles dealt with them as she went to let him in before he could ring the bell.

Whether his grin was meant to express surprise or pleasure at her apparent scramble to greet him, it bared even more of his lower lip than usual until he produced a sympathetic look. "I'm glad you felt able to call," he said.

"Why wouldn't I?"

"Well, indeed," he said as though to compliment her on being reasonable, and she had to turn away in order to clench her teeth. "Close the door," she said once she could.

The finality of the slam gave her strength, and by the time he followed her into the front room she was able to gaze steadily at him. "What's your taste?" she said, indicating the bottles on the sideboard.

"The same as you'll be having."

"I'm sure you'll have a large one," she told him, and managed to hitch up one corner of her mouth.

"You've found me out."

Whatever answer that might have provoked she trapped behind her teeth as she busied herself at the sideboard. Perhaps after all she would have a real drink instead of pretending a tonic was gin; his presence was even harder to bear than she'd anticipated. Already the room smelled as though it was steeped in the aftershave he must have slapped on for her benefit. When she moved away from the sideboard with a glass of gin and tonic in each hand she found him at the window through which she didn't know how many times he might have spied on Laura. "Please do sit down," she said, masking her face with a gulp of her drink.

"Where will you have me?"

"Wherever you're comfortable," said Claire, retreating to the armchair closest to the door. As she'd handed him his glass she'd touched his fingertips, which were hot and hardly less moist than his underlip. The thought of them on Laura almost flung her at him. She forced herself to sit back and watch him perch on the edge of the nearer end of the couch.

"Strong stuff," he said, having sipped his drink, and put it on the floor between his wide legs. "So it's a financial discussion you're after, was that what I understood you to say?"

"I said profitable. Maybe beneficial would have covered it better."

"Happy to be of benefit wherever I can," Gummer said and showed her the underside of his lip, which put her in mind of a brimming gutter. "Do I recall the word company came up?"

"Nothing wrong with your memory."

"I wouldn't like to think so. Not like my mother's," he said, and glanced down between his legs while he retrieved his glass. Once he'd taken another sip he seemed uncertain how to continue. She wanted him in a state to betray himself by the time Wilf came back. "So what kind of company do you prefer?" she said.

"Various. Depends."

"Whatever takes your fancy, eh?"

"You could say that if the feeling's mutual."

"Suppose it isn't reciprocated? What happens then?"

"Sometimes it is when you dig a bit deeper. You think there's nothing, but if you don't let yourself be put off too soon you find what the other person's feelings really are."

Claire brought her glass to her mouth so fast that ice clashed against her teeth. "Suppose you find you're wrong?" she said, and drank.

"To tell you the truth, and I hope you won't think I've got too big a head, so far I don't believe I ever have."

"Would you know?"

"I'm sorry?"

Claire lowered her glass with as much care as she was exerting over her face. "I said, would you know?"

"I hope so this far."

His gaze was holding hers. He still thought they were discussing a possible relationship. While she swallowed an enraged mirthless laugh she won the struggle to form her expression into an ambiguous smile. "So what are your limits?"

"There's always one way to find out," he said, and revealed his wet lip.

"You don't think you should have any."

"As long as one takes care, and we know to do that these days. It isn't as though one's committed."

"Wouldn't it come down to not being found out even if you had a partner? I know you're good at not being."

"As good as I need to be, right enough."

That was almost too much for Claire, especially when, having planted her glass on the carpet to distract herself, she looked up to be met by the sight of his dormant crotch. Wilf ought to be home in a few minutes, she reminded herself. "And what age do you like best?" she managed to ask.

"Nothing wrong with a mature woman. A good deal right with her, as a matter of fact, and if I may say so —"

"Nothing wrong about younger ones either if you're honest, is that fair?"

"I won't deny it. Teaching them a thing or two, that's pretty special. There again, and you'll tell me if I'm flattering myself, sometimes even when it's a lady of our generation —"

"You bastard."

"Forgive me if I expressed myself badly. It wasn't meant as any kind of insult, I do assure you. Mature was what I meant, not so much in years as —"

"You swine."

"I think that's a little much, Claire, may I call you Claire? I'm sorry if you're touchy on the subject, but if you'll allow me to say this, to my eyes you —"

"I remind you of a younger woman."

"My feelings exactly."

"A young girl, in fact."

"Ah." He faltered, and she saw him realise what he could no longer fail to acknowledge. "In some ways that's absolutely true, the best ways, may I say, only I suppose I thought that under the circumstances —"

"You loathsome filthy stinking slimy pervert."

She saw his lip draw itself up haughtily, and was reminded of a snail retreating into its shell. "I fear there's been some misunderstanding, Mrs Maynard," he said, and rose stiffly to his feet. "I understand your being so upset still, but my mother will be wondering where I am, so if you'll excuse me —"

Claire was faster. She swung herself around her chair with the arm she'd used to shove herself out of it, and trundled the heavy piece of furniture into the doorway. Having wedged it there, she sat in it and folded her arms. "I won't," she said.

"I really must insist." He held out his hands as if to demonstrate how, once he crossed the yards of carpet, he would grasp her or the chair. "I'm truly sorry for any error."

"You think that should make up for it, do you?"

"To be truthful, I don't know what more you could expect."

He didn't believe he had been found out, she saw — perhaps the idea hadn't even occurred to him. "Maybe you will when you see your mistake," she said and made her arms relax, because her breasts were aching as they hadn't since they were last full of milk.

"It'll be easiest if you tell me."

"You think I should make it easy for you, do you?" Her mouth had begun to taste as foul as her thoughts of him, and she would have swallowed more than the taste if her glass had been within reach. "Try this for a hint. Maybe you should have kept your mother out of my way."

"You've drifted away from me altogether. Let me suggest in your interest as much as mine —"

"Or found a way to stop her talking. You're good at that, aren't you?"

"Some understanding can usually be reached if it has to be. I assume that when you decide to let me go you won't be telling —"

"Like Laura never did."

"Well, really, Mrs Maynard, I must say that seems rather an unfortunate —"

"Unfortunate!" Claire ground her shoulders against the chair rather than fly at him — ground them so hard that either the chair or the doorway creaked. "That's your word for it, is it? How unfortunate would you say she looked the last time you saw her?"

He took a breath to give Claire yet another swift response; then his mouth sagged before clamping shut. He rubbed the side of one hand across his lips, and she imagined how he might have wiped his mouth as he sneaked away from the golf bunker. She stared at his face to see what would come out of it next, until he spoke. "It was you."

This was far less than the response she wanted, in fact nothing like it, and she continued to stare at him. "It was you who kept ringing off, wasn't it, till I was there to answer. What didn't you want my mother to hear?"

"Maybe I shouldn't have rung off. For all I know she's good at keeping secrets, especially if she thinks she's protecting her son."

"Why should she think —" His eyes wobbled and then steadied as though Claire's gaze had impaled them. "My God, that was you as well. You didn't just call us."

"Seems as though I might as well have."

"You tried to put the police onto me."

"If only they'd done their job properly. You wouldn't be here now. You'd be somewhere, but I'd have to put up with that being less than you deserved, I suppose. Only you are here, just the two of us for the moment, so —"

Gummer turned to the window as if he'd observed someone — Wilf? The street was quiet, however, and it occurred to her that he was considering a means of escape. She lurched out of the chair and grabbed the bottle of gin by its neck. "Don't bother looking there. You're going nowhere till I've finished with you," she said.

"Mrs Maynard, I want you to listen to me. I know you must —" He was almost facing her when he stopped and rubbed his lip and gave her a sidelong look. "Finished what exactly?"

"Guess."

"I don't believe I have to. Profitable was what you said this was going to be when you rang, wasn't it? If I may say so, God forgive you."

"You mayn't. You'd better —"

"Whatever you think about me, you were her mother, for heaven's sake. You're expecting me to pay you to keep quiet, aren't you? You're trying to make money out of the death of your own child," he said, and let his mouth droop open.

It was expressing disgust. *He* was daring to feel contemptuous of *her*. His wet mouth was all she could see, and she meant to damage it beyond repair. She seemed less to be raising the weapon in her hand than to be borne forward by it as it sailed into the air. His eyes flinched as he saw it coming, but his mouth stayed stupidly open. She had both hands on the weapon now, and swung it with all the force of all the rage that had been gathering for months. "Claire," he cried, and tried to dodge, lowering his head.

For a moment she thought the bottle had smashed — that she would see it explode into smithereens, as bottles in films always did when they hit someone on the head. Certainly she'd heard an object splintering. When his mouth slackened further and his eyes rolled up like boiled eggs turning in a pan she thought he was acting. Then he fell to a knee which failed to support him, and collapsed on his side with a second heavy thud. As if the position had been necessary for pouring, a great deal of dark red welled out of his left temple.

When it began to stain the carpet she thought of moving him or placing towels under his head, but she didn't want to touch him. He was taken care of. She peered at the bottle, and having found no trace of him on it, replaced it on the sideboard before returning to her chair. She supposed she ought to move the chair out of the doorway, not least to bring her within reach of her drink, but the slowness that had overtaken her since the night she'd found Laura's body was becoming absolute, and so she watched the steady accumulation of the twilight.

In time she had a few thoughts. If Mrs Gummer was awake she must be wondering where her son was. She'd had decades more of him than Laura had lived, and soon enough she would learn he was only a lump on the floor. Claire considered drawing the curtains, but nobody would be able to see him from the pavement, and in any case there was no point in delaying the discovery of him. The discoverer was most likely to be Wilf, who would still have to live here once she was taken away, and she oughtn't to leave him the job of cleaning up after her, though perhaps the carpet was past cleaning. When she narrowed her eyes at the blind mound of rubbish dumped in her front room, she couldn't determine how far the stain had spread. It annoyed her on Wilf's behalf, and she was attempting to organise and speed up her thinking sufficiently to deal with it when she saw him appear at the gate.

It wasn't guilt which pierced her then, it was his unsuspecting look — the look of someone expecting to enjoy the refuge of home at the end of a long day. He couldn't see her for the dimness. He wasn't as keen-eyed as a patrolman should be, Claire found herself thinking as she stumbled to face the chair and drag it out of the doorway. That was as much as she achieved before he admitted himself to the house. "Claire?" he called. "Sorry I was longer than I said. Some old dear thought a chap was acting suspicious, but when I tracked him down would you believe he was one of our patrol. Where are you?"

"In here."

"I'll put the light on, shall I? No need for you to sit in the dark, love." He came into the room and reached for the switch, but faltered. "Good Lord, what's... who..."

Claire found his hand with one of hers and used them to press the switch down. "My God, that's Duncan Gummer, isn't it?" he gasped, and his hand squirmed free. "Claire, what have you done?"

"I hope I've killed him."

Wilf stared at her as if he no longer knew what he was seeing, then ventured to stand over the body. He'd hardly begun to stoop to it when he recoiled and hurried to draw the curtains. He held onto them for some seconds, releasing them only when their rail started to groan. "Why, Claire? What could —"

"It wasn't half of what he did to Laura."

"He —" Wilf's face convulsed so violently it appeared to jerk his head down as he took a step towards Gummer. Claire thought he meant to kick the corpse, but he controlled himself enough to raise his head. "How do you know?"

"His mother lied about his alibi. Either she said she was awake when she was asleep or she knew he wasn't at home when he said he was, when — when he..."

"All right, love. It's all right." Wilf veered around the body and offered her his hands, though not quite close enough for her to touch. "How did you find that out?"

"She let it slip one day and he tried to shut her up."

"Why couldn't you have told the police?"

"I did."

"You — oh, I get you." He was silent while he dealt with this, and Claire took the opportunity to retrieve her glass, not to finish her drink but to place it out of danger on the sideboard. Gummer's body seemed such a fixture of the room that she was practically unaware of blotting out her sense of it as she picked up the glass. The clunk of the tumbler on wood recalled Wilf from his thoughts, and he said almost pleadingly "Why didn't you tell *me*?"

"What would you have done?"

He stepped forward and took her hands at last. "What do you think? When the police didn't listen, probably the same as you. Only I wouldn't have done it here where it can't be hidden."

"It's done now. It can't be helped, and I don't want it to be."

"I wish to God you'd left it to me." He stared around the room, so that she thought he was desperate for a change of subject until he said "What did you use?"

"The gin. The bottle, I mean. It did some good for a change."

"I won't argue with that."

Nevertheless he relinquished one of her hands. Before she knew what he intended, he was hefting the bottle as though to convince himself it had been the weapon. "Don't," she protested, then saw her concern was misplaced. "It doesn't matter," she said. "Your fingerprints would be on it anyway."

"So would yours."

"What are you getting —"

"Just listen while I think. We haven't much time. The longer we wait before we call the police, the worse this is going to look."

"Wilf, it can't look any worse than it is."

"Listen, will you. We can't have you going to prison. You'd never survive."

"I'll have to do my best. When everyone knows the truth —"

"Maybe they won't. You used to think he was sniffing round you. Suppose that got out somehow? I know how lawyers think. They'll twist anything they can."

"He wasn't interested in me. It was Laura."

"You say that, but how can you prove it in court? Your instincts are enough for you, I know that, for me too if I even need to tell you. But they won't be enough if his mother sticks to her story, and if your lawyer tried to break her down too much think how that would look, them harassing an old woman with nobody left in the world."

"All right, you've shown me how wrong I am," Claire said, feeling not far short of betrayed. "Any suggestions?"

"More than a suggestion."

He reached out and drew his hand down her cheek in a slow caress as he used to when they hadn't long been married, then patted her face before sidling around her into the hall. She had no idea of his intentions until he unhooked the phone. "Wilf —"

"It's all right. I'm going to make it all right. Hello." Though he was gazing so hard at her it stopped her in the doorway, the last word wasn't addressed to her. "Detective Inspector Bairns, please."

"Wilf, wait a minute. Ring off before he can tell who you are. Don't stay anything till we've —"

"Inspector? It's Wilfred Maynard. I've killed the man who took our daughter from us."

Claire grabbed the doorframe as her knees began to shake. She would have snatched the phone from him if it hadn't been too late. Instead she sent herself into the room as soon as she felt safe to walk. She could hardly believe it, but she was hoping she hadn't killed Gummer after all. She fastened her fingertips on the wrist of the sprawled empty flesh. She held it longer than made sense, she even said a prayer, but it was no use. The lump of flesh and muscle was already growing cold, and there wasn't the faintest stirring of life within.

"I'll be staying here, Inspector. I give you my word. I wouldn't have called you otherwise," she heard Wilf say. She walked on her unwieldy brittle legs into the hall in time to see him hang the receiver. "Wilf," she pleaded, "what have you done?"

"Saved as much that we've got as I could. I know I can take prison better than you can. Quick now, before they come. Help me get my tale straight. How did you bring him here? Was he just passing or what?"

She thought of refusing to answer so that Wilf couldn't prepare a story, but the possibility that their last few minutes together might be wasted in arguing was unbearable. "I called him at home."

"Will Mrs Gummer know?"

"He said she'd be wondering where he'd got to."

"You hadn't long come in from gardening, had you? Did anyone see him arrive?"

"Not that I noticed."

"Just say he stopped when he saw you gardening and you invited him in. And when you'd both had a drink you accused him over Laura, and I came home just in time to hear him say what?"

"I don't know. Wilf —"

"'You can't prove anything.' That's as good as a confession, isn't it, or it was for me at any rate. He was shouting, so he didn't hear me, because I let myself in quietly to find out what the row was. How many times did you hit him?"

"Do you have to be so calculating about it? I feel as if I'm already in court."

"I have to know, don't I? How many times?"

"It just took the once."

"That's fine, Claire. Really it is." He offered her his hands again, and finding no response, let them sink. "It'll be manslaughter. I heard Laura's name and him saying you couldn't prove it, and that was enough. There was a moment when I lost control, and then it was done and there was no turning back. That's how it must have been for you, am I right? They'll believe me because that's how these things happen."

He must be trying to live through her experience, but she felt no less alone. "Do they, Wilf?"

"Wait, I've got it. They'll believe me because I couldn't have had any other reason to kill him. It's not as though I could have imagined anything was going on between you two, even if you did imagine he fancied you."

Even in the midst of their situation, that felt cruel to her. "Thank you, Wilf."

"I have to say it, haven't I? Otherwise they might get the wrong idea. Look, there's a good chance the court will be lenient, and if it isn't I wouldn't be surprised if there's a public outcry. And I can't imagine I'll have too bad a time of it in jail. It's his kind that suffer the worst in there, not the ones who've dealt with them."

"You sound as though you're looking forward to being locked up."

"What a thing to say, Claire. How could anyone feel like that?"

As she'd spoken she'd known the remark was absurd, yet his need to persuade her it was made it seem less so. "Why would I want anything that's going to take me away from you?" he said.

Claire had a sense of hearing words that didn't quite go with the movements of his mouth. No, not with those — with his thoughts. Before she could ponder this, she heard several cars braking sharply outside the house, and a rapid slamming of at least six doors. "Here they are," Wilf said.

The latch of the gate clicked, and then it sounded as though not much less than an army marched up the path. The doorbell rang once, twice. The Maynards looked at each other with a deference that felt to Claire like prolonging the last moment of their marriage as it had been. Then Wilf moved to open the door.

Bairns was on the step, and came in at once. Five of his colleagues followed, trying to equal his expressionlessness, and Claire didn't know when the house had felt so crowded. "He's in the front room, Inspector," Wilf said.

"If you and Mrs Maynard would stay here." Bairns' gaze had already turned to his colleagues, and a nod sent two of them to stand close to the Maynards. He paced into the front room and lingered just inside, hands behind his back, as a prelude to squatting by Gummer's body. He hardly touched it before standing up, and Claire felt as if he'd confirmed her loathing of it. "I must ask you to accompany us to the police station, Mr Maynard," he said.

"I'm ready."

"You too, Mrs Maynard, if you will. You'll understand if I ask you not to travel in the same car."

"In that case do you mind if I give my wife a cuddle, Inspector? I expect it may be her last for a while."

The policeman's impassiveness almost wavered as he gave a weighty nod. Wilf took hold of Claire's shoulders and drew her to him. For a moment she was afraid to hug him with all the fierceness in her, and couldn't quite think why. Of course, he'd scratched himself with his patrolman's badge that night on the golf course. The scratches would have healed by now, not that she had seen his bare chest for years. When he put his arms around her she responded, and felt him trying to lend her strength, and telling her silently to support his version of events. They remained embraced for a few seconds after Bairns cleared his throat, then Wilf patted her back and pushed her away gently. "We'd best get this over and done with then, Inspector."

Bairns had been delegating men to drive the Maynards. He directed an unambiguously sympathetic glance at Claire before turning a more purposeful look on Wilf. Wilf was going to convince him, she thought — had already convinced him. She had never realised her husband could be so persuasive when he had to be. She saw him start towards the front door, matching his pace to that of his escort as though he was taking his first steps to his cell. Her sense of his persuasiveness spread through her mind, and in that instant she knew everything.

"I'll drive you whenever you're ready, Mrs Maynard," a youngish policeman murmured, but Claire was unable to move.

She knew why Wilf had seemed relieved at the prospect of the sentence he was courting — because he'd been afraid he might be jailed for worse. Everything made its real sense now. Nobody had been more obsessed with the way Laura dressed and was developing than Wilf. Claire remembered accusing Gummer of being attracted to a girl as a preferred version of an older woman she resembled. The accusation had been right, but not the man.

"Mrs Maynard?"

She saw Wilf's back jerking rhythmically away from her, and imagined its performing such a movement in the bunker. For a moment she was certain she could emerge from her paralysis only by flying at him — but she was surrounded by police who would stop her before she could finish him off, and she had no proof. She'd nursed her rage until tonight, she had hidden it from the world, and she could do so again. She felt pregnant with its twin, which would have years to develop. "I'm ready now," she said, and took her first step as her new self.

Wilf was being handed into the nearest police car as she emerged from the house. Shut him away, she thought, keep him safe for me. His door slammed, then the driver's, but apart from a stirring of net curtains the activity went unacknowledged by the suburb. As Claire lowered herself stiffly into the next car, Wilf was driven off. One thing he needn't worry about was her confirming his tale. She would be waiting when he came out of prison, and she could take all that time to imagine what she would do then. Perhaps she would have a chance to practice. While she was waiting she might find other men like him.